## *The St*[illegible]

"Part western, part romance, part [illegible] ...ion of American womanhood, *The Star Garden* is well researched and manages to be at once entertaining and thoughtful. Sarah's independent streak and sometimes wily nature will endear her to contemporary readers."

—*Publishers Weekly*

"Atmospheric . . . authentic, robust, and perfectly executed." —*Tucson Citizen*

"An authentic tale of courage, determination, and audacious will on the frontier. The matter-of-fact tone of Sarah's diary entries underscores her amazing resilience in the face of everyday hardship and extraordinary adversity."

—*Booklist*

## *Sarah's Quilt*

Finalist for the Willa Cather Award

"Nancy Turner has scored again. *Sarah's Quilt* is even better than *These Is My Words,* and that's saying a lot." —Tony Hillerman

"Authentic in its detail, the novel's pace and intriguing cast of characters are reminiscent of Larry McMurtry's *Lonesome Dove.* A sensitive, vibrant story about the strength of love and family told in the voice of a woman who must be reckoned with." —*The Denver Post*

"All the enduring elements of the mystery that is life on earth can be found between the pages of this book. It is a perfectly authentic story, beautifully executed by its author." —Michael Blake, author of *Dances with Wolves*

"Older, tougher, wiser, Sarah enchants with her plainspoken energy and honesty. The title may suggest a gentle tale of domestic comfort, but the book is as straightforward, gritty, and persistent as the woman who inspires it and as memorable as the landscape where she carves out her life."

—*Publishers Weekly*

"Gritty Sarah Elliot, who lassoed our hearts in *These Is My Words,* proves that women as well as men tamed the West. *Sarah's Quilt* is as satisfying as 'riding watch at sunup.'"

—Sandra Dallas, author of *Tallgrass*

"Robust, authentic, and exciting . . . a vividly conjured picture of her place and time."

—*Booklist*

"If you want a picture of what life was like back then, look no further. Authentic in feel, [this] is convincing historic fiction. The armchair traveler is in for an exciting trip."

—*The Santa Fe New Mexican*

"Hard times, danger, love, well-defined characters, and a strong sense of place all merge to form the heart of this realistic novel."

—*The Dallas Morning News*

"Action-packed. . . . We'd trust [Sarah's] judgment if a wildfire were running straight at us. We're in good hands, calloused and strong. Turner has lived in Sarah's landscape and writes with a sharp eye for the fine points of the times."

—*Tucson Guide Quarterly*

"Sarah is a pioneer of the truest spirit, courageous but gentle. . . . *Sarah's Quilt* conveys with honesty and accuracy what it was like to be a pioneer woman at the turn of the century, and is certain to delight Turner's fans who have been eagerly awaiting the return of the indomitable Sarah Prine."

—*Gaston Gazette* (Gastonia, North Carolina)

"Sarah Prine is the real article. Every westerner will recognize in Sarah at least one woman whom we know. Sensitive, loving, and nurturing, but tough as rawhide when needed, and indignant over any injustice . . . the kind of woman that any real man will cherish, if he's lucky enough to find her, and smart enough to know it." —Don Coldsmith, author of the Spanish Bit Saga

# *These Is My Words*

Winner of One Book Arizona 2008
Winner of the Arizona Author Award
Shortlisted for the Arizona Reads prize
Finalist for the Willa Cather Award

"A compelling portrait of an enduring love, the rough old West, and a memorable pioneer." —*Publishers Weekly*

"Incredibly vivid and real." —Rosamunde Pilcher, author of *The Shell Seekers*

"A lushly satisfying romance, period-authentic, with true-grit pioneering."
—*Kirkus Reviews*

"Readers come to admire Sarah, to share her many losses and rare triumphs. If even half these events are true, she was an amazing woman."
—*Library Journal*

"A great book . . . says more about America than *Gone With the Wind.* I'd put it up there with *To Kill a Mockingbird.* It is moving, funny, and rings very true." —Mary Stewart, author of *The Crystal Cave*

"A beautifully written book that quickly captures readers' attention and holds it tightly and emotionally until the end." —*School Library Journal*

"Jack Elliot and Sarah Prine are as delicious a couple as Rhett and Scarlett. The three-hankie ending to their long love affair will definitely make you give a damn." —*USA Today*

"An entertaining—at times harrowing—reading experience."

—*Fort Worth Star-Telegram*

"A vivid picture of one woman's true grit on the frontier."

—*The Dallas Morning News*

"A powerful, compelling tale of a young woman's search for identity, independence, and happiness while coming of age in the Pioneer American West. It is a powerful adventure—and a romantic love story—experienced with a passion and yearning by characters whom the readers will never forget. *These Is My Words* is rich in love and sorrow, grit and grandeur. . . . Turner writes with insight and sensitivity . . . in the grand tradition of epic quest novels, yet [also] on a deeply human, personal scale. Opening this book . . . is like opening an old trunk in the family attic and finding a treasure."

—*The Williamson County Sun*

"Incredibly vivid and real and almost as though everything has been found, complete in a box somewhere." —*The Washington Post*

"Nancy Turner has spun a frontier novel that teeters on the fine edge of truth and fiction." —*The Arizona Republic*

"*These Is My Words* belongs on your must-read list. In her first book, Nancy E. Turner approaches the fine qualities of Larry McMurtry's Pulitzer-winning *Lonesome Dove*. The two books share unforgettable characters, a grand sweep of history, adventure, love, and emotion so real that you feel it. *These Is My Words* is a book not to miss." —*Omaha World-Herald*

"Nancy Turner knows the land of the nineteenth-century territories, as it must have been, and she knows the landscape of the heart as it was then and always is."

—Meg Files, author of *Meridian 144*

# The Star Garden

## *Also by Nancy E. Turner*

*These Is My Words*

*The Water and the Blood*

*Sarah's Quilt*

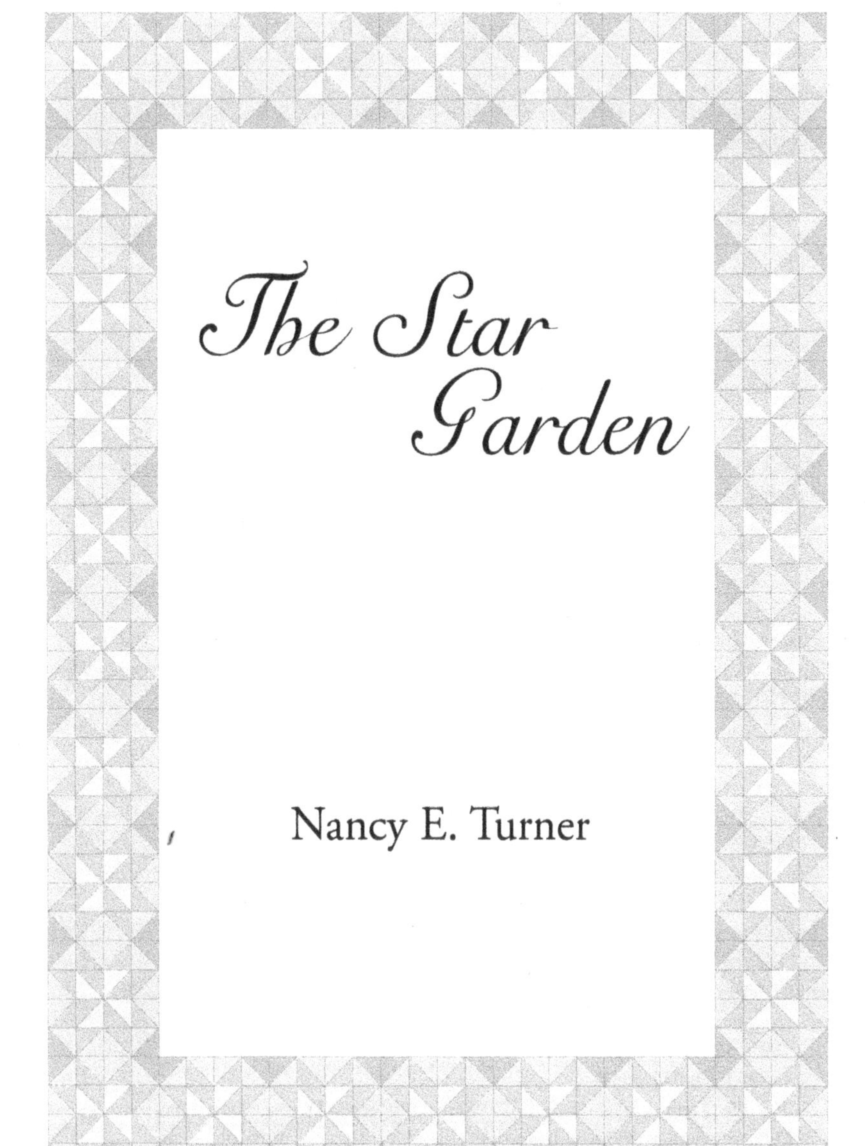

# The Star Garden

Nancy E. Turner

Thomas Dunne Books ♜ St. Martin's Griffin
New York

This is a work of fiction. All of the characters, organizations, and events portrayed in this novel are either products of the author's imagination or are used fictitiously.

THOMAS DUNNE BOOKS.
An imprint of St. Martin's Press.



www.thomasdunnebooks.com
www.stmartins.com

Library of Congress Cataloging-in-Publication Data

Turner, Nancy E., 1953–
The star garden : a novel of Sarah Agnes Prine / Nancy E. Turner.—
1st St. Martin's Griffin ed.
p. cm.
ISBN-13: 978-0-312-36317-8
ISBN-10: 0-312-36317-6
1. Prine, Sarah Agnes—Fiction. 2. Women pioneers—Fiction. 3. Arizona—Fiction.
4. Domestic fiction. 5. Diary fiction. I. Title.
PS3570.U725S73 2007
813'.54—dc22

2007020507

D 20

*For John*

# Acknowledgments

No process so singularly solitary as writing can come to fruition as a published novel without people along the path who shine brightly enough to make a difference in the writer's passage. I consider those who have helped me in the creation of this novel both friends and colleagues. My husband, John, has encouraged me every step of the way, with at times amazingly creative insight. Many thanks go to John Ware, supreme agent and one-man cheering section, who has seen this project through from its inception with suggestions that show keen appreciation of the characters that live in my imagination. At Thomas Dunne Books I have had the privilege to work again with a great editor, Marcia Markland, who always asks the right questions, and her capable, efficient assistant, Diana Szu, who always finds the right answers, both of whom have a rare talent for shepherding a book through the publishing maze. I also want to thank Marilou Groves for independent editing help, Jannett Dailey for story and place confirmation, and the Arizona Historical Society, along with the Pima County Public Library system, for invaluable research assistance, especially including Martin Rivera, reference librarian at the Mission Branch Library, for last-minute linguistic help.

# Chapter One

*December 9, 1906*

I watched the Wells Fargo stagecoach tip up on two wheels then roll on its side while a cold wind whipped my hat against the side of my face. From where I sat on my horse, there was no sound as it fell, sliding toward the place we call Sandy Cliff, southeast of my house. In the strange slowness of its tumbling, I considered for a time that the wind had tipped it. The box quit rolling at the very last point from which it could hold; another inch and it surely would topple over. A full minute seemed to drag by before the blanket of quiet was torn by the sound of mules squealing. When the noise came, it was a roar of sound: cracking wood and shearing metal, people crying for their lives, the animals' awful bray, stirred and blended by a wind that threatened to tear every leaf from every tree, every tree from every root.

My horse and I had come to a stop to listen for quail at a stand of brush that marked the foot of Sandy Cliff when we saw the ruckus high above. It was a long climb up the side of the shifting powder that faced the cliff. I'd long ago discovered a series of irregular clumps of rock that made the only reliable route, and it was only manageable afoot. Riding the long way around would take half an hour or more, for in this weather my horse thought every branch that swayed was a spook coming at him.

I kneed Baldy through the brush and untied the morning's hunt, a clutch of headless dove and quail tied by their feet in rawhide and hanging from the pommel of my saddle, found a broken branch high as I could reach, and hung them there. No telling how long I'd be climbing and no sense making wolf bait out of my horse. I left his reins hanging loosely from a stump where he could rest and forage, then started up the hill, shotgun in hand, working my way across the irregular rock clusters. Nearer the rounded edge at the top, there was nothing I could do but scramble on my hands and knees, trying to keep the muzzle of the shotgun clear.

When I could see the coach, I called, "You folks all right?" The voices that answered could have been men or women or both, hollering for help; a tormented howling mixed with the mules' bellowing. I saw the poor animals now, kicking at the coach and like to killing themselves and the folks inside. While the front pair scrambled and fought for footing, lodged sideways in the loose sand, all but burying their rear team, the back pair of mules groaned and fought, slowly dying of their broken bones under the cloud of reddening dust.

I hollered again, saying, "Where's your driver?" Another flurry of voices answered me, none of it I could make out. When at last I stood upon the edge, I thought for a bit that I was dreaming, for I've had a troublesome nightmare of being trapped in a coach or a wagon while it slid down a slope with me tumbling inside and helpless. The Butterfield nine-seater had lodged itself sideways, deep in the sand, and looked to be in danger of toppling the rest of the way. One of the rear mules was already dead. His harness mate was wild-eyed and foaming. One look at him and I wished the poor animal had died of fright before I got there.

"You be still until I loosen these animals," I said, quieter now.

A man's voice hollered, "Get me out!"

I laid the shotgun to one side and took my small .32 from my pocket. Three bullets quieted the tortured mule, but commenced all manner of howling from the humans in the contraption.

The front axle had broken and every wheel was cracked. The tongue was still fixed to the coach and the doubletree pinned the rear team fast, twisted and wrenched as it was, and all the chinks and buckles of leather and rope were knotted. I figured there was no way I could unharness the living mules. They were tangled and caught, and one dead mule was on top of part of the lines. The two living, frightened animals would surely work themselves to death if I didn't loosen them from their trap.

I pulled the hatchet I'd brought for the birds from the sling at my waist, and went to chopping at the leather straps holding the mules. I had to shake my head at the waste of gear I was cutting; that'd cost Wells Fargo a pretty penny when this was righted. Reckon I'd make good on a couple of these straps for them, since I was the one cutting them. I saw the lead reins were half-hitched to the rail next to where the driver's feet usually rested. Well, I got the two living mules up and standing and, for that few minutes, there was nothing but silence coming from the people in the coach. I leaned over as far as I dared and looked off the cliff, then I circled the place, hunting for the man or men who should have been driving from the seat on top. There was no sign of anyone, so I sucked in a breath and hitched up my split skirt, getting ready to climb up for a look inside. Tender at first, I gave the coach box a wiggle, to see if it was bound to slide off the edge. I determined that if it should start to go, I would jump clear, and not try to ride it down, as I believed the thing would likely tumble. It seemed steady, so I climbed up on the leaf spring, setting the shotgun on the coach's side which was now its roof. There was a loud cry from more than one voice, "Robbers! Highwaymen! You can have my watch and chain, but don't shoot me!"

"Hush, all of you," I said. "This isn't a holdup." I slid the shotgun to a place it looked like it would stay, and got myself up on the side of the coach where I could stand. The walls were painted and finished up slick and now were covered with sand that made them slippery. I yanked on the door. The whole rig was racked at the corners and the door stuck tight. A man on the inside pushed while I tugged, until it finally came open and fell against the side. Someone inside gave a cheer. I pulled off my hat and stuck my head in the doorway. All I could see of the inside was a dark jumble of clothes and faces. "Any of you too bad hurt to get up here and climb out?" I said.

"Merciful heavens! It *is* a woman," said a man's voice. "Have *you* come to rob us?" The fellow looked to be standing where he could nearly reach the doorway. There were two women, one sort of hiding the other, and another man. The standing man seemed to be young and pretty stout, but the other fellow was old, probably older than my father-in-law.

"Give those ladies a hand up here, mister."

"How do we know you aren't going to shoot us where we stand?" he said. I pulled back and sat up stiff. "Seems more likely I should be worried about you, the bunch of you running hell-for-leather across my place. How come you decided to head this direction? Across this way there isn't any road at all, just a cow track. You're not even headed to town."

"Ask the driver. If you can sober him up. He got up drunk this morning and has been surly the whole trip. Now let me up."

I ignored the fellow's outstretched hand and stood again on the slick wall of the stage. I knew all of the drivers who regularly came this way. Some of them, I knew their families, too. None of them were the kind to go wild and drunk down the road. The Company surely wouldn't put up with that. I hollered down, "Who was driving it? Mr. B, or was it Dailey? Where's he at?"

Three people looked back and forth, shaking their heads. I looked as far as I could see from up on top, standing up. The bushes at the side of the trail were undisturbed. If the driver had fallen, it had been before the mules charged up this sandy hill. "My name's Sarah Elliot. I'll go hunt your man. Mister, you and that lady help her friend stand up there," I said. "Are you able to get up? How about her? Is she faint?"

"Oh, my Lord," said the woman, "I think she's dead." She drew away from her friend. "Get me out of here, please," she cried. She was a young woman, probably no older than twenty or so. I reached in through the doorway and she took my hand but she had no strength in her grip. She'd got a good crack on her head and blood seeped down her face onto her shoulder. I had to take off my glove to get hold of her hand.

I said, "Give her a leg up, men! Don't stand on ceremony." With a good bit of pushing and pulling and a genuine struggle by the poor woman, she was finally up with me. However, soon as we were both on it, the side of the coach began to sag and cracking noises came from the wood. "Get on down there," I told her. "Take that step on the spring there and lift up your skirts so you don't tear them. Go on, pull 'em up or you'll trip. No one's here to see you." Then I turned to the young fellow. "You better pass the other lady up here next."

His eyes widened and he stammered, "I won't. I—I sha'n't." He looked to be some kind of bona fide sissy. Eastern clothes, a fresh white collar hanging by one button. Afraid of a poor dead woman.

"Well, I'm not helping *you* out if you leave her in there. There's nothing to be afraid of." The other passenger looked to be a man every bit as fancy as the young one, though scuffed up quite a bit more. The lady standing next to the wheel, I couldn't rate, but she seemed genteel enough. I turned to her and hollered, "You there, hand me those cutoff rigging lines. We'll tie up a sling and lift her out."

"Get me out of here," the young man demanded. "I insist you get me out first."

"Then who'd tie up the girl?" I said. "What if she were your sister? Wouldn't you bless some kind man who saved her mortal remains and removed her from this unnatural coffin?"

The woman standing below me spoke up. "Oh, she's not his sister, of that you can be sure, miss." She passed me the leather and I squatted on the coach's side, pulling up the length of it and searching for a usable stretch.

"Please," said the old gentleman from inside the dark chamber. "A bit of decorum. Miss Castle is dead."

The woman made a face as if she might cry, and said softly, "It's only that I knew her and Mister—*Doctor*—Fairhaven there. That's all."

"You're a doctor?" I asked him. "What in tarnation kind of doctor is afraid of a dead woman?"

The young man puffed himself up. When daylight hit his face, I saw he was not so young as I'd first imagined. More thirty than twenty. He said, "Of letters, not medicine. Philosophy. Literature. The study of higher thought, wisdom of the ages . . ."

"Ah. Wisdom of the ages," I repeated. I shuffled down the leather straps into the coach and tied my end of them around the axle's broken nub. "Well, that ought to have built in you a sound philosophic respect for the dead. Loop this around her middle."

With the strap in his hands, he seemed resigned now to do as he was told. After a bit of commotion, I could hear him muttering something about what part of a woman exactly *was* the middle, but I didn't think it was worth the breath to argue. It's part of the confounding humor of Providence that the scalawag had lived and the woman had not. As I know folks, likely she'd have made two of him in kindness and decency. The young woman helped me pull the strap and we laid her friend on the ground. Miss Castle's neck looked to be broken. I got back on the side and motioned to the old man next.

"I believe my arm's damaged, madam," the old man said. "May not be broken, but it hurts considerably."

"Help him up, there, Mister-Doctor Fairhaven." I could see Fairhaven was in no mood to be accommodating, but again, he did as I ordered. I'd about got the old fellow halfway through the door with his one good wing twined around my right arm. Dr. Fairhaven gave him quite a shove and the struggle of getting him on top of the stage knocked the shotgun from where it lay across the window. The thing spun around, pointing straight at me and the old man for a second, before, slicker than a raindrop it slipped down the side of the stage and landed butt down on the ground. The jar caused the works inside to jump, for both barrels went off straight up and like to deafened me for life. I let out a holler and covered my face with my arms. No one was hit directly but the shot went near straight up so we suffered the hail of bird pellet for some minutes. The two mules, which had been calmly eating forage nearby, took off for kingdom come.

Our perch began to slide. For a long, long second, I held fast to the rim, hoping to shove myself clear if it should begin to roll, but the man had me by the waist and was clinging tight to my shoulder in fear. He'd pull us both over with the rig if I couldn't shake him loose. The stage moved a good foot farther over the side toward our final judgment. The man inside yelled. We held our breaths like they were one thing all connected. Then the movement stopped.

The old man sighed as he clambered down the overturned coach. "I do apologize, miss," he said. "I very nearly finished the rest of us off. Thank you, kindly, miss.

"Mrs. Elliot."

"Ah, thank you, Mrs. Elliot. Professor Osterhaas. Let me try to be less nuisance and more help. Professor Fairhaven, if you put one foot against the seat back, you'll do well." The coach slid another inch. Professor Osterhaas said, "Posthaste, man!"

I reached in a hand for the younger fellow and, although his palms were soft, I found him pretty wiry. He came right out of there like a cork in a bottle. We settled ourselves on firm ground and the stage gave a mighty shake, like it had been wakened from a doze, and lifted itself up, giving one good roll, and planted itself solidly upside down on the steepest edge of the cliff. I coiled up the leather straps, glad to find something to do with my hands to keep them from shaking.

I needed to get three hurt folks and a dead woman back to the house. I surely wished the mules were around to ride. They might be as far as the next leafy bush, or they might have hightailed it for home. I'd have to get Baldy from below, anyway, as I wasn't about to try to load a dead body on a strange mule; I value my teeth where they are and my brains likewise. Baldy would put up with about anything, and I figured with the cold weather, he'd not mind overmuch. I told the folks to wait and I set off, half walking, half skidding around the sandy slope, and well out of range if the stagecoach decided it needed another turn.

Down where the horse ambled under a cottonwood, I took my day's kill from the mesquite branch and fastened it to the pommel. Then I rode around the hill and up the ridge to where the tinhorns waited. The dead birds wobbled against my leg. It crossed my mind that with three extra plates at the table, I'd need to either add more birds to the pot or mix it mighty thin, and I hoped my boy Gilbert had had better hunting than I had.

We got the dead woman tied on like a pack. Professor Fairhaven thought I ought to go on home and fetch them a carriage, but I told them there was nothing for it but to start walking, as they'd be purely miserable waiting here in the cold and wind all that time without moving. My buggy wouldn't hold the lot of them anyway.

We took the long way around where the footing was firm. There we found Mr. B, whose real name was Bennecelli, nearly half a mile from where the stage had tipped over. None of the passengers said they'd heard Mr. Bennecelli fall, and they hadn't noticed any change in the ride. There was not a mark on him except for a few light scratches that we could lay toward him having tumbled from atop the stage. For all I could tell, he'd died in his seat. And there should have been a man riding beside him. Fairhaven had said Mr. B had acted surly and drunk, but he's one of the nicest fellows around, so if he'd acted sour to those folks, he must have been sick. He didn't smell like drink, and I'd never known the man to touch liquor. I figured he must have tied off the reins and the mules, trained as they were not to stop for fear of highway robbers and Indians, and the animals never knew they were driverless. They'd continued in a fairly straight path, too, missing the bend in the road where it goes north by my mama's place.

Mr. Bennecelli used to sing fancy Italian songs he knew from his home across the ocean. I think he liked that I took the trouble to say his name proper instead of calling him B the way some folks did. He was fairly stout, too. Baldy wouldn't carry two and none of these were in any shape to haul him. It was a sad thing to leave the man crumpled in the dirt like a tossed-out blanket.

I pointed in the direction of my house. I said, "Yonder it is. You all can rest at my place for the night. Then we'll see to your belongings and getting you to town."

My house was already fairly crowded with folks, despite that it's a nearly new house with eleven full rooms. My mama lives there, too. She goes by Granny to most everyone around. Then there's my youngest boy, Gilbert, and my father-in-law, Chess, who's been here since my husband died some years back. My little brother, Harland, and his four children have lived with us since his wife died of cancer in Chicago this last fall. My oldest boy, Charlie, is a lawman for the Arizona Rangers and last I heard he was up in Holbrook. At least he's a Ranger until he gets back, for the talk around town last week was that they'd disband by the end of the year. Maybe then he'll see fit to return to school and set an example for his younger brother. We reached the yard. Gilbert was out by the chicken coop with the kettle and a bag to catch feathers, skinning some game birds.

"How many'd you get?" I called.

Gil looked up, and a minute passed while he took in the parade I was leading. Finally he spoke as if it were the most natural sight, and he knew I'd explain by and by. He said, "Fifteen. Grampa is already peeling potatoes." He looked back over his shoulder at some hens pecking in the chicken yard. "I think Brownie looks like she wants to set some eggs. I put a couple more under her and turned the nesting tub over. You bring home some company?"

"Stagecoach wrecked," I said. "These folks were inside. Mr. Bennecelli's dead." The passengers stood shivering in the wind while I was all but glowing from all the work I'd done wearing this heavy coat. I handed Gilbert my string of birds. "When you get cleaned up, go ahead and start them cooking with some salt if there's any left."

I led the strangers into the parlor, stoked up the fire in there good and hot, and told them to rest, and that I'd bring them coffee soon as I could.

My father-in-law, Chess, was cutting up carrots for the stew, and with a scowl on his face he went back over the ones he'd just cut and diced them up finer, making a regular rhythm like a clock. "We don't need more mouths to feed," he said. "For once I thought we'd have enough supper."

"I know it." I also knew Chess had been cutting his own helpings pretty small. The man was looking drawn and old. We'd been living on our hunting and the remnants of last summer's canned goods for a month, and winter hadn't even set in good, yet. "I'm going back up the hill to fetch Mr. Bennecelli."

"Hurt bad?"

"Passed on."

Chess stopped his angry chopping. "You'll need help."

"I was going to ask Gilbert."

Chess held the knife before him, staring down at the hilt. His hands trembled all the time now, and I saw his fingers whiten against the wooden handle before he said, "I'll go along."

"Chess, I'd rather you stay and sort out the company. The older gent there, Dr. Osterhaas, says his arm's bad. Might be broken. You look after him."

Chess said, "Harland can see to that." He pushed the vegetables into a pile, laying the knife atop the mound. "Blessing!"

Harland's little girl, my niece, was but five years old, born the day after my thirty-eighth birthday. Blessing came into the room carrying the rag doll Granny had made for her. I was right fond of the child. And I never ceased to wonder at Providence for bringing her to this house, for I'd never have known her or her three older brothers had not the earthquake destroyed Harland's architecture practice in San Francisco last spring, and the cancer destroyed his wife this fall. Blessing carried her bundle as if it were a live baby. With all the consternation of a new mother, she put her finger to her lips and whispered, "Grampa Chess, Molly is sleeping."

Her words drowned out his foul mood like water on a fire. "Blessing, my blessing," Chess said, "you put your baby down now and cut up these potatoes. Cut 'em real small, we've got to spread the gravy thin tonight."

"Poppy says there'd be more 'tatoes if Aunty Sarah'd let him buy us some."

I knew my brother would gladly buy anything we needed, as I'd heard him offer, but this was not California and even in town there were no potatoes to be had this time of year. Chess knelt in front of her. He patted her shoulder and said, "You ever leave this table hungry, sweet dolly-do-lolly?"

"No, sir, Grampa Chess."

"Well? The Lord provides all you need, then. That's all anyone can ask. Mind your fingers with that blade."

When Chess and I got the wagon hitched up and started back up the hill to get Mr. Bennecelli, I shook the reins and said to Chess but toward the horses, "The Lord provides all you need, too. It's an ornery old cuss that won't take good food when it's put in front of him." He grunted so I kept talking. "What good's it do you to skimp on your rations? Last night there were beans left over."

"Dogs has got to eat, too."

"That's why God made mice."

"You're a hard woman, Sarah Agnes. Now quit your fussin' at me. Show some respect. There's our old friend."

We laid Mr. Bennecelli under a canvas tarpaulin in our flatbed wagon. We pulled it next to the house where the fence would keep the wolves away and wrapped Miss Castle in an old sheet and put her there, too. The cold tonight will freeze them and those stage passengers can haul them to town tomorrow. I expected to take further stock of our guests and see which of them I'd trust to bring my wagon back before I let them take it to town.

We had supper at my table, the three tinhorns sitting across from Gilbert, who is now nearly twenty, and Chess, who is a good thirty years older than I.

I just hit forty-three, though it feels like last week my sons were small and carefree as puppies. Reckon I don't include my girl April in that feeling because if I think about it for a while, my April was born old. She had seen murder and shooting and too much blood spilled before she was two years old, enough to last a lifetime. She grew up worrisome, not like my boys. Never seemed like a child. My brother Harland is thirty-six and is also old before his time, what with caring for his wife and now his babes.

Harland's three sons are a surefire ruckus in a grease can all by themselves. After a couple of weeks of being good and quiet, they have turned back into regular children and they are a handful. Always squabbling about a tin soldier lost or a bigger piece of pie. Tonight, in honor of the strange company before them, they and their little sister, Blessing, had put their manners back on as if they'd slipped into heavy overcoats.

By the time we got washed up for supper, Harland got Professor Osterhaas's arm rigged up in a sling. Harland said while it looked bruised, he didn't expect it was broken. Professor Osterhaas, like Professor Fairhaven, was a doctor of letters. The two professors had been on their way to the university in Tucson from California. The woman, Miss Charity James, didn't say precisely what her purpose was. Most women would state right off that they've come to visit their mother or to take water cures at the mineral springs or *something*. I began to think she had no repute but a foul one, but then she said she'd been traveling with Miss Castle who was a milliner and who had planned to open a shop in town. Still, the things she didn't say about herself made me wonder all the more. The cut of her dress was new and stylish, like I've seen my daughter April wear, but the whole thing was done up in flimsy cloth that looked cheap to me.

"Will you be staying in town?" I asked.

"I don't know, ma'am," Miss James said. "I was only coming along to help. She had all the learning smarts with the banking and taxes and whatnot. I was a lacemaker before. And a seamstress. I'd hoped to dress hats. I've done a few before. The one in the coach, did you see it? I could make you up a nice hat."

Professor Fairhaven spoke up then. "Perhaps you should return to your lace factory in California."

"Oh, I couldn't do that. I can't ever go back there," she said. Miss James studied the tablecloth real close.

I said, "One thing about the Territory is, a woman can still do what she wants here. If you've a mind to and some grit and backbone, there's always folks around who'll help if you need it."

She kept on staring at the tablecloth, and picked at a biscuit crumb she'd dropped there. "Dr. Fairhaven, you should mind your own business . . . He doesn't even miss her. Look at him," Miss James said with a whimper. "Miss Castle was a good person. She believed him. Now she's dead and gone and you'd never know it by him."

Fairhaven scowled. Professor Osterhaas looked pained. The air in the room seemed heavy and bristly.

Harland looked in my direction and said, "Well, time to hear your recitations, boys. Truth, Honor, and Story, go wash the sorghum off your chins and let's have a good showing. Our guests will like a little entertainment after supper."

The boys traipsed from the table in the order of their names, but after they left the room we heard a commotion and a scuffle and one of them hollering, "I called *I* was first! Gimme that, you."

"Poppy?" said Blessing. "I have learnt all the words to the Running a Race poem."

"Yes, she did," I said. "She recites it eloquently." Our guests looked at me as if I'd grown horns. "You folks fill up your coffee cups if you'd care to, and we'll go to the book room."

Well, we filed into the room Harland has called the library, although in this heavy adobe house surrounded by saguaros and serenaded by coyotes, I'd think it could just as well be called the book room. I've seen a real library in town up at the university, and even given them some books from time to time. The ones I've got here are dear to me and old, and they cover most of three walls in the room. I suppose I haven't got the brass to call it a library. Besides, I'd skin anyone who attempted to loan themselves a volume.

We pulled up chairs and stoked the stove, then Harland's boys Honor and Story chanted one after the other through the stanzas of "The Charge of the Light Brigade." Truth read an essay he'd written about liberty being a precious possession. Then Blessing recited a poem I'd taught her from my *Peerless Reciter* about a tear and a smile both racing down the face of a baby. When she came to the last line, where the smile won the race and the baby was happy, she looked about with utmost seriousness at everyone gathered before her. Raising her finger, she said, "And *I* think a real, live baby would be the dearest thing ever I could see and pet and kiss. And that *someone* in this family should get *a baby*. Hopefully a girl but a boy baby would do if he's precious and smiling. I've asked everyone and they *all* say no. Poppy, can't we have a baby? Please?"

The fire crackled a full minute. The clock ticked. I looked at Harland.

I was embarrassed, and for a moment thought he'd scold her, guests or no. Harland stared at our unfamiliar company. Chess knotted his chin and lips up in one hand. It was my brother's place to chide his daughter, but he seemed lost in thought. The wind howled at the window, rattling the glass against the wooden frame.

"Blessing Prine," I said, "babies come from heaven in their own time. Little girls who say such things aloud will never get their wishes. You must only think it to yourself if you have a wish like that."

Blessing glared at me and ran to her father. Harland crushed her to himself. Tears spilled from his eyes. The poor man was still grieving too hard to be embarrassed over what his girl had said in front of strangers.

I said, "Thank you, children, for your very nice recitations. I'm sure these folks will be glad to rest now." I stood up, feeling odd in my own house. "As you can see, we have a full house and all the bedrooms are taken. You two professors, we'll put beds in here for you, in the book room. Miss James, you can stay with me. Harland? If you'll see to the children, let's all get some sleep."

Harland sent the children to their room; the two oldest boys, Truth and Honor, shared a bed, Blessing slept on a settee made up with a blanket and pillow, and Story slept in a moving crate that we'd made a straw mattress for. It took us a half hour to set up pallets for the men in the book room. When we were done, Harland followed me toward the kitchen. My brother's face, standing a head and then some taller than me, flickered in the dim light of a covered candle. As I fixed up the stove for morning, banking the coals down good and tight, he said, "Sarah, I want to talk to you."

"What's on your mind?" I asked. He had been hinting for two weeks now that he could move to Tucson and hang out his shingle. He thinks a fancy San Francisco architect could make a good living in Tucson. I had told him Tucson was a rough old cob of a place, but he showed me where the *Weekly Star* says that Tucson is the most important city between St. Louis and Los Angeles. I'd told him, "Tucson may well be the best city between St. Louis and China, but it still isn't much." Why, he'd never make it there.

"I've been thinking—now don't get flustered, hear me out—about the children's education."

"They're learning so quick, I can hardly keep up with them," I said. "Regular scholars."

"Sis, they're pulling a switch on you. Story and Honor both had that poem a year ago in school. And Truth wrote that essay a while back, too. They all made believe they were new and pretended to learn them. And they're not doing any arithmetic except a few sums."

What more do they need? My children and Albert's had all come here for school. Every one of them had come up through my book room knowing all they needed to get into college. "They're doing Latin and planetary motion."

"Their manners are atrocious. I'm raising a pack of rogues."

All four of them were pretty spoiled, that was true. I never felt it was my place to do more than fuss at them, though fussing surely didn't change their behavior much. Harland barely noticed what they did, back-talking and laughing at grown folks, fighting with each other like wildcats. I said, "They won't be better behaved in town. You won't even have me to help you look after them and feed them. Are you going to have time to teach them etiquette and wash their duds and cook and sew, *and* draw diagrams of parlors and keeping rooms?"

He put his arm around my shoulders. "You've taken great care of all of us. You feed us and keep everything clean and fine. The only thing that's wrong here is that life is not what my children are accustomed to. There's so little structure. So much is expected, you see, in a private school and home with a governess. Discipline and control . . ."

I let out my breath. Discipline and control? Did he want to raise soldiers? And was he telling me the only things he thinks I do are cooking and cleaning? I was mad enough at his words that I'd like to see him on his way. Harland's arm lay heavy across my shoulder, and my anger was tempered with the weight of that arm. "Little brother, you know you're welcome to stay. I own that house in Tucson. If you want it, you can live there and try your luck."

"First time you actually sound like you'd let me go."

"Keep telling me I don't know how to mind children, and I'll mail you to town myself with a stamp from my boot. General delivery. Why would you want to take your children to town? They'll be exposed to all kinds of diseases. Rough characters. Unfair teachers."

"They tell me you're a mean teacher."

"They tell me you can whistle out your eyebrows."

He laughed. "You know, that house of yours was the first whole house I ever built."

"Did I ever pay you for that?"

"I recollect I billed you a peach pie and a haircut. Believe you paid twice."

I patted his arm. "When you leaving?"

"I don't know. Thought I'd have more trouble convincing you than that."

"There's no rush."

Later, I showed Miss James to my room. Then I handed her a night shift and set about tightening up the ropes under my bed to pull the sagging middle up flatter. When I'm alone there's no harm in letting it sag. I don't mind sharing with someone but with another woman in the bed, I'd as soon we didn't slide toward the middle all night long.

I turned down the lamp, and as I was getting in, Miss James rolled away from me. I faced the opposite wall, too. I was thinking about Harland and each of his children. Thinking what they'd need, how they'd fare in town, how much better they'd be here in the fresh air.

Miss James's voice startled me. "Miss Castle thought he was going to marry her. That's all. I saw you looking cross when her name was brought up."

It took me a minute to put that into place. "Professor Fairhaven?"

"She said he talked to her of marriage and having a family."

"*Did* he talk of it?"

"Well, she was going to have a . . . no matter what she did, she was my friend."

"I see." No matter what she did. Going to have . . . what, a little visitor? The story played out in my imagination. The learned Dr. Fairhaven had seduced Miss Castle and talked her into leaving her business behind and coming with him with no promise of marriage or support. As if when he got tired of her company he could tell her to go set up a shop somewhere.

Miss James sniffled, and after a bit, said, "Do you really?"

I never could see how a woman could give over to a man, without reservation, without a ring or a parson. Still, there wasn't any use in being harsh toward Miss James so I said, "She must have loved him."

"She told me I had him all wrong and that he was real smart and fun to be with and clever, and she wanted to marry him, I know that."

I saw no grief in Professor Fairhaven's eyes. Disdain, that's what I saw. A far cry from Harland's deep-cut pain. "You don't think he loved her?" I asked.

"Oh, I said that before, but how can you tell? Maybe. Love? Well, maybe. As a man does, I s'pect."

"I'll tell you what, Miss James," I said, turning in the dark to look over my shoulder and face her. I saw little sparks of moonlight reflected in her eyes. "If he did, you and the whole world would know it." I lay back down, facing my wall, and went on, "I've been loved both poorly and greatly by two different men. A woman who dreams of a good home with a man who holds for her only a poor love is putting a fifty-dollar saddle on a twenty-dollar horse. She'd be far better off single than riding with him."

At that, she said no more and soon I heard her breathing hard, sleeping. Well, I had had a way of stopping all conversations this evening, that was the pure truth. Reckon there wasn't any more to say anyway.

# Chapter Two

*December 10, 1906*

Completely separate from the newcomers to our house, from the family busting at its seams, and from the ranch barely earning feed for chickens, apart from all and weighted by it all, I live my life in a state of hushed desperation these days. Under my skin I feel an urgency, a need for hurrying through everything I touch, while on the surface, I work as calm as ever, moving through each day, doing one thing at a time. I used to take pride in what I accomplished, but now each chore is little more than a task to put my hands to, with no meaning of its own.

We weren't planning yesterday to travel to town, but now with a day's hard travel ahead of us, there followed the usual commotion of packing up clothing and setting up who'd stay to feed animals and deciding what food we'd take along. With the extra folks to carry, we'd have to borrow the big surrey from my brother Albert and his wife, Savannah, who live up the road a mile. While Gilbert went to do that, I checked off the morning's chores with no more thought to my overnight guests than if they were a few stray cats roosting in the courtyard.

This past fall has been a season of great changes for me. My old house was torn down by a tornado, the new one built and filled with all its new occupants, then adding to it, the loss of the familiar faces of my son Charlie gone to be a Ranger, and my nephew Willie, hung for cattle rustling and murder. Charlie left to find Willie and took up with the Arizona Rangers, and he's been gone ever since. Maybe that's why I feel so all-fired rushed, as if so much is happening so fast, and I can barely stay equal to each day.

There is one thing that slows me down and settles my troubled soul. One person, that is. He came to this area out of the blue, last summer, bringing my brother Ernest's remains home from the war in Cuba to rest here in my graveyard on the hill. From the beginning, Udell Hanna seemed like a decent man, and lonesome, and the two of us have sheltered our lonesomeness more and more in the comfort of our clasped hands.

Where my Jack had been all fire and storm and tumult, Udell Hanna is slow to rile as a pool of still water. Savannah keeps asking me if I plan to settle down with him, as I confessed to her that I've kissed him. Savannah is mighty pious, in all the best ways, and she believes all kissing should be reserved until after betrothal. I don't know about marrying him, though. I like keeping company, is all. I really like keeping his company. I figured Udell ought to know we were driving to town. There might be some tool he'd need, a sack of baking powder or gunpowder or such. I closed the latch on the chicken coop, my apron holding four dear eggs. It's winter and my "ladies" are slow laying. I put two under the setting hen and counted a dozen in there she's warming, plus got a whale of a peck on my arm for checking.

I put the remaining two eggs by the tin sink to clean them off. I called out to the house, "I'm going for a ride."

Granny looked up from snoozing by the stove in a chair and said, "Is that the parson from town?"

"Who, Mama?" I said.

"The one with the black hair. He's sweet on you."

"No he isn't, Mama. He's some professor of letters from the university and a rapscallion I'll be glad to be shed of."

"You said suchlike before. About that soldier fella."

To compare Professor Fairhaven to my dear Jack Elliot was like putting a three-legged mule next to a racehorse. I felt instantly cross and was about to tell her so, but the tumult I felt under my skin has also had the effect of numbing my tongue when I've felt any lack of patience toward her. My mama could barely see at all, much less discern some attraction between me and that flapping, sputtering Californian. "I never got shed of Jack," I said. "I married him."

"I'll be riding in the buggy with you."

"It's awfully cold out, Granny. You'd best stay home. We'll only be gone a couple of days. Savannah's going to send Mary Pearl here to stay with you and

Grampa Chess." I thought of something quick to make my point. "Harland and the little ones will need you."

"No, I just heard you say you were going for a ride. Just you hitch up the two-seater and we'll go down together to that Hanna's place. He lives on that feller's land south of the rancho. That's what I mean. You're not going down there without a chaperone!"

"Mama, I was just going down for a bit to share the eggs with him. You stay here and be warm. We can't leave for a couple of hours. It's going to take Gilbert a while to fetch the freight and grips from the stagecoach. May as well be neighborly."

"You want folks to talk?"

I felt a sudden heat swelling from my breastbone to my chin. "It's not like I'm still a girl," I said.

"Well, it ain't like you're a old cob, neither."

"Mama." Nevertheless, I hitched the buggy myself, and wrapped Granny in three blankets plus the lap cover. As we drove along, I could hear her humming. The cold burned my face. I didn't want her to fall asleep and freeze to death, so I talked a blue streak about the weather and the look of the sky, what we'd do in town and if she meant for me to bring something back special for her. After a while, I asked her again, and still she didn't say anything. Finally, I said, "Mama? Can't you hear me under there?"

She said, "Sarah? I'm thinking. Hush." After a while, Granny said, "This here Rudolfo Maldonado's land?"

"It's the quickest way to Mr. Hanna's place."

"Well, go around! I won't ever set foot on Maldonado land again. Not after what he pulled last summer. I don't care if he builds you ten houses, he ain't going to ever pay you back for running off the cows and pi'soning the well."

I sighed. I'd as soon whip my old friend Rudolfo Maldonado as see him, but chances were good he wasn't even here. More likely to run into him in Tucson than at the hacienda. And strictly speaking, Willie had taken the cows, not Rudolfo. But Rudolfo was the one who'd paid a cowboy to poison my south water tank; thankfully the wells by the house were safe enough. It was him feeling guilty that made him foot half the bill to put up the adobe place we live in now. "Well, stay in the buggy, Mama, and you won't be setting foot on his ground."

"You're awful quick to forgive and forget."

I said, "I'm not forgetting. I'm just not grudging the land, only the man that owns it." It was four miles from my house to the Hannas'. About two miles of it was across Rudolfo's land.

"Tried to starve us out of business." Granny leaned to the side and spat. "That's what I think of you and all your kin!"

I laughed under my kerchief and chucked the reins. A hard place in my chest suggested I was neither forgetting nor forgiving the size of that wound. We were silent the rest of the way.

Long ago, after my first husband Jimmy died, left me with this place, and I was running ragged trying to keep it going alone, I'd even considered marrying Rudolfo's twin brother, Ruben. Ruben Maldonado had died at the hands of an Apache warrior before I gave him my answer. That would have made three for me—three dead husbands instead of two. After that rascal Jimmy died, well, along came Jack Elliot and I never looked back. I shook the reins again, hurrying the horses across the scarred ground of my memories.

Here, on this higher, grassy slope, I shed all thought of the strangers troubling my house. My heart gave a stir when I laid eyes on Udell, chopping rows in the earth with a pickaxe behind a wire fence. I knew him by the coat and hat, but also by the regular method to his movement. When he turned to see who was coming, the warmth that had ringed my throat rushed upward to my hair, and I knew I was all a-blush. I was thankful for the kerchief around my nose and cheeks and the Stetson hat pulled low.

He tipped his hat as I pulled to a stop. " 'Morning, ladies," he said.

" 'Morning," I said. Granny only nodded. I continued, "I won't interrupt your work. Just wanted to know if you needed anything from town. I forgot the eggs."

Udell reached up for Granny while he said, "Come in and I'll stoke the fire. Was just going to make a pot of coffee."

She didn't move, so I said, "Mama, don't you want to go in?"

"Well, I'm about froze to death," Granny said. "Naturally."

Instead of the line shack Udell uses for a summer house, we went into the tent he had built around his stove. When his house burnt down last season, he and his son, Aubrey, had taken the stove outside and left it clear of the first lean-to he made, afraid the stove's heat would burn the lean-to, also. By himself, the stove was too heavy to move, so he'd pulled up an army tent and pitched it around the stove. It was a pretty good setup for winter, warm as a summer's day inside.

Waiting for the water to boil, Udell told us about a garden he was digging and we talked about planting for a winter crop. I watched him drop the coffee into the boiling water, and caught his glance for a moment. He turned away quickly, studying the coffee grounds. For a long spell, no one spoke. At last, when the smell started to welcome us, he got some cups from their nails on the wooden tent frame and handed them out. "Kind of soon for you to be going back to town, isn't it?" he said. "Sugar?"

"I'd take sugar," Granny said. "Thank you."

"No, thanks," I said. "Stagecoach turned over. The passengers are at my place and I'd rather drive them to town than feed them. Driver's dead, and a woman."

He took my mama's cup and carefully poured in the coffee, set it down, and passed her a Mason jar full of chunks of brown sugar. "It wasn't Pancho Dailey, was it?"

Granny fished into the jar with two fingers, pulled out a lump, and said, "Bennychelli."

"We're leaving before noon," I said, "I want to get there before dark. Gil and his grampa are going to decide which among 'em is going and who's staying. I meant to bring you an egg. I plum forgot."

"You asked Chess about the weather?" Udell said. His hands touched mine as he filled my cup. His brows lifted slightly, and the twinkle in his eye was as sharp as the sun in June. "I don't know about his rheumatism, but by my shoulders, I'd be ready for rain."

"Maybe that's why he's been so crotchety lately," I said.

Udell sat on his haunches, blowing over the top of his own cup for a minute. "You can probably beat it to town. Long as you're going, I could use nails. Five pounds. And three iron strap hinges, six- or ten-inchers, whatever they've got. I'll give you cash so you don't have to lay out for it." From under the bedroll in the corner, he pulled a tin that had once held salted fish.

"I'll bring your change," I said.

He put a five-dollar note in my hand. "Whatever's left, use on beans. Even if it's only a pound or two. My sack got mold."

Granny went after the sugar in the bottom of her empty cup with one finger. Pretty soon she looked up at me and said, "What?"

"Good coffee?" I said.

"Ain't had sugar in a spell," she said. "If you're going to kiss anyone, feller, you best go on get it done. We've got tracks to make." She licked her finger again.

I said, "Mama!"

"It ain't like you're a little girl, I heard," she said. Udell looked at me. I don't know if my face was as red as his, but it felt as if it were. Granny said, "That's what we come for, ain't it?"

I shook my head. "I came to see if he needed any goods from town," I said.

Udell smiled broadly. "Well, now, Granny, usually someone charges a fee for delivering goods. But a kiss? It seems a fair bargain for fetching my hardware. I'd gladly pay it. Do we have a deal, Sarah?"

I handed him my empty cup. "I'll not be bargained for nor fiddled with by my own mother. If you want a kiss from me, Mr. Hanna, it had better not be traded for nails and hinges but for something of equal value to the kiss itself." I smiled, then said, "Sun's a-wasting," and stood and straightened my hat.

He squinted at me, then said, "I assure you, Mrs. Elliot, my intentions are pretty honorable. However, the kiss I intended was not for you." He bent and bussed my mama's cheek loudly.

"Oh, fiddlesticks!" she said, swatting at him with her bony hands. "Rascal!"

I laughed as I put his five-dollar note in my glove, and while I was putting on the glove, Granny lifted the tent flap and headed for the buggy. Udell bent quickly and brushed my lips with his. I took one step toward the tent flap with him on my heels, and when I turned my head, he was there. It was just a moment's kiss, a debt paid in kind, the trade goods for the kiss before it. I hadn't had sugar in a long time, either.

He called, "Godspeed," as we drove away. Granny and I pulled up our kerchiefs to keep the cold from freezing our noses.

A ways down the road, she pulled the calico off her face. "What's wrong with him?" Granny demanded.

"He fixed *your* wagon, didn't he?"

She pushed the kerchief over her nose and got quiet again, but I smiled the whole way home.

We got those folks loaded into Albert and Savannah's surrey, and Gilbert and Chess packed up the flatbed, putting everything above the bodies on a false bottom that sets on a rack. Chess had won, or lost I suppose, the right to drive the wagon, and he drove behind me while I handled the surrey. I could have let one of the professors handle Albert's team, but I knew the horses better than I knew the men, so I drove. I tied Baldy on behind, to have a saddle horse when we got to town. Savannah and her daughters Rebeccah and Mary Pearl had packed us apple butter sandwiches made on thick chunks of bread. I took the basket and bid them farewell, and we started down the road toward Tucson.

We got about an hour down the road, and from there, we were higher above the rest of the road toward town. The town of Benson is off in the distance one direction, and Tucson is the other way, though you can't see it from here. Another hour along we'd come to a place we call the "arroyo grande," a wide and deep gorge that leads up toward Pantano Ranch. It stays dry most of the time, but when it runs it's a tumult. The smell of rain had been in the air since we left. I pulled the horses to a stop, and Chess brought the wagon up alongside. The sky north of us loomed gray and heavy, as if clouds sat right down on the land. The mountains that should have been due north were swallowed in the dark mantle. A chill wind broke through the flaps of my coat and burned my neck.

Chess pursed his lips. "Raining pretty good up there."

I studied the sky. The time it would take to get both these rigs across the arroyo grande, we were still six hours from town in good weather. "Let's get to Pacheco's crossing," I said. "Then I'll ride up and see what it looks like before we take the wagons and the folks the rest of the way."

He nodded and snapped his reins, moving ahead of the surrey. My three passengers seemed to take no notice of the pause in travel. Whether it was boredom or aggravation that kept them quiet, it didn't matter to me. We pulled up at the round in the road, a place where the stage will turn sometimes to let passengers out to stretch their legs. It was the best place we'd find to head back for home if we needed to. I put the brake on and untied Baldy, slinging myself onto his back.

Professor Fairhaven put his head out from one of the curtains on the surrey. "Why are we stopping?" he said, and then a little panicky, he added, "Where are you going?"

"Checking the road ahead," I said. "You have a stretch but stay close by. Last time I came this way I saw lion tracks." I nudged Baldy and took off toward the arroyo at a pretty good clip. We scared a herd of four white-tail deer, down from the mountains for winter, and I slowed him down as we approached the crossing. Mist fell against my face, damp and cold. Baldy's breath formed flags of steam around my knees.

Stopping at the highest edge of the crossing, I got off and led him down the wide path that traverses the side and switches back halfway down. Farther on lay a foot-thick barrier of fine sand which we have kept passable by constantly feeding it heavy lumber ties. Last fall while I was in town awhile, Udell, Charlie, and Albert fixed up the bottom so it was good and sound, near to a bridge as it could be, planted there on the ground.

Rain fell in earnest by the time I reached the switchback. Running water covered the boards. I dismounted and stepped into it. It barely covered the toe of my boot, but it was frothy and greasy looking. That meant this water had come a long way, washing through the chaparral; miles and miles of creosote bush pounded by rain against the rocky ground had turned the water to soap.

I rode back and when I told the folks what I'd found, well, you'd have thought I said they were all to be cast out there in the road, there was such complaining.

"Just how deep was the water?" Professor Fairhaven demanded.

I tied Baldy on and climbed into the seat. "Couple inches, but running slick. It's not how deep it is now," I said, "it's how deep it could get before we can get out the other side. A flood coming down that narrow gorge could sweep the wagon fifteen miles before we know it."

He stiffened up. "I say we press on. I should have been in Tucson yesterday. I have a meeting tomorrow morning. I won't be delayed by three inches of water."

I snugged my hat down. "Not in the stage you wouldn't. Empty, they're half a ton or more. We've got less than a quarter. Yesterday, it was probably dry. Today, I'm not crossing it. Sign's bad. Gittup, there." I snapped the reins and we jerked into motion. I pulled tight on one side and got us turning in a circle.

I could hear the consternation in Fairhaven's voice at my back. "I say we vote on it! How many of us would rather go on to Tucson? We have a majority. Turn around."

"*Mr.* Fairhaven," I said, "you may have a majority, but *I* have a surrey." I pulled to a stop. "If you are inclined to walk your majority to town in the rain, you go right along. I'll stop long enough for you to get out. Watch your step there."

"It's raining."

"And it's freezing," said Miss James.

"Well, so it is," I said.

"It's *Professor* Fairhaven."

"So it is. Mind your step, Professor Fairhaven. I want to get the dead folks to town as bad as you do, believe me. You'll see the lady gets to town, too, of course?" I grinned like a jack-o'-lantern.

He hadn't moved, but shrank into his seat. "There's no call to be irascible."

Likely he didn't think I knew that word. "Irascible? Why, not a harsh word came from my mouth, sir. I was being most amiable."

"It's barely sprinkling."

I steadied the horses. "Mostly it's Easterners that get washed away in the arroyos when they flood. I'll have to make a note that Californians are susceptible to it, too."

At that, Professor Osterhaas laughed and said, "Mrs. Elliot, we're in your debt already. Perhaps we should bow to your obvious experience with Arizona weather patterns and accept your hospitality one more night."

I nodded. Fairhaven was sputtering as I took off the brake. Miss James covered up her head with the blanket. I chucked the reins and we headed for the house. By the time we got there, it was raining solid and gray. Chess and I were soaked through our coats, skin deep. We were all looking forward to some coffee and we tore into the apple butter sandwiches while we waited for the water to boil. I left the surrey and wagon loaded except for the personal things of the "majority," and put the horses away while Chess got on some dry clothes.

There was nothing to do then but turn everyone loose in the house to read or amuse themselves. Professor Osterhaas went to the book room with a quilt around his shoulders and stood looking through the books, last I saw him. Miss James took some tatting from her carpetbag and found a chair near the light. I went into the kitchen where Granny snoozed by the stove with the calico cat in her lap. I didn't know what I would serve this horde of folks for supper.

I pumped water into a kettle. I put a log in the stove and pushed at the coals. A swirl of sparks rushed upward, turning black then quickly disappearing in the damp air.

"Sarah?" Granny's voice said behind me. "I want to go home."

"You are home, Mama."

"I was thinking about another place."

She does go on. I stared at the rows of canned goods lining my pantry. They were Savannah's hard work, not mine. Everything I'd put up last summer had been broken when the walls came down. It still makes me sad to see things and remember what used to be my house. Reckon sometimes I long for home, too. I said, "Where's that, Mama?"

"Why don't we move to Texas, like your pa said? It's greener there. Better grazing."

I'd given up trying to understand when she was like this. I said, "No critters left to graze. I'd go get some bacon if I didn't have to get wet to do it. Maybe Harland wouldn't mind going out for me."

"Harland is in Kentucky."

"Mama, Harland is in the parlor teaching his boys to play checkers."

"That's not right."

Harland had been in San Francisco for years. Then he took Melissa to Chicago where she died in a hospital. Granny had been by her side and then came with him back here. "It's all right, Mama," I said. "Playing checkers won't hurt them. It's not gambling."

"I mean it wasn't Ken-tuck. Rufus. He was in Kentucky."

I sighed. "All right, Mama."

Gilbert came in then, dripping, carrying something under his coat. He pulled off his hat and opened the jacket. "Thought you might use this for supper," he said, grinning.

At first all I saw was that it was meat and I was relieved not having to trudge to the smokehouse with its dwindling supply of hanging meats. Only the poorest bony portions remained. "Son, you have read my mind," I said.

"Aren't you going to ask me where I got 'im? Look here, what he is. I didn't cut him up so you could see the size of him." He held the carcass up by the hind legs. It looked to be the biggest jackrabbit I ever saw, fully the size of a good dog. Gilbert said, "It's old Rotten."

"No!" The long-legged hare we called Rotten Rabbit. When there were no children about I called him some other things, too. That rangy jackanapes had scourged my garden for a year. He'd grown fast and fat, living on my hard work. I took the thing from Gilbert, thinking what a fine table he'd set, all buttered up with lima beans.

Gilbert said, "I waited by the garden where I found a hole under the fence. Soon as the clouds came over and the rain had barely started, here he came, heading for the pole peas. Got him with one shot."

"Buckshot?"

"Nope. Thirty-two."

I grinned. My youngest living son was fixing to turn twenty years old. Looking more like a man every day. "I'm proud of you, boy," I said. I pulled a big skillet off its hook on the wall. "I'm going to brown him up this minute. Then we'll give him a nice long simmer, and start some dough rising."

We passed a nice enough evening. This time instead of the children reciting, Professor Osterhaas found some poetry in my book room and he read forth in a fine style such as I've never heard, waving his good arm and even holding the volume in his sore hand. Not to be outdone, Professor Fairhaven gave us a speech from *Hamlet,* then one in pure Latin, all from memory. Professor Osterhaas praised my books and said he'd been too worn and pained to notice the night before. He wanted to know how I'd started collecting books and which ones I'd read. He was surprised when I said I'd read every one. I didn't tell him I had read them several times, for I was suddenly taken with the notion he'd think me stupid to have to read a book more than once. I can't imagine owning a book you hadn't read at least once. What's the sense of having a book at hand and not opening it?

Then, as he was feeling less uneasy about these folks than before, Gilbert took down his guitar and played us several tunes. Chess played checkers with Story while Harland watched Truth and Honor drawing on their slates. Blessing dressed and redressed her dolly in Granny's lap. Miss James stared into the fireplace. The professors read, and I took up my sewing basket and went to work on the elbow of one of my own waistcoats. After a bit, Miss James said, "Do you know 'Keegan's Lament'?" She began to sing, and taught Gil the song, and pretty soon he'd found chords for it. He played and she sang it again, staring at the fire, while her voice seemed to travel right out of his fingers as he picked across the strings in a pattern.

Then Miss James said she knew one about a magic animal called a Silkie. She sang that one but Gilbert couldn't find all the chords to it. Professor Fairhaven asked if anyone knew any *other* music, as if what he'd been hearing wasn't to his liking. So Gilbert started picking out the tune to "Dixie," which didn't make the professor any happier. Gil followed it with a dance tune and then he wanted to try Charity James's songs again. She asked him for the guitar and what do you know but she played some, too, and showed him the place for his fingers on the Silkie song. I liked that one.

Gilbert went back to "Keegan's Lament" and then played one like it we have out here called "The Drover's Lament." Listening to Gilbert singing, I hummed with him. If I didn't hum, those old songs would take me back in time and I'd get weepy. I knew as much and didn't care to visit the past in front of those people. It was a fine time, though.

The rain let up the following day. After a stack of flapjacks, Gil rode up to the wash but came back saying it was running so hard there'd be no crossing it. One more meal for all these folks. So I got out the sack of beans. When he saw me cleaning a bowl of pinto beans to soak down for our supper, Professor Osterhaas asked me if I couldn't kill one of the chickens instead. "They aren't mine," I told him. "Those chickens are Savannah's. I borrowed them to start new chicks this spring. They've got to last through winter." He looked disappointed but didn't say more. I suppose some folks aren't partial to beans. Dressed up with some red chili and onions they go down all right to me.

That night we gathered around the supper table where I'd laid out risen biscuits and tortillas, red sauce and piccalilli and beans. I noticed Gilbert held out the chair for Miss James, then took a seat right next to her. I'd be happy enough to be soon rid of these strangers. For a while, everyone was eating and it got quiet. Then Harland up and said, "Sarah? Clover and Mary Pearl came by with the mail while you all were gone. Rachel's written back. I . . . I've hired her for a governess."

Granny said, "A girl can't even vote, son. How do you expect her to be the governor?"

He smiled. "Mama, she'll watch the children after school. Tend to them. Give them lessons in town. I've decided not to wait any longer. Sarah has offered me her house there. When we take these folks in, I'm going, too. Going to hang out my shingle."

Gilbert said, "Town's growing."

Harland went on, barely hiding the excitement in his voice, "Houses going up like weeds. Macadamized roads. Gas stoves. Horseless carriages all over."

I pushed the plate full of biscuits toward him. Everyone got quiet. Chess said, "Folks may not need an architect. They generally just order up a house from the Sears and Roebuck or draw a square and start hauling rocks."

"Well," Harland said, "if it doesn't work, I guess I'll go on home to California."

Then all three of our guests started in with Harland, discussing all the grand places they'd seen in California, painting the place up like a new barn, as fancy and flowery as the Garden of Eden. The only part of California I'd seen was San Francisco and the memory of that destruction was printed in my mind like a lithograph: sludge and mud and rain, smoke and disease and desolation. It truly sounded as if they were talking about some other, far-distant, airy and lovely place—the Hanging Gardens of Babylon. Listening to them chatter, I began to think they were all in cahoots with one another, even my baby brother, working up a gullywasher of a tall tale.

Finally, there was a quiet spell and I said, "You don't need to go yet."

"I can make a living in Tucson. Pay you rent on the house. You'll have money coming in, enough to live on."

"That's what this is about. We aren't starving."

"Well, not entirely. I can't go on here. It—it makes me feel invalid. I need to get back to work. You need the money. It's good all around."

"So's castor oil." I felt as if I could run from the table. The company had grown silent. No one dared move.

"Sis?"

"Oh, go on, then. Never mind I need you here."

"I don't do anything here. I'm no good at all the things you make look slick and easy. All I'm doing is collecting dust."

I felt that same rush of heat under my chin, but this time it hurt and threatened to make my eyes water. I looked toward the window and stared at the reflection in it. A kerosene lamp, lit, on the table, made an arrow of light under an image of Harland's head.

He smiled kindly. "Sis? I'm good at what *I* do."

I'd lost the battle. In front of strangers, too. I frowned and said, "I charge a mean rent. And inspections every Thursday."

Harland grinned. I'd rarely seen him smile since he'd come here, other than the wan tremor he used facing his children's eager faces, trying to approve their small accomplishments. Now here were two at one meal. He was coming back to life, that was it. I remember coming back to life after Jack died. I needed to do things, work at things, too. If I kept Harland here, it'd turn out no good for any of us. Judging from the spunk I saw in his eyes, there'd be no keeping him.

I wish I knew a word for that kind of righteous ache that weighs down my insides when I do what I know is the right thing to do, though it goes against all my normal leanings. I suppose I could quit aching if I quit trying to do right. I said, "Tell the children to put out anything that needs washing and we'll do it tonight so you'll have a few things to last when you get there. I've got work to do." I left the table and went to pump water in the washtub. I added salt water to it, I reckon, as a couple of tears fell in the water before Granny came to help. She pulled out the hand wringer and the scrub board and brush, never saying a word. Then I wiped my face and mumbled something about the water splashing on me.

Well, the whole lot of folks followed me into the kitchen, and lingered about while we washed and rinsed, talking about Tucson. Harland's boys were happy enough, I suppose, to be going to town, though I wondered about the littlest one, the only girl, Blessing. Those professors couldn't hear enough about town then, and wanted to know anything Gilbert could tell them about the college. Harland went to talking about how he meant to start his business going. Granny and I set rows of little duds on wires hung near the stove, and I felt as if I could give over to lonesomeness right in front of them all.

Before we were finished, Harland sent the children to their room, the professors went to the book room to read, and Granny left for bed, too. I reckoned if the whole household was going to town, now, I'd better plan to stay a few days and help Harland get started. That meant I had to pack my own things. I told Gilbert to bank up the stove for morning, and I left him with Miss James overseeing his work.

In my bedroom, I took the box of odd buttons from its place on a shelf over my sewing machine. Beside it lay the waistcoat I'd been mending. For a while, I sat in the dim light of one small lamp and hunted something from the button box that might match the other buttons on the shirt. Nothing came close enough in both color and size. It had been pure silliness to put fancy buttons on a shirt of mine. They wear out and come off the same as the cheap kind. I bit my lip. Everything tears down and goes away. Eternal fire, I thought, I wish they'd all leave this very minute. Maybe I'd send Gilbert packing, too. High time that boy got out on his own like his brother.

I threaded a needle with black thread and bit the end off the spool before I tied a knot. I pushed the needle up from inside the sleeve, through the cloth, through the button, over the top and down. It has been the abiding hope of my life to know someone who came to stay and wanted to be with me. I know I have got an ornery streak in me, and some of my bones seem to be made of cast iron. Nothing about me ever gentled down and got soft and motherly like my brother Albert's good wife, Savannah. I'm sure it is because she is of righteous makings that she has had Albert to take her along life's path. No one has ever been my strength and shield. Nor even wanted to. I've stood on my own feet and fought my own fight. Even Jack, who I loved with those same iron bones, was never content to stay put and let me lean on him.

Miss James came in to go to bed. I had my torn pocket inside out and was working away on it, when she came over and turned up the flame on the lamp. "You'll hurt your eyes," she said. She put on the nightgown I'd loaned her, and sat on the end of the bed and watched me sew for a minute. "I can do that hem for you."

"I'll get it myself, thanks," I said.

She picked up the waistcoat I'd put the odd button on. Holding it up in her hands as if she were considering wearing it herself, she said, "You've got a nice figure. My waist has never been very small."

"Where are your folks? Don't they mind that you've gone so far from home?"

Without answering the question, she said, "Are you feeling poorly, Mrs. Elliot?"

"Bone tired, is all. This is finished. Put out that light, will you please?" I got myself undressed and got into bed. I could hear her breathing next to me.

After a bit, she said, "Did I do something to make you angry?"

I did feel mettlesome. I wanted these strangers out of my house. I wanted things set to rights. It was these strangers gave Harland the notion to up and leave. I said, "I'll go in the morning and see if the water's down yet."

"Your brother seems like a nice fellow. How long has his wife been dead?"

I flew out of that bed. Stood there, stiff as the iron fence I pictured made up my ribs. Stared at where I thought she'd be, in the dark. Before too long, I started shaking. I would not share my bed with a slattern and a hussy. I couldn't turn her out of my room, for then she'd be free to approach someone else for a place to lie. I kept my voice low. "To think I've fed the snake in my own corn crib," I said. I fumbled for the matches on the highboy but couldn't find them. Light from the moon outlined her form.

"I didn't mean it thataway." She flustered, pulling the coverlet up to her chin.

My feet felt as if they were drilled into the floor. "You best not be putting designs on him or you'll answer to me."

"I only meant he seemed like a nice man. Nicer than Professor Fairhaven."

There was no way to tell what she meant in the dark, nothing but the sad whine of her voice. A person could make any sound come from their throat, but they'd have to go a long ways before they could hide what's in their eyes. I wanted to shout and chase her from my room, but I'd better keep her right here so there wouldn't be any foolishness going on. I said, "He is a nice man. His wife was dear to this family. He's not looking for a wife right now."

"Professor Fairhaven began to make advances toward me so I come to bed."

I sat on the edge of the bed. "What'd he say? I'll throw him out of the house."

"He didn't say anything. It was the way he looked at me."

"Just get some sleep," I said. I rolled back in and pulled up the covers, trying not to touch her. After a bit I heard her sniffing at odd times and I believed she was crying. I kept quiet. When I awoke before dawn, she was deep asleep and I slid out of the bed without waking her.

I did the feeding with Gilbert. The eleven head of cows we ended up the season with were all in a fenced pasture close to the house where I could watch for rustlers. That meant they had to be fed and I was deep into Albert's pockets for that. I'd kept all my horses, too—against my own common sense—because Albert put his foot down and was buying feed for them, too. Our pa had us raising horses before any of us could walk, and Albert said someday we'd need 'em again. He just couldn't bear the idea of me selling off the two dozen horses, though their feed bill is triple that of the cows. If all my life fell into perfect step-in-time for the next five years, I'd see things back the way they were. For now I was counting on family and neighbors to keep my place off some banker's mortgage blotter.

Hot breath curled from the nose of El Capitán, the prize bull, forced out in gasps between holding his breath as he tried to take a lion's share of the hay I tossed out, and he made thick noises as he chewed. I tapped him on the side and chanced to rub his great head. There was a crusting of frost on all the cows. The only thing on them that looked warm were their wet and steaming noses. Capitán stepped sideways and I jumped quick to keep from getting my feet broken. The old fellow had gotten pretty tame, being fed and petted. Better to have a bull that only wants to kill you half the time instead of all the time. Most of 'em see anything moving as standing between themselves and two minutes of true love. That made me think of that Professor Fairhaven. I'd sure be glad to have these strangers gone.

I left the household to cook their own breakfast while I rode to the arroyo. I wore a pair of Gilbert's pants under my split skirt. Udell once told me he thought he could sell sheepskin coats in Arizona. I'd laughed at him. What I wouldn't give for a heavy fleece coat this morning.

The sky had cleared overnight and the morning world was coated with heavy frost. Puddles on the road were frozen near solid. Baldy had been sassy when I was trying to saddle him before full daylight, and now he acted foolish, stepping in frozen puddles like a little boy will do, just to hear the ice crack. Never saw a horse do that before. At the arroyo, there were still three inches of water in the bottom, but it was sludged over with silt and branches, the last tracks of a rushing torrent. As I stood in the bottom of the gorge, torn weeds and shredded trees showed the height of the flood that had come through. The water had been higher than the tips of my fingers, with my arms stretched as far as I could reach. We'd have all been dead if we'd been in it. I headed for home and gave the horse his head. He was still feeling his oats so he got me there in under an hour, though my nose was near frozen.

We lined up the rigs and took stock so we could load all the people and baggage from the stage, plus Harland's family and their few possessions. Albert's surrey could seat eight people if two were small. Gilbert hitched my dusty old buggy that hadn't seen daylight in ten years or more, being too small for a family. Then Chess pulled up the buckboard with the two dead folks. None of us dared a look but we decided they'd be frozen pretty solid, judging by the layer of ice on the tarpaulin covering them. We rigged up a platform on the sides and piled the freight on top. Then it was time to sort the people.

I supposed it would be best to insist Miss James ride with me to keep her from making cow eyes at Harland, but she preferred to ride with Chess, sitting over the dead ones, on top of the boxes and baggage filling the buckboard's false floor. Professor Osterhaas took off his hat and asked if he could have the pleasure of riding with me.

Fairhaven did not look happy about riding with Harland's children all the way to town, which gave me a guilty pleasure thinking how the children would surely entertain him. Gilbert was to stay home and mind the place, but he walked us out of the yard holding the side of the buckboard, until we turned the corner toward Albert's place. Harland wanted to stop a minute and say farewell. Albert will follow us tomorrow and help drive all these rigs home. It was nearly ten before we got on the road.

One thing about a long trip with a stranger, if they're inclined to talk and be genteel, it can be interesting and pass the time right along. Professor Osterhaas knew a great many things, but he was also every bit as interested in what *I* knew, and asked why I read so many books and all. He declared he had been up most of the night reading, and didn't even seem surprised that I taught my children and all my nieces and nephews until they went to town for university studies.

"But you've never been, yourself?" he asked.

My double team was made up of one fairly sober horse on the left and an ornery one on the right that always thought she should pull left. If I put her on the left, we did nothing but turn in circles as if she were hard of seeing in one eye. I shook the reins. It helped to make her pay attention that I was the one holding the harnesses. "Nary a whit."

"May I ask where you took your prior education?"

"Took it, sir?"

"Normal school, or grammar, that sort of thing?"

He had a colorful way of stringing words, this professor of letters. Why, under threat I would not admit to a stranger that I'd never passed through the door of a schoolhouse, except the day I took my twelfth-grade examination by mail order. I was plenty tired of these folks, and I surely didn't want this one clucking his tongue over my ignorance for the next eighty miles.

Then I remembered my papa making me sound out letters and words from our old family Bible, and then Savannah giving me a piece of newspaper to practice on. "Private," I said. "I was schooled privately."

"Excellent. What a fine governess you've had, then. What was that good lady's name?"

"Most of the time I'd like to not be asked so many questions, Professor Osterhaas."

"Beg pardon, ma'am."

"How's your arm?"

"I think it's better. Still black and blue."

"Starting to knit up, then."

After a spell of silence he said, "I must say, it has been a relief to be free for a few minutes from Professor Fairhaven."

"How so?" I said.

"The man's an intemperate rounder. A popinjay."

"Well, I had him called, then. I'd have thought someone who's a professor—"

"It has been to my continual . . . ah. If we had remained in California I'd have recommended him for censure. When I found out the unfortunate Miss Castle was not his bride, you see, I was put in a dreadful fix. As we had been hired together, I was forced to extend professional courtesy as a colleague."

My team tussled with their rig. I said, "Tell me about going to college. All my boys tell me about is the pranks they pull and how awful it is, but I saw from their books what they get to read."

Reckon I hit on Professor Osterhaas's best subject. He expounded for a good hour on everything a person could study and do and see and all in the name of education. Hearing it made a tingling run from my hair to my shoulders. At the same time disappointment made itself hard in my throat. While he talked, I could imagine the school buildings before me, picture folks from all over the territory waiting for a professor to come tell them about Chaucer or the Alps or Gregorian music. There were student meetings after class, discussions of philosophies from distant lands, clubs and societies for this subject or that, convocations to attend, displays of bird species and lectures on chemistry and real microscopes to look through, and what he called "savoring the search for truth" with poetry and tableaux and violinists from New York.

"All that," I said, "takes place here in Tucson? In the Territory?"

"It took place in Philadelphia. I'm sure the university here is quite the same."

"My daughter and her husband lived in Philadelphia for a while. She never mentioned a university."

"Well, it probably wouldn't interest a married woman. She'd have many other concerns."

"Raising babies. She's got three already."

"And that young man, Harland, he's a brother, not your husband?"

Well, he'd whittled things out of me without my knowing. "Professor, I've put two husbands in the ground by that big tree at our place. Here's the arroyo. You hold on to the sides. This gets to shaking, but it's not going over."

It took our train the better part of an hour to go down one side and back up the other. Professor Osterhaas turned whiter than a sheet a couple of times, but I drove that team hard against the sides, and the footing was wet and soggy but did not give way. At the bottom, we unloaded the buckboard, and while I drove, the men pushed it uphill. To the last, each of us wore half our weight in mud by the time we got back on the road.

The professor must have been some orator for he started in again, and kept me in a spell with his words about learning. If anyone ever wanted to hear a fine speech, they'd do worse than to pay a nickel for his time. A long time later, when we could see the outlines of Tucson in the distance, Professor Osterhaas said, "I suppose you're quite caught up in household affairs. Pity. With your educational background, you'd make a fine student."

I gritted my teeth against a quick, sharp pain in my chin. "Sir, my educational background was only this side of Abe Lincoln's spade. The honest truth is that I found some books cast off by the side of the road. That there was the lock, stock, and barrel of my school in between washing diapers, baking bread, and fighting Indians. I'd no more fit in that classroom full of young thirsty minds—as you put it—than I could wear feathers and fly to Constantinople." I snapped the reins. The buggy jerked forward as the horses picked up their feet a bit. A fine student! Long ago, I'd dreamed of it, but I'd been a girl. Now it was pure tomfoolery and nonsense.

My eyes watered up and I couldn't see. Tears slid out of place and tracked down my cheeks. I turned my head away and wiped them, hoping he wouldn't notice. I had a ranch to run. Work to do if I was going to drag my place out of the ground again. It might never be what it had been when Chess first came with his gift of a cattle herd. The children were small. Jack was here. The work was keeping track of breed stock and branding and hiring and such. Now there was just hoping and scraping and trying to get the garden up and keep the chickens safe from coyotes, both four-legged and two-. What would make a man I barely know think he could talk to me of my secret dreams as if they were no more hidden than a pinto pony in broad daylight?

"Still, any woman who's read *Theories of Planetary Motion* without benefit of instruction, why, deserves a chance—"

I quit crying. "I reckon you're trying to be polite, Professor. I've always longed to go to school and there's no one that's thought about it more than me. It just ain't going to happen, so I wish you'd let go of that rope and just let the dust settle on it!"

"Pardon me, madam." He was quiet the rest of the way to town. It took me a long while to set my face to rights, feeling so torn inside.

Chess called a halt to our travels and Miss James climbed into the surrey with the children. Then Chess turned off the road toward the undertaker's. Harland followed me north of town to finally take leave of our company of travelers.

When we got to the university steps to let them out, that buzzard professor says to me, "It *was* a simple spade he used. I seem to remember he dug a good, long furrow with it, too. President Lincoln, that is," and took his bags with not a single word of thanks for all I'd done for him.

# Chapter Three

*December 13, 1906*

By the time we pulled up to my house in town, the sun had dropped behind the mountains past Sentinel Peak, and long shadows followed our weary horses. Jack and I had built that house when April was little and the boys were babies. Two more children had been born there. The baby boy never took a breath, but little Suzanne grew to be two years old. She'd skinned her nose once, toppling off the porch when she was learning to walk. Scarlet fever took her from us before she was three. There were a lot of memories in that place. I watched Harland's "band of rogues" bundling up the steps, impatiently waiting for me to open the door. I suppose I hadn't even thought of the place as sad, but there was nothing like the clatter of children to wake a wooden house up. Truth, Honor, and Story bolted through the empty place, whooping and scrambling up the stairs, and for a long while we could hear them stampeding across wooden floors high overhead.

We'd barely gotten in the door when Blessing dropped to the dusty floor and started kicking her feet against the boards. She yelled and hollered until Harland was beside himself trying to get her to hush. Finally, I said, "Harland, follow me," and led him out the door. We left her crying on the floor and went around the yard. "You'd better either cut a switch and use it, or ignore that, much as you're able," I said. "Soon as she sees you're not paying attention, she'll quit."

He looked a little nervous, but paid attention while I showed him how to start the pump to get water to the top floor, where the ash hopper went through the wall, and where the valve was to get the gas going into the pipes for lights in the parlor. The whole time, Blessing followed us, sniffling, at times crying, but we ignored her until she came and put her arms around Harland's right leg.

"Poppy? Carry me."

He took her in his arms, where she sagged against his neck, quiet at last. Harland said, "And how can you tell if all the lights are down? Isn't there a main switch? I'd put one in."

"Maybe you should. I always worried about the gas and mostly used kerosene. We never ran gas lines to the upper floors because I was afraid the children would leave one open and unlit." I felt as if I were abandoning my little brother to take care of himself. Then I remembered he was only a couple of years younger than I and he'd been doing just that for twenty years. I took Harland's arm.

I'd left a couple of cots in the place, where Albert's and my offspring usually slept while they took classes at the university, and a rugged old table and a few beat-up chairs furnished the kitchen. Otherwise, the house had more spiders than furniture. Well, Harland said he couldn't possibly do up the place without a woman's help, so he asked me to stay another day and help him buy some things. I told him if he wanted real style, he'd do better to ask April to come along, as she has lived in Philadelphia and her house is the grandest thing I've ever known.

That evening, I fixed us a simple supper and we all pitched in to clean and sweep the kitchen and make up spare fixings for tonight, with the promise of better things tomorrow. The children were none too happy with just a blanket to curl on, to be sure. But I circled them up and made up a story for them, about four children on a great adventure who could ride their bedrolls like a cloud in the sky, and wherever they wished to go, they could go. The kitchen was the only warm place in the house, so Harland and I let them eat their suppers sitting on their blankets around the cookstove. They made up a game and shouted out fantastic things we'd eat from their magic bedrolls, like popcorn-ball-picnics held deep under the ocean and animal crackers over the moon, flying fish in India and noodles in New York. Truth said he'd prefer camping in the kitchen to having a regular bed, anytime.

Harland gave me a stiff argument about the rent, insisting he'd pay $52 a month. I got him to settle on $38. It was fair enough, since he'd helped me build the house years ago. Then he paid me in cash, six months in advance. I'd never taken money from my family, except for when Granny paid for my well and windmill this fall. I took that money—$228 in folding money made a wad too big to put in my pocket—and as I held it in my hand, it poured an awful and strange torrent of feelings through my soul. I was glad to have it, sorry to take it, happy to know we'd eat through Christmas, and mortified to need it, all at the same time. He said he'd fix up a room so I'd always have a bed in town.

First thing we did next morning was to pay a call at April and Morris's house. I let my brother talk to my daughter—and she went on and on about furniture and wallpapers and fancy new linoleum floors—while I went upstairs to find her children. Vallary was nine now, Patricia was six, and Lorelei was three. How I love to see those three grandchildren of mine run to my arms! As they smothered me in kisses, I thought of Professor Osterhaas's foolish suggestion. Schoolgirl grandma—what a hoot! When we came down, April sent their maid for some tea and cookies. She looked pale. When I gave her a hug, she said, "Oh, Mama, please don't. Oh, my—" and then hurried out of the room. Well, I followed her a ways and she only made it to the conservatory door before she let up her lunch into the potted fern there.

I went past her and found a clean towel in a stack of folded ones. I ran water over it and brought it to her to wipe her face. "Honey," I said, "you'd better get out of that corset and lie down."

She mopped at her brow and held the cloth to her face. "Oh, Mama. I'm expecting another baby."

I smiled. "That's just wonderful. When's it coming?"

"May or June."

I held her hands. "I'll get to be with you for this one," I said.

She groaned and said, "I'm faint. Would you undo my stays for me?"

"Let's go upstairs."

"Right here. I don't think I can make it upstairs."

I opened her buttons and loosened her stays. I couldn't stop smiling. I saw the skin of her back had grown puffy, already ripening. She gasped for air when the bands came loose. By that time, the children found us, and I threw my shawl around her shoulders to hide her open dress. April told her son, Vallary, to go fetch their maid to throw out the poor fern.

It was settled that if she were able, April would accompany us the next day as soon as the stores opened, to help her uncle choose the right chairs and such. I've never known finery except the things Jack ordered mail order. Just a few short years have turned Tucson into a big place. There are stores selling things I didn't even know I could want.

That afternoon Albert and his boys, Clover, Ezra, and Zack, along with Mary Pearl, arrived. Savannah and Rebeccah had stayed at home for want of the surrey we'd used. Albert said they had some errands to do for Savannah, but he drove to fetch Rachel from the schoolhouse where she lived and worked. We'd have one more night on the floor, and then a busy day tomorrow.

Rachel has been small and frail compared to her twin, Rebeccah, ever since she took rheumatic fever a few years ago. Her frame seemed as delicate as Granny's, though her eyes were bright and her mind plenty quick to handle all these children.

As Harland introduced them to their new governess, Story piped up with, "Does this mean we can go to regular school again, or are you our teacher like Aunt Sarah?"

"Regular school. But if you got the measles and missed a day, I've been a teacher and I'll help you out."

I saw Harland's boys cut eyes at each other. No telling what their experiences had been in San Francisco with schoolteachers, but it didn't look as if they were pleased to have one for a governess. Small as Rachel was, I figured the children would be in good hands. She was Savannah's daughter, after all.

Next thing, I went in the kitchen to start supper and Harland got a newspaper to see if there was an advertisement of someone wanting to be a house girl. While he went to visit a lady who'd run a notice, I started up a big pot of soup and made myself a list of things I needed to buy to take back home. I counted out thirty dollars and folded the bills up tightly, tied them with string, and put the money in my pocket for tomorrow.

April and Rachel decided they'd stay at the house and visit, so I told them to keep the fire going, then took up my cloak to go back to town and get my own errands done. Just then there was a knock at the door. Two women in dark hoods and cloaks stood there, their arms loaded down with baskets of bread and cakes. The Methodist ladies were having a baked-goods sale to raise money. The taller lady said one fund was to put a new stove in the parson's kitchen, as his wife heated it so hot the top sank in and none of her pans will sit up straight nor hold half a pint of water. Well, I told them to tell her to just cook in the yard on a spit, the way I grew up doing. Folks who think they have to have a stove need to think again. Then the shorter lady said they had another collection, which was to take food and building supplies to the townspeople of Clifton. They said the entire town had washed away in the recent rains, and the money was to help them move and rebuild everything higher up on the hills.

One powerful storm and all my memories had been pulled from under me as if they were no more than sand. Harland's, too, when he'd lost the house in the earthquake. I knew exactly what the people were feeling. Flattened out like dried leather. No idea where to turn. I felt the lump of money weighing down my skirt. Harland's little ones and Ezra and Zachary, Albert's youngest boys, crowded about my back, sniffing the air like foxes. Those boys would eat cake any time of the day, any day of the week.

"Would you try the cinnamon cake? It's my grandmother's recipe. She always claimed it was very good for warding off the grippe, too. It must have been so, since I never had it until I left home."

The children made appreciative noises. My neighbors had built me a house and given me more than a roof. They'd made it a palace. I needed the money in my pocket, but here were neighbors I didn't know in straits I knew all too well. "How much?" I said.

"Fifty cents for a cake. But it's for charity."

As I untied the string I'd just fixed, another flood of feelings swept through me. I said, "Let us have two. We've a lot of children here today." I handed over the cash and took two cakes. "And would you please send along an extra dollar—two dollars?" Those poor folks needed the money, but still, I had to think that three dollars gone was a day's wages for a man. A week's worth for a poor one.

"Oh, do take another cake for it."

"No," I said. "You sell that, and two extra dollars will buy a few pounds of nails. Mind, this is for the people who lost their houses, not for the parson's wife to melt her stove."

"Yes, ma'am. And thank you," she said.

The children crowed with happiness as I carried those two big cakes, still warm and smelling like Christmas Day, into the kitchen. They hollered when I told them they had to wait until after supper to eat them.

Then I left so I could run some errands of my own. Might as well find Udell's hinges and get some goods for the ranch before nightfall so we could head home in the morning.

First I went through Sharp's Candy Store and got some horehound in case the ague or the quinsy made the rounds of our family again this winter. I got some Foley's Honey and Tar Cure, too. Nearby was a store I dared not go in. Corbett's books and toys was as spellbinding a place to me as it was to the smallest babe in the family, for they had books for sale. Everything I owned I'd read at least twice, some several times. I stopped and looked in the window. There was a large volume on a display stand, propped open, bound in heavy leather and illustrated with amazing watercolor paintings.

The man behind the counter saw me at the door, came right outside and said, "Well, good afternoon, Mrs. Elliot. How lovely to see you." He took my arm and led me in the door. I must admit, I didn't resist the tug much at all, but fell into that den of sore temptation like a common drunk toward a saloon.

"I'm just thinking," I said. "Looking and thinking."

"You know your credit is always good here. No need for cash. You can pay next summer after the cattle sales."

I pictured my horde of nephews and nieces languishing in front of those cakes in the kitchen with the same tortured hunger I felt standing in this store where the air was perfumed with the delicious fragrance unique to an unsavored book. "Thinking," I said, "that it's a nice day, and I've got more shopping to do."

The man's face fell for an instant, but he said, "We have the most complete line of toys and dolls. Santa Claus is coming, after all. There *must* be some apple of your eye deserving of a gift on the tree this year?"

I sighed. "Many, many children." I could see beyond the books now, to where charming dollies stared, unblinking, their china heads longing to be loved by some little girl. Beyond them, baseballs and leather gloves and carved wooden bats hung over tin trains and lead soldiers, paint sets and hobby horses. "I'll be making them shirts and pinafores for Christmas."

"What about a nice volume for yourself? *The Family Mark Twain* is popular. Have you seen the *Peerless Reciter Or Popular Program*? Rich with tableaux and readings for young and old. Briar Rose, Romeo and Juliet—"

"I've got those." Nearly worn them out, making all the children read.

He pulled a different book off the shelf and opened it. The back of it made that lovely sound, pages starched and perfect as a man's new shirt collar, too stiff to lie flat, loosening their grip on each other. "Here we have *The Advance of the British Empire*. Are you interested in Egyptian secrets from the tombs of the pharaohs?"

I reached for the book, then took my hand away without touching it. "Oh, yes. I'm sorry. I never really meant to come inside. There's a man over there wanting to buy that flashlight machine." I left the store fast as my feet would go down the boarded walk. I'd better do my dreaming in a general store. I had a family to think of.

Christmas *was* coming. I'd need more whole cloth and ticking. Knowing the cash in my pocket was all I had left caused that now-familiar surge of nerves to awaken, and as I ordered things off the list, I spoke slowly, watching Mr. Griego stack goods on the counter, all the while feeling on the verge of panic. What if the flour got weevils, the beans got mold? Should I buy twenty pounds and risk mice eating it up?

In no time I had a bolt of muslin, boxes of nails, bags of beans, sacks of Indian flour and wheat and coffee. A new paper of pins. Five cards of buttons. Axle grease. Hide glue. Baking soda and liniment. I paused in front of a pyramid stack of five jars of Hagan's Magnolia Balm, where a sign underneath said the stuff was guaranteed to keep a woman from looking old and worn. I shook my head, wondering how a woman knew when she looked old and worn. There was a handy mirror right next to the balms, just to check. Instead, I took a box of headache powders. When everything was totaled up it was nearly twenty dollars' worth. I paid off the credit I owed Mr. Griego, too, another three dollars and eleven cents. I tied my string around a thinner roll of bills.

Well, I was ready to leave when I spied a peculiar item under the glass at the register. "Will you show me that?" I asked Mr. Griego. It looked to be some kind of kitchen tool I'd never seen. A metal box with a glass inside.

Mr. Griego squinted and felt around until I nodded when he took hold of the box. He said, "A spirit level, this one? A spirit level is a tool for men to put on things they building. To see is she flat and square. See these air bubble in the oil? When she's lined up in these line, you got you a flat place. It's not flat, it's no good. House going to fall down. Got to be level, and only way is to put this on and see. Keeps everything straight. Just like, you no like when the floor go sideways and the stove don't stand up straight. This fix it. Don't build her crooked."

I set the spirit level on his counter. It was off by a quarter bubble. "A person needs this to build a house?"

"*Sí.* This *mesilla,* she is too many peoples leaning their arms."

"Level would be better. Makes sense to me."

"*Sí.* Less than two dollars for a tool she is *indispensable.* Is good price. Fine instrument."

I couldn't possibly give Udell Hanna a shirt the way I'd do for my own family. That was far too personal. But this, this was the kind of thing a man might use if he had it. A better thing than another pair of gloves, fancier than a hammer. Useful but unusual. I counted out the dollar and ninety-one cents very carefully. I tucked the spirit level into my pocket next to the rolled-up bills, where it bumbled back and forth as I walked to the buggy.

Harland had been busy, and he'd found a lady to cook and clean, too. The place began to feel less mine with every tick of the clock.

Next morning, Harland and I fetched April and off we went. He bought over two hundred dollars' worth of furniture and rugs and lamps from Caldwell's store. Their wagons were loaded and sent to the house in quick order. April said she felt fine and that her baby sickness came on her some days and not others, so Harland took us to lunch at Bell's Pharmacy where we had sandwiches and phosphates.

The wagons full of goods arrived that afternoon, and then we were all a-flurry, setting things right. Rachel had brought her own bedstead and two chests, and we prettied up a room for her on the second floor. With everyone helping out, it began to look like a real home in no time. I had become a guest in my own house. It smelled different. Looked different.

I sent Zack, who is ten, to the attic to sweep so there'd be a clean place to store the few remnants of my furniture. Then I told Ezra to go around all the windowsills with a wet rag. Well, before long I heard them howling up the chimneys at each other, when suddenly Ezra came tearing out of the parlor like a scalded cat, stringing dust and dirt from his hair as he galloped up the stairs threatening to hang Zack out a window. Pretty soon, down they both came, Zack just ahead of his brother, when he tripped and went nose over like a barrel down the stairs. He landed at the bottom with a thud and sprawled, unmoving. Truth and Story came on his heels, with Honor a few steps behind. Those three were cheering and hollering like wild coyotes.

Ezra ran to Zack, shouting, "Get up, you. I'm gonna make you eat a pound of dirt. Just you blink one eye, you yellow dog. Just you breathe one snort."

The rest of us watched in horror. "Zack?" everyone called at once. The boy didn't move. Albert went to him. "Son?" he said.

Zack opened one eye. "Don't let him pound me, Papa. I didn't know he'd stuck his big dumb head up the chimney. I was doing my chores like I was told."

Ezra said, "Ah, I knew he was playing possum. You bum."

"There'll be no calling names," Albert said. "Now, boys—"

Zack crossed his arms and said, "He was owl-hooting up the chimney like he was being some ghost."

"Was not."

"Was, too. He said Uncle Jack's ghost was walking around up in that attic and if I moved the dust, the ghost would get me. Then he starts—"

"You were bragging you didn't care about being up there. Bragging's a sin."

"—hooting up the chimney like he was a ghost. The only way to see a ghost is when they walk through dust, so I dusted him."

Albert held both of them by the collars of their shirts. He said, "Ezra, go outside and shake that out of your hair. Then you sweep every speck of dust you spread through this house and finish the attic yourself." Albert went on, jostling Zack by his neck, "You apologize to Aunt Sarah, then get in that kitchen, find the stove black and start painting that stove. And don't you spill one single drop."

I turned around to keep from laughing at their antics, but I kept a strong face while Albert scolded. A couple of men were busy tying netting over an oil painting of a river where cows grazed under a big tree. Even they were laughing.

In the midst of it all, I spied Blessing sitting at the top of the stairway. I went toward her, but she hopped up and ran for one of the bedrooms. She closed the door before I got there. I stopped outside the portal, wondering what I should do. Blessing had been her mother's darling. Her father's, too, I'd reckon. Far too headstrong and willful for a child. I thought of Harland hiring Rachel. An inexperienced girl would have her hands full with this bunch. Far as I could see it wasn't the lack of a governess that caused them to be sassy and spoiled. My brother had put aside his responsibility for rearing them because it was easier to see them through eyes of pity than courage.

"Blessing?" I said, opening the door. "I want to talk to you."

"Yes, ma'am," came a little voice. She was seated on a rocking horse, staring out the window.

"Well, that's not the reaction I expected, after you ran away from me just now."

"Poppy said I have to say 'yes, ma'am' to you for my own good, or I'll go to hell when I die."

"Ah."

"Poppy says we have to live in your house now and we should be thankful."

"Are you thankful?"

"I want to go home to our own house. Mommy's there waiting for us. She doesn't know where to find us, or she'd have come. I don't want to live in *your* old house. It's too far for her."

I sat down on the window seat next to her. She turned her head and stared out the window in another direction. I said, "You know your house burned down. Remember the earthquake?"

"No."

"Remember how sick your mommy got? Remember she was in bed in that awful tent and then you went with her in a train to Chicago, waiting for her to get well?"

"There wasn't anything to eat."

"I know."

"Poppy said you came to take us to a safe place. To save Mommy. Where did you put her?"

"Blessing, you know your mother went to heaven with the angels."

Blessing turned a red face toward me. Tears shot forth from her eyes and a slick of spittle came from the corner of her mouth. "She did not! She did not! She's lost and she's looking for me. My mommy would never go to heaven without me. She needs me. She said so."

"I know she needs you. You were her favorite little girl in the whole world. You were a special gift to her from God. But He needed her up there with Him."

"I hate God! He doesn't need my mommy. *I* need her. I'm going to run away and find her. You'll see. I'm leaving."

There are people I know who would spank a child for saying to an adult anything so impertinent. But I knew how she felt. "Shall I help you pack?"

She made a choking sound and nodded "yes."

I pulled her valise from under the new bed all decked with fluffy down coverlets and stuffed toys. "What would you like to take? This bear?"

"No."

"You'll need some drawers and stockings. How about one of these dresses?"

"I hate that one." She slid off the wooden horse and pulled open a drawer on a chest between the windows. "This is my favorite nightie." She folded it carefully and laid it on the bed. It was an old one that had belonged to one of Savannah's girls that I'd restitched for her when she'd gotten to my ranch house. For some reason, it warmed my hands to touch it. "I want my dolls from home. Poppy said I can't have them."

"They are all lost, honey," I said. I tucked the nightie in, along with stockings and two sets of pantaloons and the brand-new tortoiseshell hairbrush from her dressing stand. "Do you want the doll Granny made?"

"All right. Bring Molly. And my red cape. Poppy reads me 'Little Red Riding Hood' when I wear it."

I folded the tattered cape. She'd had it on when I found her and Harland's family in San Francisco, living in the filth left after the fire. It had taken me two washes to discover it had once been red. "If you leave, of course, he'll never read it again."

She glared at me, the look on her face one of suspicion and accusation. "Yes he will."

"No he won't. If his Little Red Riding Hood is gone."

"I'll be with Mommy. He can read it and come find me."

"Do you want to take a buttonhook? How about a toothbrush? Are you all set, then? Shall I drive you to the train depot?"

"Yes." She nodded firmly, a horse trader having made the best bargain of the day. I carried the valise through the house past workmen and movers, the maid and the cook. Harland was calling from a back room for men to put a piano in the front parlor. Truth, Story, and Honor were in the backyard prowling through crates and cartons, hiding and jumping out to shoot each other with their fingers. Out of habit, Blessing took my hand as we swept past them all and got into the buggy I'd only half unloaded. No one noticed that we pulled onto the road, nor waved or called as we drove toward the depot.

Two miles down the road we turned at a corner, and another mile went by before we pulled up at the station. It was quiet at the moment. I tied off the horse and helped Blessing down. "Sit there," I said, and went to talk to the stationmaster. Then I returned to her. "It's all set," I said. "You have permission from the man who runs the trains to get on. All you have to do is wait for the next one. Good luck. It's getting dark. Try and find something to eat along the way. There might be something left on the floor after someone real sloppy is finished. Don't forget to brush your teeth once in a while so they don't fall out. If they do, be sure to get some false ones that don't clack too much. Goodbye and farewell." I smiled and waved as if she were only skipping next door to see a friend, then I climbed into the buggy.

Worry took her face, but she sat still. I shook the reins. The wheels turned. The horse took two more steps. I heard a squeal of alarm. "Wait!" Blessing shouted. "Wait, Aunt Sarah!"

I stopped the horse and turned to see her. "Was there something we forgot?"

"Are you going to leave me here?"

"Well, yes. You said you wanted to go."

There was panic in her voice. It came out a shriek. "You can't leave me here to wait all alone. I'm a little girl!"

"Well, if you're leaving, I've got to go tell your poppy and brothers. They'll be awfully sad, of course." I gave a great sigh. "Maybe he'll find another girl someday who wears a red cape and wants to hear the story."

"He can't do that."

"Oh, well," I said. "He is already so sad, with Mommy up in heaven and all, having to lose you too will just make him cry day and night. Maybe I'll read 'Little Red Riding Hood' to *him,* so he'll remember you before you left him."

"I wouldn't leave him! Poppy needs me."

I turned the buggy around. Blessing stood at the edge of the platform. A train whistle howled from the west; the evening Santa Fe was pulling into town. "He needs you more than ever," I said, "but you want to leave. He's too sad right now to tell you to behave yourself. He doesn't scold you or paddle you when you're naughty because he misses your mommy so much. He might forget that underneath the tantrums you can be a good girl. Who is going to remind him of how good you can be, if you aren't there? Why, he might keep crying until he's old."

She put her fists into her eyes and rubbed, crying loudly. "I want my mommy," she crooned between sobs.

I got out of the rig and went to her, kneeling. "Blessing, Mommy can't be here. She's looking down from heaven, hoping you'll help her take care of Poppy. She'd want you to come home."

Suddenly, she threw her arms around my neck, nearly sending me sprawling on the platform. "I want my poppy. Mommy needs me to be with Poppy."

"Yes, she does," I said. Tears brimmed over in my own eyes. "Shall we go now?" The air began to hum with the low rumble of the train approaching. "Train's almost here. You could get on it."

"No!" She crushed my neck. "Don't *let* me go away. I want my poppy."

I picked her up and sat her in the buggy, her valise at her feet. We drove back to the house, and the whole way there, Blessing nestled against me, sniffling and whimpering. Soon as we got to the yard, she called her papa, and hopped down so fast when she saw him I had to brake hard and haul back on the line for fear of running over her.

I went to Harland, who looked exhausted. He patted Blessing's head as she clung to his knees. He said, "Oh, Sarah, there you are. Can you please help me and watch her for a bit? Just do something with her to keep her from underfoot."

"She was running away from home," I said.

He stopped short. "Running away? To where?" He picked her up.

Blessing said, "To find Mommy. But Aunt Sarah said you'd have to read

'Red Riding Hood' to someone else because I was gone away. So I comed home."

"You comed home?" he said. Harland looked over her head at me.

I said, "She was at the train depot. Fixing to get on the seven-thirty to Lordsburg."

"You need me, don't you, Poppy?" Blessing asked.

He looked puzzled and sad. "Yes, of course."

"Where's Mommy?"

Harland shuddered. "Go in the house, precious. Be a good girl. Find Rachel, and play with her. Go upstairs and . . . play. Wait until I can tell you the story again."

She went. I handed him the valise. "Here's what she was taking," I said. "She may try this again. I think she wants to believe she can find her mother, so much that it might happen. Like a child sitting on a rug waiting for it to fly like a magic carpet."

My brother scratched his head. "I'm making a mistake, aren't I? I can't do this without you."

I forced myself to say, "Yes you can. This moving commotion will be over. You'll have your work in the front room there that you've made into your office, and Rachel will see to the children. You won't be far away. I won't be, either. Melissa will be just over your shoulder, too. I was sorry to see you leave the ranch, but life in this town will be more what your little ones are accustomed to than at the ranch. They'll have regular schooling. Friends to play with. Epworth League at the church. It'll be good."

"But not the same."

"Harland, nothing ever is. Will you come down for Christmas?"

He sat on the edge of a wooden crate and picked at a loose thread pulled from the weave of his trousers. At last he looked at me and said, "We'll bring the goose."

"Fine," I said.

Well, instead of playing with Rachel, I found Blessing sitting on a chair next to Chess, who was warming his hands at the kitchen stove. She was recounting her trip to the train station and he nodded now and then, repeatedly asking, "What happened next?"

That evening I repacked my purchases to be ready for the drive home, and waited for my supper as if I were some royal personage in a castle. Likely to get plum spoilt, having all that work go on without me. While we ate, commotion went on overhead as some fellows hoisted the last two beds into place upstairs.

It wasn't a bad meal that Mrs. Ramsey cooked, it just wasn't enough for two people, much less the twelve of us. Everyone had a taste of the potatoes and carrots and peas, and a morsel of meat. If I hadn't made the soup, we'd have all gone hungry. The dessert was a single pie. Only eight inches across and cut into twelve pieces, it was little more than two bites each. Well, everybody is new at something once. Mrs. Ramsey would have to learn her job, I suppose.

After supper, Harland's children were sent to the parlor where Rachel read them stories. The last workmen left and then Harland went to his study and started sorting things. I climbed the stairs slowly, feeling foreign as a daisy in a rose garden in this old familiar place, now all done up fancier than I'd ever seen it.

In the washroom I closed the door, ran the water, and had a good soak. From the tub, I stared at the mirror high over the washstand. How many times had I stood there, talking to Jack's reflection as he worked that straight razor across his neck and face? After I dried off, I went to the mirror and touched the place on the washstand where Jack's shaving cup had sat. When he was eleven, Charlie once knocked off and broke the shaving cup his father had carried through the Indian Wars. He'd had to buy a new one out of his allowance. I remembered the smell of Jack's shaving soap tinctured with oil of bergamot and eucalyptus.

The room was cold. I dressed quickly and went to my new old room; it had been transformed, too. The cot was gone and in its place was a fine bed. Against one wall was an armoire, and a cushioned chair waited beneath the window with a companion table. The chair was padded and fat, and made a nice warm nest for someone to curl up their feet and have a good think. The bed had been laid with linen sheets and new blankets.

I put out the light. The almost dozen other people in the house managed to get themselves to bed without me, and I didn't mind it a bit. In that fancy, soft bed, I stared into the darkness. If Jack were here right now, I'd make him love me and then wrap himself around me so we'd stay warm all night. The house got quiet. It was my house no longer. Felt different, sounded different, smelled of the new furnishings. It took a while for all the memories I knew of Jack in this house to fade into the night.

# Chapter Four

*December 15, 1906*

The ruckus of our return home was equivalent to watching the Sixth Army abandon its post years ago, and it appeared we were taking half the town with us. This being so close to Christmas, it seemed as if a migration had begun to points south. Since we were traveling with all those folks, for once there was little worry about highway robbers and bandidos.

At last we came to the fork that leads to Granny's old house where we homesteaded years ago, and from there we could see the sprawling rock home that Albert and Savannah have built over the years. Albert and his boys dropped off our train then, and I was left to drive on with Chess.

"You've been quiet," he said, as we pulled into the yard.

I thought I'd been purely friendly, waving to folks on the road. "How so?"

"Nothing to come home to but old folk. This house is plum empty."

"This house is this house," I said.

"Less washing now."

He wouldn't look in my direction. So I said, "Go on in and I'll unload this."

Granny came out the door just then. She must have been watching by the window. She raised her hand and called out, "That feisty girl is about to make supper. I'll tell her to lay a couple more plates."

I knew who she meant. Mary Pearl did tend to flit through the house like a bird, too full of energy to sit still. "Afternoon, Mama," I said. "Go tell her we're here, then."

I heard her voice from the open door, calling, "Put some water in the beans, Mary Pearl. The folks are home!"

Chess loaded up his arms and we piled things near the pantry. It was all I could do to keep up Chess's pace. Soon as we were done, without saying a word, he drove the rig to the barn and disappeared while I stocked our shelves. Maybe Chess was the one who hated the empty house. While I was trying to keep all those little ones clean and fed and teaching them schoolwork every day they were here, he was the one holding Blessing on his knee as he spun a yarn about a magical bear that outsmarted a hunter. He was the one teaching Story, Honor, and Truth how to make a slingshot and aim it true. I'd been thinking they must surely have tried his patience, but maybe it had been the opposite. I had been too busy to see it.

*December 16, 1906*

Sunday, Savannah held her usual Sunday School. I sat in my best dress in her parlor, listening to her read aloud from the Bible. Albert was next to her and Mary Pearl next to him on the settee. Granny sat near Albert and Savannah's son Clover. Her eyes were closed as if she were in prayer, but I believe she was snoozing. Chess was between Ezra and Zachary, both of them full of Mexican jumping beans. Three hours of not squirming was easier for them to withstand if they were kept apart from one another, and far easier than the chores that would be heaped upon them if they showed signs of disrespect, too. I laid my hands in my lap and stared at them, trying hard to study upon the words she read.

In the corner of the room, Udell Hanna's hands were also folded in his lap. He was clean shaven and had a piece of cotton tied around the smallest finger of his left hand, as if he'd needed a bandage fresh this morning. I wondered if he was thinking of the Scriptures, or daydreaming about his son Aubrey, who should be driving up from Tucson in time for dinner to pay a call on Mary Pearl. I wondered, too, if his people kept Christmas. Had I been too forward, buying him a gift? I could give it to him now, simply because I bought it, and it wouldn't be a Christmas present, so he wouldn't feel obliged to return me one if he hadn't already thought to. How could I keep it another two weeks, anyway?

I couldn't wait to see the pleased look on his face. Lands, I had plenty of sewing to do. I planned to start on it first thing tomorrow, cutting out shirts for the fellows. I hoped I'd bought enough buttons. Udell's face looked deep in thought. I wondered what he was thinking.

Savannah had stopped reading. I turned toward her. She was staring straight at me as if I'd interrupted the Scriptures or sneezed or something equally awful. "Now?" she asked.

"You go on ahead," I said. I had no earthly idea what she'd asked me to do. Albert began to pray and we all bowed our heads. Prayers. Of course. I listened hard. Then all was quiet and that's when I began to let go of the people in the room about me and thought about our trials, feeling thankful we'd kept our heads above water. I also prayed I'd gotten the right number of buttons.

Prayers were signaled to a close by a knock at the door. Aubrey had come, leaving a nice horse and buggy tied up at the rail, and carrying a handful of roses, reds and pinks, mostly, with one white one which he presented to Savannah. Red and pink roses! If a man gave flowers of those colors to a girl, his passion was said to be unbridled! Heavens, I hoped Savannah wouldn't send him scalded from the house. I heard Gilbert, Clover, and Joshua clear their throats. Then Aubrey said, "I stopped to admire them, Mrs. Prine, and the lady of the house said I should take some. Please don't suspect I have hidden artifice in them, as they are the shades she had growing in her yard. She was quite embarrassed, asking me to take them, because of the colors, but they smelled so nice, and I do declare that no clever meanings are attached."

Savannah held the roses and smelled them. She smiled at the young man, and said, "God made all flowers equally beautiful."

Once dinner was over it was time for quiet work, reading or stitchery. Aubrey had come to spend Christmas with his father, but along with that, he'd come intending to take Mary Pearl for a drive. Savannah pulled back the curtain at the parlor window so she could see his new buggy, and said, "Your father should drive, Mary Pearl, and take our surrey."

Mary Pearl's face showed no disappointment, though I do suspect she would have considered driving alone with a man in the afternoon if her mother hadn't spoken. She was seventeen and prettier than a girl has any business being. Mighty headstrong, too.

Udell stepped up and said, "Miss Savannah, if you'd allow, I was planning to ask Miss Sarah to take a drive with me. How about if she and I were to go? We'll provide the children with plenty of company."

Mary Pearl stared at the ceiling as if her mother's answer would come from it. Savannah pursed her lips. Udell had done a good thing making it seem like they needed company instead of watchdogging. I said, "I don't mind spending the afternoon," trying not to sound too anxious myself.

"We'll go, too," said Zachary.

"Yeah," Ezra echoed.

I suppose Mary Pearl and I are closer under the skin to being two buttons on a single card—she wasn't just my niece, I felt more like her older sister. At this moment, we were conspirators in crime, even if the crime was only a few innocent minutes alone with a fellow. Having Ezra and Zack along to ride herd on us would take all the frill off the afternoon. So I said, "Don't you two have lessons to write?"

"We already did 'em," Ezra protested.

"Never mind," Savannah said. "You fellows are going to read a chapter apiece from a work of inspirational thought. Then you may play outside. There will be no riding this afternoon."

The boys turned angry glares at me, dead sure they were surrounded by adults who delighted in keeping them from having any fun whatsoever.

Udell and I sat in the front of Albert and Savannah's old surrey, with the two young people in the back. Udell drove south past my place and farther on, where Cienega Creek runs toward the San Pedro River. This place is so hilly it's like a wrinkled bed. Cross one hill and another and nothing lies before you but another hill. If you go west a bit and south, there's ever flatter and grassier land, but here the rocks and crags fight for a place amongst the grassy slopes. Trees were coming back from the range fire of autumn.

Everybody hereabouts had lost plenty in that fire, except for Rudolfo Maldonado. His family had been on that four sections for three generations when ours came, sometimes trading with, sometimes fighting off, four different tribes of Indians. In the years since my brothers, Savannah, and my mama and I drove up in our rattling single wagon, El Maldonado's parents have passed on, as has his wife, Celia, and the four-room adobe has grown to a twelve-room hacienda. He has hired servants enough to start his own town, and every form of finery that can be shipped to this territory fills his place. But, though we were both young folks at the same time, and have grown older together, while I have had a home and fine family, I believe Rudolfo's riches have not made him satisfied. His new wife, Leta, is a year or so older than both our Mary Pearl and Elsa, his oldest daughter, who he's sent to Tucson to the convent of the Sisters of

St. Joseph of Carondelet for safekeeping. Some days I long for the old times when his first wife, Celia, was alive—when I could call him friend.

It was cool but not cold and, though the air was not bitter, we were all under lap blankets. You'd have thought they were still caught up in prayer, silent as the two were back there. At one point, I managed to need a good long look at a red bird flying by, just to have a reason to turn behind my seat. As the bird flitted off to one side I caught a glimpse of Aubrey and Mary Pearl. They stared into each other's eyes, their faces flushed.

When Udell finally stopped the rig, the two horses snorted several times. We were near the top of a rounded hill. This range was open grazing land, most of it beat into worthless desert by too many cows run at one time. Barrel cactus poked up their ugly heads all around like badgers, daring any animal to get close. A horse stepping into one would be crippled on the spot as those finger-long hooks tore tendons from bone.

My cows were gone. Out of the eight hundred or so head I'd had, only a hundred and twenty were sold. Most of the rest were stolen when my nephew Willie took a bad road and went with some rustlers toward Mexico. The few remaining were scattered to the very wind by that range fire. I had twenty-one left. Udell had bought ten from me, to start himself a place, too. We shared the old bull, El Capitán, so I figure we each own ten and a half stock animals. Silly thing is, I've got twenty-three trained herd horses for watching ten and a half cows.

"Care to take a stroll?" Udell asked, with his eyes toward Aubrey and Mary Pearl.

"I'd be pleased to," I said. He put his hands around my waist to help me down, and I pulled my shawl close. "You two mind if we stretch a mite?"

"No, ma'am," they said on top of each other's words.

Udell handed me a bag of oats and took up another. We looped them over the horses' ears. I said, "Care to come? It'll warm you both up."

"We're warm under the blanket," Mary Pearl said. "I'd rather stay here."

Udell called, louder than he needed to, "We'll be right nearby."

We walked a long way without a word. He stopped when a yellow-eared jackrabbit darted out of the brush and hightailed it farther up the hill. Udell's foot slipped on some gravel, so he turned to me and smiled and offered a hand, which I gladly took. We stayed on the trail that rabbit had taken, up a well-used path, not that we wanted a skinny old hare, but for a clear way to the crest of the hill.

"It's nice walking when it's too cold for snakes," I said.

Mountains to the north and east were capped with snow. The air was frosty but the sun felt warm. Udell put his arm around my waist and held on as we reached a flat area below the top. "I don't miss the snakes," he said. Then he nodded toward the white peaks. "But I don't miss that kind of snow, either."

"Worst I ever saw was when I was a girl up on the Little Colorado—breaking ice on the spring with a pickaxe so horses could drink, them always picking some sleety night to drop a foal. Pure misery."

We talked a while then, about when we were children, where we lived, how our parents lived. Udell's parents were both gone, as was my pa. Of course, Granny was still with us. A cloud drifted by the sun and I felt a shiver. "Do you need my coat?" he asked.

I felt warm inside as if a bed of coals had grown good and red. "Thank you, but I don't really."

He pulled a paper from inside his coat, and proceeded to unfold it before me. "Sarah, this here is the plan of a house your brother Harland drew for me. Just the start, anyway. A couple of rooms and a kitchen. But eventually, it'll have two floors. It'd take some doing to get it built. I had been thinking of putting it out here. Dig a new well. Start on raw ground."

"After you got all that bottom land plowed for a spring garden? Why would you go to the trouble of this when you've got the place already going where it is?"

"That one's too close to my borders, I suppose. Too close to—"

"Maldonado's?"

"I like my freedom." He walked away, studying the ground.

I tagged behind him. When he stopped I said, "Tell me about your wife."

Expressions flitted across his face like the shadows of a flock of birds. At last, his face softened. Then, as memories crossed his mind, his eyes crinkled at the corners.

"Frances was only sixteen when we married. Mercy, I was just twenty. Aubrey is twenty-eight, an old bachelor compared to his pa. Both of us, our fathers were stationed at Fort Laramie. Only hers was a corporal and mine was a rancher trying to keep enough sheep alive to feed the soldiers a good meal once a month. Her pa figured it was quite a comedown, sending her off with me. But the Sioux were defeated. Land was there for the taking. We built up a place, she and I. Aubrey was born in less than a year. We had six other children, all lost. One to typhus, two to measles. One died of great pox before he was two. Callie died in the same coach accident with Frances."

I put my hand on his shoulder and hung my head. "That's not—I'm sorry. I meant, what was she like? Did she bake cakes? Go to women's suffrage marches?"

He put an arm around my waist and drew me a little closer. "No, nothing like that," he said, smiling. "She always said she wanted nothing more than to keep house and hearth together. She sewed for some spending money, though, fancy dresses and crinolines. She had eyes the color of water in a glass, pale blue with a dark rim, like, like—" Suddenly his face turned dark. His mouth quivered and he looked away.

I held him and he pressed me close, and for a while we didn't move or speak.

Then, he said, "What about your man, Jack?"

"What about Jack?"

"Did he go to suffrage marches?"

I laughed against his chest. Then I inhaled. He smelled of shaving soap, the kind with the faintest touch of oil of bergamot. I said into his shoulder, "He was a soldier first and always. He was tall. His hair was brown and wavy. He was bent on protecting folks who couldn't protect themselves." I held Udell closer. Jack had had a jagged scar on his right arm from the blade of a Comanche knife. He had two healed-over bullet holes, too. One was on his side and the other made it hard for him to ride sitting down for a while. Jack Elliot carried my heart with him in his saddlebag, every time he left me, which he did more than not. I reckon he'd always thought I could take care of myself, too, though I'd have differed with him on that if he'd asked. I looked up at Udell's face, almost surprised to see he'd been waiting for me to turn and look at him.

"Your eyes are brown," he said.

"Just like yours. I don't sew much that's pretty. A quilt now and then."

"That's all right. I never looked good in crinolines."

I laughed again. When our lips met, it was with the air of a well-practiced act, tentative only for a moment. I sank against him and he surrounded me. The man was shorter than Jack, just taller than I was, and while he kissed me I began to think how convenient it was to kiss a man not so different in height. Had I lost my love for Jack? Panic swept through me. I pushed Udell back, saying, "We'd better get back to the carriage."

But as I tried to pull away, he held my arm and slid his hand down to my fingers. "Sarah," he said. "There's something I want to say to you."

"Tell me in the carriage."

He tugged on my hand. "Were you happy, being married? Did you love him?"

I rolled my eyes and tried to pull my hand from his. He pulled again, insistent. "Of course," I said.

Udell squinted as if he were trying to read something written on my face.

I said, "I was happy and miserable. I loved him so much because he loved me. He was my very life and, well, what did I know? I was young and he was handsome and brave. Just like a prince in a story."

"Did you feel like *you* died?"

I stared at the ground before me and gulped, waiting for my heart to start beating again. Gravel, burned bronze by the desert sun, had been kicked aside where we stood as we kissed, and the gray-white underside showed. A tear dribbled to my chin but I didn't brush it away. I said, "Lord, yes. For weeks. Months. Then, I had a family to raise. My boys. My ranch to run. I couldn't lose another minute wishing for that man to come back."

"I thought I had, too. Crawled into a bottle of whiskey, hoping I'd never come out. All that did was make me sick. Aubrey dragged me home from an alley one night, left me in the cellar and called me a coward and a liar because I'd promised him I'd take care of him when I got home from the war. He was already a man then. When I got my feet under me, I realized he'd been right. So I quit then and there. Laid it all down, went to bed for a month, but when I got up, I got up sober. I don't drink. Nor gamble or carry on with fancy women."

"Well, I never questioned your character, Udell."

"Nor I yours. Were you happy?"

It took me a long time to finally say the words. "Painfully happy."

"I doubt I could ever live up to that. I don't believe I kept Frances painfully happy, unless she found it in her heart in spite of me. I'm sure fond of you, Sarah."

I felt the selfsame words ready to roll off my tongue, as if all he'd said was "how d'e do," and it was customary to return in kind. I dared not say those sacred words aloud until I was sure I meant them, for they would bind me in ways I'd already learned. That jackrabbit was watching us from atop a rock. I could hear Udell breathing. I drew in a long breath, too, my heart aching. The trouble was, I did love him. At least, I felt something. What exactly it was, I had yet to name. Long as I didn't say it aloud, it could wait until the thoughts cleared on their own, I suspect.

Then we started back down the hill toward the carriage. Udell whistled a tune as we stepped arm in arm through the brush. We found Aubrey and Mary Pearl sitting sedately next to each other. If it weren't for the flush of their faces, I'd have believed they'd been discussing the weather.

"Ready to head home?" Udell asked.

"But please, drive slow, Pa," his son answered.

We turned the rig around and had just started down the hill, Udell pushing his foot on the brake to keep it from banging the horses' legs, when I grabbed his arm. "Stop," I hissed. "I heard something."

It took two more steps for the horses to come to a halt. Aubrey and Mary Pearl had little to say when we returned, but they both leaned forward now, asking what I had heard. There it was again. The sound of horses approaching. A dozen or more.

With no thought to being ladylike and waiting for him to help me, I got down while Udell set the brake and gave the reins to Aubrey. I hurried toward the sound, stopping by a leafy ocotillo to peer around it before I stepped out from the shadows. Udell crouched next to me. Before us there played out a tableau that took away all the previous warm feelings and chilled me deep in my core.

A band of riders, Mexicans by the cut of their getup, was moving across the desert below us, at least a mile away. Ahead of them, two men on horseback charged as if their lives were in the balance. One had lost a hat, the other whipped his horse with his as they leaned toward the setting sun. Then one of the horses of the men out front stumbled, and the rumbling of many hooves was overlaid with the squeal of the animal and that distinctive crack of bone. The other rider didn't stop but kept on. The men closed ranks upon the fallen man, and two dismounted, strode up to him, and drew pistols while the others continued after the lone rider. The man on the ground clasped his hands together and his mouth moved, but we couldn't hear him. Their guns barely a foot away, they shot him through the head. When he fell, they shot him again, then shot the horse, too. The chase had crossed another rise and was out of our line of sight, but before another minute passed, we heard a volley of gunfire.

Udell took my arm, saying, "Let's get away from here." Aubrey and Mary Pearl had followed us, and hurried, too.

We ran to the carriage. Udell drove as fast as he dared, stayed on the road for a bit, then suddenly turned off by a copse of ironwood. He pulled the horses to a stop along a natural pond, and told us all to get out. Hooves approached. Birds scattered noisily. Udell said, "Spread that blanket on the ground." We laid it over the muddy bank and took the second coach blanket, too. Aubrey spread it over

Mary Pearl's lap while Udell and I put the feed bags back on the horses' heads. I pulled the rifle from under the front seat and tucked it under, too. We joined them on the blanket in a circle, taking poses and laughing and chatting as if we'd been having a picnic.

No sooner had we caught our breaths than the air filled with the din of horses. Udell pulled the rifle from my hands, putting it down the length of one leg. The men had circled the hill and were coming toward us. One of them shouted, "*¡Alto!*" and they pulled to a stop with a clatter and the drawing of pistols. The men pulled kerchiefs over their noses, but stayed mounted while two eased out from the rest toward us. One man rode his horse up against our carriage, looking inside it as if there might be someone hiding.

He reached out a hand, slowly, and patted one of our horses on the rump with an almost kindly gesture. The animal muttered into his feed bag, but nothing more. Then the man holstered his pistol, strapped low on his leg. He eyed us. A pair of vicious spurs dressed his heels, flashing in the sunlight. On his horse's left shoulder, the Bar-M brand of Rudolfo Maldonado.

I held my breath. A patch of foam hung on the flank of one of our horses. From where I sat, I could see it clearly, but from his point of view, he couldn't know we'd run those horses unless there was foam on the other side.

The rider turned, thrust his chin toward the south, and at once, the band of men sped away in a clattering flurry. We were left quaking together on the blanket, wondering what we'd just witnessed. When I tried to stand, I found my legs cold from the dampness that seeped through the blanket; my knees shook as I hurried to the far horse, looking him over carefully. There was no foam. No reason for them to suspect us of lying, other than that heavier smell of a just-run horse.

Aubrey said, "Mary Pearl, quickly, get in," and he jostled the wet blanket into a bundle at their feet. Udell's face was grim and hard. He took the reins. I took the rifle. We turned the horses toward home and made dust.

# Chapter Five

*December 17, 1906*

Last night I said good night to Udell in the dark, outside the house. The night had been crisply cold; the stars all seemed only a few feet over our heads. The moon hung like a lantern, low in the sky. He had put his hands against my cheeks but he did not kiss me. He had only held my face and said, "Be careful."

Then I took his face in *my* hands and said, "*Y tu.* You also," and I made Udell carry my rifle when he and Aubrey went home. As he mounted his horse I called, "Aim left a touch."

After that, it seemed I carried the warmth of him in my hands, and as I curled up in bed that night, shivering, trying to warm up one spot before I stretched out, I folded my hands and told myself I could still feel the skin of Udell's face. It was a guilty pleasure, craving the touch of his skin against mine. When I thought about it a little, I thought about it a lot. I wanted to press my cheek to his, and leave it there, and sleep, curled against him. If Jack walked in the door this very minute, I'd never think about Udell Hanna again, but Jack's not going to do that. So I put my hands on my own face, remembering Udell's hands and his face in the fabric of my own skin, and slept that way through the night, comforted.

This morning as I was headed out to feed the chickens, Rudolfo Maldonado rode up to my front porch. The sight of him gave me a start and I realized that I'd been looking for Udell. I pulled an old hat on, took my basket, and stepped off the porch toward the chicken coop. I wondered if he would tell me about what went on at his place without me asking. I wished my suspicions about him would quiet. Reckon once someone has crossed that line with me and I quit trusting them, they're going to travel down a long, long road to get back to where I believe what they say.

Gussied up and grinning, Rudolfo swept off his hat, saying he'd come to beg my family, Albert's family, and even Udell and his son, to come to his home Christmas Eve for a fiesta. I told him he'd have to ask each one, and that I'd not speak for others. I unwound the wire that held the pen shut and went inside.

Rudolfo watched me closely while I dumped out the hens' trough and banged it against a post to knock the gravel and trash out of it. From the corner of my eye I saw him put his boot up on the chopping block I keep by the door of the coop and lean toward me. He said, "You should have some *peón* to do this, Sarah." He let out a long breath and the steam came toward me.

"Well, I don't," I said as I measured mash in an old coffee can and spread it in three big streaks on the ground. The chickens all came a-running, making that waterfalling sound they do when they're happily eating. When several minutes passed and Rudolfo said nothing else, I turned and looked him in the eye. The expression on his face was not the slick baldness of lying I've seen on him before. Instead, it was a shade of some unspoken sorrow. Regret, maybe, or pain.

It still rankles me to remember last summer. He'll never know how close I came to accepting his marriage proposal only a few months ago. He had come to me saying he was planning to go into politics and needed a wife. He had all the land and cows in the area. I'd never worry another day of my life. I'd have had *peóns* to feed my chickens, *cocineros* to fetch my supper, *caballeros* to tend my stock. Just in time, I'd found out he'd paid a man to tear up my south windmill and poison the water tanks. Why, I'd as soon be hung as marry the likes of Rudolfo after that.

Within days of my threatening Rudolfo with a shotgun, he had married a neighbor girl. Leta was the oldest daughter of the Cujillo family; probably had figured her life was to be a spinster, until her much older *vecino* suddenly chose her from the brood to be his *esposa*. I held fast to my feed bucket, keeping some distance between us, watching him study the chickens as they clustered around the hem of my skirt. After their honeymoon he had set off with some of his hired men for Vera Cruz and Mexico City, and was gone over a fortnight. His wife, all of twenty and two years old, was home by that time and holding a bucket of her own, sicker than any girl I ever knew with a baby coming. What

I knew of her, I reckoned Leta Cujillo Maldonado made his life just about what Rudolfo deserved.

I said, "Heard there was a ruckus on your place, yesterday."

"*¿Que?*"

"You didn't know about some cowboys, Mexicans, chasing a couple of drifters?"

"Oh," he said, nodding. "There may have been some riders coming across. How many did you see?"

I shrugged and said, "All I know is, I heard horses running. Moving too fast for me to count."

"Ah. *Sí*? Only riding through."

Now I knew that look in his eyes. Too shiny. Too clever. I said, "Too jingly to be American rigs."

"I'm sure it meant nothing, my friend. You will ask your *familia* about the fiesta? I'll send escorts and carriages. You will have to do nothing but be ready." He reached toward me but drew back his hand, as if he'd thought better of the gesture.

Was his land now unsafe to cross without escorts? "I'll ask them, Rudolfo. We'll bring the beans."

"No, no," he said with a smile. "I'll provide. There is much to celebrate this year. Things I would like to make up to you, too."

"You aren't forever in my debt, Rudolfo. You put up that house. That's enough." I hated the notion that he was going to spend his life repaying me as much as if the debt had been my own. I pulled the coop shut, working the rickety dried-wood-and-chicken-wire door into its frame.

"Let me do this, *mi amiga*." He turned to go, adjusting his hat. Without another word, the "old friend" I would have to guard against for the rest of my life went to his horse and lifted himself into the saddle. There was something about his walk that telegraphed to all the world how much he'd changed. Before I ever married Jack, Rudolfo and his brother Ruben had worked as *peóns* keeping my place going, and took their pay in tortillas and eggs. The man whose back I watched riding away was handsome but wily, still virile and strong but too clean to have worked recently, too sure of himself to have come this way simply to ask this. His clothes were expensive and impractical. His bearing was quiet and brooding, like a mountain lion waiting on a ledge.

I finished my chores for the morning, looking over my shoulder every few minutes for Udell. But the sun climbed and the day dragged with the waiting.

When I got back to the house, the stove in the kitchen was going strong. Granny and Chess warmed their tired bones beside it while I made us something for the middle of the day. I'd gotten some jarred flat beans and bacon warmed up and put a pan of biscuits in the oven when the door opened and a cold gust of wind shot through the room. Gilbert was in for dinner. Right on his tail feathers came Ezra and Zachary.

"Hey, Aunt Sarah," they said together. Ezra made a loose fist, put one knuckle against Zachary's ear, and hollered, "That's two you owe me, runt."

"Two what?" I said. Zack made a face.

Ezra said, "Mama is trying to train him to quit saying other folks' words like he was some kind of trick mind reader at a circus. Ever' time I open my mouth and his voice comes out of it, he's got to give me his dessert tonight *and* tomorrow."

"Aw, I'm not hungry anyway," Zack said.

"Tell yer stomach that when the pie comes around. Dripping with sugar and crispy on the edge where the cream soaks in. All sticky—"

"Ain't my fault your brain is strung so loose you no more'n open your trap and I hear the words knocking around behind your eyeballs before you say 'em."

Gilbert and I caught eyes. Zachary was at least as clever as his brother, though Ezra was two years older. I smiled, then I said, "Well, this time doesn't count. All you said was hello to be polite and it would have been rude if you hadn't both said it. It was an accident that it came out together. You two had dinner?"

"No, ma'am," Ezra said.

"No, ma'am, and we'd be pleased," Zack added.

I dished up plates and everything got quiet for a while. I told them all about Rudolfo's invitation as I passed around the plate of pound cake. Chess frowned. It wasn't like him to withhold an opinion about anything, so I figured he'd say something when he's ready. The only voice was Gil's. Gilbert said he was fixing to ride into town again. When I asked him what we'd forgotten, he couldn't say, but Granny piped right up and said, "He's got himself a girl," with no more question than she'd have proclaimed fine weather was upon us. Granny had been on a tear about romantic entanglements lately. I hoped she was wrong.

All eyes turned to Gilbert, who took a sudden interest in the bacon rind on his plate. He said, "I need some plate glass to fix that window for the bunkhouse. It's almost done. Just need the window glass and some paint. Is there any coffee left?"

"Well, we don't have any hired hands," I said. "It can wait, can't it?"

Ezra and Zachary muttered to each other, and I heard, "Girl? Oh, no, more girls!"

"I only want to get the job done, Mama," Gil said.

I wondered if he was intent on moving back into the bunkhouse like he and Charlie had done before the new house was built. Getting some independence without being too far from the nest. I said, "I don't want you riding to town alone. Not after what went on yesterday."

"Grampa will go with me, won't you, Grampa?"

"Your ma's right," Chess said. "No sense traipsing across the territory this time of year."

I could see more disappointment in my son's face than the lack of a sheet of glass ought to bring. I wondered if he was determined to go against my wishes. Part of me didn't want to be sidestepped, part of me hoped he had the backbone to try it. I said, "Why don't you ride up to Marsh Station for the mail? See if there's word from Charlie."

"Why's every decision I want to make somehow nailed to Charlie's shoes? I'll only be gone a couple of days. There's no chores to be done these two can't handle. Uncle Albert will appreciate us putting them to work."

"Gil's got a girly!" Zack sang.

"Weevils are evil and gir-rels are squirrels," chanted Ezra.

"Chess?" I said. "Can you spare Gilbert a few days?" Chess was seventy years old. The thought of him and Gilbert going off to town made my stomach hurt, and I regretted the cake I'd had that left a burning right below my ribs.

Chess rubbed his hands together, the dry, woody sound of his skin loud as a statement. He looked from me to Gilbert, and then to Granny and the boys as if he were about to give a speech. He shook his finger at Ezra and Zachary and said, "I want pistols in these fellas' hands the whole time we're gone. And no foolishness. You two ride with us as far as Marsh Station and then come back with the mail. Gil and I will go on to town from there. I'm trusting you two to act like men and do a man's job. No shenanigans or I'll strap you both myself." Then to Gilbert he said, "I'll give you two nights, boy. One day getting there and a day staying and a day coming home."

Ezra and Zack both opened their eyes wide. They'd never heard Grampa Chess talk to them like that before. After all, he wasn't their grandfather, but my sons'. With sober faces, the two of them nodded. Gilbert flushed red and left the table.

Later, I went to Gil's room. He folded a shirt and laid it carefully on some clean drawers. He didn't look up when I came in, so I whispered, "Is this about some girl?"

"Lord, Mama. Can't you just let me go to town? It's only a call. It's not like I'm eloping. I'm older than Papa was when he was a full officer in the army. He called on you. Aren't I allowed to call on a girl?"

What he didn't know was that Jack had already married a girl before he was Gilbert's age and had been a widower when I met him. All of twenty and busting loose. I could as much as hear the string in my pocket wrapped around that folding money coming undone. I said, "Reckon so. Don't forget the window glass. How much do you figure it'll cost for the size you need?"

"Figured I'd just buy a piece as big as the money in my pocket allowed and cut a hole to fit it."

"Well, what size is that?"

"About twelve bits. A hole that size won't let in the skeeters."

"Did I pay you this week yet?"

"I'm still working off the tuition money I lost, remember?"

"Well, a man can't call on a lady with empty pockets—she is a lady, isn't she?—what would she think, after all? You'll want to take her skating or to a supper."

"I was hoping she'd just cook something."

I laughed and hugged him. "I'll spare you three dollars. Bring back what you don't use."

He took the money from my rolled-up parcel, and as I retied the string, he said, "Thank you kindly, Mama. I won't waste it."

I reckon that was as close as a mother could get to love and affection from a near grown boy. I patted his arm and said, "While you're there, run by the dry goods and bring home ten cents' worth of shirt buttons."

So off they went next morning, Gil and Chess, with Zack and Ezra tagging to bring home the mail. It seemed a long way to town. One too young to go alone, one too old. At the last minute, I saw Aubrey Hanna pushing his horse to catch up with the bunch. He waved to me and I saw him turn in toward Albert's place farther up the road. I'd thought he was here to stay until after Christmas. And I was hoping his pa would have thought to ride with him through our place to say hello and have a piece of pie.

After watching them cross over the northeast horizon, I bundled up Granny and drove us to Savannah and Albert's place to visit a while. Rebeccah was home from her teaching job in Mexico, and she had plenty of tales to tell.

While I got Granny inside and settled under a quilt, Rebeccah said her mother was upstairs in "the girls' room," a large bedroom all four sisters had shared. I climbed the stairs and reached the landing. The door stood ajar, so I entered while giving a little knock at the jamb. My sister-in-law was staring out the window into the yard, her arms crossed, deep in thought. She didn't look up.

"Savannah?" I asked.

"Yes, honey? Oh, Sarah, it's you. I heard someone on the stairs. I thought it was one of the girls."

"Is there something wrong?"

"No, no. I just came up here for something. I forgot what it was."

The four daughters' beds lined the walls in a neat formation like army cots. Only two of them had been slept in recently, Mary Pearl's and Rebeccah's. I patted her shoulder. "Well, you'll remember directly," I said. "For the life of me, sometimes I meet myself coming the other way in my house. Was it thread? Scissors? A pencil or a hairpin?"

Savannah rubbed the windowsill with one finger, as she kept on staring through the glass. "Sarah, did you ever just feel like something was going to happen? Something unusual? Did you ever feel a sense of expecting when you hadn't ordered a package or anything, just a notion that something was coming?"

"When I was a girl and we left Cottonwood Springs. I told my mama I had that feeling. Later on, she said there was an ill wind a-blowing. That what you're feeling now?"

Savannah turned and faced me. "No, nothing like that. I can't put my finger on it. It's nothing. Just daydreaming, I suspect. Did your mama come with you? Let's go downstairs."

Rebeccah, Granny, Savannah, and I sat at their great kitchen table, where at one end a pile of men's clothes awaited mending. I thought she looked plum tuckered, her eyes red and sunken, but I didn't say anything. After Savannah poured coffee, she said she hadn't slept but an hour for two nights running, but she had gotten two pairs of pants made for Albert. We each picked a garment and threaded a needle, and passed a good time hearing about Rebeccah's teaching adventures in Mexico.

In their parlor, Mary Pearl was pushing dust around with a torn rag, openly mooning over Aubrey being gone so soon back to town on some mission he wouldn't discuss with her. He'd only stopped long enough to tell her he'd be back in three days with Gilbert and Chess, too. I saw the fire in her eyes, and I knew she only held her temper back because her mother watched her. If she'd been alone with that young man, him keeping secrets from her like she was a baby, why he'd a-left with half an ear chewed off, I reckon.

Well, after I told Savannah about the reason Gilbert was taking off to town, she said, "It's getting to that season of life, where they're all bound to head out, aren't they?" She smiled at Rebeccah, who blushed as if there were some secret in her life, too.

I said, "I keep looking for my boys, sort of expecting them to be Ezra's size, and every time I lay eyes on one, it's some big stranger who's come in and put on my children's boots."

"Have you heard from Charlie?"

"I'm hoping he'll look at a calendar and try to head home for Christmas." Then I told her about Rudolfo's Christmas fiesta.

"We'll go, if you're going," she said, "but I won't go empty-handed. You know Rudolfo was nothing but generous and kind while we built your house. Still—" She held her breath, and let the silence finish the words.

My house. I've lived there three months and it doesn't feel like home. It was big and comfortable and as fancy as Rudolfo's big hacienda, and sat there empty at that very moment except for the cat.

"Mama," said Mary Pearl, her flashing eyes peering from the doorway, "why couldn't Uncle Harland have hired me to watch the children? I'd have been as good as Rachel. You know I would have. She wouldn't have to leave her teaching position."

"Still," Savannah said, her eyes on Mary Pearl, "to let him provide it all gives me a sense of, well, I don't know just how to put it."

"As if we're the serfs gone begging at the duke's castle?" Rebeccah said.

I said, "Exactly. Reckon all I can afford to take to the fiesta will be a stack of tortillas."

"We won't go empty-handed. That's that," Savannah said.

I added, "Being flat broke doesn't bother me as much as him saying he'd send armed escorts to see us there and back."

All of us were quiet, then after a bit, Mary Pearl said, "We should take our own escorts and guns, too, just to be sure. If I were living in town watching our cousins—"

"You'd be courting every evening with young Mr. Hanna," said Rebeccah. "That's all you're after. Now Mary-pie, you're too young for such things." Mary Pearl bristled. Seventeen was not too young for a lot of things, I remember. I wondered why Savannah had done nothing to quell her youngest's longing for

Aubrey Hanna, though he was ten years her senior. "Isn't that right, Mama?" Rebeccah said.

Savannah's puzzled expression made us all watch her face for the reaction. She said, "Well, Rebeccah, you've already started a quilt for her trousseau. You said so, yourself."

Mary Pearl grimaced. "Why, Sister Rebeccah, if you keep a-pulling my leg," she said, and stumped toward her sister with an exaggerated limp, "it's a-gonna make my weddin' dress run up on one side." She giggled, letting loose her anger in silliness.

"Baby sister, I'm doing no such a thing," Rebeccah said, grinning.

"Now, Rebeccah," Savannah said, "insincerity—"

A sharp bang shook the door in its frame. The sound brought the small hairs on the back of my neck to attention just as Mary Pearl pulled it open. I saw a man, dressed in a suit of fine wool, pin-striped and elegant as any congressman ever thought of being, standing there. He held a hat in his hands. His gray hair was greased down and a flag hung from a button-pin in his lapel. "Pardon me, miss," he said. "Oh, my. Aren't *you* the beauty of the county? Is your mother at home, dear?"

Savannah and I both rushed to the door and while Savannah tucked Mary Pearl behind her, I planted my feet square on with this new stranger. "Lost, mister?" I said.

Fumbling with the hat, he bent to fetch a fancy gold-topped cane from the porch floor. "Never meant to drop the thing. Must have sounded like thunder from inside, eh?" He looked across the yard toward Granny's old, shut-down house, "No, ma'am, I'm not lost. That's the place, I believe. Do you folks know what's happened with the lady who lived there? The place does look abandoned." The fellow's face seemed nice, but he was far yonder too full of questions for this part of the territory.

"Rebeccah," Savannah called over her shoulder, "ring the bell for your papa." When they heard the supper bell at an odd time of day, Albert and Clover would surely know something wasn't straight at the house. I felt Savannah close in behind me. I watched for him to make a move even half an inch toward the open door, and held my right hand behind my back. Savannah's fingers touched mine, and when she backed away, the heaviness of a revolver remained. I kept still, waiting for him to make a move.

Finally, I said, "Mister? Are you paying a social call? Not having been introduced to you, I'd say it had to be business."

"Oh, yes, yes. Quite forgotten my manners, I have, dear lady," the fellow said, and then simpered. "May I present my card?" He reached into his watch pocket and pulled out a fancy calling card. I took it with my left hand while he proceeded to explain it to me as if I couldn't read. "Elvin Richards, special purchasing agent with the Santa Fe Overland Express Company. I represent the railroad, madam. We acquired a piece of land up the road there, a few months ago, from a Mrs. Prine. I told her I'd be returning later in the year. Almost didn't make it." He smiled again, his face gentle and sincere, but his eyes searched the room behind me. "Do you know where she's gone?"

So this was the skunk that swindled my mama out of a big piece of her homestead plot. About that time Albert came up with Clover. Albert told the fellow he could sit in their parlor and asked Rebeccah to make coffee. I slipped the pistol in my pocket when they weren't looking.

Granny was snoozing by the kitchen window, so we didn't wake her.

I declare, that fellow could charm the daylight out of the sky. We passed an hour and then some as Mr. Richards explained how wonderful it was going to be having a screeching, smoke-belching, thundering locomotive hauling cows and freight from Kansas to California through our front rooms for all posterity. He said that he was going to offer a good sum for the rest of Granny's place, soon as he could find her. Albert said there was no use making an offer, but Mr. Richards said, "Ten thousand dollars is no foolish whim, sir. It's a fortune. And to a kindly old widow with no use for that land herself, and all her worldly needs met by good, loving folks such as yourselves, it's a fortune you would eventually inherit. Think about it." With that, he said good day and left, riding off on a black horse.

"They've got part of the land and they want the rest of it," Savannah said.

Albert looked from Savannah to me. He said, "I can see how he got Mama to believe in him, last fall. That fellow could talk fleas off a dog."

I said, "He waved ten thousand dollars under our noses and as much as told us we should talk Granny into taking that money so *we* could get it!"

I squeezed my arms against my ribs and went to the kitchen. Granny's head bobbed with her snores. Her fingers looked like white wooden spindles with brown leather stretched tightly over them. That tiny person there was not just *some* old person. Never mind that she'd been driven beyond all understanding by watching her children and husband die, she was the one who'd tied my hair up and kissed my tears. I have always believed that if she could just once get enough rest, my mama would come back to herself, think clearer, be stronger. She never seemed sickly, just brain-tired.

Albert called Ezra from the back of the house. Pretty soon, Zack and Ez showed up, sweating and panting. Albert said, "Zack, you stay here with your mama and Aunt Sarah. Ezra, follow that Mr. Richards up the road a ways. See which way he turns when he comes to the west fork. Come back and tell your mama if you can't find me." Then Albert and Clover went back to work in the barn.

When we were alone in the house, Savannah said to me, "I feel like that man just brought something evil to my house."

Granny woke and jumped at us, giving us a start. "Is it Indians?" she said.

"No, Mama," I said. "It's railroaders."

"You need me to load for you?" she said, tossing off her shawl.

I said, "No, I hadn't decided to shoot him, yet."

Shortly, Ezra returned and nodded to each of us in turn; the boy suddenly seemed five years older than his thirteen years. "Well," he announced, "he didn't take the west fork at all. Went north and circled Granny's place, left a note nailed to her door saying he'd come back, and made a wide loop headed south. He didn't stop at your place, Aunt Sarah, but went straight to the hacienda." Then Ezra left to tell Albert. The hacienda. Rudolfo Maldonado.

I thought that news explained everything, but it didn't explain what Savannah did next. She said, "My head is pounding like someone is driving a nail through it. How will we fight the railroad? What are we going to do? If only Esther were home! If she hadn't run off and died—" Then she sat in a wooden chair and burst into tears. After a few minutes, she gasped out, "Lands, it's hot in here. Open a window, Sarah."

"You need a rest," I said. I hugged her but I felt uneasy doing it. I didn't know what to say or do. It seemed the addled notions that have taken my mama for all these years had suddenly jumped into Savannah, who has always been my sure foundation.

I put my arm over Savannah's shoulders as she heaved in great, pathetic sobs. Rebeccah and Mary Pearl came in to see what the commotion was. Savannah said, "Oh, I'm so very tired."

Granny looked suspiciously from one of us to the other and said, "Your mama's going through the change. Leave her alone!"

At that, Savannah cried all the harder. It was only after a good spell that she settled down and we all surrounded her and made her go to bed to take a nap. She told me then that she hadn't been sleeping for weeks, and she'd thought it was in sorrow for her daughter who was murdered, but now she was afraid she would die of not sleeping. While she pulled off her black skirt and waist, I drew the curtains in her room. The curtains were only starched plain muslin, though, and didn't keep out much light so we laid cold wet cloths over her face.

"Close your eyes, Savannah," I said. "Just close your eyes." I sat by her bed, watching tears mixed with drips of water eke across her cheeks sideways and dampen her hair. Were women all doomed to follow Granny into that gray world of half-truths and mysterious memories where real life is muddled with bits of songs and shadows and old pains that seem new? If I lose Savannah to that dark place, what will I do for a friend? When she started breathing regularly and seemed to be asleep I tiptoed from the room. I told the girls to fix her some soup for dinner, and keep quiet, then I fetched Granny and drove home. We didn't talk but I thought plenty, first about Savannah's weakness and then about how I didn't know how old my own mother was. She seemed as eternal as sunshine to me, but her hands looked so very old. Mr. Richards was sitting at this minute with Rudolfo exchanging winks about how soon my mama might die.

When I got home, one of Udell's work horses was tied up at our trough. I felt as if the burden upon my shoulders lifted, just seeing the animal.

"Rascal's back," Granny said.

I left her at the porch and drove to the barn to put the team away. I found Udell there, fixing a blanket on Hunter, my orphaned yearling colt. The place looked bright in the drawing afternoon light, and I saw he'd filled lamps and cleaned the chimneys, waiting for us to come back. He didn't look up when I came in, but he smiled at Hunter and said, "Didn't know if you went for the night, so I fed your stock. This fellow's sure a pretty piece."

"He's feeling his oats," I said. I felt my face grow hot, and I started pulling the harness off my draft horse. The two of us together made quick work of it. While we did I told him about the railroad man. "Will you stay for supper?" I asked. "I'll make a pie."

"I'd be obliged, Mrs. Elliot."

"I'd offer you to spend the night but the men are gone to town. Reckon it wouldn't be proper." Suddenly, that felt like the worst thing I could have said. "I'd better go make some ruckus in the kitchen."

I hurried toward the house with him fast on my heels, all the while thinking it was pure folly to have Chess and Gilbert both gone at the same time, and more folly still to want Udell here as much as I did. No telling which part of my heart wanted him here. Surely I'd only suggested it as any friend would do? And, of course, it was a suggestion with no hidden intent, a mere feather of a word. Nothing more. Why did the words between us carry so much weight they seemed to rattle on the floor to be tripped over?

"Sarah?" he said, breathing heavily. "Slow down. I came . . . I wanted to tell you something." He caught my arm as I reached the front door. I pushed it open. Granny was not in the front room. He followed me toward the kitchen and said, "Ask something, that is."

I turned to face him. I was panting. "Ask," I said. At first I thought he was going to ply for another kiss. I waited for it. I felt the heat of him standing there, not a foot away.

The look on his face changed. "Sarah, I admire you so." Udell was quiet for a minute, then he shook his head and said, "Just wondering what kind of pie that was you were going to make?"

"That was your important question?" I pulled the flour crock from its corner and hefted it to the table, grunting when I set it down. He sat and watched. He hadn't offered to carry it like he usually did. As if things were different between us. "Suppose I'll make a supper pie and a dessert pie," I said, eyeing him carefully. I got the can of lard and turned a spoon in it, to make a good smooth lump. Then I put in half a spoon of salt. My hand shook and spilled the salt. He went to brush at it; his hand touched mine, and it felt as if he'd stung me. I couldn't speak. He stood and put grains of salt over each our shoulders, but he was jumpy and jittery, clearing his throat, and wouldn't look me in the eye.

For the next hour we did a strange and gentle dance, Udell and I, circling behind each other and around the kitchen table and Granny in her chair, with him kindling up the stove and fetching me water, me reaching for carrots one minute and butter the next. He shelled pecans and cracked a sugar cone into grains while I beat eggs. The room warmed and stirred as the pecans and sorghum whirled in a yellow bowl. When I got both pies in the oven, the carrots and flat beans and gravy bubbled in one pie soon as the sugar and pecans bubbled in the other. Outside, the sun lumbered toward the horizon and the room was bathed in a honey-colored light, dusted with flour. Rather than look like snow, it appeared as if we were covered with the pollen of a great, fragrant flower.

At supper, Udell said over and again how he loved that vegetable pie, and thought there was nothing better until he tasted the pecan. Then he had another piece of the savory followed by a second piece of the sweet. He groaned with delight. At last his eyes settled on mine and I thought he was going to say something but he didn't. I got up to clear the dishes. For the longest time, he seemed to be frozen, and then I saw something that made me tremble, for his eyelids held a rim of tears, as if he'd looked at some dear old memory and seen in front of him only something harder and colder—me.

I collected the spoons and knives. Granny poured hot water into the wash pan. Something was as wrong as a mule wearing bloomers, and my insides felt like my dinner had turned to rocks. I said, "Granny, are you washing? Here's the last."

Keeping his voice low, Udell took hold of my hand as I reached in front of him for the final spoon, saying, "Let the dishes wait, and I'll help you with them later."

"No time like the present," I said, and wiggled my hand loose.

He struck a match and lit two lamps, putting one on the shelf near me and carried the other to Granny and set it down over the washtub. Udell stared at the flame and said, "Sarah, I'm going to Colorado for a while. Aubrey's gone to town to get me some papers and as soon as he gets back I'm going. He'll help you out with anything you need. I should be back in three weeks."

I started pumping rinse water. I held the pan wrong and water shot into a plate, dousing my apron. "What's in Colorado that can't wait until after Christmas?"

"A judge. And a vault. Frances's mother died last Christmastime. Her mother's will left everything to Frances and it hasn't been changed even though she was gone. The woman didn't like me much, so I swore to myself not to take her money, but it's just sitting there, being eaten up by taxes and lawyers' fees. I've been thinking long and hard about my life, and what I'd do over. It's no good to go away from things. It's better to go toward things. Do you know what I'm saying?"

"Doesn't seem right to have to go for Christmas. Bank won't even be open." I tried to find a dry corner of my apron to wipe my hands with. "You've been acting like there was something on your mind. Why don't you just say it clear?" I put a pat of lye soap in and filled the pan with hot water from the kettle always on the stove. I've been known to be stubborn and blind to things I didn't want to see. I've been called hard and I've lived that way. Always having to do for my own like I was a man. I'd rather he'd say what he meant to say and get on down the road.

After a long, awful stretch of silence, Udell said, "Sarah, I've been living in that tent, pretty much a failure, sitting on the mistakes of the past. Maybe trying to leave it all behind is the mistake of the present. I have ten days to claim that money, or it reverts to the bank. Frances's mother had it set up in case I didn't come back from Cuba. I've got to get to Denver before the end of the year." He went across the room then, pumped water into my coffeepot, set it on the stove, then opened the stove door and prodded the coals back to life under it. "I have to build a new house."

"You're saying you plan to get this money for a house?"

"I came to ask you to go with me. We could hitch up in town on the way. Make a sort of honeymoon out of the trip. 'Course, it will be cold, but if you're coming I'd take a train. Otherwise I'll pack a mule."

The color of sunflowers that had dazzled the room an hour earlier was gone and winter gray filled the place. "It must be a lot of money."

"Well, it pays off the mortgage and likely could put up a shack on it. Nothing fancy. Come along with me, we could see some country."

"It's Christmas. Charlie might come home."

"If it weren't urgent, I wouldn't go. I aimed to ask for your hand. I can't ask you to live in a tent, Sarah."

"Udell, you don't have to go on account of me. It's the dead of winter."

"It's a lot of money." He waited a long time, then said, "It's a future."

"Wait a minute. If you hadn't come back from Cuba, why wouldn't Aubrey inherit it?"

"He would if he'd go up there to get it. If I'm alive, it has to come to me first, and either way, the deadline is the thirty-first, but—" He stopped, then said, "It is Christmas. I didn't mean to get you riled."

"I'm not riled."

"Suppose I'm mistaken, then."

I took the coffee mill off the shelf and measured leftover beans roasted this morning into the chute. My hands trembled, so I held fast to the crank and steadied the machine against the table. I tried to laugh a little, but it came out cranky, and I said, "You sure you're not going up there to hold up some bank? If you come back jingling, tongues are going to wag."

He watched me fumbling with the grounds, spilling half of it, and took it timidly from my hands, refilling the funnel with beans and turning the crank.

I rubbed my forehead with the back of my wrist and tied the coffee bag while he ground the mill. He said, "Sometimes I don't know if you make jokes because you aren't really so angry or to hide that you're ready to spit nails."

"Take your pick."

Udell took the lid off the coffeepot and dropped in the contents of the drawer. He said, "Will you wait for me, then?" with that warm look in his eyes that turns all the hardness in me soft. "You aren't going to go and marry while

I'm gone? There are other suitors?" His words sounded teasing, but his face looked sorely pained.

"Suitors, my hind foot. See if that coffee's done. Give it a stir."

Udell did as I ordered, but turned a somber expression to me. "Be straight up with me, Sarah. I thought you had some fond feeling toward me. You wouldn't wait?"

"Wait? That's what every man I've run across wants. They, *you,* gallivant around the countryside off on some mission or other, and I stay at this place and *wait.* Just wait and wait some more. Never knowing if you're alive or dead, run over by a train or took off with a slack-jawed *señorita* from Coahuila." I started to choke on the knot in my throat and tears rimmed up in my eyes. I hollered at him, "I've waited for men and I know what that brings me. No, Udell Hanna. I ain't waiting for you nor any other two-legged jasper that wants to hang his spurs on my back door. I'm not waiting for no one, ever again."

"Sarah, you are the confoundingest woman," he said. "I believe you were mad before you knew what I was going to say."

I stacked the plates noisily and said, "Well, I aim to be confounding. It's one thing I claim right knowledge of."

Granny stood abruptly. She said, "Too noisy in here. I'm going to bed."

"G'night, Mama," I said. Wiped my eyes quickly on my sleeve. Then I turned to Udell, who'd gotten stiff as a post right where he stood. "Go on to Colorado. Traipse through the mountains in the dead of winter. I'll see you *if* you come back." The coffeepot was boiling.

He stirred the brew with a long wooden spoon, watching the grounds spin around. After a while he said, "If I'd thought it through, why, I could have made the trip a month ago. But this fall, with the fire and all—I'd forgotten the will until Aubrey got home and talked about it."

I pulled two cups from the shelf and set them on the table.

Udell took hold of my arm. "Sarah, I'm coming back to you."

I jerked my arm but he held fast. I said, "I've been told that before." There were any number of ways a man could desert a woman. So far, I've known enough of that to last me the rest of my life.

"I'm telling you that, now. Look at me."

"I'm fetching the coffee. Let loose my arm."

He circled me with his arms. "I am coming back. I promise. Look at me."

"I don't want to."

He sighed. "Well, you aren't fighting too hard to get away, either."

"I'm fed up with people leaving me."

"I know," he said, and kissed my forehead. "I know it. You angry enough I can get a kiss and keep both lips, or am I going to lose a hunk of one?" He pressed my back and hugged me close.

I said, "Oh, turn me loose, you." But he didn't. He laid a kiss square on my mouth. Still, much as I enjoyed that, I asked myself what could possess me to buckle under so easy. When he pulled away, I said, "You're leaving tomorrow?"

"After chores." He took a towel and lifted the coffeepot, pouring it partially on the table, but getting some in both cups. Then he dropped the towel on the puddle and sopped at it.

I passed him the first cup and we sat as if no strong words had passed between us. "You're staining my dishcloth." I hung it on its peg. "We'll mind your cows."

"Don't suppose you'll know if you want to marry by the time I get back?"

"You come back, first."

"No harm in just going on being friends. Anyway, it's all said, out in the open."

"Can't stand pussyfootin' around when there's a thing to be said." We were quiet for a long while. My heart quivered with pain. Sometimes I wondered why it kept beating at all, it hurt so deeply, so often.

He said, "Anything I can bring? I'll be passing through town coming back."

"Sugar. That pie was the last of it and Granny likes it. Udell, do you think that's all it comes down to, in the end? That a person is only the money they leave behind? How much or how little, that's all there is?"

"That your impression of what I'm doing?"

"Someone else brought up the subject earlier. Never thought of my mama as a cipher." I winced at my impatience with her.

"I believe your mama is richer than Solomon. She's got you. What I don't have is working cash to build me a farm."

My throat grew tight. I said, "I wish you knew her before she got so addled."

A smile worked its way around Udell's mouth. He reached for my hand again and this time I gave it to him. "I am mightily fond of you, Mrs. Elliot," Udell whispered.

I sipped the last of my coffee, then said, "It's awful late to get home. You could take Charlie's bed since he's gone." As if heaven conspired to make my point, a distant clap of thunder announced a light rainfall. "Granny's a light sleeper," I added.

Udell leaned toward me and placed a tiny, light kiss on my lips. In that small touch, so much more than the passionate one before, I could feel the stubble on his cheek in need of a fresh shave. I inhaled the smell of his skin mixed with coffee and a hint of soap and a faint whiff of sweat; the smell of a man. It would be a hard contest to decide which kiss I enjoyed more.

He went to tend his horse while I banked the coals in the stove and refilled the kettle so the steam would heat the room through the night. I carried coals in the scuttle to start Granny's bedroom stove along with the ones in my room and Charlie's. I set extra wood by Charlie's stove, too, and turned up the lamp in there.

As I carried a last lamp to my room, Udell came in from outside. From the hallway, I watched him hang his damp hat and coat, watched him reach the doorway to Charlie's room, hands outstretched in the near dark. He was only a shadow with the light behind him. "Good night, Mr. Hanna," I whispered.

I saw him turn from the open bedroom door. He said, "Sweet dreams, to you, Mrs. Elliot."

Neither of us took a step. The lamp grew heavier in my hands until I feared I'd drop it. We stood like statues, in the doorways of two rooms so far from each other he might as well already be in Denver. The lamplight sparkled in his eyes.

*Come to me. Rush across this cold floor and take me in your arms. If I take one step would I fly wantonly to you? Would you be repulsed by such a show of vulgar desire? Or would you run to meet me, pinning me against the wall with passionate caresses?* The house was empty except for Granny snoring soundly behind a heavy door at the end bedroom. My feet took root. We stayed there, watching each other in the shadows.

At last, he crossed his arms, sighed deeply, and said, "Good night, Mrs. Elliot."

"Good night, Mr. Hanna." I slipped into my room, set the lamp on the table, and inched the door into place without making a sound. Only then did I begin to breathe. From my bed, for a long, long time, I listened to the fire whisper behind the grate in the stove and watched the door, wondering if it would open.

But Udell Hanna was a gentleman. Next time I saw him was breakfast.

Udell left early and came back riding his dun horse and pulling a pack mule. He said farewell quickly and rode off. As he vanished over the horizon toward town I couldn't keep from my mind all the men I've seen ride away from me in that direction. No one remained at my place but me and my mama, now. Nothing I could ever do pulled them back, made them stay. My insides filled with a darkness I couldn't name, watching his packhorse finally drop out of sight. I figured I'd never see the man again. It was that easy to lose someone in the Territory. Same way he'd come across that hill last fall, looking more or less concerned and bringing my brother Ernest's remains home from San Juan, here he was leaving, not seeming too concerned about that, either. I decided right then I couldn't figure that man any more than I could figure the other ones around me, so I left off trying.

Gilbert came home that afternoon with a grin on his face and the buttons I needed. Chess said nothing to me of the girl in question. Over the next days, I set about finishing the shirts and pinafores I had cut for all my family. Chess all but disappeared into his workshop in the barn, where he, too, worked long hours, probably at the same motive I had, to make some token gifts for our loved ones.

Granny and I worked side by side until we no longer felt like two lost spoons in a box. Hazy clouds kept the house dark; though I lit lamps, nothing seemed to brighten the daylight. Hour upon hour, my ankles ached from making that sewing machine dash through the cloth. My backside felt like it took root to the chair. It was worse than riding roundup—at least a saddle is shaped something like a person's behind. Granny said she'd make the buttonholes for me, and for that I surely was thankful.

Mary Pearl spent two days helping me wash and iron the boys' new shirts. With her here, Aubrey stayed underfoot. But still no word from Charlie. I worked extra hard on his shirt, and gave him two pockets instead of one, and did his buttonholes up myself, in hopes I'd see him wearing them.

At last, when I had all my gifts starched, ironed, and neatly folded in packets tied with string, I stacked them all in the traveling chest I keep at the foot of my bed. With a sigh, I put Udell's gift, the spirit level, in, also. At first I laid it on top, but it was heavy enough to wrinkle the crisp shirts, so I pushed it down the side, burrowing it under my quilt scraps at the bottom where it, and my heart, would wait for his return.

# Chapter Six

*December 23, 1906*

The morning dawned clear and brittle, one of those so cold I have to break the ice on the troughs and watering pans for my critters. I put Udell from my mind as if he'd never existed. Savannah came after her morning chores with five pounds of sugar and a jug of fresh cream, and we are trying our hands at making taffy candies from an old receipt she found in a newspaper long ago. She came upon it yesterday after going through a trunk, and we are having a fine time. We are set up in my kitchen for some long boiling and stirring of sugar syrup. Then we plan to get everyone in for some pulling.

Ezra, Zack, the big boys, and Albert have put Christmas trees made out of cholla skeletons up in their house and mine, and they are stringing popcorn and dried chilies on the branches right now in the parlor. It will be a fancy Christmas tree, but I wonder if old Saint Nick will know it, as it sure doesn't look piney. At any rate, we have a new pup, and he was getting a good sniff at the thing, yapping at it and strutting around as if it were some danger he was guarding. Buttons is a spotted fellow, all mottled up like no dog I ever saw, some kind of breed mixed with sassafras and tumbleweeds and no telling what. When Albert got him in November and held him up to see if he was a girl or not, on his chest were three black "buttons" like he had on a waistcoat. Well, Albert meant to keep him for a yard dog, but Buttons ambled over here one day and just took up residence, so now he's my dog.

By the time we got the boys worn out pulling taffy, we had talked about our children and our dogs, our distant loved ones and those long dead, our woes and our hopes. We had crossed every bridge of our lives more than once. Then we set about cutting the taffy in bits to cure. While Savannah and I washed up, Granny wrapped each piece in white paper that she oiled with clean lard. Savannah told me all that was wrong yesterday was a touch of the melancholy, and not the change Granny was talking about, because nothing had changed. Granny just stared hard at her and went on wrapping candy.

I ran water in one of the pans that was still coated with sugar cooked on, and let my dogs drink it. Nothing here is overfat, so it won't hurt them to have a treat, I reckon. Old, crippled-up Nip and Shiner took their drinks, now and then letting little Buttons in for a taste. After he'd had a good drink, I sent him outside with the other dogs. Then Savannah and Albert's family went on home so everyone could get on with their afternoon chores.

### *December 24, 1906*

It's Christmas Eve and I declare, I feel purely childish and pouty about Udell being gone. Still no sign of Charlie, either. What law puts a star on a boy's chest and a gun on his side and sends him away from home on Christmas? I took Charlie's new shirt out of the stack of others I'd made and ironed it again under white paper, carefully refolding it. Then I put on Charlie's old coat and went to the barn. Gil was out there helping Chess, so I hollered to them that I was going hunting, pulled Baldy to the post and saddled him. He snuffled at my pocket, hoping for sugar. I gave him an apple, and while he ate, I went and petted my colt Hunter and the old horses I keep inside. Rose has been with me many a year, and she was happy to see me, murmuring and tapping her feet. I left her an apple, too.

With both the .410 and the rifle, I rode north of the house on a long curved path that leads to Albert and Savannah's place. I veered off the trail toward the sandy cliff where the stage had turned. Its hulk was gone now, dragged up and salvaged for the hardware sometime while I wasn't paying attention. The Cienega was running and a red bird flickered out of the bosque. It called and seemed to be dancing in the sunlight. Finches twittered nearby, too, and the birds were having a Christmas feast. I pushed Baldy through the water at a shallows and we climbed the backside of the hill. I could hear quail and doves, too, hoping to get a covey so a single shot would bring down enough for dinner.

Farther on I turned back toward the creek, and then I got down to look at the ground. Deer track led through some fine gravel and I followed them on foot a good distance. I reckoned there were at least three. Where the trail turned back down into the thick of the bosque, I stopped to see which side of the wind I was on before going after them. I picked my steps carefully, remembering how Jack used to tease me about being able to sneak up on an Indian scout. I carried both the weapons, in case I needed them.

In a clearing no bigger than a bathtub, a buck and two does nuzzled at new grass. The buck was young but husky, and one doe had swelled as if she were in foal. The other female was middle-sized and slender, perfect for several meals, but she ambled around with her tail toward me so I didn't have a decent shot.

I laid the .410 on the ground and pulled the rifle up, working the cartridge in slowly, not to make any noise. The deer kept on eating. There was no way I could move to either side without rustling the brush, so I waited, hoping she'd nibble around and turn. The other two were good shots, as if they were posing for me, but I didn't want to leave the does unprotected, nor take the foaling one. After a good long bit, I heard a flutter in the brush to my left, and I re-sighted, hoping the herd would move.

Well, like they do sometimes, a great commotion of dove and quail rose up at once, a squawking, wing-beating riot of feathers, scared by some whim. They flew between me and the deer, all three of which went in different directions. The doe I wanted got wide-eyed and darted forward, then turned on a nickel and sprang to the right five feet in the air over the brambles that enclosed them. I squeezed the trigger but she kept on going. The other two vanished.

I headed after my supper through the ironwood thorns, catching my skirt wickedly in the brush, and then came upon the animal, stone dead, six feet from where it jumped. I was glad it had been a clean shot, but when I looked around and saw where the animal landed, I knew it was going to be a piece of work to get our Christmas dinner off this hill and home.

It took me three hours to get the animal field-dressed and tied onto Baldy so it wouldn't fall off. And on the way back through the Cienega, I flushed out another mixed covey and fired two shotgun blasts quick enough to bring down nine birds. I'd make a good pot of greens to go with them and hang the deer for us to have later. Now I could go to Rudolfo's shindig with food in hand, not "begging at the castle," as Rebeccah had said. That red bird peeked at me as I collected the game birds. The pretty red one quit singing, watching suspiciously as I tied the quail feet with twine. I told it I'd never eat a red bird.

On the way back to the house I came across a mule wearing a collar and dragging a piece of rigging. It was one of the team from the stage wreck. He wouldn't let me catch him at first, but I drove him ahead of us and then caught his tether and tied him to my saddle, too. He pulled a bit but then quit, maybe remembering that people meant hay and water. We may never find the other, but I'll take this one to town and hand it over to the Wells Fargo, next time we go. It was a good Christmas Eve. All I needed then was my Charlie to come home. And Udell. But I determined with all my strength not to think about him.

Chess helped me hang the deer and he and Gilbert worked at doing the rest of it. Aubrey decided he'd watch from afar; he didn't have much stomach for cleaning a deer. Chess is going to put it on a spit and start the fire right away so we'll have it tomorrow. While they were busy with that, Mary Pearl and I fixed up a row of pie tins and we cooked up those quail for tonight. Granny had started a pot of beans going this morning, with three marrow bones. She got into the kitchen too, and fixed up the crust all fancy with pinched edges. Each one of us got a bath while the beans and pies baked, then they'd call me and I'd take out the pies while the next person filled the tub. By the time it was my turn, we had six steaming pies on the table and the sun was down.

I wore my best new dress. It's a fine black skirt and shirtwaist in a new style, with a lavender blouse and a hat that matches. It makes me sad to see it, though. Fine as it is, it was made for me by April's seamstress, on the occasion of my nephew Willie's trial for rustling and murder. I pushed each of the thirty tiny buttons through their holes, thinking of that day. I set Willie's memory aside, with all the other hurts of my life, and took a deep breath. I tried to remember what Udell had said, about how going toward the future was better than just leaving the past behind. I couldn't see much difference in the two, especially when everyone's future seemed to be taking place somewhere else.

I let out a long breath and looked in the mirror. I wished I could go to Rudolfo's place looking like I had some sand and vinegar in me. I felt low on both supplies. My hair was an ordinary brown color with no curl except for a wave where my hat presses. Even fresh-washed, it has no shape but the braids I put in it. April does hers with curling irons, but I hadn't got one and I'd probably burn myself bald if I did. Savannah buns her hair at the back of her neck, but the new way to wear it is with a rolled cushion of hair around the face, and some ladies carry that as big as they can get it, but that took hair rats and combs

I didn't own, either. What I could manage was to braid it, raise it up tight and slack off a bit, then tie it pretty much like I always had. I got it pinned up about the time Chess went out to load the buggy, put my dressy hat on and ran the pin through, hoping that at least in Rudolfo's sitting room, it would pass for a nice run-up.

Granny opened my bedroom door, and said, "They're here. Get the shotgun."

"Who, Mama?"

"Maldonado's outlaws."

"He sent a buggy. Aren't you going to wear your other dress?" I asked.

"I'm going to sit here with a pistol and wait on you to get home."

"Mama," I started. If she didn't go, one of us would have to stay here with her. I wouldn't leave her alone on Christmas Eve, even for a couple of hours. I looked in the mirror again. What was I doing all this for? I didn't owe Rudolfo the pleasure of my company. I'd much rather serve up those beans to my own kin and enjoy our spare bounty. There was a knock at the front door and I heard Gilbert greet someone.

I heard the voices of Albert and his family, and then a tapping at my bedroom door. Savannah came in looking fresh-pressed and fine. But when she found out Granny wanted to stay home, Savannah said, "I'll keep Granny company. You take my pecan cake and go to the dinner."

Well, it wasn't much later that I headed down the road in one of Rudolfo's fine carriages, accompanied by Mary Pearl and Aubrey, Albert, Gilbert, Ezra and Zachary. Chess, Granny, and Savannah stayed at my house. We divided up the beans and quail pies before we left so they'd have some supper, although Savannah said it wouldn't do to send a cake that had been cut, so it was offered up whole for the feast.

I can't say I expected what we found at Rudolfo's hacienda. I never saw such a spectacle. The yard was strung with trails of candles nodding in the breeze, and lanterns hung from every post and beam. *Guitarristas* played melodies continually, crooning songs I'd never heard before, most of them in Spanish but with accents I hadn't known in these parts, like the musicians were from somewhere far south of here.

Inside, every corner of every wall was draped with festoons in bright colors. Candles glittered on every table, so thick that the air hung with heavy smoke and the smell of wax was dense enough to taste. Men smoking cigars gathered in the main hall, a room not unlike my own new parlor, and I saw again how

Rudolfo had been a major factor in building that house for me, how like his house mine was. No duty-bound wife greeted us, though. Leta was hiding in her room, I reckoned, banished for the crime of being swollen with child.

Rudolfo introduced us all around to several gentlemen wearing fancy finery and gold lapel pins, even neck ribbons hung with gold medals like army citations. They stood and kissed Mary Pearl's and my hands. These fellows all looked too alike to miss that they were a breed apart from me and my kin. We had indeed come as country *peóns* to the nobility's feast. They nodded and smiled at each other with an air like they were a string of Thoroughbreds forced to welcome a boxcarload of hacks.

There was a priest there, a *padre* I didn't know, though I thought I knew all of them in these parts. He gave me a cold shiver when he shook my hand rather than kiss my fingers like the others. His eyes had no more feeling in them than if I'd been a sack of flour.

General Reyes sat by an American named Doheny, and next to him, wearing more gold than the rest put together, was a genuine dude going by Von Wangenheim. One short fellow was named Madera, and he bowed and smiled at me, just charming as you please, while next to him sat that man Richards from the railroad. Rudolfo, waving his arms around, called them all *"los demo-cráticos y científicos."*

Then Madera starts talking to me in something I think was French, but I didn't understand. I talk American and I talk pretty good Mexican Spanish, so he might have been talking Bolivian Spanish or French or pure Russian, for all I knew. I'd been to this kind of test of my understanding only days before with those fancy-dress professors. I waited for a moment, thinking how rude he was despite being dressed rich as a king, and I answered that fellow, saying, "*Pietas requiro sulum agnosco.* No one here speaks your lingo, so please, *por favor,* either talk in Spanish or American, sir."

Laughing gently, looking almost fatherly, Madera said, "You are as profound as you are beautiful, Señora Elliot."

Rudolfo ushered us to seats. His smile looked hard and set like stone as servants scurried every which way. Before us the table held delicacies I could only guess at. There was a large fish in the center of the planks, swimming in a pool of clear sauce and sort of decorated with leaves and strips of orange peels until it looked monstrous. Where they got a fish that size in this desert I couldn't even guess, and I silently noted that dish and determined to keep a safe distance. There were jellied aspics on little plates covered with some seeds. At the head end of the great table, an entire deer's head, antlers and all, looked out upon the crowd from an arm's-length-wide silver platter. The head was surrounded with fruits, with a pomegranate held in its teeth. Right next to it, as if laid with some kind of purpose, was my crock of humble pinto beans. Opposite that were the little quail pies. On either end, eleven bowls of different hot vegetables plus three kinds of potatoes, lay in front of at least twice that many sauces in gold and silver chargers. Candles flashed and their flames danced as the servants paraded the whole lot around the room like a river of temptingly rich food, then loaded our plates using silver spoons and lifters.

There were steaming bowls of hot cider, and boiled milk with vanilla, bottles of wines and other spirits I couldn't guess at, and what looked like dozens of little goblets and silver cups at each place. A whole table of sweets waited behind Rudolfo, where candlelight danced across lacy tablecloths loaded with glistening brown Christmas puddings and sugared fruit, chocolates stacked on delicate plates, and sugar-rimmed compotes and bowls of punch. In the center, a place of honor, but looking so plain it was clearly out of place, sat Savannah's little cake on a heavy crockery plate.

Everyone helped themselves to the foods laid out, and the gentlemen took great helpings of my pies and the beans with marrow bones. Each one proclaimed how they admired them, too. I smiled, but somehow that filled me less with pride than suspicion. In the next room, just loud enough to be a fine side dish, someone was playing a guitar and a fiddle, and everything seemed merry. It wasn't long until the music stopped and the children, even Mary Pearl and Aubrey, were sent to another room, and then the cigars were lit again and the talk got quiet. It was pure business, but told in shaded words with smiles and gestures that I knew meant things to those present. I could see there was an old fuss-fight going between that fellow Madera and the one named Reyes.

The one thing they all agreed on was that they needed the railroad to cut down from the Southern Pacific lines south of Benson straight to Sonora. I asked that Mr. Doheny why they couldn't use the switch rails near Charleston, but he only smiled and squinted his eyes at me as if I were a child too silly to care about such things. I asked the question again, facing Doheny but saying all the words in Spanish, then Doheny quit grinning. Everyone quit talking.

Rudolfo said, "Ah, my dear Señora Elliot. We are here to offer you a business proposition, with these most respected men. Changes are coming that will pour money through our hands"—he opened his hands toward me as if he were catching something flowing from the ceiling—"and some of it will land in yours! All we have to do," he said, clenching his fists around his mystical riches, "is take it. Sarah, I have been buying land. From Cananea by Bacoachi to Arizpe in Sonora, now almost ten thousand acres is mine below the border. I'm going to connect my land there with my land here."

Von Wangenheim looked from Rudolfo to the other men. "Frau Elliot," he said, then drew a breath through his cigar, and spoke through the smoke as he exhaled it toward Doheny. "Herr Maldonado is making his point well, but you, I see, are a woman who speaks plainly. What we want, Frau Elliot, is to let you in. Share the profit with you in exchange for the unlimited use of your land."

I didn't answer, so he continued.

"We have already sent horsemen to this area to protect our interests. Soldiers in our cause, so to speak. You see, we are going to move a large quantity of supplies by road and rail south to Mexico, and we are ready to do so very soon."

"Whether I join with you or not," I added.

He smiled a bitter, thin slit of a smile. "Of course, we would covet your cooperation. You would be compensated for the use of your land."

"Why do you need my land? Why don't you cut through Maldonado's?"

Rudolfo grinned at me under stony eyes.

"Tracks run best over flat terrain," Von Wangenheim said. "The parcel of land owned by your family north of your house is a prime example. The west side of your southern parcel lies in a direct route to the lovely village of Arizpe."

I stiffened my back. Arizpe had been in the newspapers as the scene of a terrible battle between copper miners and *Federales*. A hundred and fifty miners had died on the orders of the Cananea Copper Company. "That's a fair piece," I said. Three of the men laughed softly. Madera did not. I sipped my tea, and checked the eyes of each of them while I did. Albert got real stiff and quiet.

Doheny said to him, "You're the one, mister. You give the word and the little lady will do as you say."

Albert shook his head and nodded toward me. "It's Sarah's land you're talking about, isn't it?"

Rudolfo held his glass of wine toward the light on the table next to him, and seemed to study the flame through the red liquid. "*Amiga mia,* I have told them you are *la mujer de negocios excelente*. You must not overlook that these generals and directors know more about situations in the government than you. It's very far south of here, Doña Sarah. But there is a route from there to Tucson that could become *el camino de oro*. We are talking about much gold."

Doheny said, "Call it *El Dorado del Norte* if you wish. Hell, call it anything you want. Trick is, lady, it runs through your south lease."

I heard shuffling around the room. Rudolfo said, "I need the lease, Sarah. You need cash. You have the best connection from Baca Loco to Pantano. I have gold."

Rudolfo had wanted himself a governor's chair last fall and I always thought he'd meant Phoenix, though territorial elections were not due for a couple of years. At last it dawned on me. It wasn't Arizona but governorship of Sonora he'd been interested in. Never have been handy with shadows and slick smiles. It touched off sparks inside me I had to fight not to show. I said, "El Dorado? Isn't that a fancy name for some burned-out cow pasture? And what about my mother's land?"

"Ah, *sí*. It is only a little track. Worth nothing. If you don't wish to share in our venture then allow my friends to purchase a small section of land. We offer you a thousand dollars of American gold. In return for receiving this money, you will receive a hundred times over, into the future. You see what this will mean, my friend? *Tu familia?*"

Friend? Like a rattler had just woke up under the floor and started shaking his tail, my insides fluttered and a keen wariness overtook me. Albert raised one eyebrow when I looked at him. Around the room, where doorways had seemed empty before, there were men all about, watching. Men in white uniforms like they were cooks and houseboys stared in at the group. They wore servants' clothing, but they stood too ready to spring, and to a man they had hard, steely eyes, like coyotes, like they'd maybe been the very *caballeros* who'd killed the two men on Rudolfo's land. The *padre* sipped his wine in the silence. A spot of light, reflected off the cup, showed a spider web of red lines and an old scar high on his left cheek.

Then Reyes said they had twenty-eight train cars loaded with goods, ready to pass this way, and for every one that passed I'd get another hundred dollars. While he talked, I wondered just how Rudolfo had gotten enough money to buy ten thousand acres in Sonora. My land didn't extend halfway to Naco. But it did lie between here and Pantano's place as a crow flies. He was going to good lengths for it, so what would he do for the rest of the passage of his Paso Dorado?

As if he heard me thinking, Rudolfo added, "I'll fence the whole distance. For safety of your stock, you see."

The varmint knew I had no stock roaming that range. My windmill stands guard over nothing but hungry coyotes and mangy javelinas. This was a test far beyond shaking foreign words at each other to see who'd flinch. These men were up to something I couldn't put a name to, but it frightened me down to my core.

"What's it all for, Rudolfo? The Southern Pacific doesn't need this, really. Why do you men need a rail line to Mexico?"

Von Wangenheim talked about how the political future of Mexico was at stake. That Germany was behind everything they did, too. That we could count on his government for any support—and then he paused before adding—necessary. How we'd all band together for the good of the people who'd brought prosperity to Mexico. And then he said no one who'd come to this meeting could ever be apart from it again. A cold, hard iron formed itself in my back, and I breathed very lightly, just as if I were hunting and testing the wind lest I give some sign of my aim.

I thought about those men who'd chased down and killed the other two fellows. Now I knew who the murderers were, at least: part of this deal with these villains before me. It's been in the paper now and then that revolutionaries planned on raising an army and taking back the Gadsden, then reannexing everything from the Pima County line back into Mexico. He was talking about starting a war. That meant politics and bullets, and governments taking land; the greedy and powerful always winning the lion's share. This land was mine and I'd have no part of Porfirio Díaz taking it, nor ride with the men who plan to take it from him as soon as he did. Rudolfo had brought my family into his confederacy by trickery. We could be linked to these dark and dangerous men by attending this supper. Never mind we came out of sheer ignorance.

I happened to glance at Madera as he looked at me. He had a strangely sad look around the eyes for a moment. Then he turned a vicious stare toward Von Wangenheim that disappeared as quickly as it came, returning to his politician's suave expression, aimed at Rudolfo. Rudolfo's face proved there was nothing he wouldn't do to get what he wanted. Somehow he needed me for it. The more desperate he was, the more I didn't want any part of it.

Why was Albert saying nothing? I dared not look at him. He'd already made them think I was *La Mujer* of this family, the matriarch, though I never thought of myself that way. I took a deep breath, worked out the best excuse for a smile I could manage, and stood, causing every man in the room to leap to his feet. Very softly and very firmly, I said, "*Señor Maldonado, y los caballeros,* I say to you, *Feliz Navidad, adiós, y buenas noches.*"

"But Sarah," Rudolfo said, "your answer? Perhaps if I explain again?"

The room bristled. Firelight danced from a thousand candles. The men's fine clothing glowed. All was aflame except for the eyes of the *padre,* cold and hard above the scar on his cheek. I decided not to do them the favor of speaking anything but my own language. Last I heard, the Gadsden had a border yet. I looked Rudolfo square in the eyes. "The question is complete, and so is the answer. Good evening, señores."

We were carried home with the same courtesy we'd arrived with, as if nothing more than a fine evening had passed. Mary Pearl and Aubrey were curious about what had happened in the "meeting," but I told them it was nothing much, and they went back to making soft eyes at each other in the back seat. Beside me, Albert whispered and told me he'd been thinking the whole time about how to guard his house and his family from soldiers should a war break out with Mexico. I didn't want him to know I believed the same thing, so I said, "Isn't this just a feud between the Maldonados and us? What makes you think there's going to be a war between the countries?"

"This is bigger than that. It ain't going to go away, either."

"I know it."

"Might be better if we did have some soldiers around."

"No, brother, I don't think it would. You sure kept awful quiet in there."

"Nothing much to say to a bunch of strangers. And it was your land they wanted. I couldn't tell 'em yes or no for you. You seemed to have a handle on it."

"Still, I wished you'd-a spoke up. Might have added some oil to the fire."

"Naw. You got it said. Them fellows heard every word, too. Better'n if I said 'em."

The carriage arrived at my front porch where Albert's rig awaited our return, and Albert helped me down. He was just a minute going in to fetch Savannah. They left quickly with no more than a wave. We would certainly talk tomorrow.

From my porch I saw in the darkness the gleam of Mexican silver conchos on the rigs of three riders who had followed the coach. The riders waited on a hill with the moon to their side and signaled to the driver as he passed them. I wondered if the jinglings of their tack were the first drums of war. As I stared toward the sound in the deep night air, one by one they turned and followed the coach back to Maldonado's hacienda.

# Chapter Seven

*December 25, 1906*

Christmas morning Albert and Savannah's family joined us at my home to have breakfast, sit around our spindly cholla-skeleton Christmas tree and sing carols and tell stories, and share our gifts with each other. We passed around food and a special treat, a crate of oranges, with a whole one for each person. I kept Charlie's shirt in my lap, hoping the dogs would bark, the door would open, and in he'd walk, but as the sun rose and the smell of the roasting venison filled the place, he still hadn't come.

Chess went out to tend the roasting venison while Savannah and the girls joined Granny and me in the kitchen to fix the big supper for the afternoon. First thing, Savannah pulled out a knife and cut us each a slice of a pumpkin bread she'd been up three hours making. Well, I poured us coffee and put on water to boil for more, and had a taste of that bread. It was bitter as an old root, and I looked from one face to the other, trying to swallow it.

Savannah's eyes grew wide as she chewed. "It isn't right!" she called. "Don't eat this, it'll poison you."

"Land-o'-living!" hollered Granny.

"Savannah, what did you put in this?" I said.

"Just the regular. Flour. And mashed pumpkin, of course. Salt. Alum and soda. A teaspoon of . . . glorious heaven. I put in a teaspoon of sugar and a whole cup of salt." She jumped from her chair and swished about the room, taking the bread from each woman's hands. "Don't eat another bite. Goodness sakes alive. I moved the sugar jar to be closer to the counter and washed out the salt cellar and left it . . . and then put the salt in a bowl with a blue ring on it just like the sugar jar. Whatever has possessed me?" Her hand flew to her mouth. "Oh my!"

"What?" we all said at once.

"That cake I sent to Rudolfo's. Did you taste it?"

"No. We left before they served sweets."

"It was made the same way. They'll all be sick."

I grinned. "Are you sure?"

She looked pained. "Likely."

"Oh well," I said, "if they hadn't got the sense not to eat a salt cake, they'd deserve it. Don't worry. I'm sure there was plenty of other things."

"I've just spent three hours boiling and mashing pumpkins to come up with this mess."

Well, we all had a good laugh and started in making apple and pecan pies, light bread, boiling potatoes, carrots and greens, and corn bread for sage dressing. Every time any one of us went to measure the sugar or salt, we stuck a finger in the bowl and tasted it first, to be sure!

Two big surreys arrived before noon, and spilled out Harland and his children and April and Morris and theirs. True to his word, Harland had brought a crate containing a roast goose, baked yams, cinnamon rolls, and chocolate candy. April had salads and confits and fruit for two feasts. It was a great commotion of love and noise, this ever-growing brood of people who make up my family. As they were putting things in the kitchen, moving furniture around to make room for our bounty, I slipped out front and stared down the road for the hundredth time, hoping for a glimpse of Charlie, risking a fussing-at by Granny for wasting time watching a pot that wouldn't boil. I put his shirt back in the chest to await his receiving it. The house felt lonesome. I know Charlie will leave home eventually for good, but for now, it still seemed to me that he belonged here on this day if no other.

We had cheese pies and oranges for lunch, holding off on the big feast for the end of the day. After that, all went out to play baseball; everyone except Savannah and Granny got into the game. As we lined up to hit the ball, I counted noses, then went through the house and caught Mary Pearl on the back porch by herself, frowning at the very air. I said, "First time I've seen you alone since Aubrey got home. What's wrong, honey?" I said. "Are you ailing?"

"Aunt Sarah, Aubrey says he wants to buy a house for us in town."

"That's nice," I said, trying to read her face.

"But he already said he'd buy me the Wainbridge ranch. He said he'd got it weeks ago so we could live there next to Mama and Papa."

"Well, can't you have both?" I said. "I've got a house in town, too."

"Yes, but you don't live there. Aubrey says a lawyer can't make a living out here, that he has to be in town where people need him. I told him he could help out on the farm, and he just laughed. He laughed!"

"Oh, honey," I said. What could I say, that he and his papa may both be filled with feathers, the way they'll take off on a wild-goose chase over one thing and another?

"He wants to sell Wainbridge's, for 'capital' he says, and buy some house close to the courthouse on Church Street."

"It's up to him to make a living for you," I said. The words nearly caught in my throat. "If you're going to marry the man, you have to live where he lives and works."

"You haven't ever lived clear away from Granny."

"No, that's true," I said. Was I ready to live where Udell lived? Follow him if he got itchy feet like my pa and set out for greener pastures? Had I thought it out clearly? I patted her shoulder and said, "Why don't you let it simmer for a while? Think on it and go see the house. Everyone I know ended up different than they expected. Fate, you know. It'll settle in your mind."

"What if it doesn't settle? What if I hate it? I—I wanted to go to art school, and there aren't any here, so I'll have to go someplace else. He said he'd wait for me to go, maybe two years. Now he's buying this house and it seems like it's going too fast. What if I don't want to live there?"

"Well, I don't know just what to say, honey, but you aren't marrying a *house.* And he's not a pair of pants, you're marrying the lawyer that's in 'em. You'll have to decide whether you want to wash and mend them the rest of your days, not me, nor anyone else. He's the one to choose where he can make the best living for you. You talk this over with your folks?"

"Mama tells me I'm betrothed and that's as good as married. Papa says that a mistake only half done is twice-easy fixed. Aubrey's not a mistake. I love him, truly, but he *told* me he was buying the Wainbridge place. Next to Mama and Papa."

I grasped her hands and turned them in mine. They were delicate, firm, and strong, but still white and unweathered except for a line of callus across the palms. I had seen those tender fingers put a steel blade into a fencepost from across the yard, and pull a trigger on wild game and coyotes. To me, she had everything a girl could want going for her, and no one ought to try to change the course of the river that was Mary Pearl except herself. I said, "I always took you for a girl who could think for herself. A man can sure turn your head, that's a fact. You do what's right for him *and* for you. That's all."

She sighed, fell against my shoulder and hugged me, and said, "When I think about him, I can't think at all. It's worse than being kicked in the head by a mule."

I laughed. Then we went to see how the roast was doing. After a bit, Mary Pearl and I got into the baseball game. At my turn, I clipped a good lick on that raggedy ball with the board we used for a bat and took off for the rock that was the first base, hiking my skirts up so I could run. Albert yelled, "Shameful!" and everyone laughed at me.

Gilbert scooped up that ball and tossed it to Ezra, who was pitching, then hollered out, "She's been practicing that swing on my back pockets since I was little, I tell you what."

April laughed and called to him, "No, no. I got the worst of it!"

When Mary Pearl got her turn with the bat, she hit it a lick that nearly took Ezra right out of his shoes, but he caught it so she struck out. I couldn't read her face but it seemed to me she didn't care about getting out so much as knocking that ball into next year. Later, Ezra hit up a ball that Gilbert missed catching so Rebeccah and Mary Pearl both got to run to home plate. We had a fine game, what with no real teams and everyone winning.

Finally, Chess announced the venison roast was ready, and we descended on our feast like jackals. Thank goodness April had also brought dishes. I didn't even have enough plates to go around. As we all settled down I counted all those folks and added up my riches, right there, like Udell said. We were a fine bunch, I'd say. Anyone who didn't get full at that meal didn't half try. When we were stuffed to the gills, we started in on the sweets.

Then the grown-ups and the babies slept, while the children ran loose as chickens. The sun was low on the hills to the west when I saw a movement in the east. Two people rode horseback, moving at a gentle pace as if their horses were tired. They pulled a pack animal behind them. It was a man and a woman.

We all turned and stared. Zachary muttered, "Say, looks like Mary and Joseph showed up late, Ezra," but Albert heard him and snapped Zack's ear with his fingertip for blaspheming.

Pretty soon, the man held up a hand and waved, then spurred his horse onward, holding his hat in one hand. Both of them came on a gallop. It was Charlie! Charlie and a woman.

I ran toward him and he hopped down. He was clean and shaven except for a mustache, and looked all a-glow. Tall and filled out good, too, as if he'd been eating well and had finally quit growing. "Mama, oh!" was all he got out, and gripped me in a bear hug that took the breath out of me. The woman's horse caught up to us, then, and the rest of the family gathered.

Her clothes were simple, the kind Savannah wore. On her hands were light gloves, new and likely just bought for the trip, although she rode well accustomed to a saddle. Though most of her face was hidden under a stiff shawl, the chin I saw was firm and deeply cleft, and brown.

"Well, son," I said, "introduce us."

Charlie grinned, not the least embarrassed or shy, reached up and lifted the woman from the saddle as if she were a child. He held her hands in his for a moment longer than the lifting down took, and gave her a sincere look as if he were reassuring her this meeting would turn out all right. I remembered in that fleeting instant the time I first met Chess and what a scallywag he'd been to me. Charlie turned to me and said, "Mama, you remember Elsa, don't you?"

"Elsa?" I said. The woman pulled back her shawl, revealing a delicate face I vaguely knew.

Mary Pearl squealed with delight, "Elsa!" and flew between her brothers. The two girls hugged each other and kissed each other's cheeks again and again. Mary Pearl cried, "Elsa, my dearest, sweet friend!"

Elsa Maldonado. I stared at Charlie. My mouth dropped open and my heart felt as if it had stopped. Rudolfo's oldest daughter should have been cloistered in the convent in town. Then I sighed with relief. Charlie was simply escorting her to her folks for a Christmas visit. Naturally they came by this way first.

The clothes Elsa wore were plain and featureless, but by no means were they a habit of any order. She was trim but buxom, and had a manner about her that made her seem ten years older than I knew she was. Plus, I sensed some fear or pain in her bearing that, now that I knew who she was, I was sure did not come from meeting us.

"Well, come on and have supper," I said. "Sun's going down and we've cooked the livelong day. There's a feast for an army. You have to stop and eat, Elsa; let us get a look at you before you go on home."

Elsa smiled, whispering, "Thank you, señora," before she turned to Charlie. "I hope," she said, and paused too long, I thought, before she continued, "I *am* home."

"Mama," Charlie said, "folks—everyone—I mean, Elsa and I were married in town before we left yesterday. We'd have gotten here sooner but we lost a horse. I knew you'd be looking for me at Christmas. I tell you, we spent a cold night down in that arroyo." He laughed nervously.

Granny seemed to be studying her shoes. Chess let out a whistle and everyone kept silent for a long minute. Savannah's girls all whirled in for the rescue, surrounding Elsa and Charlie and giggling, kissing, embracing the bunch, happy as birds in spring.

Charlie had married Elsa Maldonado, connecting us to Rudolfo in a way I never to my last breath would have imagined. It would be polite to congratulate my son and his new wife, all of seventeen or eighteen years old. It would be right to hug her and kiss her, myself, and welcome her to the family. What I should have done was to smile and cheer them, but what I did was only to look into Savannah's eyes and say, "Does your father know about this?"

"Now, Mama," Charlie started.

Elsa pushed through the circle made by Rachel, Rebeccah, and Mary Pearl and faced me squarely. "No, he does not. I tried to write to him, but his letters to me in reply were only orders to stay where I was. He would hear of no choice for me but the Sisters' convent school. I—I had to leave there. I had to. I wanted to come home, but—"

Charlie interrupted her. "Anyway, it's done, and legal. And that tough old padre in the mission was mad at her, but Elsa and I, we—" He turned his hat around in his hands, fiddled with the band around the crown, and smoothed it before he kept on, saying, "Well, we've known each other since we were kids."

Granny said, "Just like Harland and Melissa. Only Melissa didn't have a whippersnapper of a pa waiting to put a bullet through Harland for taking her away from him."

Charlie grimaced, but seemed undaunted. He'd been an Arizona Ranger for several months, had lived in the desert heat by his wits and his guns. Not many people could make the fellow squirm. I felt a swell of pride in him that was outside the circumstance before us. I said, "The truth of it is, son, talk to Rudolfo if you please, but the Maldonado ranch is not a place to ride up to tonight with news of that sort. He's got men stationed around, guarding, and watching for, well, strangers. They mightn't recognize you. You two had best bunk here."

"I aim to get his blessing," Charlie said. "It was because of me he sent her there."

Had Charlie made known to Rudolfo some affection toward his daughter that had angered him? And that I never noticed?

Chess grumbled. Then he hissed, "You'll be more likely to get his buckshot."

Charlie laughed, but the hard resolve I saw in his eyes made me know he wasn't about to back down from any man standing.

So the evening meal was a long and windy one, with so many things to tell Charlie, so much I wanted to know from him and Elsa but couldn't ask. I'd always thought if a girl went into that convent, she was as good as gone and likely to be sent to South America. She was a pretty girl, too. Pretty enough to turn a young man's head.

Mary Pearl kept trying to tell Elsa about things *she* was interested in, like fashions and school and that time she stomped on a snake last summer. But to all her questions and prodding for conversation, Elsa only nodded. It was as if she had been utterly locked away from any kind of girlish frills for those two years, as if Mary Pearl's words were foreign to her.

In between everything, we got the story of their secret romance, and how just before Thanksgiving Elsa had left the convent after what she called a grievous ten days of prayer and penance, convinced she was not called to a life's vocation. Together they told how Charlie'd stopped in the market to find a gift for me. Pausing by Elsa's table, thinking she was only a girl selling embroidered handkerchiefs, he discovered her anew. Gilbert kept quiet, now and then looking up with a dark flush to his face.

After we washed up, made more coffee, and pulled out blankets to bed down the children, it got quiet as the little ones turned in. April went to bed, too, being worn out and looking swollen with her next babe. Only then did we tell Charlie and Elsa about last night's Christmas Eve at the rancho south of here, the railroad man coming to the house, the *políticos* and *científicos* gathered around Rudolfo's table. Elsa's eyes grew wide and dark with fear.

I reckoned my Charlie had caught himself a timid little cottontail rabbit, used to being bullied by her papa. Snagged her right out of the jaws of an old lion that Charlie was going to have to battle as long as he lived. Then something changed in Elsa's face. She sat rigid, gripping her coffee cup as if she warmed her hands on it, and looked quickly to Charlie before she said, "All the time I've been gone I prayed to be united to Christ, but my heart is not a Sister's. For three years my friend Esperanza secretly brought letters from Charlie when he was going to the school there. She carried my messages to him, too. Then when he left, I was crushed. I didn't know why he was gone and couldn't get word to him. I thought he'd left me. I tried to forget Charlie, though I'd loved him since we were children. I left the convent and I'd been living in Tucson for a month and a half at a widow's home, sewing and washing, doing odd tasks. When Charlie came to town and we met by a miracle, so perfectly ordered that I knew it was no accident, I . . . I'd already accepted his proposal before he made it. That's how certain I am that I love Charlie.

"I have had plenty of time to think and begin to understand my father. His strength is also his weakness. Much as he has built his wealth on hard work, he is very much afraid to lose anything. If he will not bless our marriage he will lose me. If we have to leave to keep you safe, we will, but I think he will be too afraid of what he will lose to make a decree to us and lose me forever. This is what I think."

"I'm ready, too," Charlie said. "If we can stay here a bit, I'll work for you, Mama, harder than I ever did, for our room and board. If not, I've got a job waiting for me up toward the Mogollon as a deputy sheriff out of Springerville. Word is they're breaking up the Ranger outfit come summer, and anyhow ranging's no life for a man with a wife."

"No, don't go. Of course you can stay." Lands, if they went that far away, I'd never see them. There could be babies born, just like when April was in Philadelphia, that I'd not see for years. I turned to Albert, Chess, and my mama, lastly to Savannah. Her eyes were misty and she nodded slowly. I felt as if my jaw had frozen.

In the midst of my thickheadedness, I remembered my gift. The last shirt I'd ever make for my oldest son. I rushed to my bedroom. Opening the chest, I took up Charlie's shirt. I had no gift for Elsa. What with thread and cloth so dear I'd barely managed something for those at hand; I hadn't done extra. In that chest was the remainder of the pinafore material, waiting to be cut up for quilt scraps. I trimmed it up square and folded it carefully. I found a piece of lace in there, about two yards long, raveled out at one end, but I trimmed it smooth and folded it onto the cloth. Folks were talking in the other room. I laid a long spool of white thread on the stack, though I had not a single button to spare except some big round ones that go on men's pants fronts, nothing a lady would wear. Hunting for more, I lifted the quilt at the bottom of the chest. There was the spirit level I'd bought. I refused to let myself look on it or think on the man I intended it for. I was headed for the door when I spied the assortment of odd things jumbled on top of the highboy chest, and from it I took up my best new thimble, adding it to my gift to Elsa. Couldn't it have been anyone other than Elsa?

I gave my son and his new wife their gifts for Christmas and they were kind and said their thanks. Though I replied, I could barely speak above a whisper. Elsa grabbed my shoulders and hugged me and I think I smiled but, Lord, I wanted to cry. I wished them a house full of healthy children and all, but I couldn't leave off thinking my boy Charlie had married the only girl in the Territory who could bring to this house the tender femininity possessed by a leaky keg of blasting powder.

# Chapter Eight

*December 26, 1906*

I got my saddle blanket on a green-broke pony and rode north across the Cienega toward the sandy cliff. The cold that seeped through the seams in my old coat cut into my ribs and chest. I came upon the place where the stage had turned over and I kept going. My mount, a small bay named Hatch, was shy of the shadows, and danced as she walked. I'd left the family to make their own breakfast and had gone to the barn after only a cup of coffee. Chess offered to come along wherever I was going as I shouldn't be out alone but I told him to stay put. Maybe he thought I was going to see Rudolfo. Have some words with him. Truth is, I didn't know where I was going, I just needed a ride.

By now, Udell should be in Colorado, and maybe caught up with the end of the rainbow he's chasing. I gave Hatch her head and went up the stage road to where the bend went toward Granny's place. Two miles up, I found a wooden stake beaten into the ground with a strip of a red handkerchief tied to it. The horse snorted at the fluttering cloth, and pulled on her reins. I pulled up that stake and tossed it into some brush. I made her settle, and then we cut far around by a washy place where the sand had become frozen and hard. It broke in U shapes with each step of Hatch's hooves.

Far upwind, the slow-rising call of a wolf spooked Hatch and she hauled up into the air about three times before setting off on a dead run. I jerked the reins, held on for my life, and got her to plant her front feet, but nearly went over. The wolf gave one more howl as I jumped off and pulled that horse's nose to my chest, talking low and steady. Hatch's eyes were white all around and her ears laid back. Without me on her, she could barely keep her feet on the ground.

I should have ridden Baldy. Leastways I'd be free to think of my own worries instead of his. I should have used a saddle instead of just a blanket, so this lunkhead cayuse would mind. We set off walking, me pulling Hatch's chin lead, across the frozen patch of sand to the cobbled gravel beyond it, knowing I'd left footprints behind me. I watched the ground closely, finding a path where the greasewood was far enough apart Hatch wouldn't have to rub her sides on it. Ornery horse. I wanted to be somewhere else and I didn't much care where it was.

I pictured my papa when I was a girl, the day he came to the house and told us to bring in the herd because he'd got word there was better grazing in San Angelo, Texas. He's buried there, now. Savannah's papa and sisters had stayed there, too, farming, all except Ulyssa, who died at the lung asylum here in the Territory a couple of years ago. How had Papa come to choose moving instead of staying? If he'd known it would cost him his life, would he have gone pulling up stakes and leaving the only home I could remember? I had visions of the curly-stemmed grass that used to get into my stockings when I was a girl, in the place I grew up, Cottonwood Springs, and the way the wind blew constant for days rather than coming in gusts and storms the way it does here. Had he ever felt part and parcel of the land he wanted to leave that day? Was it easy to ride away?

Then I got right down to my sore spot, and pressed it. If I were a man, I might just leave. Strange what a man can do that a woman would break apart doing. Maybe there's more to being a woman—other lives were intertwined with mine like the bougainvillea that had long ago become part of Albert and Savannah's front porch. I was caught between Rudolfo and the railroad, with a load of dynamite just moved in, as near to flat-out broke as I've ever been, lonesome for a man I barely knew, and responsible for too many people to just run away. Unless I packed the lot of them along, too.

There weren't any Apaches or Comanches left in the Chiricahuas. It's winter. There'd be water past El Paso. I had no reason to move to Texas other than that my pa had wanted to go there. I knew nothing about the place, didn't even remember it, except for Chess's ranch, that's probably overgrown with mesquite and cedar. We could head to Austin and pick up Chess's old place, buy it back from his daughter, who's a widow now and not running anything on it but some chickens. Or I'll sell out and take up life in town. Raise chickens and sell some eggs, myself. Then again, I wasn't ready to ride a rocking chair the rest of my days. Right now, though, I could leave this ranch with nothing to show for the life I'd led but some footprints that will blow away when that sand thaws. I was too young to just sit and wait to die.

I turned Hatch to the south and stopped on the ridge again. Above the house, smoke curled in earnest from three stovepipes. A rooster crowed, almost in time with the windmill's creaking. West of the main yard, below the black, leafless branches of the jacaranda tree, the graves of people I've loved lay under a haze of frost. My dead babies, two husbands, an assortment of cavalrymen including my brother, and my crosscut nephew, Willie. Smoke raised a line from the stovepipe, straight up over the house to where it met some kind of breeze and there it spread in a fan. From the very first timber Jimmy Reed cut, that place had belonged to me. These double adobe walls were sturdy and solid, and bound to be pleasant in the summer, but though I've lived here near three months, the place didn't feel like my home.

I put Hatch in the barn. Chess was tinkering with something and set it down to pull the saddle blanket down. We walked toward the house. I asked him, "Was it hard to leave your place and come here? Did you just reckon this was your new home?"

He stopped in his tracks, his head nodding with a rhythm he can't control. He said, "What're you driving at?"

"I'm feeling like pushing on. Maybe head back to Texas, where my pa always wanted us to live. Reckon we never gave that a chance, just up and left because Albert and I were only young'uns and didn't know what to do with ourselves but run back."

After a few steps, he said, "Always thought our boy Charlie had more sense than to do what he done."

"What man's got sense when he loves a woman? Or woman, either."

"We'll see how it fares, soon as the old boy finds out. So you reckon not to stand up to Maldonado again, that it's better to up stakes? Let him win it all?"

I took a few more steps, slowing to keep pace with him. "Suppose I don't want to fight this battle."

"Reckon not."

"Maybe you'd like to go home." I stopped. "Chess?"

He turned. "You asked me to stay the day we laid Jack in the ground. It ain't about the roof and windows."

I'd have hugged him, except he'd have ducked away. I said, "Maybe Rudolfo will be all right. Maybe he'll even be happy. Nothing like a grandchild to melt a heart."

" 'Til they grow up and go off Romeo-ing with some Juliet."

"I should never have let the boys read Shakespeare. Wonder which one of us is the Capulets? I could swear."

"Well, go ahead. You don't get profane often enough, Sarah Elliot. It'd do you better than leaving. And what about that Hanna fella? Don't you owe him no fare-thee-well?"

"He isn't Jack."

"Naw. But you ain't the kind to fiddle with a person. You got grandchildren, too. Look at that houseful. So, no sense turn-tailing. I reckon old Charlie'da got the notion some otherwise. I'm hungry. Let's quit jawing and start eating."

We stepped through the door into warm air perfumed with cooking. I've stuck on this land through fire and flood, gale winds and Apache raids, and though Rudolfo's hand in the building of the house itself still rankled me, I wouldn't be chased off this land. Especially not by my own fears.

### *December 28, 1906*

Long before dawn I went out to get eggs, and when I got back to the kitchen, I found Blessing sitting in the chair that Granny usually occupies when there is a good fire going. The child was shivering, but she said nothing when I came in, so I gave her a minute to open up while I set down my egg basket and put up my hat and coat. When I turned around, she had gotten out of the chair and had a chunk of firewood in her arms. "Aunt Sarah?" she said. "Ain't I big enough to make this stove up for you?"

"Well, I swan, you are at that. But before you put in that old log, you'd better add some kindling." I bent and poked in the depths of the stove with an iron, moving banked embers to the front while she picked up some twigs. "There, lay it on top of the coals. Don't get too close. It'll scorch you."

She poked a few slips of split shaves and twigs in while I pushed over the coals. Blessing said, "Poppy says we have to go home, but I like it here. There's a mommy *and* a daddy here. He says we're too much trouble for you. I could help you light the stove ever' morning. You might need that. I'm real helperful."

I tried not to grin. It hadn't been long since she'd hated my very breath. I sat in the chair and held out my arms to the girl. She climbed in my lap and laid her head against my shoulder. I said, "You aren't ever going to get over missing your mama. I know it."

"Miss Cousin Rachel is mean. And she's not my mother."

"Rachel is trying her best. She's new at being a nursemaid and maybe you have to give her a chance."

Blessing straightened. "Nursemaid? Poppy says she's the giver-nest. She givers us castor oil, and givers lectures, and scolds Story about scratching his behind in Sunday School, telling him he mighta caught worms and that if he don't tuck in his shirttail for the fifteenth time today, she's gonna sew lace doilies on it so all the boys can see. I don't see what's wrong with scratching what itches in Sunday School. It ain't his fault."

"Isn't. You say 'isn't his fault.' "

"Well, at school some girls say 'ain't' all the time. I heard Granny saying 'ain't' and Grampa Chess says it." She sighed and moved her legs around, holding her stocking feet toward the stove. "Why don't you come to our house and be our giver-nest? You tell better stories, and you don't scold so much. I wish I was your little girl, now that Mommy's gone to heaven in Chicago."

"I wish you were my little girl, too," I said. For the blink of an eye, my tiny Suzanne was in my lap, prattling away in baby talk over a string of wooden beads. Suzanne died of scarlet fever even before Jack was killed. Blessing's mother died of cancer and left this child sitting here in my lap on this bitter cold December morning. I kissed the part in Blessing's hair and the past vanished. As Blessing rhythmically waved her left foot toward the stove I rocked the chair for a while, without either of us saying another word.

## December 29, 1906

The year is drawing to a close and I for one am glad to see this one put in the barn. It has been one of the toughest years I've faced, with famine, flood, and fire. Reckon the only thing missing was pestilence, but then I thought, I have Rudolfo Maldonado, so we've endured plagues enough. Harland and his little ones left this morning, as he had to get back to his practice, and they had to return to school shortly.

Elsa, April, and I have washed clothes all morning and hung them outside to dry. Every few minutes we take a look at some gathering clouds, but still no sign of rain. They also helped me put on some bread to rise and three of the loaves have cinnamon and raisins rolled into them. What a fine treat we'll have this evening. Keeping the table full for this big family has been near as hard as riding a roundup for a week.

About noon, April went out to check the clothes on the line and hollered, "Sprinkling!" so Elsa and I ran to help pull them all in, dried or not. We got shirts and pants and drawers laid around the book room, and lit a fire in the stove in there, then we worked up some lines in the kitchen and every bedroom, too. Patricia and Lorelei thought that was great fun and ran, whooping, beneath the hanging clothes, surprising each other and dashing through the house.

Once we got this little army fed and put down for naps, the rain started up with more purpose. All we females settled in the kitchen for some tea and cookies, and to watch that bread rise. April put her feet up on a second chair and pulled off her shoes, rubbing her swollen ankles. Granny snoozed in a rocking chair. The calico cat rose and arched his back with a flick of his tail and hopped from Granny's lap to April's.

"Elsa," I said, "you have to sit and rest with us now. You've been working all morning."

She looked from April to me. "We're all working," she said.

April laughed. She said, "Mama doesn't want anybody to best her, is all. Get down, cat. Why don't you name that old thing, Mother? Hand me another of those cookies. We'll get them cleaned up before the boys get in here."

"I'll save mine for Carlito," Elsa whispered.

"No you won't!" April crowed. "If you don't eat it, I will. With this baby, I'm so hungry all the time! Besides, there's not enough for all of 'em and Charlie gets all the food he wants. Come on. Hand it over." She laughed, but she meant business.

I watched Elsa's face closely. She frowned. Then she sat up straight and pushed out that strong chin, and put half that cookie in her mouth at once. I laughed and said, "Now you girls, do I have to give you a talking-to or will you behave?"

April and Elsa laughed, too. Elsa greedily chomped on the rest of the cookie while April said, "Mama, are there any left in the crock? Just crumbs? I'll take them. I'll make some more. Elsa, we'd better be good now. Mama's talking-tos can pin your ears back for a week."

"No more'n you deserve, young lady," I said.

She giggled. "You haven't called me that in a while."

Elsa said, "We can make more cookies. Granny said she likes them, too. Come here, *gatito*." She held her hand down toward the cat with a tiny piece of cookie on one finger. She'd made a friend, I could see, and the calico curled up on her lap, then, to stay. "Charlie and I want to start our family soon."

"Well, I'm not sorry about that," I said. "I think grandchildren are the best part of being a mother. Twice the fun and half the worry."

Elsa peered under lowered lids from me to April. "How, how *do* you know if . . . ? How can you tell if . . . if there is a baby? Can you tell before it comes?"

"Well," April began, "I always get a brown spot on my left hand, right here, and my ankles puff up. Then I have a sour stomach nearly every day for a month. That's a sure sign."

Elsa studied both her hands. "It could be a spot there. My stomach, sometimes."

"I never got spots," I said. "Backaches, that's what I had."

Elsa rubbed her back. "It hurts a little," she said. "Does it hurt a great deal, when the baby comes?"

I tried not to glance at April, but the two of us locked eyes almost like clockwork. "Well," I said, "it's different for everyone. It's hard. But it doesn't last forever. If you can think about the work you're doing and just go to doing it, it gets done quicker."

"Oh. Like laundry. I hate laundry," Elsa said. Then the three of us laughed enough to wake Granny. Elsa sputtered, trying to regain her composure. "They made me do so much laundry at the convent I thought I would perish from my cracked and tortured hands."

April got up and went stocking footed to the pantry shelf, returning with a can. "Here," she said, "rub your hands with teat salve. Mama doesn't keep a milk cow but this is good for plenty of skin ailments."

We passed that can of salve around, along with more cups of tea, and then put that bread in the oven to bake for supper. Elsa rose from closing the oven door and kissed my cheek, hugging me warmly.

December 31, 1906

The bustle in this house has not slowed one bit, what with April's brood of three. Her boy Vallary is a pistol, and he, Ezra, and Zachary are wilder together than my two ever thought about being. Spurred on by the number of new faces, Savannah and Albert's children from youngest to oldest have all but moved in here and shirked their chores, having to be gotten home by Mary Pearl or their brother Clover, regularly. Little wonder that by the end of the year of nineteen and aught six, my patience with the number of people in the house was wearing thinner than the gravy made from my last ration of flour, and when April announced she and Morris were taking their family home, I was not truly unhappy to see them go. She begged me to go along. I was sorely ready for some peace and quiet, but I needed feed and supplies more than I needed quiet, so I will be accompanying them to town.

Gilbert will be riding along, too, for he wants to see his girl again. I have asked him when I can meet her, as I'm not looking forward to yet another surprise wedding, but he only says soon, and then goes to talking about the cows we've got swelling with calves or the size of the moon, or some other thing. Gilbert is pulling at that spare mule that belongs to Wells Fargo, and the thing is giving him quite a time. Finally, we put him and the ornery critter up front ahead of the rest, and he moves along just fine as you please. Must be used to being the lead, and I know some animals never can do aught but what they learned the first time. Mary Pearl is also coming to town, intent on seeing Aubrey and the house he proposes to buy for a home. She's more than lonesome lately, and put out by Elsa's conversation, which has pretty much been about Charlie since she got here.

Charlie and Elsa are staying put at the ranch, along with Chess and Granny, and I reckon the two young people will be glad for at least some measure of quiet privacy, the both of them having camped amongst the bunch in the book room and parlor floors, at far ends from each other for a week now. Granny mostly sleeps around the clock, and Chess stays busy, so things should be all right for the new married pair. After plenty of talking last night, we made them promise they will not pay a call on Rudolfo until I get home with Gilbert, so the bunch of us can go together for strength.

Last night we came to an arrangement where Elsa and Charlie can use the plaza and one of the other rooms for their own kitchen and then take Charlie's old bedroom and the book room for a small apartment. While I'm gone, Charlie is going to move all my books to the parlor and fix them up some quarters. I figure soon enough they'll be getting their own house, but we'll wait until the big *confrontación* with Elsa's papa to see how far away it may need to be. I looked toward him as we drove away, but his eyes were only on her. Charlie Horse, his papa called him when he was first born. The boy was skinning his knees one minute, shaving his face and married the next.

April's house was just as lovely as ever, and thankfully, she is not suffering as much with the baby coming now. We settled right in as if the party had only changed locations.

Two days after we got to town, both April's girls, Patricia and Lorelei, woke in the night with fever. Patricia held her neck and said her tongue hurt. I rocked her and held her, while April tried her best to comfort Lorelei. The little one cried weakly, and when the sun was up, Morris went to fetch a doctor.

Influenza has stricken the babies. Patricia barely eats, and Lorelei eats but vomits. By the next day, Morris was down in bed, too, and the third day, Vallary came downstairs with sore ears and throat, and now Gilbert is coughing and crouping. It seems we wait each day to see who will come down next. April, Mary Pearl, and I are tending everyone, with the help of April's maid Lizzie. Toward afternoon all the sick ones seemed to be sleeping at last, and so I made April lie down, too. I was planning to get to town and buy a few things but I was met at the front of the house by two men in long black coats looking like they were a matched pair of undertakers. They nailed a big sign to the door that said it all in one word: QUARANTINED. The house is locked up like a prison with us inside for no less than four weeks.

I told them I had a ranch to run, chickens to feed, old folks to care for. But one doctor said that if I left, I'd take the influenza to the old folks and they'd likely die. No matter that I still felt well, he said, it had been microscopically determined that people could carry the sickness and spread it like dysentery or trail fever. Someone could bring us things from any store we wished, as long as we waited until the baskets were delivered and the messenger left before opening the door. I can't say why this all made me feel somewhat ashamed, but it did, as if we'd done something criminal or vulgar, and were being shut off from the rest of town like we were unclean.

Fortunately, we are allowed to send letters, and so Mary Pearl has kept up letters with Aubrey and with her folks back home. Then, one day as she was sitting at April's desk and busily writing, she asked me to keep a secret, and she told me she wrote away to the college for artists in Illinois at a place called

Wheaton. I didn't like keeping secrets from her folks, but she said she was convinced that if the teachers will let her into that school, she'll tell her mama and papa, and things would be all right, and if they didn't, she'd take it as a sign she should stay home and marry and keep house, forgetting her other dreams. Mary Pearl insisted if her mama knew she was applying to the school, she'd be here in an hour with more speeches about betrothal and all.

Mary Pearl sent them five small drawings she had done with pencil and paper. One of them she figured was her best shot, though it was on lined letter paper turned sideways. To me, any big fancy college wouldn't give her a second thought for sending something like that but I didn't know if I should say that or keep quiet. I told her to ask April for a nice piece of paper, and then just take some time and draw it over again. So she spent a couple of hours, pronounced it not as good as the first one, but enclosed them both, so the teachers can choose whichever one they like.

Well, after the littlest children had been sick a week, they were starting to be well enough to be restless in bed, and we had a time corralling them. Just when it seemed the rest of us would miss the beating that half the family was getting by the illness, though, April woke one morning in a terrible state with fever. I was plenty worried about her, for I had been sick once with fever and it cost me a babe. I sat by her putting cooling compresses on her most of the morning. I felt ragged myself, but not sick, just tired, and so there was only Mary Pearl, Lizzie, and myself tending things, until that afternoon Lizzie took to her bed. Morris put on a robe and tried to help, and we made soup and boiled sheets from morning to night while he kept the children still.

By the next day, though, I reckoned I had done too much lifting, as my arms ached deep inside the bones, my head shook with misery, causing my teeth to rattle, and after fixing breakfast for those that could eat, I could barely lift a single spoon to wash it. Mary Pearl told me to go upstairs and lie down, and that she was going to send for help from the doctor who'd penned us up. I don't know how the girl did it, but I do know that before long I heard strange voices and footsteps, and I was ordered to stay in bed by a woman in a dark blue uniform.

I could hardly argue with her. My throat burned day and night like I'd swallowed a branding iron. Every hair on my head throbbed, my eyes felt glued shut, my feet shivered and no blankets could keep me warm. In between fretting over April being tended so she'd keep her unborn child, I sank into the sickness for I don't know how long. I had fierce dreams of being trampled by horses, having birds pick at my skin while carrying April's unborn baby in my arms, trying to run to save it, and not able to move because my feet were clamped in leg-hold animal traps. I knew these night visions were from the bone aches of sickness, but I'd awaken feeling tortured and afraid to sleep, then immediately fall asleep and eventually drift into some other terrible nightmare. It seemed days passed, while I struggled to breathe, asking the faceless forms that passed me if others were well, but receiving no answers, and sleeping first in shallow spells and then frighteningly deep periods, as if my bed were half a step from my grave.

*January 17, 1907.*

Seems waking from the depths of the influenza meant coughing my lights out. I couldn't remember being so aggravated by coughing since I was little, and though the fever was gone along with the aches and stomach disorder, the need to stay absolutely still to avoid coughing kept me in bed. I tried to get information on the health of the rest of the family from the doctor and the nurse that stopped in the room, but when they said anything, it was only a few vague words clouded with sanctimony.

At last, I awakened and decided to get out of bed, driven by hunger and an empty water glass which had mercifully remained clean and filled for no telling how many days. I knew it was daylight outside, but I had slept long after dawn, and dreamed of someone calling me with a voice that echoed from a long way off. I rose and dressed myself, putting on two pairs of stockings without shoes, which seemed too much effort to bear.

As I ventured into the hallway, the house itself seemed to sigh. I tiptoed from door to door finding no one. By the head of the stairway I heard children's voices quietly whining and someone hushing them. At the fourth step I had to stop for a coughing jag, then I headed on toward the voices. They had come from the parlor, and I made my way there, growing more troubled about the curtained windows, the fearful, unnatural silence in a house I thought was sheltering eight people.

I found Morris sitting with Vallary, Patricia, and Lorelei all in his lap. He wore a dark blue coat like I've seen in store windows downtown, the kind for "gentlemen of leisure" which I always thought meant rich and lazy. Apparently even a working man like Morris might own a sort of coat to wear indoors rather than putting on a shirt and collar. The children seemed happy enough, not crying or anything, although instead of April, a nurse in a uniform was standing over the trio of babes with a large spoon and a brown bottle. Morris was trying to cajole the children into taking the medicine by promising them favors and candy. He smiled when he saw me.

"Oh, Mama Elliot, you are up! What happy news. See, children, I told you we will *all* be well soon enough." Then, with the same smile on his face, which I saw in a moment was only for the children's peace of mind, he said, "The last and healthiest young person in this house has now been taken by the mean old influenza. They've set up temporary nursing in the dining room." His face grew darkly serious and his eyes bored into mine. "If you have the strength, I'm sure Miss Mary Pearl would love to see you. She is in there."

Dining room? What in heaven's name was the girl doing tending someone in the dining room? Was it April? I felt the floor sway under my feet, and held on to a nearby table for strength. I didn't ask what he meant, but immediately went to the dining room where instead of a table, a bed had been set. Thick as a fringe, a line of people surrounded it, all softly murmuring. I searched for Mary Pearl amongst the crowd, and was surprised to see Savannah, Albert, and even Aubrey Hanna and April standing in the circle of nurses and doctors.

"Savannah?" I said. "What's happened?"

She turned and flew to my side. "Sarah, you shouldn't be out of bed. I told them not to wake you, but Albert said she'd want to see you. Sit down here." Albert fetched a chair and no one had to tell me again to take it, as I was purely worn out, traveling this far from my own sickbed.

"Savannah, Albert," I said, surprised at the raspy sound of my own voice, "you and Aubrey shouldn't be here. You'll catch this awful sickness. Where is Mary Pearl?"

One of the doctors came and whispered with that soft, serious tone that never brings anything pleasant, "Mrs. Elliot, you may see her briefly, but it will be to her own good for the girl not to know of the gravity of her illness. We believe her passing to be imminent. Her parents have been summoned despite the quarantine."

The bed was a pretty, four-poster arrangement with a feather bed a foot thick, quilts and lacy counterpanes piled high upon it. From that great mound of bedding a tiny head poked, resting small and dark on a pale calico pillow. It took me a moment to recognize Mary Pearl, so shrunken and drawn and pale her face had become. Her breath came slow and shallow, rattling and raspy, and each one seemed to be an effort that took her whole frame to make. She grimaced and struggled for air as if the blankets were strangling her. She couldn't open her eyes when I spoke her name, but reached a hand from under the covers, and I took it immediately. There was no strength in her at all, and while I couldn't believe what the doctor had said, I saw that the fight had gone out of her.

I leaned toward her and softly said, "Mary Pearl, there's work to be done. Have you saddled up your horse?" Behind me, Aubrey gasped, and Savannah sniffed and gave a slight moan.

Mary Pearl's face moved into a tiny smile, and she opened her eyes. Her eyes had taken that dark look of a newborn babe's, no color and no inner circle of black. They say a dying person is so close to heaven's gate they see again the world of angels that they saw shortly after they were born.

Savannah had retreated from the bedside and now was leaning against the wall, sobbing into her handkerchief without a sound, her shoulders shaking hard, her face red and tears soaking the blouse she wore. As I watched, poor Savannah sank to the floor and clasped her hands. Her prayers made a sort of soft music in the room, as her voice was so faint it seemed to come from some distant place and drift around in the pall of sadness that hovered over us.

I had watched too many people die. I've seen it from every way there is, I reckon. It filled me with such shock and anger that old Death was now hovering at the arm of Mary Pearl. She closed her eyes, and I pressed the back of my hand against her glowing, fevered brow.

I turned to Albert and said, "Has there been any mail?"

He looked at me with a hurt expression. Silently, he shook his head, and turned back to his daughter.

I went fast as my shaking legs would carry me to Morris, where the children had obviously all gotten their dose and were eating licorice candy. They smiled with blackened lips, but I had no time to laugh. "Morris? Morris! Is there mail? Have you gotten any letters or notices or packages, anything at all, for Mary Pearl?"

"Surely she's too ill to sit up and read."

"Grandma, Grandma, watch me, I can write my own name," Patricia said, pulling at my skirt. "I learnt while I was in sickbed."

"But Morris, is there something for her?"

"Yes, on the receiving table by the front door."

I hurried to the place, with Patricia tailing, saying again and again, "Grandma, watch me write my name." There at the table, I found a note addressed to Mary Pearl. Feeling a taint of guilt, but a bigger dose of desperation, I carefully opened the paper, trying to wish the best news from it before I read it. "Grandma, come watch me," Patricia said again. "Please?"

The note was nothing but some invitation from a friend of hers to a tea party. Nothing. I wanted to be the one to carry her the message of her longed-for schooling.

"Patricia." I turned and lifted her in my arms, saying, "I'm very proud of you, Patty-cakes. You show me after I get done visiting your cousin."

"She's sick, Papa told me. We have to be very quiet."

"Scoot along now, and find yourself a pencil while I take this letter to her. It might make her feel better."

"I know! I'll write my name for her. I can't wait for her to get well and see it."

As I returned to Mary Pearl's bedside, the doctors and nurses retreated to another room, quietly conversing with Albert and Savannah. Aubrey was there, holding her hand, gently pressing it to his cheek. He stood and sighed, resting both his hands against his eyes.

"I'll watch for a while," I said. When he went to the corner and sat, I leaned in over her face. In a tone I used to tease her with when she was small, I said, "Mistress Mary P? Open your eyes, Miss Mary-Quite-Contrary. Your friend Monty Hershey wants to have a tea party and sent you a note. She's having six girls from town in for a tea party next week. You'll need a new dress, won't you? That'll make you look so smart. How about a modern skirt, with those plackets on the side?" Then I leaned down close to her ear, and whispered, "Don't you slip out of here without getting your chance at school. You know you've got to try it, if you were willing to disobey your mama just to go."

There was a glimmer of sadness in her expression though her eyes remained shut, and she said, "That's why . . . being punished . . . wickedness."

I felt as if I knew Mary Pearl as well as I knew any human being. If there was anything honest in me at all, I'd swear on the Good Book that Mary Pearl had less wickedness in her than anybody I could name. She was clever and headstrong, but being full of vinegar and spunk was never what I'd call a bad trait, when a person had their head stuck on right and their heart squared up even all around.

"Now don't go putting that rope around it," I said. "You aren't wicked and this isn't punishment. This is just illness and it comes to man and beast alike. Judgment doesn't come this way, except in silly novels. You aren't going to perdition on account of a wish for a grander future than what you can see before you. I've been wishing it all my life, and looking forward is how you keep on moving in this world. If you stopped wondering what was around the bend, why you'd just have to go sit in a rocking chair and wait for the end of your days. You think Mr. Thomas Edison is going to damnation because he wanted to read his newspaper in the evening without smelling kerosene and wondered how to make a light? Wondering is no sin. It isn't. I know it."

"I'm going to die," she said. "That's why they're all here. That's why they're shouting at me."

For a moment I wondered if she did see angels because no one in this house was shouting, but then I reckoned it seemed overloud to her, being so sick. I lowered my voice and said, "I'll tell them to talk softer. Shall I read something to you?"

"No, that's all right. Mama's been reading Psalms until I dream about turning into a deer and tightrope walking across . . . I wish it would rain."

"I'm praying for rain, right now, honey."

Mary Pearl nodded and slept. For three more hours, we took turns at the chair by her side, and she stayed deep in that sleep. I should have been on my knees praying for her. Instead, I thought about rain. Prayed for rain, wished for rain. Anything, so as not to think of her dying.

Late that afternoon, the doctor arrived again and brought a new tonic. They dosed Mary Pearl with brown syrup, and she seemed revived for about an hour, and ate soup, then sank back on the bed and slept as I must have done, feeling so close to the edge that my own breath echoed from beside my grave.

There was no sunset. Clouds that had been hovering like white swans here and there spread and thickened, grew dense and low, and a heavy rain began. It beat against the windows in the dining-room-turned-hospital. It drummed the porch roof and the gutters started funneling it to the numerous barrels at the corners of the house. The evening closed in, April and Lizzie came with lamps lit, and the night seemed for all the world like the dreary type that accompanied folks' dying in books that I've read. But it's been my true experience that folks die on any given day, sun or cloud, heat or cool. Besides, every last drop of rain that falls in the Territory of Arizona is the answer to a hundred prayers, no matter what time of year, no matter if houses washed away. Someone, somewhere, was always hurting for rain. To me, rain was not a message of gloom or despair but of bright hope. Life.

I felt almost cheerful when we went to a quiet supper of our own soup and hot biscuits. Then I went with Savannah to watch at Mary Pearl's bedside, and again we gave her some tonic and again she revived for an hour, even talked with us, then slept. I wondered if I should tell Savannah about Mary Pearl's letter to the school. Maybe together we would contrive to tell Mary Pearl she'd been received and was pledged to go, and that would cheer her enough to bring her back to us. We'd have to admit when she was well that it was a lie, and I'm sure Savannah would perish herself rather than do that. Savannah certainly wouldn't propose that I lie to her daughter. But if the promise of some future could bring my youngest girl back from death's dark portal, I'm sure I would welcome it. I couldn't decide what to do, and because I couldn't decide and felt so drawn myself, we listened to the rain at Mary Pearl's bedside without speaking.

Years have passed and times have changed so much since Savannah and I were girls, when all a girl needed besides being able to shoot straight and ride hard was to sign her name and do sums. By nine o'clock, I'd begun to feel as if I had walked a thousand miles, and Savannah said I looked so faint she feared for my life and to go to bed at once, so I kissed Mary Pearl's face and took myself to the stairway toward my own bed. "Call me, if," I said, and she nodded.

## January 19, 1907

If there was ever a time when I thought I might have seen a ghost it was in the small hours of this morning. I awoke to find Mary Pearl, pale and shivering, dressed in a white wrapper, patting my arm. "What is it?" I asked, half terrified that an eery moan would be the reply.

In a weak voice, Mary Pearl whispered, "I don't think I want to get married, even though I let Aubrey kiss me. Mama'd never forgive me if she knew I kissed a man. If I don't marry him, it's better to go away to school, isn't it? To let her simmer down a while?"

I sat up. "Honey, let's talk about this in the morning. You have a fever. Your mind is playing tricks on you."

"I just can't stand the thought of having a baby. Is that so wrong? Aren't betrothed girls supposed to *want* to have babies?" She sat on the edge of my bed.

"Did you climb all those stairs just to ask me this?" I wrapped my coverlet around her trembling shoulders.

"Aubrey's real handsome and all. But he asked me if I wanted to have a family, and—promise you won't tell? I told him I did, but I'm so afraid of it."

"No need to worry about those things now."

"I can't wait until morning. Mama will be up. You know I can't talk to her about this. She won't listen. If they don't let me in that school, I'll *have* to marry him. I'm a coward."

I'd kissed Aubrey's father. Did I *have* to marry him? I patted her hands. "Babies," I whispered, "and the getting of them, are a different matter altogether. You aren't being a coward. But, I reckon if you aren't looking forward to nursing and diapering and three-day crying jags, you oughtn't to marry yet. You might feel different after a year or two. No harm in that. Even if you don't go to school, you can let off courting with Aubrey for now. I kept Jack Elliot waiting nearly five years. If they're worth having, they'll keep. As for your mama, tell your papa first. Let him break the news. Ready to go back to bed?"

"Yes'm." She pulled the coverlet around her and stood.

We tiptoed down the stairs and I tucked her in. "Want some sugar water?" I asked.

"What I really want is a baked potato and corn relish."

"Must be feeling better. Maybe in the morning." As I poured water for her, I saw by the kerosene lamp that the dark hollows had left her eyes.

"Don't tell Mama."

"I won't tell anything you ask me not to." I kissed her goodnight, though I felt shaken as I made my way past the parlor. Halfway up the stairs, I stopped. Could that have been only an apparition of Mary Pearl, coming to say farewell? I'd read of such things. I returned to the dining room and raised the lamp while I touched her forehead. She was warm. Satisfied, I wrapped myself in the coverlet and sat in the rocking chair, watching over her until I fell asleep.

January 21, 1907

I have sent Morris straight to the post office to check for a letter from the folks in Illinois State. Nothing has come from Wheaton or anyplace else. I have questioned myself whether or not to discuss it with Savannah, wondered if it would matter or only cause discontent. Then I decided if the folks in Illinois State had a-wanted her to come, they'd a-said by now.

Mary Pearl has been having her tonic every three hours, and someone must provide it, so while she was wakeful, I sat with her, reading aloud. After hearing about her sickness, Mary Pearl's town friend Monty Hershey sent over a book she loved, so Savannah reads her the Psalms and I read often to our little patient from Elizabeth Browning's *Sonnets*—a book which her mother would have none of, if she knew, but it cheers Mary Pearl, and I will do all I can for her. Savannah and I take turns waiting at her bedside with the Coca-Cola syrup.

It was while we were changing the watch before dawn this morning, that she began a coughing spell.

"Mama?" Mary Pearl said. "Do you think you could make me a baked potato?"

Savannah grasped her hands to her own throat and then touched Mary Pearl's forehead. The fever had broken. "Oh, thank heaven," Savannah said. "Now, now, all will be well."

"Go on and rest, Savannah," I said. "I'll stay. It might spread to you with her coughing, and you need some sleep."

"I haven't slept in three days. But I'm not really tired."

With that, I had my own short coughing jag, and it reminded me just how badly I had felt. The sun broke over the Rincon mountains and suddenly I saw Savannah's face more clearly. Her eyes were weary in a way I'd never seen before. If there was ever anyone who was weakened enough to ride this influenza to its last depot, she might be the one. "Go on, I'll stay." I said it forcefully, not as a suggestion. Savannah left the room, feeling ordered out, I suspect, but it was for her own good.

We coughed so much that by lunchtime, Savannah said Mary Pearl and I sounded like two coyotes barking at each other. Terrible as it was to hear, it signaled her returning to us, so I welcomed her coughing as if it were a song. I said nothing about the letter writing, because it seemed a lost cause and not near as important as the victory we'd won over that old Specter.

On the twenty-fourth of January, our quarantine was lifted, and the children were running us ragged, having recovered too soon for the rest. For myself, I am coming back to health. Best of all, Mary Pearl is being more ornery and feisty than the littlest children, and plum full of herself like a yearling colt, so that we constantly remind her to sit still, take time, not wear herself out and risk a relapse.

It seems the fog of illness has not drifted to the lungs of those newly arrived, Savannah and Albert and Aubrey. The smells of the sickroom have been replaced with the smells of barley and pea soup, roasted chicken, glazed vegetables, and risen bread. The rain continues to fall yet the feeling in this house is one of hope and happiness, as we have weathered the worse storm indoors.

# Chapter Nine

*January 25, 1907*

This morning from the window upstairs I saw Udell coming up the walk before Lizzie let him in the door. I reckon I'd expected him to show up in a twelve-dollar suit, for all that booty he was supposed to bring home from Colorado, but he wore the same work clothes, same heavy lambskin coat and slightly broken hat. I heard Lizzie tell him to wait in the parlor, and heard Vallary, Lorelei, and Patricia all greeting him, him answering back, showing interest in something or other they were doing. I had seen some strain on April's face, too, and I thought how tired she must be of all this company she had welcomed a month ago. It was time to go home. And Udell was back.

I didn't wait to be summoned, but went right down to the parlor, although I set my face to be stern. Part of my heart wanted to run down the steps and rush to his arms, as if I were a girl, young enough to be not Mary Pearl's aunt but her sister. April's children were playing with a set of colored wooden animals in one corner of the parlor, and they ought not to be witness to some wanton spectacle. After all, that rascal had been gone more than a month and hadn't written a single line.

When I came in, there was a flurry of greeting by the children again, aimed at me as if I'd been gone a week rather than upstairs for an hour, then I sent them to their toys.

" 'Morning, Mrs. Elliot," Udell said. He held his hat in both hands, moved with the stiff solidity of a fellow who worked hard and close to the ground. Unlike the lanky, sword-swinging horseman Jack had been, Udell's shape and gait was nothing that would draw him a second look anywhere. His brown eyes were not sparkling with mysterious laughter, but frankly honest and easily read. He watched me with a bit of hesitation, as if I somehow might not have recognized him after a month and three days.

"'Morning, Mr. Hanna," I returned.

"Heard you been sick," he said. "Mighty glad to see you up and around."

"Thank you."

"I got home two weeks ago. I couldn't call, you see, folks being quarantined and all. Been working on the house. It's just some scaffold and rocks now. It's going to be pretty good, I think. Your brother Harland is helping me." His face flushed deeply as he said that last, though the words had nothing I could see to make a man blush like a girl.

I couldn't help but see we were about five feet apart. All the times I've leaned against him, kissed the lips he spoke to me with now, pressed my face against that face, and at this moment it felt as if we were hollering across a canyon. *Ignore the children and sweep me into your arms.* One touch might convince my stubborn head how my heart truly felt. I said, "Harland is a pretty good architect. Did he draw you a house?" Little voices giggled across the room. My heart banged like a drum. "I'd like to see the picture."

"Oh, better than that," he said. "He's out there hauling buckets of cement with his own hands. Nice fellow. Oh! Forgot to mention. Got my well in yesterday, so I finally had a bath—well, that isn't a proper thing to say to a lady. So I finally got dressed up to come calling."

April appeared at the door that came from her conservatory and called the children to lunch. She smiled at Udell and me, and said, "We'll serve luncheon in the dining room for the grown-ups in half an hour." Then she closed the great, sliding door behind her.

We were alone. "Udell," I said, "was it a good trip? Weather all right?"

He took one small step toward me, saying, "I headed north through the Salt River Canyon but I couldn't bring a wagon back through that. Came down through Santa Fe and Lordsburg. Sent three wagons on ahead. I've been ten days, starting to build a shed and all, to shelter the goods."

I nodded.

He said, "Got the well in," again.

"I should have asked you to sit. I'm all flustered."

"Y' look fine to me." He smiled, a move that made the corners of his eyes tighten around lines deeply etched there. "The children are gone."

"It's broad daylight. And my daughter's house. I wouldn't—"

"Kiss me, here in the parlor?"

"Mr. Hanna!"

"You are some kind of woman, Mrs. Elliot."

"Is that so?" I felt myself almost simpering at his attention, and couldn't keep my face straightened out for anything. I could hear him breathing, and I was suddenly aware that he was listening to my breathing, too.

He drew a deep breath and said, "Mrs. Elliot? Ever hear tell of a bower bird?"

"It's from Africa, I think. The fellow builds a house for his lady bird."

"Yes, ma'am." He took two steps closer to me. Dropped his hands to his sides. The hat to the floor. "Mrs. Elliot, Sarah, I plan to build my love a bower. I—I know I haven't known you very long. I spent some time thinking on this trip and decided it's not a thing to take lightly. Different than with Frances. Loving a different kind of woman, someone who takes my breath away and keeps my head spinning and makes me feel so simple that it's a wonder she even looks my direction. Makes me proud and humbled at the same time. I'm going to build it strong and safe on the outside, with gardens and trees and plentiful water, and put every kind of pretty in it. Just like one of those bower birds. I'll fix it up until you like it enough you're willing to come there."

I turned from his earnest face to where a Regulator on the wall started to chime noon. Not even Jack had made such an offer. Jack let me build my own house and came and went as it pleased him. I loved him with every fiber of my being, but he never once considered building a nest for me. Suddenly, I felt very much afraid of Udell Hanna. Afraid of how much I could love him if I let go of the reins and just gave over to the feelings that were turning my neck scarlet. I peered at him from the corners of my eyes, and startled myself when my voice wouldn't come out louder than a whisper when I said, "I don't know what to do with you, Udell Hanna."

"Come see it, that's all, when I get it built." He leaned toward me, raised his hands, and I reached out with mine. I could almost feel his kiss on my lips while we were still far apart. At the moment our fingertips touched, the conservatory door slid open on its grumbling rail.

"Mother? Mr. Hanna? It's already done." April said. "Won't you come in?"

At lunch, we told Udell about the quarantine we'd endured and he told of the travel he'd done. He said he was surely happy that Mary Pearl was not going to leave us so soon, and that Aubrey would certainly have come apart at the seams if she had. Then he said he had come back with some furniture his wife's mother left, and the sale of her house had brought cash, too.

Udell offered to take me shopping before driving home. I'd gotten the doctor to write us a note to the druggist so I got some of that Coca-Cola tonic for influenza, with directions how to use it. It was pretty much settled that we'd leave for home on Monday. Mary Pearl was going to stay another week with her folks in town so she would be recovered enough to go home. I would go back to Albert's home and relieve Clover of taking care of Ezra and Zachary, and move the three of them to my place. I'd been gone long enough that Charlie and Elsa may well have gotten the notion to go on their own to seek her papa's blessing. If I know my boy, it's the kind of thing he'd have done. A year spent as an Arizona Ranger has put iron and steel where his backbone used to be. I told Udell about Charlie and Elsa, too. He didn't have good feelings about Rudolfo's daughter being on my place, either.

*January 28, 1907*

Udell drove his old freight wagon, loaded with lumber and bags of nails and hinges. I sat next to him wearing my old coat and one of his warm shearling ones, too, with a big woolen blanket across our laps, binding us together. Behind us, Gilbert drove the wagon I'd come in, filled high as we could get it with food and goods. Udell had insisted on adding things to my pile of goods, niceties I didn't usually go in for, like fine white flour and white sugar, raisins, and plenty of extra coffee and oats and ointments for horses. He even bought me a whole bolt of fine muslin and half a bolt each of a summer sky-colored calico and a green-and-black plaid.

I watched Udell's strong hands driving that team of mules he'd come home with from Colorado. As I sat next to him, so close our knees sometimes bumped, my heart had lost the fire that I'd felt in April's parlor. Tempered by a morning in a church meeting yesterday, discreetly sitting on either end of a pew with Savannah and Albert between us, the feeling today was a familiarity as gentle as if Udell and I had already been married for years and were just returning from town—as if we'd made this trip seated close on a wagon seat a hundred times before. It was a feeling of simply belonging, and that, too, made a ripple of fear run through my spine. And I never quit thinking that Gilbert drove a second rig right behind us. That influenza had taken the starch plum out of me. Before we reached the arroyo, I felt weak as a bale of loose string.

After a while, he said, "You seem tired."

"I'm all right," I said. "Just wrung out. Tell me more about your trip."

"Pure-D lonesome, most of it. Rode through some snow that like to kept me from making it by the end of the year. Or the century. I got there in time, though."

I nodded.

"Fixed up for the future a little better than before. Don't suppose you had a chance to think on anyone or anything except the sick ones at the house there?"

"Only to wonder if you were coming back."

He didn't say anything for a good while. Quail scurried in front of us as we interrupted their steady march to forage. We had a sorry time crossing the arroyo, with the wagon loaded as it was. The ground was wet and the mules ornery, and we had to let off some of the lumber for them to make it up the far side. After we got to the top, when it'd seem like a fellow would let off some steam, all Udell said was, "The other day in the house, I'd a-thought it was . . . well, then. What led you to think I was leaving for good?"

"Can't say. Just thought that, is all."

"I've got all my teeth," he said with a grin. "See here? Sound as a dollar."

I laughed at him. "What'd you say that for?"

"I believe you to be a clever horse trader, and you'd naturally like to know, that's all. You aim to only throw me a bone for the rest of my days?"

"I expect more of a man than I do of a horse."

"I've been giving a great deal of thought to winning your affections, besides the house. Bought books on cattle husbandry, farming processes, fertilizers."

"Udell, I'm looking at my boy Gil, and thinking of Charlie and your Aubrey and Mary Pearl, and, well, marriage is for young folks. What would be the sense for you and me? And what about children? Have you thought about children? Why, you've got a boy older than mine, and I've got grandchildren already."

His face was red and he turned his head, shocked, I suppose, at my brazen talk. Then after a bit he said, "But Sarah, you're young yet. And beautiful. What would be the matter with children? Maybe have a chance to raise some whose pa'd had the sense knocked into him by then. And not have their ma fighting Indians like you did. Children brought up safe and whole, just like your girl April is bringing up hers. With the better things of life, that's all."

"I'm trying to be practical."

"Ah. I thought you were trying to bedevil me. I'll tell you a poem I made up while I rode that nag to Denver. There was an old feller from down by San Pedro, who turned on a road headed north. He waded through waters and canyons on foot; though lonesome and fool he might be . . ."

Without conversation, Udell began a tale that rhymed and went along just as perfectly grand as if it came from a book, about a sad and lonesome cowboy who went to Denver to dig up a treasure chest, so he could buy his lady love a golden ring and take her to his castle in a land where the sun shone ever after. I smiled at it, but squirmed inside as the story went on. It was surely about him wanting to marry. He'd made up a tale that made me seem like some exotic princess in a far-off land, too proud to love a poor cowpoke.

In every stanza of the poem, the wanderer did a new and wilder thing to get the girl to love him. Every so often he mentioned that word "bower," too, as the perfect home for the princess. Udell recited it all patiently, as if he were a boy in school doing his recitations. When he came to what seemed to be the finish, he said, ". . . and his heart it soared like a cloud on high, to his Maker he loudly called 'bless!' when with the lady's dainty sigh, she happily, truly said . . ." Then he left off reciting and didn't look at me nor ask me anything again, the rest of the way. I felt so disappointed at wanting to hear the end of the story, I plum forgot it was about me. He left it unsaid to bedevil *me*.

Why in heaven's name would I want to spend more of my days ironing some old rusty fellow's shirts? I was purely put out by the man, and when we got unloaded at my place and Gilbert took his team to the barn, I felt almost glad to see Udell Hanna crossing the horizon heading away from here. Bone-deep wished him to stay, too.

# Chapter Ten

*January 29, 1907*

I was glad as I could be to be at home again. At least it was away from the bustle of Tucson. I put the tonic on the highest shelf in the pantry, behind other jars where it can't get broken. Nice thing to have a receipt that actually seems to do a person some good when so many of them are nothing but moonshine and kerosene.

Elsa and Charlie were quiet, blushing, and every few minutes looked for one another and made signs with their eyes—just happy as two ducks in a pond. She cooked and cleaned as if she had something to prove, and the place hasn't looked this sparkly since it was built. Even the glass in the windows had been scrubbed. Well, soon enough, her hands will be full of children and the windows will go back to the way I generally keep them—dusty prints of doves who had no sense of direction making a crazy-quilt pattern between crusted and dirty rain splatters.

First thing they said was now that I was home, they wanted to invite Rudolfo to come here for supper. To celebrate their wedding, and let him see how happy his daughter was. I thought of his other girls, especially Luz, now passed over as lady of the house by the new wife, Leta Cujillo, and how angry she had been, thinking I would come to their house instead of Leta. I told Elsa this would only do if we invited Rudolfo and all Elsa's sisters. And, Leta. Lord a-mercy. *Son familia*, my kith and kin.

We discussed, too, whether to tell Rudolfo the reason behind it, or let him come and find out at my door. It's purely against my nature to plan a secret attack on a person, and other than Christmastime, I'm mostly bad at keeping a secret. I reckoned that if Rudolfo were angry about the situation, he might show restraint in front of his girls, all decked in their party finery, whereas if he knew in advance, he might arrive with his armed *caballeros* to do some harm. It was my intention to let him know that Elsa was here and why, along with the invitation to supper.

Then Chess said, "Sarah, you know I ain't telling you how to run things. But look who you're dealing with. No matter what, he's liable to come gunning for the lot of us."

Charlie said, "It's not like I stole her, Grampa. I asked her to marry, but she had a choice. More than she did when he put her in the convent. I say we have Elsa come from some other room after he gets here."

I said, "Reckon it's no different than Rudolfo himself would do. Using Christmas supper to railroad me into selling land to his pack of snakes."

So it was settled, a secret, and a date two days from now. As underhanded a plot as I'd ever been part of, far worse than just knowing Mary Pearl wrote a letter and didn't get any answer. Charlie, with Gilbert and Chess, would go and deliver the invitation. Having just come from town with a load of flour, I had plenty of things on hand to have a first-rate fiesta, and just maybe a well-ordered and generous feast would soften Rudolfo's heart. Deep in my soul, I doubted that prospect.

The fellows got back and told me they just naturally invited Udell Hanna to come to the fiesta, too. Well, I don't know what was so natural about having him around, him and his unfinished poem. Maybe I'd bother him to tell it again and he'd get to the end of it because there were other folks around. Reckon I'd have to make some of those butter pecan cookies he is so fond of. I set the men to putting up tables in the central plaza and collecting lanterns, while Elsa and I, with help from Granny, started making foods that could be done ahead, near every kind we knew.

Granny said more than once, looking at Elsa, "Who is *this*?" And ever again, I explained that Charlie had married while he was in town. When my mama pressed us for more details about who Elsa was, I told her she was Rudolfo Maldonado's daughter. Then, minutes later, Granny would ask with a different emphasis, "*Who* is that?" as if she were settling in her mind the connection to the *haciendado* on the south road.

*January 31, 1907*

I am thankful, now that the day of this ambush party has arrived—for ambush is the only way to think of it—that Albert and Savannah, Mary Pearl, Rachel, and Rebeccah are still not home. If they were, they'd have to be invited. It is better that if any trouble comes between the Maldonados and my bunch, that it doesn't include all the rest. However, as determined as I am to have nothing but a fine time tonight, I talked with Charlie, Gil, and Chess, and we have loaded pistols and rifles but hidden them from sight. "I know," I said, "that Rudolfo wouldn't dream of bringing any but his family, or causing a ruckus, but I will have more peace tonight if we are prepared for calamity."

The weather has favored us and it has been a mild day with a fresh but gentle breeze hinting of spring being just around the corner. The sounds of my home surround me and I love a spring morning like this, with the windmill reassuringly creaking on its axles, the chickens muttering in their yard, the bull and cows in the near distance, now and then letting out a low hum. The beauty of the day made me feel even more sinister, as we prepared the feast for this family of ours so recently expanded. Can't say whether Rudolfo and I will ever feel like friends again. He's likely never to forgive my rejecting his offer of marriage in that stubborn way a man can—never mind that it was only about taking my land for himself—to him it will always be an insult. Still, I know enough to enjoy every minute of a day such as this, for there are too few fresh breezes in the Territory.

Udell came early, as if he'd finished chores before noon, and when he came a-hollering up to my front porch, I was shaking a towel off the side, making a white cloud of flour. "Fair weather, this morning," he called. Strange, how that voice made warmth spread through me, and I drew a deep breath, feeling my worries ebbing away. Udell tipped his hat with one hand while stepping down from his horse.

"Yes, 'tis, Mr. Hanna. How's work going on your house?"

"Bottom main floor is about squared in. It's going slow now, but Harland says it will pick up once the timbers come for the upper floor and roof."

"Is he out at your place? He should come to supper, too."

"No. I meant last time he wrote."

"Don't you have timbers for the bottom floor? I thought you drove home with a couple of wagonsful."

"I'm only using the wood framework to hold until the cement sets. The bottom floor is built of solid rock. I thought maybe this afternoon, there'd be time to ride back and see it. If you'd care to. I know you've probably got something on the stove, though."

I gave the rag another flip in the air, snapping it loudly. "I've got bread rising. Rest is pretty much ready. I reckon between Elsa and the boys and my mama, they can manage if I'm gone for an hour. Will your horse take two?"

He pondered the animal. It was a heavy draft horse. "He's got the wind for it, but I don't know about the temperament. I'd better get you—"

"Baldy. I'll get him from the corral." Only I didn't need to fetch the horse; he'd come on his own given the right bait. Whistling that melody I'd heard Gilbert and Charity James singing, I fetched an apron full of apples, then hollered to Gilbert to let the gate down. When he did, I whistled a shrill for Baldy. That good rascal came along pretty smart, expecting an apple or two for his good manners. I fed him two, gave two to Udell's horse, then I slung myself up on Baldy's warm, bare back, and off we went.

Udell said, "He'll mind with a cotton halter?"

"Oh, Baldy'll mind even without a rider. He's about my favorite, now that Rose is retired."

We talked about horses on the way, about how I got some of them to do so well, and I don't allow Mexican spurs on the place. I'd seen *caballeros* leave a horse bloody and scared to death in an hour, and have to have a new one ten times a day, as they rode them so hard. Myself, I'll work on only one horse or two, most of the day, but I don't ask him to kill himself for me, and I reckon they know it. Udell allowed it was good to have a horse know who was boss, but it was sure better to keep them in good spirits.

It was a nice time that early afternoon, with the wind soft at our backs, and me smelling so much of fresh-baked bread like a fancy perfume, and him all cleaned up and shaved with witch hazel and soap. I notice how a man smells. It'd never be right to say it to anyone, and I don't know if all women do, but I notice. I reckon that is part of the many mysteries women must keep secret, part out of decency and part because it would seem plum foolishness to tell a man I liked the smell of him. I found myself hoping he'd take the liberty he'd come so close to taking in April's parlor, too.

We passed the field where his herd of sheep had been killed in the fire, tied in their tracks by one of Rudolfo's men, so the poor animals couldn't even run. The ground was damp and haired with green shoots. One end of the plot of land was dug up and a row of three barrows stood waiting to be filled. Farther on, where the hills rose and fell away and rose again, we passed the trees where we'd hid from the bandits that day not long past. And then, rounding a curve in a road that Udell had been slowly etching into the ground toward his new place, I saw the hill where we'd followed the jackrabbit that day, leaving Mary Pearl and Aubrey behind in the buggy.

An ugly, rugged structure grew from the top of the hill, thick and squat, with narrow windows and wide doors, built completely of rock. It was about the sorriest thing I'd ever seen. Not fit for a chicken coop, it seemed to me. My heart sank. Then I thought maybe this was a barn. It would be natural to build a barn first. So I looked around with better hopes that this was not the "bower" meant to tempt me into marriage. The walls were about six feet high, braced here and there with frames and struts of wood. Strange openings were on one side of the big square thing, and a pile of cut bricks showed where he'd been creating an old-fashioned fire box and hearth. We rode around the whole of it. Udell talked about difficulties he had overcome in the building here and there, bracing and timbers and callused hands, and about how he'd hired some fellows but they had gone home at noon and wouldn't be back until the first week of February. He made it clear that this stack of broken rock and concrete was the house itself.

Beside the half-built walls, a windmill turned merrily in the light breeze. It was a new Aeromotor, and a painted one at that. Pretty as a quilt, all red and white, it looked like an incredible flower in the sky. Whoever had put in his well while I was quarantined in town had done it slick and fine.

We got off our horses and I listened while he pointed here and there some more, talking about what he had in mind for raising a crop and more cows. I kept turning back to those rock walls. The man believed he was building something beautiful for me and that heap of rocks had less charm than an army camp. I didn't know rightly what to say. Maybe this was the foundation foot he was building, and got it too high, but then the firebox would be in a basement. I felt as if a shadow from some unseen cloud passed across my heart. This wasn't a place I could ever love. Nor live in. Maybe I was fooling myself into wanting this man. Maybe I have been blinded by lonesomeness into telling him I'd come here.

As if he could hear me thinking, Udell said, "Well, what do you think?"

I said, "It's looking fine. But I thought you said you had the house started."

"This here's the house." It had all those holes in it, not like any kind of house, and though I only know a wood house and adobe, I started to wonder what on earth he was building. I even wondered if he'd lost his mind on it, and if Harland had designed this, what had gone with my little brother's reason, too. He said, "Sure gonna be a beauty. Come on up here and see. It's an easy step-hold, the way we left it. The rocks there will hold the next layer better when they're all in stairs, and I can start fresh with the wet cement over the dry because the weight of them holds it down. Walls are a good two foot thick. It'll be safe as a bank vault, and cool as a spring morning in the summer, warm in the winter. This—watch your step there—is going to be the kitchen. And that wall run with a lead pan up on top? Windmill takes a pipe no bigger than your little finger, and sends a fine drizzle of water down it any time you want. That kitchen will stay airy all summer long. Feel the breeze that comes up this side of the hill? That's what convinced Harland and me it'd work. Those slots there will pull in the air all you want, and you can close them off in the winter with iron furnace plates."

Standing on the walls, I held his hand just to keep balanced. The strength of his grip, the warmth there, pushed the clouds back. I held my face toward the sunlight. To the north hills, I could see smoke from the two ovens going at my house. There was a clear sight of the road we'd come down, too, especially where we cross under the twelve-foot-wide ocotillo that marks the corners where Udell's and my land make the junction with Rudolfo's. To the west, I could see the fields, the rows of barrows that now obviously looked as if he were hauling that dirt one bucketful at a time to some other place. Eastward, we got a clear sight to the Rincon Mountains; below that, a place where the clear-cut canal supplied water straight from the San Pedro to Udell's land. A road I'd never known, older and grown over, cut across the landscape here and there. And to the southwest, so small it seemed no more than a matchbox on a ledge, but clearer than a picture postcard, was Rudolfo's hacienda.

Udell had stopped talking. He stood on top of the wall close to my side and took my arm. We watched the scurry of a couple of men riding up to the hacienda, dust rising only high as the horses' knees. A large fancy wagon with a team of four perfectly matched buckskin horses stood out in the yard.

"Maldonados are fixing to head to our place for the supper," I said. It would take him forty minutes or more to drive that slowly to my house. We had time, and we were only a ten-minute ride away, on horseback. I turned to Udell.

I looked down at the rocks under my feet, all carefully laid in two rows with a sandwiched layer of scrabble and cement in the middle. Then it dawned on me from something I'd read long ago.

He was building, not a gentle, kindly nest, but a formidable castle. A fortress, like the ones from before the Norman Conquest. I looked downward, able to make a better judgment of what I was seeing than before. Like a miniature of the castle at Edinburgh in Scotland, this house rose from a three-sided hill. From what seemed to be its ramparts, he could see anyone coming from below in the distance long before they'd see him. I turned back to stare in the direction of the hacienda. The tight feeling in my chest relaxed. I said, "You come along, too, if you will. There's food for the Sixth Army waiting for supper. We could use another man on our side of the table."

"I'll come just for that reason, then. What do you think of the house so far?"

I didn't want to say. It looked more like a dungeon than a castle to me. "It's going to take you some time to get this finished. Maybe a year." That way, I'd have time to think plenty, figure this way and that, whether I wanted to live here.

"Could be. Don't think I'm going to be in it by summer. Wearing my fingers clear off is slowing me down. Mixing that stuff, I thought I'd hit something with red dirt in it, and then I found it was my hands bleeding into it. The only luck of it is the cement seems to stop infection." He held his hands out for my inspection. "My workers will be back next week, and Harland's coming out again. I think I'll have a roof on by July. Between toting rocks and planting a field in April, I'll read all those books about cattle raising in between hauling topsoil from the sheep field."

I saw Rudolfo's rig head up the road. I wanted to postpone this supper as long as I was able. "You need a can of teat salve. Show me again, how you are going to cool off this kitchen," I said. The homely stack of drab rocks and mortar began to look less ugly. Then I asked him what was the measure of the place, and how many rooms he expected, and where would he have the stairs and all. We walked around the place on top of the wall as far as it would go, and back again to where the wall stepped down to the ground.

He said, "Well, I figure—if we, that is—that Chess will need a room, and your ma, and then I don't know about Gilbert or Charlie and Elsa. They're welcome but Charlie's likely to want his own place."

"I reckon if I came here to live it would just be with Chess and Granny.

I . . ." Suddenly a pain as deep and threatening as an arrow went through my ribs and made me clutch at my sides. I felt all the losses I've ever known crowd into my soul at that moment.

"Are you ailing?" he said.

It was hard enough to lose the living. But to never again look out the kitchen window and smile toward Jack and the others? "My graveyard is on the hill where I can see it. Back there. You can't see it from here. I've always been able to see it from the house."

"I'll build it taller so you can."

The pain went into my throat and I held both hands at my collar. I could barely breathe. "You don't understand. I have—babies buried there. And . . ."

"And Jack?" Udell's eyes pierced mine.

"Yes. No, it's not that," I said feebly. Udell pulled on my arm and I let go of my throat, put my hands on his shoulders and let him surround me with his arms. But it was Jack. Jack waited there, always at hand in case I needed him. I held tightly to Udell's shoulders, nestling my face against his neck. When I looked up at last, he smiled at me and kissed my forehead. Then he kissed my hair, right over my ear.

"It's all right if it is that," he said. And then he kissed my mouth, sweetly and gently erasing all other thoughts of longing and loneliness. His eyes held mine and with a shared pain he whispered, "I know. I know. Let's get along, now."

I pressed Baldy too close with my knees and he bolted out of his tracks, trying hard to do what he thought I wanted. I had to circle him around to ride alongside Udell's workhorse. I had to get my mind back on the horse, and not on the fellow next to me, or Baldy would likely take off for Texas, the way I felt. I wondered if I had taken up loneliness for a habit, and was too addled by it to recognize the end of it.

We weren't home a half hour before that fancy trap pulled by the four yellow horses came up to the edge of the yard, and I knew our siege was on. There was no more time for musing on either the past or the future.

Rudolfo grandly presented his four other daughters and an eight-year-old son, who I rarely have seen, and they all formed a line and curtsied or bowed. The boy wasn't like any I'd had around, and it occurred to me that Rudolfo rarely mentioned him and I couldn't for the life of me remember his name. It wasn't too long that I came to realize the child was blind. Nearly mute, too, though he did whisper softly to his sisters, but he was led around by first one then the other, and helpless if no one touched him. Luz stared haughtily at the furnishings, and taking a seat in one chair she finally deemed suitable, stiffly said that their *madrastra preciosa* greatly regretted her health required her to stay at home. I knew Rudolfo's new wife was great with child, and wondered if that was Luz's regret, too. The two were the same age. I also knew the sneer on Luz's lips was hidden from her father by her position in the room, the voice perfectly sweet and light.

I said to Rudolfo, "Well, aren't you going to ask that fellow, that driver, to have supper, too?"

Rudolfo smiled that too oily smile of his and didn't even turn toward the carriage. A man, very small in stature and with a mild, unmoving face, stood holding the reins of the lead horse. He had on the clothes of a deep-country peasant from Mexico, loose white cotton pants and shirt and a plain brown serape over his shoulders. His hat slid forward, then, as if he were asleep on his feet. "Caldo? He is only *el chófer,* and eats with the men when he is done working for the day. Now, dear friends, let us be merry and celebrate the return of our trust in one another, and how happy I am that you have opened your *cocina* for the joining of our *familias* at this time."

He couldn't know what those words meant! However, everyone was on their best behavior, and so we went to the supper table. Granny come from the parlor to the dining table just then with a hard, angry look on her face, and a cold chill ran up my spine. There would be no guessing or shushing anything she might say, so far was she beyond the spell of normal conversational regimens. However, without another word, my mama announced she'd be going to bed as she didn't feel up to taking a meal. I was saved from her springing an untimely announcement on Rudolfo, but not from her glare, equally as furious as Luz's had been, and hers she freely turned on everyone in the room before she left, including me.

Outside, a stiff breeze had come up. Chess and I brought out bowls of hot vegetables and plates piled high with tortillas and risen bread made with that fine white flour Udell had given me. We set it out with the best doings I could lay up, that is, a good sharp knife and fork, even for the blind boy, and napkins at each place, too, starched and ironed flat with creases by Elsa Maldonado Elliot just that morning. Then I carried in two plates heavy with roast chicken that had baked slowly with onions and pomegranate juice. I wasn't the cook in charge of it this night, and I'd never cooked it that way. Usually I'd just roast it and take the drippings and make gravy, and still have to beat the boys off it so there'd be enough to feed us all. Never anything so fancy and elegant. Elsa had put her touch on the finery by making the chicken that way. Charlie said he'd give her a signal after he told her papa she was there, but to wait in the kitchen.

Well, we were just bursting with polite talk about nothing in particular, and all Rudolfo's family made continual compliments on the food. All the while, Elsa was listening for the right time to come out. That fancy chicken, though, changed the state of everyone in the room. Rudolfo took one bite and looked up at me. While he chewed, the expression on his face went from happy to puzzled, suspicious to angry. He took a drink of water. Glowering, he put down his knife and fork and raised one hand, lowering it to the table. With that movement, all his children noisily put their utensils down, too. He did not smile as he said, "Señora Elliot, the graciousness of your hospitality knows no boundary. There was only one person in the world to create *pollo granadita* in this way. You have never served this at your house before."

I'd had enough. This was just plum wrong. "Rudolfo, let's have a talk. There's something I got to tell you, and this here was supposed to make it easier but it's not. I haven't felt right about this all along. Now—"

"It's just chicken, Señor Maldonado," Charlie interrupted. "There is someone special here who wants to see you." He was about to go on talking, but at those words, Elsa hurried from the kitchen door, her eyes bright with sentiment, her arms open wide.

When I saw Charlie's expression, I knew he hadn't meant for her to come out yet. His face was darkened by some kind of passion I feared could be anger, but I wasn't sure. My son was no sniffling boy, of that I *was* sure. Rudolfo let a smile flick across his expression, then he looked around the room at all of us gathered there. He stopped Elsa in her tracks with another raised hand. "What are you doing here?" Rudolfo asked. There was no happiness in his voice.

*"Papá!"* the girl said. Elsa drew herself up, her arms still lifted. Took in a long breath. I reckoned she'd been going over her speech for this minute all day. Maybe for weeks. Elsa said, "I've left the Sisters, *papá*. I am not a novice anymore."

Luz had tears in her eyes, no longer the haughty and bitter one, and the other children looked expectantly toward their oldest sister, waiting only for their father's sign to rush her and smother her with kisses. Chess put his hands in his lap. The man had never eaten a meal without both elbows propped in plain sight. Gilbert shot a look at Udell, who sat up straighter but said nothing.

Rudolfo glared at me. As if each word struggled to come from his lips, he said, "And these . . . friends . . . of ours. You betray me, and betray the Virgin, and you are so ashamed you have come to their house instead of your own home? You couldn't come to your father's house, where you belong?"

She fastened her gaze to the ring on her left hand, turning it as if to check its roundness. "I have come to my husband's house, where I belong. I love you, *papá*."

Rudolfo stood and angrily swept his napkin to the floor. Then his every word got louder until he was shouting and gasping, "Who is this husband? Who takes my daughter and makes her God's whore? Who dares to impale the finest flower of my house, stealing her virtue and mine? Let him show himself. Let him come forward and be strangled for his crime! Let him be torn apart and pitched into . . . *malo que el diablo* . . . Where is this fatherless son of some cursed—" He stopped short. His eyes nearly shot flames as they settled on my face.

Silence dropped into the room as if the air had turned thick as pudding. Elsa's brow was damp with sweat, and though she didn't cower or shrink from Rudolfo, her eyes were red and brimming over. Luz had a cold expression as she watched her sister come undone before their father. Rudolfo's children's eager faces turned from joy to horror. They clapped hands over their mouths in fear. Tears slid down Elsa's cheeks and printed blots on the front of her black bodice. "I've wanted to see you. I wrote you, *papí*, that I was not happy."

"It is not a daughter's place to be happy. It is a daughter's place to obey her father!"

Charlie stood then, not touching Elsa but close to her. "She did obey you, Señor Maldonado, as long as she could take it. But you couldn't keep us apart. Elsa and I have married. This is her home, now. With me."

Rudolfo trembled visibly. My mouth went to cotton. The food from the table seemed to cry out then, that we'd staged this betrayal and that it was cruel. The telltale sauce in crimson loops around the chicken was getting a film over it as we stood, all of us frozen. Silent. Before this very moment, the supper had seemed a fair enough way to tell him of the elopement and not get shot for the trouble of being a messenger. I surely regretted that we hadn't come up with some better way. Something easier for the man to take. I felt lowdown and mean.

Rudolfo said, "No!" Then he turned his glare to me. "So you sent your *cabrón* to—to filthy my house, my daughter."

"I won't have that language in my house, Rudolfo. They were in love long ago."

"I know what is best for my own daughter! Not you."

"They married without telling any of us."

He stared hard at me. "So you wait, with your trap, you wait to take, to keep, what, Doña Elliot?"

*"Papá?"* Elsa said.

Rudolfo raised his hands, looked into both palms, then clenched them tightly into fists. "Magdalena, Luz, take Cedric. Margarita, all of you, go to the coach."

The girls, except for Luz, began to whimper. Cedric cried aloud for Elsa while being led away. Luz led the parade toward the door. Elsa watched them go, and called their names, one by one. Only Margarita turned and waved to Elsa, but Luz pushed the child's hand down with an angry slap.

*"Papá,"* Elsa said, "please, dear *papito,* let me sit at your knee, just like long ago. Let me bring you coffee and the flan I have made for you, just the way you like it, the way *mamá* made it, with rose essence I saved so long to buy, just for you."

Rudolfo took a step toward Elsa and Charlie, and quick as that, Charlie tugged Elsa behind him and put up a hand to his defense. But Rudolfo did not strike him. He pulled his hand short before it even got close.

Elsa stepped forward again, too boldly, I'd have to say, and smiled through her teary expression, begging, "*Papá,* come and sit . . ."

Rudolfo's face grew darker still, and it seemed as if lightning crackled in his eyes. He squinted at her face and leaned over, closing the distance between them, then said, "All *my* children . . . are in *el coche*!" Then he whirled around, stepping squarely on the creased napkin lying on the floor, left the room, left the house, leaving the front door hanging wide open, and from it we felt a cold blast of air that carried on it the sound of horses being whipped furiously as they drove from the yard.

Elsa sobbed and ran from the room. Charlie looked helplessly at me; I nodded toward the path Elsa had taken and he followed her.

"It's a wonder he didn't throttle someone," I said. "I don't blame him for it."

Udell sat back in his chair, looked over the remains of the uneaten supper, and said, "There wasn't any *good* way to say it. The man's dangerous, and now he's mad like a wounded bear. It'd be one thing if Charlie was some worthless saddle tramp. Give old Rudolfo time. He'll see Charlie's a hardworking, God-fearing man. Fine sort."

Chess nodded. "He's right, Sarah. He'll warm up to it after a while. Like you said before, when that first baby comes along."

As the night wore on and we cleaned the supper fixings off the table, the wind that had been fussing at the windows turned into a cold blast that shot rain hard as hail against the glass. I told Udell that he'd have to stay the night, as I wouldn't even have sent Rudolfo home in a storm like that. He didn't put up any argument. Likely we'd all heard enough harsh words this night to last us a month or more.

# Chapter Eleven

*February 18, 1907*

At long last, Savannah and Albert have brought Mary Pearl home. I saw their surrey coming up the road, and I went to the chicken coop to find a couple of pullets for supper to have ready to take over. They'd need something made after that long drive. Maybe I'll put in a sweet pie, too.

Well, just as I sat plucking the chickens and had a mess of feathers flying across the porch, here came Savannah, dressed in the dress she usually wears for Sunday, and wearing her best white cap and bonnet. I waved to her and smiled, but I was too big a mess to get up and hug her. "Come on over and set a spell," I called.

Savannah stared at the chickens, one lying headless at my feet, the other in my hands, nearly naked of feathers. She didn't speak.

I said, "Thought I'd fix you some supper. Ezra and Zack are—"

"Sarah?" she said.

"Mary Pearl's all right, isn't she?"

"I've always trusted you. Always thought I could count on you."

A feather flitted up and whisked at my face. I rubbed my nose with the back of my arm. "I count on you, too," I said, and nodded, pretending I didn't register her word "thought." She seemed upset as ever I have known.

"Never thought you to be the kind to go behind our backs. To approve of her taking off like that. I trusted you with my children but I see that was a mistake.

I should be wary of your influence with them, should never have let you have them around so much that they lose their good sense and upbringing."

"Savannah, what's got under your bonnet?"

"You encouraged her to go off and leave her betrothed behind, like some . . . some . . . trollop! You contrived with my daughter to send her away to some *school* at the far end of the country, away from her beloved and her family, away from her . . . her home."

I stood up. "Now wait just a minute, Savannah. I didn't contrive anything. Mary Pearl wanted to write to the school. She asked me about a picture she drew. I told her if she didn't like it to draw it again."

"You didn't think it was important enough to tell her parents that she was planning this foolishness? You didn't think to stop her? Talk reasonably with her? You couldn't tell us so we could reason with her? Is that because you knew it was wrong?"

"She was sick and we thought she was dying. What was the use of telling it? Then, why, I was sick, too. It never crossed my—by the time she started getting better, they never wrote back, so I figured it was not going to happen anyway. I thought about telling you at first and then I forgot. Seemed like it was over and they didn't want her. I simply forgot."

"You forgot? Well, they do want her. And she wants to go, just like that. *And* her father is allowing it! You have been pushing her toward this all her life just like your own children, always insisting everybody ought to go to college. Telling her that's the most important thing. Well, it isn't necessary for every girl to go to school—it's not even in this Territory!—or boy, either. She's got her reading and writing and plenty of education, and has no need to traipse across the country, a betrothed woman. He'll have grounds to put her aside, same as divorced. He'll marry some other. I thought I made that understood to you!" She turned to leave, but stopped short and whirled around at me. "Don't think I will let you have your hand in the teaching of my children anymore, from this day on. I'm perfectly capable of learning my own children all they need. And if you have need of a Sunday School lesson, which I think you do, you should make the effort to study the only book a woman need concern herself with."

With that, she walked away, and her every step beat her fury into the ground of my yard. Even Savannah's back looked angry.

I sat over the bloody mess of chicken feathers and guts. And I cried. Deep, long, childish gulps of agony swept through me and racked me until I thought I might vomit. Elsa came out the door then, hearing me, I suspect. I handed her the pullets, and walked and walked, through the yard and out the gate and over the hill. There I sat on the cold ground and sobbed like the child I felt—scolded and scorned. Savannah and I have not had harsh words with each other in the twenty years I've known her. Now she felt betrayed and maybe rightly so. It seemed all I was good for lately was back-shooting people I had cared about.

I walked to the banks of the Cienega and rinsed my hands in the icy water. She'd worked hard on that speech. Just like Elsa had done trying to please her papa, Savannah had practiced her scorn. I felt so forlorn, it was near as hard as when Jack died. Worse, almost, because he didn't have a choice about dying. I stayed there, shivering and miserable, not ready to go to the house, not able to move. It wasn't long, however, before Albert came up on horseback. He got down, sitting on his haunches next to me. I sniffed, staring hard into the water.

After a while, Albert said, "Savannah told me what she said to you. She said she only meant to ask why you'd not told us about Mary Pearl writing the letter, but she got angrier and angrier as she spoke and said it got bad. She's pretty torn up. I'm sorry."

"What's the good of you being sorry, Albert?"

"Well, she's upset."

"I figured that."

"I come to get you."

"Go home, Albert."

"At least let me take you to the house."

"I've just been shot with both barrels. And Savannah didn't send you to apologize for her, you only said *you* were sorry. Go on home and leave me be, brother. Go on."

"Sarah?"

"Get!" I said, and stomped off toward home. By the time I got there, though, I felt just awful, and I went to bed, without explaining anything, without a kind word, just straight to bed. There I relived the afternoon again, seeing it this way and that, one time hearing this thing said and one time that thing, until the room darkened and I fell asleep.

### March 2, 1907

A light has gone out in this land, oh, my soul, and darkness overtakes me, and my soul cries out to Thee and Thou hearest me not. Something like that, Savannah read once. I can't even find my Bible. Likely it's gone somewhere for some good purpose but I can't lay my hands on it. I know how that one felt, though. King David just crying out and no one to hear, and not even God gives a dang about it.

I never felt so forsaken. Never thought I could be so torn. Why, I'd have hurt less if Savannah had died. I haven't heard from her since that day, nearly a fortnight. Lands and heavens and earth and vexation, all is vexation and brokenness of spirit.

I went to their house today, and Albert received me in and the children were sweet as could be and polite, but Savannah wouldn't come from her room. I'm as shunned as if I had murdered Mary Pearl with my own hands. I said to Albert, "You and the children come on over any time you choose, but I won't come here until I'm invited by Savannah herself. I can't cross this bridge she's torn down unless some of the ties come from her side. So you tell her that. I'm waiting."

Since I said those words my every footstep wants to turn toward their house, to hug Savannah to my bosom and cry on her neck and beg her to love me again. I don't understand this nor cotton to it in any way. I can see being angry with folks. Shoot, I'd about hang Chess on the laundry line any day of the week, but I don't shun him. Shunning's no way to get over and done with your fussing. It just drives in a sword that won't come out unless the person holding it pulls first. So every few minutes, I look toward their house and sigh. And I don't go over there.

It is March and Mary Pearl may be getting ready to leave for school or for a wedding and I won't know.

I only know I have work to do.

### *March 11, 1907*

All morning, Elsa and I have been turning soil in the garden, working side by side. We got down the end of a long row that had overgrown with goat thorn, and when she pulled back the dried weed tops with a hoe, she let out a gasp.

"Snake?" I asked.

"No, Doña. A big hole."

I came closer, a long-handled shovel in my hands. "Step back. Let's have a look."

We peered carefully. The hole was four inches across. Elsa leaned over it. "What do you think it is? Rabbits?"

"Well, there's no mound outside it. Not rabbits. Nor foxes."

"Snakes?" she asked.

"Or ground squirrels. Nothing I want taking up housekeeping in this garden."

"Let's dig it up carefully, and see."

"You stand far back as you can, lest it is a snake hole." So we tugged off the weed cover and tossed it over the fence, then began to gently remove dirt from the top of the burrow. When a little of the rim caved in, we could see which direction the tunnel went, and started scraping in that line. Before too long, another hole fell in, and we had a shallow spot nearly two feet wide. Under the dirt, something moved and made a shriek. With a dusty flurry of wings, two little owls burst from the soil and headed straight up overhead. I raised my arms in defense as I shouted, "Ground owls!" but I was only startled, and immediately felt foolish, for the little things were no threat to anyone.

Elsa asked, "Are those bad?"

"No. We want these here. They eat mice and packrats. Look. Eggs. I'm sorry we've bothered their nest, now. Let's see if we can fix it back." Well, with a piece of a board and a chunk of greasewood over the little clutch of eggs, we carefully repacked the dirt and laid the torn sticker bush across it.

Elsa crossed herself and prayed aloud to Mary for the owls to return and to forgive us for tearing apart their home. Then she turned to me with tears in her eyes and said, "Are *you* sometimes very lonely, Doña?"

"What do you mean?"

"Have I torn apart my papa's home, by marrying?"

I scanned the sky for any sign of the owls. "No. The rend in Rudolfo's tent comes from the inside out, honey."

She nodded. Then she touched up the edges of the little burrow with her hands.

I said, "But you're right. Sometimes I feel awfully lonesome. I reckon it's just my lot in life." Savannah's face whisked before me, along with all those I've lost.

Elsa bent again, sizing up our work. "These owls may not come back."

"Depends on how much they want those eggs, I 'spect." I pushed the goat thorn back into place a little more. "Does that look like how we found it, to you? A nice little home for an owl family?"

Elsa stood and hugged me close, and I patted her on the back. Then she said, "I see now why my mother called you her friend, more than I knew before. We'll watch and pray for them to return."

"We will," I said, and headed down to the other end of the garden to start on a new row.

*March 18, 1907*

These days, most of my family spends their time when they aren't doing their own chores helping Udell raise his house. The days of winter rain are past, and so, it seems, is Rudolfo's temper, as we have had no more brushes with bullets from his end of the Territory. Still, it is obvious that every day there is enough commerce of some sort taking place on Maldonado land that it would put Fishes' Mercantile to shame.

When he's not building, Udell has been sticking by me as much as he can, and the both of us are puzzled by Savannah's actions. I told him some things I knew about how her mother died, and her sister Ulyssa who had the consumption, and how much she looked like Mary Pearl does now. Of course, he already knew about her daughter, Mary Pearl's sister Esther, eloping with a hired hand from Rudolfo's gathering, and being murdered only a few weeks later. Maybe Savannah feared that Mary Pearl would die like Ulyssa had, or like Esther had.

Udell said maybe she simply feared losing all her children to their growing up. Well, one thing I knew about Savannah was that she had always been sensible. "No," I said. "Reckon I betrayed a trust. All her children spend near as much time at my place as they do at their own, and I as much as lied to her about something important, by keeping quiet. The fact that I had a reason or that I forgot is no excuse."

That was two people I had betrayed. The lowest thing I could think of to do. Blamed if I didn't know how to come back out of this hole I'd dug for myself. Now I had enemies on all sides of me. The worst part was, the one person I always thought I could trust was me. I felt more like cussing it all and running to Texas with every passing day.

I fill my days and nights with work. And every day, I think of Savannah less by five minutes. In a year or two, I won't think of her at all.

Last night, Albert came to the house for a bite of dessert. I asked him if he'd take cream in his coffee, and if he thought it would rain soon, and if he's seen my new calf. He answered, "Would it make you feel any better to know that she's more mad at me than at you?"

"No, it wouldn't."

"Well, she is. Savannah can't . . . well, it wouldn't do to talk behind her back. I think . . ." Albert said, "give it time. Not forever, but a while."

"Patience is my middle name, don't you know?"

Albert laughed, only a bit at first, then loud and merry. Then he said, "Mary Pearl will be leaving in a few more weeks. She wants to take her horse with her. Savannah is having a fit over that, too."

"Well, a girl has got to have some transportation. Does Savannah think they have a trolley on every corner?"

"I don't know. Reckon we'll send Duende along with her. It costs another forty dollars to send the horse and two dollars a month to board him there. Only twelve dollars more and I could send another student! I'll tell you, he'd better get good marks or I won't pay his tuition another course." He got fixed to leave, then stopped and said, "Have you taken Udell up on his offer of matrimony yet?"

"If I do, you'll be the first person I tell."

He went home, humming, but with his shoulders hanging down in a dejected sort of way. Likely he reckoned the tempest in his own parlor was going to be a long one. I grieve for the death of our friendship, as dear to me as the true life of a living person. The days stretch endlessly and dreary without Savannah to console me in the pain of missing her—but in my two score and three years I have become well accustomed to grief and how to bear it. Five minutes at a time.

## *March 19, 1907*

Next day, Harland got here about noon to see how Udell's house was coming. Business was growing already, in town, he said, and he was real proud that he had taken the step to put down roots there. I allowed as I was proud for him, too, but truth was I was lonesome. It was better having too many people than too few. Especially when one of them was Savannah. If Harland moved back here, I'd have his children to look after. I had a talk with Harland and he wants to buy my place in Tucson and put down roots to stay. I'm happy about them staying, and it seemed the right thing to do. Marriage or no, the $2,000 he offered on the house will get me through two years, and by that time, I ought to have eight or ten new calves to sell, and I'll be back in business. Remembering how foreign it felt to me when I was there, it wasn't as hard to let go. I reckon one reason to build up property and houses is to have something to see a body over in a storm.

I asked him, since he knew about creating houses, if he knew about land rights. He said no matter who I married, my ranch would all belong to my husband. I laughed a little to show him I wasn't worried, and said I wasn't planning to marry. I want my own land. With no house in town, and all my years of work belonging to Udell, I'd be in a worse fix than Granny! At least she's still got title to her land. The other reason to build up property is to pass it on to the family when you cross over, but the only way to do that was to sell my house to my children. I believe I know what kind of fellow Udell is, but yearning for someone isn't the same as giving them over your entire lot in life. I believe this is the biggest quandary I've seen in all my days. Harland had dinner at my place, and he chuckled when I said he should just move back here to the ranch with me, then right after that, he went on down to Udell's to oversee some more building.

## April 1, 1907

Today dawned clear and beautiful, one of those perfect days that makes me wonder why I would ever think of leaving this place. The breezes moved my skirts. Trees budded at Albert's farm. My rosebush shouts beauty to the world. There have been no stray bullets flying this way from Maldonado's place. I have decided, for today at least, to forget and forgive myself for my many transgressions and get on with things.

Two batches of new chicks have hatched in my coop, and they toddle after their mama hens just as dear as can be. The other ladies are back to steady laying, so we are fixed with eggs for now. I worked all last month laying in my early garden and I spent last week stretching strips of cloth across the seed beds because we still could get a killing frost until the end of April.

We got a later start than usual this morning because Gilbert and Charlie were up half the night with a cow having her first calf, and we have a new addition to the herd. Udell's six that were carrying have all dropped pretty calves, too, the last one three days ago. I decided to go check on them, so I put on a freshly ironed dress and took some pumpkin bread and a cup of butter in a basket, and started toward the barn.

Baldy didn't look happy to see me. Though he'll put up with just about anything including butterflies and gunfire, he's never liked a basket. I had a dickens of a time trying to get on him and hide the basket at the same time.

When I reached Udell's place, he was alone, sitting on a stack of fire bricks laid over with a tarpaulin. He looked up at the sound of Baldy's hooves, and waved, calling, "Mrs. Elliot! Help me make this decision, will you? Your brother tells me the place where I planned to build my biggest hay barn is not stable enough. He says that plot would be better for a garden needing drainage, and I've been weeks hauling topsoil to this side of the house, where he says it'll get too much shade. Now, with what you know about horticulture and all—seems to me the sun is so hard on man and beast, I meant the herbs to have some shade—don't you suspect I could put a garden here? I'd like to get some corn in before summer comes along."

I looked over the land he pointed at. "Well," I said, "let's walk it. You're already behind if you haven't planted. Summer can't be more than a week or two away." We looked closely at every weed, every rock, every greasewood bush. Standing still in a place a dozen yards from where he'd laid all that topsoil he carted from below, I said, "I think he was right. Over here's cut off from the morning sun by the shadow of the house. Here's a better place, shaded from the afternoon with these mesquites and all this sage. Look at that dead paloverde tree. See the dirt under it, how soft and dark it is? You've got loam that will sprout wheat and beans and squash all out of the same hole, given water. But you don't want them right under a live tree or they'll catch a rust. Put tomatoes out here and pumpkins here. If you want some drinking gourds, you have to plant them way down the hill somewhere."

"So I'm not going to get a garden in this spring?"

"Not if you're going to move all that soil you dragged up here. Why don't you move half, on the shadiest side, and plant in a couple of days? It won't be too late to get some good carrots and broccoli, long as you put up rabbit fence. Squash'll come later, with cucumbers and lettuce, which ought to shoot right up. I can barely get an ear of corn to produce in my garden for love or money. It isn't corn country."

"What about the barn?"

I studied the lay of the land around the house for the hundredth time. I thought it was odd he hadn't built the barn first—what I'd have done. "What did Harland say?"

He pointed. "He'd put it there. I'd wish it was closer by when there's bad weather, but that's pretty rare."

"Let's walk it." So we started down the shallow slope, the only way now, up to the house. It went southeast and curved a bit, then met up with the road. Farther east, the Cienega split off a rivulet that was bubbling and flowing, but would be dry come summer. We went toward the trees and stepped off the distance from the windmill, talked about where to put a water tank for the animals. "If you put your barn here and a cistern beside it with some gutters off the roof, I think you could make use of this stream in the winters and after the *sudestadas*—those summer rains."

We went around the house farther downhill, then upstream where the flowing water disappeared in the streambed for a few feet. Every few steps we stopped to look back at the house and judge a place to put a barn. When we got to the shallow where the stream came aboveground again, we turned toward the house. From this angle, those ugly, plain rocks had grown from homely to handsome. The place was a fortress, but it had white painted trim and the doors and shutters were a dark, velvety green. "It's becoming a fine-looking house," I said. He was talking on and I didn't catch it, as his voice seemed to be just one more murmur in the hum of the spring air.

Udell said, ". . . and if I put the barn between that mesquite there with the cholla under it—the one that's blooming, not the other—and the road? Then a corral that comes over to this creek and a waiting pen closer to the house? With the slope on that hill, which looks to be mostly rock, I could put an entry on two floors and not have to use a hoist. Could even store a buggy up on top."

"I like that idea, Mr. Hanna. I like it fine." Suddenly it seemed as if we'd been talking nonsense and both of us grinned foolishly at each other. I declare, one minute I am head over for the man, the next I don't care for him at all, and then I'm as addled as a colt. My head felt stuffed with wool.

He searched the sky for a moment. "Mrs. Elliot, I thank you for your opinion. There," he said, "I aim to put trees of our own. Pecan if you like, as Albert said he had some seedlings ready to transplant. They're good shade in the summer, he says. And maybe a few others. Peaches suit you?"

"Oh, peaches suit me. Kind of mosquito-y, though. You might like them farther from the house, pecans closer. But do what you'd like; it's *your* house, Mr. Hanna."

We walked to the stream and got near the place where we'd hidden from those bandidos last fall. All was quiet now. Birds chirped happily at us. A red bird swooped past. The early wildflowers were on full display, and some wild iris had braved the rocky banks of the Cienega to make purple stars in the grass. "Aren't they pretty?" I said.

"If you like them, I'll dig 'em up and plant a hundred by the door to the house."

"They might not like the sun. They're blooming here in the shade."

"Then, where it's too dark for tomatoes, it should be right for purple stars." Udell found a flatter rock, and he motioned for me to have a seat on it. "Take a look from here. I come here every evening, to see the progress. Sometimes you can't tell much, because things change on the inside while the outside is the same."

From my perch, the house did look more elegant. The drive to it was trimmed with rocks, small blue-green boulders alternated with white chalky quartz. Udell's house had rooms for my mother and my father-in-law on the ground floor so they are not made in their old age to climb stairs. An enormous stone hearth warms the old folks' rooms and the kitchen and dining area. It has rooms for my books and my sewing, a visiting parlor and a reading parlor, plus separate bedrooms for four extra people. Even an indoor privy upstairs that meant no midnight trips to an outhouse. Yes, Udell had built me a bower, and here he was, suddenly on one knee in front of me, shyly studying a seam on my gloves, though he was brazen enough to be holding my hand.

My heart swelled. The papers were on my desk at home to sell my children my ranch. If the deeds were in front of me at that moment, I'd have signed them over and married him that minute. I smiled at him, and he turned and stared at the house. So I knelt beside him and tried to ponder it, again.

Keeping his eyes on the house, Udell said, "Sarah? You know I'm a plain man. And you know I care for you truly. There's those who think once a man and woman have had their first true loves, well, they should be done with that and go into their twilight years alone. But I don't see the sense in that. Why, it could be a long time 'til twilight for you and me. Have I done any one thing that makes you not think I'd be true to you, and loyal, and kind?"

"No, not a thing," I said. Oh, Lord. Where I'd been willing a second before to swoon into his arms, I felt a surge of alarm at the way he talked. Was he going to argue me to the altar with him? I got my back up. I was ready to say to him, *Listen, Mr. Hanna. Press me with kisses or tempt me with spring flowers, but don't argue me!*

"I'll gladly buy you a gold ring. Any you chose; I know you're particular.

The roof will be finished by the end of July, long as I'm able. We could go to town together before long. Hitch up."

Those words flung my anger from me as if it had been an old blanket that didn't fit my notion anymore. I didn't say to him not to think of that. I couldn't. I felt like my thoughts were riding a waterfall over a scoop in the rocks, churned at the bottom only to ride over another crest again.

We sat side by side in the grass, listening to birds splashing in the pools. A dozen quail lined up in a row crossed an open place in front of us. There was no reason I could think of not to marry Udell Hanna this very day. If he wanted to argue, I'd be ready. But if he didn't, my only argument was that I didn't believe he knew just exactly how ornery to the very core I could be.

He stared at the house, at the ground, then the sky, looking all around, as if he'd plum forgot the train of our conversation. After a while, he picked a stem of grass and peeled it, then used it to draw a circle on the leg of his pants. "Sarah," he said, "I've talked every way I know to ask you to marry me. I gave up a couple of weeks ago, figuring it was no good. Then, after Harland came out last time, I thought to try one more thing. I know it wasn't right to talk about you behind your back but we did, some of your kin and me. Wasn't their fault, it was me asked 'em. I learned some things about you from your boys and Harland. It gave me the idea, so I went and did something. It can be undone if you don't want it, but it's done and ready if you do. Now, here's the thing. One of those times I went to town for supplies, well, I stopped at the college. And I know you might say you won't, but hear me out."

"Udell, you're talking in circles."

"Yes'm, I am." He breathed deeply and started again. "There's one thing the boys told me I could give you that no one else ever gave, nor did you have the chance to take. One gift that might mean more to you than a box full of solid gold. And so . . . and so I put your name in at the college and enrolled you as a student. Unless you swear right now that you don't want to, Mrs. Sarah Elliot, you are going to the university in Tucson this fall. Fully enrolled. It's a betrothing gift to you. Latin, English composition, algebra, and general science. Girls are required to take cooking, too, isn't that a hoot? You could teach them a thing or two. You'll have to be there come August."

The breath went out of me. My heart came to a complete halt. I stammered for words. I looked at this man sitting in long grass beside me, still facing the house, his eyes on the sky above it. I trembled so hard my teeth chattered. I said, "Aw, you're just teasing."

"It's the gospel, Sarah. On my life."

"Udell," I whispered, brushing my lips with my fingertips. "Oh, Lord. Udell Hanna."

To the sky, he said, "I'll expect you to make passing marks, of course."

He turned to me, and I kissed him as I'd never imagined doing. Rapture sent my arms to his neck and my lips to his mouth again and again. We fell into the grass, returning the other's kisses as if there were no night or day, no world around us. *Oh, Lord, stop me!* The birds chirped "University, University!" and we kissed each other as if we were to become the other, melting together like candy under glass. We rolled on the grass until my hair came loose and spread like a great feather fan I could feel with my cheek when I turned my head as he kissed hard at my neck. *This, then, was love.* Crushing his chest into mine with my arms, I closed my eyes against the morning sun and my surrender didn't seem wrong, or sad, or anything else but heaven-come-to-earth to lie with him there in the grass, finding each other, tumbling together, knowing his body and him knowing mine, and all the earth coming to a stop at this place and this time, the sun shining like a halo on his hair as he raised over me, the very breath he breathed making my heart sing. *Merciful heaven. Oh, perfect bliss.*

We awoke cold. Under the grass, the ground was damp with winter dew and our skins not used to so much daylight and cool air. Faint and still trembling, I straightened my skirts and then my hair, combing grass from it with my fingers while he turned away, doing buttons.

Add this to my list of sins and I was truly unlovable, a betrayer of enemy and friend alike, and now, no better than a common strumpet. By having succumbed to my foolish loss of all reason, I will have lost his respect, lost the future he meant and has so earnestly planned for, and lost my life's dearest secret dream. All because of the fulfillment of that dream. Savannah was right, I had no business thinking I could teach anyone's children. Yet, I loved him more, wanted his touch more than before, as if this act had tapped at some secret doorway, too long shut, that I craved to fling wide open. *I will know when he turns around.*

As I tried to get a small burr worked out of my hair, he shook his head and swept his hands over his clothes, brushing off bits of grass. Udell turned at last, with a deeply embarrassed expression on his face, and reached toward me to help me stand. It took me some doing to look him in the eyes. I felt craven and low, and at the same time would have offered my lips to more kisses at the least invitation. When at last I raised my face he seemed worried. His lower lip trembled as he said, "Please forgive me. Oh, please, Sarah, I never meant to take advantage. I'm so sorry. Only say you'll not hate me—"

I drew a breath so sudden and deep it felt as if my ribs had taken a life all their own. "Hate you? Oh, Udell, do you hate me? Do you scorn to see—"

"That you love me, too? That I've made you happy?"

"Beyond all my dearest hopes, Mr. Hanna." I kissed his cheek, in a sisterly way.

"We ought to marry, then, Mrs. Elliot. It's only right. I never meant to hurry . . . but it's only right. We can ride to Benson by dark. I'll stand by you. Do the right thing." He kissed me deeply. Nothing brotherly about that one.

Nearly in a swoon again, I stepped back, blushful and gasping. I couldn't believe the words spilling from my own lips. "It's only right," I said. *It was all sliding away—washed down the river like a petal from a fading flower. School. College. Books and wonderful teachers and unsavored colloquiums awaited me.* "I need to think." I walked in a small circle, making a tent with my fingers pressed tight, searching inside them for some kind of wisdom I didn't feel at all capable of finding. I said, "If, you see, if there is no child that comes of this, this . . . today, then I might still go to school, mightn't I?"

"Well, yes."

"But if—married—this were to happen on a regular basis, even if there were no child today, that might be something that *might* happen."

He nodded, looking as dazed as I felt. "It might be likely. If you didn't mind. *I* don't mind." He lowered his voice, flustered. "I mean, well, I don't mind."

"I don't mind, either," I said. My cheeks flushed anew at the depth of his loud sigh. "But for a few months more, if I could go to school, just for a while, just a few months, Udell, I'd never forget it as long as I had breath. I'd better go home. I have some work to do. Plans to make. Packing, and all."

We rushed to each other. I inhaled the smell of his skin, the soap he'd used, the shaving lather, the very sweetness of his lips and a lone stickery whisker he'd missed near his chin. We kissed long and hard until I felt compelled to sink to the grass again, but held my ground with more strength this time. Let the birds sing "University" all they wish, but even a precious baby would certainly sing, "Not for you, my loving mama!"

I said, "We'll wait, then. I'll dream of school for a couple of weeks, and by then we'll know. There will be time enough to marry, and I'll not be sorry if we do. I think I'll not be sorry one bit, Mr. Hanna. For two weeks, though, I'll have my dream."

"I'll not be sorry, Sarah. You forgive, then? I aim to do the right thing."

I held out my arms and he wrapped me in his. "Oh, Udell. There is nothing to forgive. We're not children. We will marry in the future, whether nearer or farther, that's the only question."

Udell and I rode to my place, me sitting in front of him on the workhorse he had named Dodger. We tied Baldy on behind, which didn't sit well with either horse, but after a mile they settled. Udell's arms around me fit just fine, and I leaned my head back against his shoulder while he held the reins, both his hands around my middle. We got to the yard and I felt guilty and rumpled and plenty glad no one was there at that moment. He turned that horse to go home and gave him a good kick, sending him running, Udell hollering, "Wahoo!" at the top of his lungs like a boy.

I fairly flew to my bedroom and closed the door, going through the house to the *baño* at the back to run a bath.

For two solid days I sat with myself and my thoughts, not letting much of anything interrupt me, and had some good long thinks and some not so good. I thought of Mary Pearl's fear. Of how Miss James seemed, instead of low-down and mysterious, just frightened and confused. Of how Miss Castle—rest her soul—seemed not trashy, just sad. I tried to figure out what I'd done with myself, what had happened to the person I thought I knew that I'd so recently misplaced and replaced with this new one I couldn't get a rope around. Why, I barely recognized my own reflection in the mirror.

Latin and English, he'd said. No doubt heights of examination in those languages that I'd never dream. Intellectual things. College things. General science? I wanted to study *specific* science! Didn't Charlie have that geology book, and would they take up geology in "general" science? Gleeful shivers ran up and down my spine. And why not some Greek history, too? Would there be room for Plutarch and Homer? India. China! Maybe I'll learn about China. But would there be room for a woman who might have grandchildren but the heart of a hussy? And would that day's indulgence be the last bar on the door for me? Would the miracle of my own body take away that chance with the coming of a baby, no matter how dear? Udell was an ordinary man, I thought, but a man with an extraordinary way of thinking. That was truly worth more than gold: extraordinary thinking.

The next two nights I dreamed not of school but of nursing babies. Sometimes two at a time, always with golden halos in their hair like pictures on the Jesuit mission's walls. Like Udell's. I was happier than I could remember being in a very long time. Silly as a goose. Couldn't stop grinning. Couldn't think any more at all. That waterfall had become a torrent and I was head over heels under the stream of it.

### May 11, 1907

"Mama?" Charlie said. "I've asked you four times now. Do you need anything from town? Elsa and I want to take the buggy. She's wanting some fresh vegetables."

"No, I don't mind," I said. "What's Gilbert doing?"

"He went to get mail, but he wants to go, too. I reckon it's a good idea, to let him ride shotgun, if you can spare us three or four days."

"Surely that's fine," I said. I felt purely stupid. Too happy, too sad at once, too confused to make any sense at all. I had discovered—the way women do—that there was no child to come from lying with Udell on the banks of the Cienega. My eyes were on Charlie hitching the rig, but my heart was blanketed with warm sunshine of that afternoon ten days ago, the light that surrounded every living thing, the joy that drew me to a man. And Udell has been only tender and gentlemanly ever since, so that nary a notion has crossed my mind that I have lessened in his esteem. He worries the opposite, he has said, feeling it was a great fault in his character to have let it happen.

How could I blame him? There surely wasn't any cry of "no" from me. But no baby. *How I covet to hold a baby. How empty not to expect that miracle.* Yet, an expectation of other joy has come in its place. I plan to ride to Udell's place this afternoon when I've finished my chores.

Gilbert brought in a small stack of paper envelopes. I asked him what they were and he only hollered from the hallway, "I don't know. I have got to take a bath!" and disappeared. Well, his going must be about the mysterious girl, I speculated.

My sons left with Elsa. Chess was out in the barn, Granny worked on her quilt. The house was quiet. I put the mail under a bowl on the table to wait for later.

About an hour after the boys left, the dogs started barking. Then I heard hoofbeats, coming at a fine pace but not a full run. I stepped outside to see Mary Pearl riding up on her three-year-old stallion. She slipped off his bare back before he'd stopped, and looped reins at my porch rail, hurrying to me.

The girl grabbed my shoulders and hugged me. "Mama will scold me if she knows I'm here, so I have to ask you to keep quiet again. If you won't, or can't, say so now and I'll leave."

I said, "Glad to see you, Mary Pearl. Is it a sin now, for you to talk to me?"

"Are you going to tell?"

"No."

"Then I'll stay. Aunt Sarah, Mama is driving me to distraction, she's so peeved at me for going to school. I have thought and thought until my head aches, and I finally figured a way to settle it. She is giving me lectures until you'd think I was only born to get married to the first man that came along. I do love Aubrey, but, you know, he said he'd wait for me. If he won't, then he's not the kind of man I'd care to marry anyway. Don't you think that's right?"

I wasn't sure just what to say. Her coming here had jarred me, and it seemed as if the threads of my thoughts were hard to gather. "Come have some lemonade and tell me how you're going to fix this." I led her inside where we spent a few minutes admiring Granny's quilt blocks before we began to talk.

Mary Pearl drank a whole glass of lemonade in one long, thirsty draft. She sat in a chair opposite her grandma. Then she addressed both of us and said, "I have written a letter to Aubrey, just as formal as I know how—because he is a lawyer and knows more than I do, and Mama says we are legally bounden to marry. She pulled a wrinkled half sheet of paper from her pocket and held it to her face and read, "And it says, I hereby request that we conveniently agree to null our betrothal for the good of any and all, for the duration of my schooling, to be hence and forthwith reconsidered at which future time I shall return to the Territory of Arizona and all its legal confines.' How does that sound?"

I said, "Well, I'm not sure. Why do you want to do that? In a letter, I mean."

"Because I'm only seventeen. And do you know how old Aubrey is? Twenty-eight. He'll be thirty when I get done."

"Thirty is a good age," I said. Jack was thirty. Lands, I wish I'd married him the first minute I laid eyes on him. But I saw real fear on Mary Pearl's face.

"Mary Pearl, sit down here, honey, and catch your breath," Granny said.

"Granny? Mama says I have made a commitment to God, being betrothed, and I'd have to get a divorce to go to college! I can't get a divorce—dang, I'm just seventeen. Aunt Sarah, I just can't. It would be the ruination of our family. I'd be so ashamed."

Granny said, "Don't you like the rascal?"

Mary Pearl's face reddened and her chin crimped hard when she said,

"I love him. I *kissed* him. But I've been thinking about art school for a whole year, and Mama won't let me go to school betrothed. She and Papa have been squabbling on it for days."

"Did you send him this yet?" I asked.

"No. I want you to mail it for me. Mama'll want to know what I'm mailing anyway. She'd make me read it to her." She held her rumpled letter as if it hurt to gaze at it. It looked more childish than the lessons Zachary usually brought to me. Seemed to me that she was feeling like a cornered kitten.

I said, "If I did that, I'd be going behind your mother's back again. It's one thing not to tell her something I didn't think would matter, but this would matter. Is that all your letter says, honey? Doesn't it say that you care for him?"

"That's pretty much the whole thing except for 'Dear Mr. Aubrey Hanna, Esquire' and 'your true friend,' me. I wanted it real formal."

I said, "Why don't you write another letter? Explain it in a kinder way. Tell him you care for him but you are too young to bind him to such a pledge when you are headed off for two years. Tell him you respect him and admire all his good qualities, and that if God and nature allow for you to meet again and you find that you're still in love, then you will happily make a reacquaintance with his promise. Or some such."

She smiled. "Can you tell me all those words again?"

"No, you make up your own. And then tell your mother you want to send it."

"Oh, no."

"Oh, yes. If you're woman enough to go to college clean across the States, you're woman enough to tell your mama you want to. You aren't running away like Esther did and you sure aren't hiding behind my skirts to do it. Don't be sassy, just brave up."

Granny said, "About time somebody went over and talked to her," pointing her gnarled finger at me. To Mary Pearl she said, "Child, get yonder and start to writing. Then you, Sarah, get your best dress on and hitch the buggy and take me visiting. Is my purty bonnet washed?"

I said, "The boys took the buggy."

"Fiddlesticks. I'm going to see Savannah and Albert. Are you ridin' me over, or am I walking?"

I did not want to fuss with Granny, nor face Savannah. I wanted to pretend there was no quarrel and go on forgetting her five minutes at a time, but I could only do it if I stayed away from Savannah. Granny wouldn't let it rest, and she kept on at me while she got her bonnet on. I didn't have any choice, really.

Much as I didn't want another scene with her—deep down, I knew Savannah was right, although she wasn't giving me any quarter—I reckon I would rather face her and say the things I ought to say, than keep on being squeezed by folks I love to take one side or the other.

Chess helped me with the hitching, then got in to drive, too. When we got the buckboard pulled to my door, Mary Pearl sat busily working on her letter at the kitchen table, with Granny coaching her every word. When she was satisfied with it, Granny and I climbed in while Mary Pearl got back upon Duende. I watched the wheels turn and my heart thumped against my ribs in time with the squeaking. Why, I'd been stubborn! I had the gumption to go tell her so. No sense carrying on a fuss-fight when we could just be friends again. I'd tell her straight out I was sorry for waiting so long, too. It isn't like me to be so stubborn, I'll say. Why, I'll tell her everything that's happened. She will have gotten over being mad. Surely she will have.

We found Savannah kneeling in front of their porch, working a hand spade around a flower bed. I thought about Udell's trouble with shade and wondered if I should say something. That kind of talk would have to come later. We had some fence to mend first. Savannah stood. I could read the consternation on her from across the yard. All these years she and I have cared for each other like sisters, nursed each other's wounds and brought forth each other's babies, and here she is still mad at me after all these days. I stood there by the buggy, pretending to fiddle with the brake and get the reins tied up real tight. Clover helped Granny to the ground.

Mary Pearl slid off her horse and headed toward the house, but Savannah stopped her, saying, "Where you been? You have chores to be done."

"I know, Mama," Mary Pearl said. "I wanted Aunt Sarah's advice on a letter I want to send to Aubrey. She helped me fix it."

Savannah looked from Mary Pearl to me and I saw real hurt in her eyes. She said, "I see. So you're writing him to break the engagement? You'd rather do that on a whim than live up to your promise?"

"Savannah," I started. She held up a hand to quiet me, the same way Rudolfo had stilled his children. The move made me angry but I kept quiet. She stared at Mary Pearl.

"Mama," the girl said, "I've been thinking about art school for over a year. I haven't known Aubrey Hanna for six months. *He's* more a whim than schooling. And it is a short time. I'll be home. You let the twins go off and Rebeccah went clear to Mexico before she came home, and Rachel's in town minding Uncle

Harland's children. Why, once they were there at school, you didn't see the twins for months on end and you sent letters to them, and they to you, and I can do that, too. It's no different than the twins, Mama. And a far sight better than what Esther did."

Stone-faced, Savannah said, "You've no call to say anything about Esther, Mary Pearl."

Mary Pearl drew herself up and took a deep breath I could hear. "I'm not running away and I'm not going to get killed. I'm doing this in front of you, not scheming behind your back writing to some fellow you wouldn't approve of. Seems to me I've got two things you do approve, and all I'm doing is choosing them, one *after* the other. Couldn't very well marry first and then go off to college. Why, it might be a lot of fun to walk a circle around our parlor and take Aubrey's hand and be married. But those folks wrote all the way from Wheaton that they want me to come. You always told me to look at the doors opened by the Lord and go on through."

Savannah had tears running down her face. "You're sassy."

"Rebeccah went and taught in Mexico."

"Mexico is less than half the distance to Illinois. If you must go to college you can go to town," Savannah said. "Rachel will have to mind you as well as the children. And maybe Mr. Hanna's affections won't be turned sour by your silliness. Wheaton is too far away!" Savannah said, then abruptly went into her house.

Mary Pearl stood in the yard, her mouth open, as if she were stunned that she hadn't won her point with her mother. She followed Savannah like an obedient chick. I followed after Mary Pearl. Granny had already made herself at home in the kitchen, and was sitting with a cup held out while Rebeccah poured tea into it. Rebeccah lighted up and started to say hello to me, but then turned her eyes away.

I was fixing to ask Savannah to sit and talk with me when Granny cut through the bad air in the room as easy as you please, saying, "You girls know I've come to the evening of life. I've made up my mind about some things and I've done some poor living. It ain't much, but I see this youngest girl is about to bust out on her own and I got something for her to do—"

Savannah turned around and said, "Mary Pearl isn't on her own, Mama Prine. There'll be no 'busting out' while I'm drawing breath."

Granny waited a moment and then said, "Well, that'll be or it won't, but your dying won't change it a whit. The girl's growed and I got something needs doing before I go. I put in my time here on this land. I aim to write my memories only

I can't do more than a *X* for my own name, and she's got a knack for putting down words. I want Mary Pearl to write my memories for me as I recollect 'em."

Mary Pearl's face went from puzzlement to dread. "Oh, I'm no hand at that kind of thing," she mumbled. "Rebeccah has finished her schooling; she'd do better."

"I want you to do it. And I'm yer eldest elder. You got to do as I say, this one time. These young folks galloping around like they got no thought for the old folks—it's the only thing I'm asking and I don't ask much. Now settle down a while. Learn some respect before you leave home. And learn how things used to was, when it was hard, and how your folks lived, and a poor living it was. I he'ped you with your letter, you can he'p me with mine. You fetch a quill and paper. Take down ever' word. We'll start directly."

"Today?"

Granny sipped her tea. "Needs sugar," she said.

Savannah seemed to be mulling this over. Myself, I didn't know Granny had a wish of this nature, and I wondered why she hadn't asked me to do the writing for her. She's so beside herself so much of the time, there was no way to figure if this was some carefully derived plan or just another notion that she'd tire of in an afternoon.

Savannah turned to Mary Pearl and said, "You heard your grandmother. Fetch some paper. You may use a real nib if you'd like, instead of a feather. Look in the top left drawer in the secretary."

Granny nodded. Then she said, "Send her by Sarah's parlor every afternoon when her chores are done. Might take all summer. Longer, maybe. She can go when it's done."

Slowly, Savannah nodded just once, then several times, as if this were going to keep her girl at home and safely married off before she turned eighteen, but it had to be weighed against the constant exposure to my surly influence. I tried to picture Mary Pearl sitting still for hours every afternoon, quietly writing Granny's words. I thought of Savannah steaming and angry, every moment Mary Pearl did it.

"Mama," I said. "If you wanted me to write this out for you, I'd a-been happy to oblige. All you had to do was ask."

"I know it," she said. "I asked who I wanted, that's all." Mary Pearl straightened three sheets of paper and opened the ink, pen raised. "Let's start now."

I looked up and caught Savannah's eyes darting from my direction. I said, "Would you take a walk with me, Savannah?"

"I have weeds to pull, while the ground's wet from the rain."

"Let's pull 'em, then," I said. She took off for the yard and I followed her fast as I could, for she seemed to be trying to outrun me. We worked in the flower bed a good long time without speaking. Finally I said, "That wild broom is about to take over the place, isn't it?"

"Yes," she said, "most of them have got more root than top."

I could see Albert, Chess, and Clover having a talk, and I saw that Albert saw me and Savannah talking, too. I said, "Well, maybe there's a point to that, though. We all sort of do."

"What do you mean?"

"Well, maybe I'm sort of a desert weed, like that. Not too fancy on top, but ornery enough and tough, and roots long enough to hold out. You know I've never been a genteel sort. But I never thought of myself so cantankerous or mean you couldn't trust your children with me."

"I never said that."

"You said I was a poor influence on 'em. It isn't the kindest thing I've heard, Savannah." I knew she took care to be honest. Somewhere deep inside, she had meant those words. Mud soaked into my best driving gloves, but I didn't mind wasting them in the hope of settling the hard words between my best friend and me. I jerked out a clump of chokeweed, and some kind of a round dumpling came up with it, looking like an onion with bark. I waited a long spell, pulling a few more brooms until I caught a finger-sized cholla in the middle of one. The fiery needles of it went through the leather of my gloves.

Savannah said, "You're taking out the bulbs, too. I just planted those! That has to go back in, blunt side down."

Thinking she should have weeded before she planted, I said, "I believe April planted hers last fall."

She snapped, "These are daffodils. They are supposed to be planted in *spring*. It's about time something here went the way it was *supposed* to."

"Well, Savannah, we had spring in February. The people that write those gardening books all come from England where it's cold and rainy. You can't—"

"I can, and I will. I'd just like for once to have flowers instead of weeds."

"Won't the javelinas eat 'em up before they bloom?"

"No."

"What's got into you lately?"

"Not a thing except wanting life to be lived in a good and righteous order. I've been too soft on those children. Too soft on myself. Pure lazy, letting them go off instead of schooling them myself. I did what came easiest, instead of what was right."

I felt myself twist inside. What did any of us do, except keep body and soul together the best we could in the Territories? Did Savannah think she could fight the weather with a daffodil root set out like a feast for rabbits and rodents? I said, "You had eight children. You did all anyone could have done. I thought I'd been helping you."

She chopped away at the ground, going over a place she'd already weeded, smoothing and straightening the soil as if it were a bed she was making. When she didn't say anything for quite a spell, I said, "Esther was prey to a criminal. It isn't anyone's fault she got killed."

"I'd prefer not to speak of my departed daughter just now."

"You can't hold Mary Pearl back from leaving home because of what happened to her sister. She's grown. The tighter you hold her, the harder she'll strain."

"She's betrothed. She'll leave home on the arm of her husband."

"You have any more of these daffodil roots? They might do in a clay pot up on the porch rail, if they got watered regularly."

"I've planted all I got."

I sat back on my haunches. "All right." She'd spent the lot on a sure-to-fail flower bed. Planting food for rabbits and wild pigs.

"She's got no reason to traipse across half the country to a place we've never been, living with total strangers whose character we don't know. You know about artists. She'd be consorting with be-*heminas*."

"Bohemians? Mary Pearl isn't going to consort at all. I know the girl."

"Better than I do, I suppose?"

I kept quiet for a bit, then I said, "Well, there once was a girl I met, all of nineteen. She come across this rusty feller still living with his folks out of a third-hand wagon without six bits to his name. He had nothing and no future, no meat on his bones and no education, nor was he too pretty to look at. She'd barely met him, too, hardly long enough to know what his character was, but she sized him up and on his say-so decided to take off to the worst badlands in North America, and then had to fight Indians the whole way to get to where he was leading her. He didn't even know where he was going. He just came to a place one day and said, 'this looks likely,' and drew a square and put up a shack. On top of that she had to live with his mother and all his brothers and a sister, and have her first baby in that shack out in the desert. Her pa told her not to go but she was headstrong and all. She wouldn't be turned away. Just up and went off, like she knew what she was doing."

"Those were different days."

"But you decided how you wanted your life to be and went and did it. That's all."

"Albert told her she can go. My opinion—"

"Matters, plenty. Now, I reckon I have warmed up to where I can say what I ought to say. That is, that I'm sorry if I've caused you trouble with your children. Never for the life of me would I have set out to do that if I'd thought that was what was happening. I thought—well, that maybe—"

"There's more than that."

"Well, I know. I should have told you she wrote to the college. I forgot about it in the fear of her maybe dying and I'm sorry for it."

"I have come to see that you have been partly raising my children all these years. Now you have this fellow Udell wanting you to marry. You'll have your own life, then. You don't need my boys taking lessons every day. And it's so much farther away, I couldn't let them go alone—"

"Is that all? Why, you'll teach them just as well. But any marrying'll be on the pantry shelf for a few months. I'm going to town for a while. Going to try my hand at this college business, too."

She sat up stiffly, spade in midair. "Well. I see. Well, you go on, then. That's fine. That's just fine." She rose and went to the house without another word.

By the time I got in the house she had gone to the bedroom and closed the door.

In the parlor, Mary Pearl sat taking notes from Granny. Rebeccah was mending a leg on a pair of boy's pants. Ezra and Zachary hunched over slates at a small table, working arithmetic. "Hey, Aunt Sarah," they said as one. I waved to them and followed Savannah's footsteps to her bedroom door, opening it without knocking. Savannah sat in a rocker, facing the east window, staring hard and rocking. She twisted a handkerchief around her fingers.

A framed print of her mother and father in wedding clothes hung on the wall near a highboy. A finely quilted, double-stitched topper was on the bed, just as straight as if it were sewn to a box—no sagging ropes on their frame. I felt as if I'd snuck into a church, and needed to be quiet. I whispered, "Are you going to tell me what you're so angry about, or do I have to stand here and guess at it the livelong day? I've got chores to do, a heifer having her first crooked tail this morning, and weeds of my own to pull."

"For years, Sarah, you have filled my children's heads with fanciful tales of faraway places. Got them imagining all kinds of things. Romantic notions of . . . of passion!"

I felt some pride in what learning had happened under my parlor roof. Many enjoyable hours in the board swing out back, where one after the other of our children recited poems and long division aloud.

She said, "That's what led Esther to take off with that Spaniard, simply because he made love in letters to her for a few months. Why, she didn't know who he was. It's what's led Mary Pearl to want to take off across the country—"

"Now, wait a minute. Joshua is across the country, too, studying medicine."

"He's a man."

"She's going to be a woman. What's wrong with drawing some pictures?"

"She's got a life already cut out for her."

"Savannah? Are you sure you aren't just angry that I'm going, too?"

With that, she fumed. Tears ran from her eyes, though she brushed them away bitterly as she said, "I can see that these bo-ho—whatever you called it—ideas have all come from one place. Your parlor, and all those books, most of which do not teach moral virtue but complicated thinking, graying of righteousness. Very little is godly in that library of yours. Far more is . . . I believe in simplicity and godliness. Honesty and cleanliness. Hard work. Girls ought to be warned against romantic notions, not fed them. This tainting of my youngest daughters is your doing."

"Well, I don't rightly know what to say, Savannah. You never brought it up before."

"It never got so out of hand before."

It was true I believed in looking past the horizon. I couldn't see how an apology was going to change what had been done over years past, in the nature of reading Homer and Groves and all the rest, in my book room. I said, "And that's your last word on it?"

"It is."

When I got to the door I turned to her, her face only half visible as she rocked that chair in bitter strokes. The wooden joints of the chair gave angry squeaks faster than the ticking of the clock I could hear from their parlor. I've had plenty of hurt in my life. Been angry enough to eat a two-by-four plank of wormwood with a bowl of nails for dessert. This here was different. This was the only sister I'd ever known, my best friend in the world, turning away from me for being who I was, after all the times she's stood by me for the same reason, too. After all we've shared, from head colds to peach preserves, this is the end of it all. There had never been any word to me about what to let her children read. And hadn't I just been thinking Charlie might not have gotten himself into such a fix marrying Elsa Maldonado, if I'd kept my children away from Shakespeare? I took a deep breath. There was a fragrance of rosemary from the sachets in the drawers on the air, but the room was cold. None of what Savannah was angry about could be undone. Don't reckon I would if I could.

I held the door open one extra second, said, "Suit yourself, then," and left without closing it. I heard the rhythmic squeaking hesitate for just a moment, then I went out the front door.

Out in the yard, Clover and Albert stood at the wagon talking to Chess. I climbed into the seat. "I'll come back to get Granny after supper." Albert watched me, wrinkled his brow and nodded sadly.

Chess chucked the reins and we went up the road. He said, "Figure out what Miss Savannah's got stuck in her craw?"

Finding it hard to open my mouth to say the word, I muttered, "Yup."

"Get 'er fixed?"

"Seems Savannah is pure sick and tired of the cut of my clothes."

"Tarnation."

"Suppose it won't matter, then, to be two miles farther down the road. Udell's building you and Granny each a room. I told him I'd marry."

"Well, I'll be."

"Yup."

"When?"

"He gave me a session of college as a marriage gift. I'm going to town to try my hand at that college for a bit. Then I'm coming back and marry him. I gave my word."

"College. Well, I'll be."

### *May 13, 1907*

Mary Pearl comes over every afternoon and takes down Granny's words. They are hushed-up about it, too, and the girl says she's sworn to secrecy by her grandma. She stays late, sometimes. We fix supper or sew, and Elsa and Mary Pearl have returned to being friends. Far as I know, Mary Pearl has not sent her letter to Aubrey yet though he's been scarce. I am of the mind that if their love is true, it will hold.

My mama told me she wouldn't have me doing the writing for her, as I had too many chores already, and she said she didn't want me to read her memories until she got put in the ground. I laughed and asked, did she think I'd be shocked and embarrassed, and she said, "Maybe so."

Mary Pearl said there was nothing left of her mother's flower bed. Javelinas have been a torment since those daffodil bulbs went in the ground, and they have had a puma lingering around hunting javelina dinner. I stared down the road toward Albert and Savannah's place, thinking about those bulbs, and how she knew it wouldn't work and still insisted on planting them.

# Chapter Twelve

*May 25, 1907*

April is lying in! I got her letter yesterday. Gilbert and I came to town soon as we could. She had summoned a midwife, so comforting words and watching the other children may be all I can offer her. What a blessing to have a real midwife at hand. Naturally, Gilbert disappeared right away. He heard one yell out of April and decided he'd be spending his time with Harland until it was all over and done.

*May 29, 1907*

April and Morris welcomed a little girl the day after I arrived. She is no more than five pounds but hearty in the lungs, and April named her Tennyson after one of my favorite writers. I think that's a crackerjack name if ever I heard one. Miss Tennyson Weingold has brought a heat spell with her, and she and her mother suffer from prickly heat. April will not allow wet burlap to be strung in the baby's room, fearing it draws mosquitoes and some dire fever from the tropics, so they are both fretting and mighty tearful. To find some relief from the torment, I have spent some afternoons with Harland in my old house. I love to hear him talk about the new houses he is building, and where land is under survey for this or that new thing.

Harland took his children and me in his horseless carriage up to the university to have a look around, getting the lay of the place before I have to go. He said he supposed I wouldn't want to live in the basement of Old Main, and offered to rent me my old bedroom for the price of a peach pie and a haircut every month. Then we had a good chuckle over how that much in trade didn't bring what it used to.

### June 13, 1907

Pleased as I was to see my precious new granddaughter into this world, after two weeks of tending April and her family I looked forward to taking the road home and getting a good night's sleep. I felt tired enough by the time we set off, you'd have thought I had been the one delivered a babe. Gilbert and I headed home at sunup.

As we headed past the Pantano place, a fresh cut of wheels went through the brittlebush headed southwest. Gilbert thought we ought to follow the tracks and see where they went, but I reckoned it likely that at the end of the tracks we'd only find a broken-down wagon or a loop where the driver had thought better and gone back to the road. I had plenty of trouble and didn't need to go sticking my nose in some other.

### June 15, 1907

Next time I saw Udell Hanna's house, the rock walls, six feet high before, were now ten feet to the top, and it looked to be as big and wide as a church. Someone had put on the front door, although the windows held no glass and a stairway ended in the sky, with the rest of the house and the roof still put together somewhere in Udell's imagination. Each window hole had two shutters with a cross cut into each one. Every thick oaken shutter had been fitted with big iron dogs to lock it closed from the inside. The floor of bricks set in sand turned at angles and made a smooth pavement. On one wall, the second floor rose from the ridge of stone in two layers of wood, one inside and one without, with rock wool between them.

I kept trying to remind myself not to think of this pile of boulders as *his* house, but *ours*. Yet, it was so drab and severe, so unlike any kind of house I ever pictured. When I saw it from afar, I turned my eyes, so that it was not as ugly as it seemed in the stark light of day. I stood on the rock walls again, this time even higher, so that the wind came up the hill toward us, and peered toward the east and Rudolfo's hacienda. The corrals out front were empty. Peculiar stillness had replaced all the usual bustling there.

I came across Udell in his garden, drenched with sweat, pouring water from a long-handled bucket onto a row of little sprouts. "My, those are looking fine," I said, leaning over the fencepost.

Udell spoke as if he were afraid someone at the neighbor's house below could hear. "Maldonado came by yesterday. Offered to buy me out again."

"I'm not sure I like the tone of your voice." I waited while he searched the horizon for some answer.

"Offered to make sure I would want to sell to him."

"Meaning?"

"Don't know rightly. Just said I'd be wanting to sell before long, and he'd make sure of it."

"Reckon he didn't expect you'd have stayed this long."

"Would you mind if we move my cows to your corral?" Without another word, we got off the walls and, on foot, leading our horses, we pushed his little herd around the bend and across Rudolfo's corner by the big ocotillo to my place. We kept them slow as the heat could kill them. The little calves and the mamas now gave him a nice fifteen head. Still, not a one could be spared.

Well, I tried to talk Udell into staying at our place, but he said he planned going to sleep in his house come Rudolfo or the Devil himself. If I were a man, I'd go there with him and spell him so he could sleep. Asking any of my family to go in my place didn't seem right. Reckon Udell would have to fend for himself. So after supper, I asked him if he'd like to take our fellow Buttons along. That dog is about half grown now, still got big feet and a skinny neck, but he's pretty good at watching. Udell said he'd tie him up good so he wouldn't try to run home and get killed during the night, so he rode home carrying Buttons in his arms.

Next day after morning chores, I rode down to see how they did during the night. While I talked to Udell, Buttons slept off his breakfast of bacon and biscuits, and I laughed at his middle sticking out like he was a gourd with legs.

*June 20, 1907*

Clover drove up in the big surrey with Mary Pearl, come to say goodbye. Ezra and Rebeccah sat in the back. They told us Clover will be going along on the train to see Mary Pearl and Duende all the way to Wheaton. Rebeccah is going to bring home some goods from Tucson, and Ezra is to do the driving back. Zack stayed home doing chores. They clambered down and filed into the kitchen. I passed them biscuits and some sorghum. Rebeccah said she'd already had breakfast, so Ezra ate his and hers to boot.

Mary Pearl watched her brothers like she needed to commit them to memory. After they ate, I asked if she wanted me to take up writing Granny's memoirs, but she said it was pretty much finished. I asked her if she wanted me to send her some new duds, but Savannah had made sure she had more clothes than she could want in ten years, all of them gray or brown and plain as a board, she said, without even a black button on them. Usually she wore split skirts cut above her boots for riding and a Cavalry-style Stetson. Mary Pearl spoke out in front of Rebeccah, so I figured she didn't have any suspicions that her sister would scold behind her back to their mother. Savannah had gone and made the girl a little starched cap of old-fashioned design, like she'd worn when we were girls.

"I got my regular hat in a box," Mary Pearl said. "So I can ride now and then."

Chess came in the room and peered at her, and pretended like he didn't know her, until it almost brought her to fuss-fighting. Charlie and Gilbert just stared until, finally, Charlie said, "Mary P, if your mama feared you were too pretty before, it ain't helping to wear that."

"This cap? I'll have to wear a bonnet on top, too, to keep from getting all freckled up and brown, and it feels awful on my neck, having a bow there."

Gilbert just snorted and said, "Shucks, Mary Pearl. Ain't seen you without your hat before. You already turned into a city girl. Better not be any lop-eared hooligans carrying on around you, or you write us and we'll come fix 'em."

Charlie said, "I reckon you ought to be carrying Mama's old derringer."

I put my hands on her shoulders. "Now, a young lady needs protection, but it might not do, carrying a pistol in Illinois State. You don't want to go giving a bad impression right off. Have you got your knife, though?"

The girl raised her brows and smiled. Clover and Mary Pearl exchanged glances. He said, "Mama forbids it."

I said, "But it's dangerous. A young girl in a strange town. Didn't your pa—"

"I fixed a scabbard on her boot. With strict instructions"—he wagged his finger at her as if reminding her of a conversation they'd already had—"about its secrecy."

"Wait just a minute," I said. I hurried to my bedroom and opened the top drawer on the high boy. I unloaded my two-shot derringer, the little gun Jack had called a 'lady's pistol' when he gave it to me. I took the rounds and the gun back to the parlor and placed them in Mary Pearl's hands. "Take these," I said. "Just in case."

Mary Pearl winked at me. Her dimples puckered, making me sure she'd never be safe in that far-off place. She whispered, "We're both students, you and me! Will you write me? Every week? I hope the mail will come regular. 'Course, you'll be in town, won't you? It will, won't it?"

"Yes, and I will write, every week," I said. "You tell me about your lessons and I'll tell about mine." Though I felt foolish after I said it.

"We have to get on, now," Clover said.

"It's hot. You all drive slow," Chess said.

I said, "You've got your riding saddle, don't you? I think your working one is still in our barn. Well. It's come down to this. I suppose you'd better be getting off. Here, take this." I handed Mary Pearl a new canteen I'd bought for her as a going-off gift. It had a thick canvas on it to cool it and ought to get her down the road all right. She took it and grinned and kissed my face and then she climbed aboard the buggy. A painful knot formed in my throat, threatening to strangle me as she leaned down and I kissed her once more. Of all the foolish things people might say in farewell, all I could muster was a single word. "Mind—" Then I sighed. Her face darkened up, quieting tears.

They pulled out and headed up the road, the big surrey loaded with two trunks, four grips, four brothers and sisters, and pulling Duende, a half-wild stallion fidgeting at his tether behind. I thought of Albert staying behind to comfort Savannah. A man ought to do that, when his children were old enough to push out of the nest. If things were different, I might be there in Savannah's kitchen this very minute, talking and laughing, drinking coffee, shedding sweet tears and hugging each other. He'd be driving his daughter to college.

Mary Pearl seemed cut from the same cloth as me, more than any of my own children, yet I had no claim to her. Glimpses of April clouded my eyes. How separate we were. I always expected my daughter to grow up to be a reflection of myself, but it hadn't happened. Mary Pearl, though, had always been as much a piece of me as my arm.

Mary Pearl waved for a long time, and then before they turned the corner and took the road beyond my line of sight, I saw her head come around the side of the buggy for one last glance. I watched until they went around the curve toward their place and beyond, over the last horizon to the north. She has started a journey from which she will never really return.

Then I pulled weeds and watered and trenched and fought with the soil of my garden until I nearly collapsed from the heat. No matter what I did, I couldn't work the lonesome out of my bones, and no sense dying for it, so by half past two, I went to the house. I pumped a bath for myself, and after cooling off, dressed in a cotton shift to lie on the sleeping porch and wait for the sun to go down so I could go back to work.

*July 1, 1907*

This morning while I hung the wash, Charlie came and stood around for a while, either waiting for something, or couldn't think what he wanted to say. Finally, I heard his voice through the rows of sheets and pants and shirts, "Mama, are you feeling poorly?"

"I'm just fine."

"Are you sure?"

"Yes, son."

"You been quiet."

I tugged the line down with the clothespin in my hand, so I could see his face. "A person can be quiet."

"You ain't sick?"

"No."

"Well, then. Well, Elsa is anxious to take a drive. I told her we'd take the wagon up the road and fetch mail. She says she wants to get out of the house."

I needed to be alone. "Yes. Get the mail. Take your time," I said.

"I've got work to do, but Elsa can't drive a rig, so I want to take her."

"Well, you don't have to explain it to me. I know you aren't shirking chores." As he turned, I said, "Reckon it's certain, this time?"

"Oh, reckon so."

"Acting ornery one minute and crying the next?"

"Yes, ma'am. To make me want to holler."

"Don't be surprised if you get to the end of the yard and she says that's enough. Having a baby makes a girl all nerves."

He grinned and blushed darkly. "Not for good and all, though, right?"

I hugged him and kissed his face, already leathery. Already so much a man. I said, "It's temporary." Watching him bustle around and get ready to take Elsa to the station, I saw Gilbert hop onto the back of Hatch and follow. It looked like a nice time for them, headed up the road.

I'd finished with the chickens when I heard a commotion of horses and shouting, far in the distance. Our yard dogs set up a racket, sniffing the air. I looked out the window and here came our buggy with Charlie whipping those horses, Gilbert riding hard at his side. Gilbert's horse didn't stop at the gate but jumped over the fence. He slid off as slick as if he had no saddle at all, then swung the gate open. Charlie drove them in, then jerked the brake. The wheels locked up, chucking up dirt and rocks, while the animals kept fighting their bits, wild with fear.

Before I got out the door, Chess ran and helped Gilbert and Charlie take the leads on each horse and get the buggy stopped. Almost as soon as it did, Elsa jumped from the buggy and threw her arms around Charlie's neck, then began screaming something at him in Spanish. First I thought she'd taken the maternal instincts too far, then I heard a gunshot. The dogs started barking again.

Elsa's words didn't sound angry but plaintive. She tried to kneel in front of him, shaking his pant legs and crying out, but he stood her up, not letting her sink to the dirt. I didn't catch every word but the gist of it was that she was not about to let him go alone after some outlaws, and that at least they were all safe.

Charlie said three men blocked their way with guns drawn, and one of them fired as they turned the buggy around. Gilbert said he'd wanted to shoot back, but he couldn't risk his horse throwing him for the trouble, so they all turned tail. The men chased them and got their horses in a lather, and halfway here, Gilbert's mount spotted a rattlesnake crossing the road, then it was hell-for-leather toward home, barely getting the horses stopped.

"I'm going after them," Charlie said.

"I'll get my rifle," Chess hollered, and took off before anyone could stop him.

Elsa begged, "No! Tell him, señora. Please! Charlie, you can't."

"She's right," I said. "You can't expect to hold your own against three."

Gilbert said he'd load up more guns and go with his brother. But Charlie looked at Elsa, then at me, then toward the hill where they'd driven so wild only a minute before. He said, "If they were highwaymen, they hadn't got the knack of it. They didn't chase us long enough. They're here for something else."

Gilbert said, "One of them had a big kit of some sort with him. Could be just prospectors."

Charlie answered, "Think prospectors'd greet strangers with guns drawn? They're up to something, having a look around maybe but didn't want anyone to see what they were up to. We surprised them and they figured to scare us away."

"I reckon," said Gil, "they held up a bank or a train or something."

I asked, "How far up the road?"

"About four miles," Gil said.

"It wasn't by the train wreck, was it?" People still keep coming out to look at the wreckage from the Santa Fe that went off its tracks and burned a couple of years ago. Some bring photographers' gear, and some bring shovels, hunting gold they reckon is left in the disaster. They all shook their heads. "Then it's railroaders," I said. "Sure as I'm standing here. Rudolfo's got a parlor full of them and we've chased off more than one in the last six months. They're up to something, all right. Long as it doesn't take place on our land, we'll leave 'em be."

"But Mama," said Gil, "what if they are old Maldonado's men? What if they're coming for us?"

"Well, then they'd be here by now," I said. "Your sister-in-law is Rudolfo's daughter and you won't be using that tone about her father. You *ought* to respect folks you love, son, but you make a big mistake not to respect folks you don't see eye to eye with. Elsa, you stay here with Granny and Chess, and he'll watch out for you both. I think we'd better all ride together."

Charlie said, "I don't want you up there."

"Then get Udell. You and Elsa put off your driving a couple of days. That won't hurt, will it?"

Elsa had started for the house. Charlie whispered, "They can't hold us captive when we might need to get to town. She's having a baby."

Gilbert groaned and said, "Aw, Charlie, for crying up a crick. What a thing to say." He headed for the barn, whipping his hat against his leg and shaking his head.

I smiled and bit my lower lip. "Well, son, she's not having it today."

A loud gunshot and the crack of glass interrupted us, followed by a stream of violent shouts that sounded like Chess's voice. We hurried in the direction of the noise to the side of the house, and came upon Chess covered with dust and hopping mad. He beat at his own arms and legs, knocking a cloud of dirt from his clothes just as he filled that cloud with the sorriest storm of cussing I'd heard yet. Elsa put one hand over her lips. Savannah had been right. The coarseness of my household full of men was not a fit place for a girl.

The boys tried to steady Chess by the arms. He jerked this way and that and commenced to cussing them for helping him. His rifle lay in the dirt and at the barrel end a long scuff told the tale of a round that had gone off while the thing lay on the ground. When Chess finally got settled, he rubbed his nose with his sleeve and said a no-account cat had run across his path and tripped him. Then he said I shouldn't allow so many cats around the place, what a nuisance they were and still mice in the barn and all. He swore he meant to shoot them all.

I hollered at him he'd better not or I'd make him eat them for supper. No cat in sight, either. No space under this adobe house or other place hereabouts for a cat to run to. Our five tomcats spend their time sleeping and hunting in the barn and the bunkhouse. I'll grant they're pretty mean, and not the kind for petting on your lap except the calico Granny likes to hold, but none of them are given to running around the yard in broad daylight. We were on the far side from the bunkhouse.

I figured Chess just tripped on his own feet. I eyed him closely, and he shot me back a look as mean as he could. "Chess," I said, "I was going to ask you to stay here with Granny, but I got to thinking about your army training and I think we need you with us to have a look around. Gilbert, stay with Granny and Elsa."

"Aw, no!"

I took hold of Gil's arm and said, "Wait here. Charlie, saddle your grandpa a horse." Well, Charlie took off with Chess on his heels swearing that the day he needed someone to saddle him a horse, he'd swing himself a noose from the bridge below Albert's place. I turned to Gilbert. "I expect you to do as you're told. I want Elsa and Granny watched over by someone who has got good eyes and a sense of distance."

"What if she has that baby while you're gone? Some upset or other? I don't want to be there alone with her."

"Good heavens, Gilbert, you know a cow takes near a year to drop a calf. Elsa isn't going to have a baby for months. You just guard from outside if it makes you nervous. They'll fix you some lunch and sew. You set on the porch and keep watch."

Charlie, Chess, and I toted firearms and rode in file like we were an army detachment. Then Chess told Charlie to flank off the north side of the road, and pretty soon, Charlie and his horse disappeared into the scrub like a coyote. We came upon those fellows—two men on some seedy horses, pulling a couple of others loaded too heavy with packs. The pack animals were balky and tired. These were tinhorns or they'd have used mules to come this far with that load. We pulled reins and waited while they sized us up. I had them figured right away by the slope of their hats. Easterners for one thing. Worried, for another. Waiting for somebody, was my call. Up to no good for certain.

Chess had a pistol on a belt under his coat. But he kept his hands very still and said, "You boys lost?"

I watched them turn stiff and wary. "No," the taller man said. "We're all right."

I said, "You two see some folks in a buggy with an extra rider come this way?"

"Yeah," the same fellow said. "While back."

"They head to town?" I said.

"Maybe," he said.

"Well, did they pass you or not?" Chess asked.

"Can't say."

The second man volunteered, "They changed their m-minds. Turn-turned around. Like you all should do."

"That so?" said Chess.

"Go on home, c-clodhopper," the second man said.

"I think we'll go ahead and pass you boys. You go your way and we'll go ours."

"Old m-man, I said t-t-t-turn around," the man said again.

We heard hooves. The first man said, "Here comes Luce. Listen, folks. We don't want trouble with you. Just go on. Go to town some other day."

The rider came closer. Charlie rode straight at them with his reins and a pistol in one hand, a lasso in the other. He whipped that loop around the taller man and yanked him from his saddle faster than I could breathe, and pointed the pistol at the other, telling him, "Off your horse. Now!"

After some fussing and hollering, Charlie got those fellows to say who they were waiting for and what they wanted here. The railroad. They had come with stakes and flags, all ready to set up for some new tracks.

"Well," I said, "you're going to have to tell them you failed, on account of you're on our land."

"No we ain't," the second man said. "We got a c-c-court order. Deeded and signed. One fourth of this quarter-section belongs to Señor Rudolfo Maldonado *and* the Santa Fe Railway Company."

Charlie said, "Hand me your court order, and your maps and deeds."

"Aw, get shucked. We don't gotta show you nothin'."

"Yeah," said the first man. "Who are you to be shoving us around?"

"Arizona Ranger," Charlie said, lifting his pocket flap to produce his badge. I didn't know he still had it. "These are my folks, and you're on our land. I could string up the pair of you right now for firing at me and my wife for no cause earlier on this very road. So you'd better find some manners, right quick. Hand over the papers."

The first fellow swept off his hat and said, "M' name's Bill Deacon, Mr. Ranger. Now, we'd never a-shot *you,* directly, we had our orders to chase off anyone snooping around. They're surveying up there and we was told to keep folks off the road that might come down. Now, see, but here's our problem. We don't have no papers, and we're a-waiting on Mr. Ashton Luce to bring 'em. Ranger, sir."

One thing I know is that once they get that track laid, it is going to be blessed hard to unlay it. Another thing I know is that Charlie said he'd quit the Rangers, yet he still carried the badge. Deacon elbowed the other man, motioned with his hat in hand, too. The shorter fellow pulled his cap in a move like a boy will do who's obeying because he has no choice.

He said, "Name's Tick. They calls me Tick. Short for B-b-bob T-t . . ." And then he began to say another name that began with a t but he was caught with such a fit of stuttering he seemed in the grip of apoplexy.

"Never mind, Tick," Charlie ordered. "Suppose we just wait here for Mr. Ashton Luce and let him explain them laying railroad tracks across Prine land you say belongs to Maldonado."

### July 12, 1907

Well, he did explain. Then he allowed us to the station, even clear to town, and promised us passage across our own land to home. Charlie and Gilbert went to town and brought Aubrey Hanna back, but not before they had a chance to do some checking on the town side of things.

It appears Rudolfo has gone and sent lawyers and detectives and looked under every rock and toadstool in St. Louis, and found my dead brother Ernest's floozy wife—no doubt in some brothel. Felicity "Lulu" Prine has taken money for Ernest's birthright, the inheritance of one-fourth of Granny's homestead. Ernest died in the war in Cuba and his son got himself hung for cattle thieving and murder here in Tucson. As the remaining children, when we inherited it, Albert, Harland, and I would have split that parcel in thirds. Then—this was some kind of seven-legged horse—the railroad claimed it has bought from Felicity the right to build right through Mama's land north of my place, clear to the bounds of where Rudolfo's land meets mine. It looked legal on the papers, to us. Chess stuck them up to his nose then held them as far as his arms would reach, and said the same. I don't know if it's possible to sell a birthright, but you'd have to own it first. A judge in town had declared that Felicity abandoned Ernest and their marriage dissolved before Willie got hanged.

Railroaders surveyed every inch of Granny's place.

Thing was, *nobody* could inherit a square inch of that land. Granny wasn't dead.

# Chapter Thirteen

*July 28, 1907*

Once they finished the survey, the rail crew cleared out. All stayed quiet, else I'd not even venture on this crazy notion of schooling. Last night, too hot and still to sleep, I laid awake and stewed it over. I decided not to go. Whatever possessed Udell Hanna to give me that? To say it? Whatever possessed me to react the way I did? Lands, deep inside, I must be every inch a strumpet. Then this morning, every other minute I ask myself what on earth I should do, stay or go. In between those questions, my heart sings like a red bird, as if my thoughts were cutting slices of pie out of the air and gulping it in with my eyes so wide I could see until tomorrow. Now the rain clouds gather in the distance and the air smells of lightning, so I know this heat will go and tonight will be blessed and cool. It gave me the courage to decide to go. Dread and hope crowd my heart at the same time.

It has been hot enough today to kill my chickens. Leastwise, that was all I could figure would put half of them down at once. We were due for a gully washer, from the stillness of the air and the weight of it. The dogs were poorly and we were all mean as snakes, waiting for rain. I needed Savannah to talk with. I looked toward her house as storm clouds gathered in the south and rumbled this direction.

As I heard the first close-up crash of thunder, I kept thinking there must be a way to talk to her. A cool wind swept aside my hair, and I breathed in as if I'd been holding my breath all day. I'll write her a letter.

I raced to the book room and took a paper and found a good pen. Then I opened the ink and tipped the jar to fill the little dam so's I could dip easy. I wrote: "Oh, Savannah. I yearn for your friendship. How long will you hate me?" Rain began to pelt at the windows, so I had to pull them down, leaving just two inches open so the fresh smell and breeze could come in. The letter flew from the table and I set it back. The words were so childish. I turned the page over and began again. "Dearest Friend," I wrote. Wasn't she my dearest friend? The rain became a sizzle like bacon in a pan. I should just go to the house of my dearest friend, but crossing the Cienega in this weather could be treacherous. I wrote, "please forgive me and let us put this fussing aside. If you will let things be and . . ." I tried two sentences and quit. My letter sounded like either a whining kid or a scolding hen. The smell of rain on the greasewood perfumed the house, filling my head with a pleasantness that made it impossible to write any letters at all. I went to bed, leaving the letter unfinished where it lay.

This morning the air was still again, but cool and lovely. I got out early and went down to Udell's place. The rain had softened the garden ground. There he and I planted the rest of his garden, squash, beans, and muskmelon. It may be too late for any good to come of them, but slim chance is better than none. I couldn't talk to him about school. I couldn't question his notion of giving the present or my accepting it to him. I didn't talk to him about Savannah, either.

By noon, we finished and went to my place; he sat on my porch with the door open, brushing mud off his boots. I soaked my hands in soap and water, trying to get dirt out of my calluses. I spoke to the walls in the kitchen, to Granny, Chess, and the calico cat curled in his lap. "I have decided I cannot go off to school. Not with this railroad business hanging over our heads." Through the open door, I saw Udell's back straighten when I said that, but he didn't speak.

Chess said, "Sarah, we can handle things here. Likely if you're in town, you can do some nosing around. If you go, it'd be all right. Charlie's going to be here, n' Gil."

"Where're you going?" Granny said.

"Town, Mama."

"Get me some gingham. Red, if they got it. Or any color'll do."

Udell stood in the doorway, put his boots down at the jamb outside. "Have you changed your mind about wanting school, or do you think your staying here would make Maldonado play any straighter than he's already done?"

I tried to read his face. "There'd be all that driving, every weekend. It's too far."

He turned at a sound in the yard, a cat making way past the sleeping dogs with a hiss and a spit. "It isn't so far you couldn't get home if you had to," he said.

"I don't feel it's right. There is too much trouble going on."

"No one's heard a peep out of Maldonado. You go if you *want* to."

I looked at all their faces. None of them were begging me to stay. Finally, Granny repeated, "If you *want* to. Hear that? A girl don't never get much chance to go her own way, do her own mind. Might be nice for a spell."

"All right, then."

I spent the rest of the week sewing, mending, trying to set things up right so I could be gone four months to town. My heart raced in bursts of excitement, and then I like to cried for lonesomeness, and I wasn't even gone yet. Once in a while, I wondered if I wasn't gone addled too far to figure, and that I was lost in a mix of my past wishes, my mama's "otherland," Savannah's anger, Mary Pearl's new dreams.

Saturday evening, I took a ride bareback, trying to get Hatch to settle, and wandered toward Albert and Savannah's place. After I passed the bend in the road, I could see smoke from their chimney. The wind shifted. The breeze waved the warm salty smell of their supper this direction. I spotted Ezra and Zack a-playing in the yard. I missed those fellows. The scene seemed like a picture painting that moved, and with the lowering sunlight, changed colors. The boys became little figures Mary Pearl had drawn on a paper taken from April's desk.

I asked, "Does she ever think of me?" Hatch looked back in confusion. After studying the ground a bit, I clucked to Hatch and we rode for another half hour, then headed home. There weren't any tracks in the road leading from her place to mine.

## August 10, 1907

Tomorrow I will move to a room in Harland's house, the one Charlie used to sleep in, to be ready for school. I spent a long afternoon with Udell, walking and talking, giving each other directions as if we were both leaving on some adventuresome journey. Finally, he said, "I'm going to miss you, powerfully. I'm sorry I suggested this. It seems like a long time for you to be gone. Do you need me to go with you? Or come fetch you home once a week?"

"Oh, no. You'll have some peace and quiet, I reckon."

"I'd rather hear you hollering at me."

"I didn't holler at—"

"Now, Mrs. Elliot. I remember some pretty cross words aimed at my skull, once."

"You didn't deserve them. Have I said 'thank you' for this you're doing?"

He blinked a couple of times and grimaced. "In a manner of speaking." After a deep breath, he went on. "I'll mind your herd. What else can I do for you? Buggy got wheels? All of 'em round?"

"The boys will look after the cows and Elsa will see to Granny. Mind Chess."

"I'll ask his help sanding all those doors. It'll serve us both."

"Udell, have you been to a university? What's it like?"

"Grammar school was my stock and trade."

*Couldn't we relive that moment you told me, again?* "I promise I'll study."

"Will you promise to . . . come back?"

"Why, of course."

"Aubrey told me Mary Pearl isn't coming back. To him, at least. That she'd changed her mind. Said she sent a letter."

"She told me she wanted to be older before she married him. Not that she didn't love him still."

"He took it pretty final." He looked at me, searching my face, it seemed. "That letter didn't leave much doubt."

"I didn't read the final one. She showed me her first one and I told her to try again. She's young, though. Mighty young. You know I'm coming back."

"To me?"

"Yes, Udell. To you."

Then for a while we didn't need words to say what we needed to say.

## August 26, 1907

Granny and I have moved into two rooms in Harland's house. We spend our days taking his and April's children to the park or plays and sometimes the public swimming pool. Most children played in their old clothes, but there were grown women in the water, too, wearing short-legged skirts and gathered bicycle-pants with half their legs showing. It looked cool and wonderful, but I would never dream of that out in public!

Gilbert will be taking Granny home soon and that will be fine with this household. She has been putting up a mighty fuss, wanting her quilt, worried about influenza, wanting everything from the ranch that I could not bring to town. Blessing acts as if Granny frightens her, and I figure if my mama would do less caterwaulin' and more polite conversation, she'd fare better with the girl.

Today Blessing has brought me a book she wrote herself: eleven pages of a story about a top that fell in love with a dolly, and it asked the little girl who owned them both to marry them. The girl set up a little wedding for the toys. Blessing said she needed a cake. After she asked and then demanded, Rachel refused to make it for her. Blessing said, "Miss Rachel declares it is a unnatural event to have a wedding between a top and a doll. What does that mean?"

I put my finger to my lips and looked about the room secretively. I whispered, "Miss Rachel doesn't believe toys could fall in love."

"Oh!" Blessing gasped.

I nodded.

"Doesn't she know?"

"I suspect her toys never fell in love."

After a bit, Blessing said, "Maybe they did and she didn't pay no attention."

We nodded as conspirators do, and then Blessing read me the story again. Blessing was six. She drew all the pictures and wrote the story, put a cover on it and stitched the pages, just like a real book. There wasn't any rust growing on this child's thinking gear. This book gave proof Rachel wasn't shirking her teaching. If Rachel lacked Blessing's appreciation for the spiritual natures of the toys in one's own cabinet, it was a small failing. Myself, I wish I could wrap Blessing up in cotton candy and gobble her down, as she is far too clever to be easy to manage. That will be her nature all her life, I can see.

Twice a week I visited April and her family. Often Granny and me, but sometimes Story, Truth, Honor, and Blessing went to visit April's children, too. In the evenings I wrote letters to the fellows at home and to Mary Pearl. I feel as if I have been gone forever, but it has only been two weeks. Every bone in me rings with alarm, telling me it is time to go home, but I'm staying here. My uneasiness grows daily and I am quarantined to town for having caught education.

Udell came to town for supplies. Gilbert rode along with him, so we are having a wonderful reunion, eating watermelon and grapes and hard biscuits in the shade of April's back porch where we all pray for a breath of wind. April has recovered from her lying in and she flitted around, making sweet noises like a mockingbird to everyone there, as if she'd arranged a happy play party. She made her children do recitations for us, and served our fruit lunches on white china plates I'd never seen before. As she put the girls down for naps, Gilbert said with a grin on his face, "Mama," he said, "you won't mind meeting my girl for supper, would you? At Uncle Harland's house? I asked him."

Lands, the boy sounded fearful. I swapped a gaze with Udell, and said, "It is his house, I suppose."

"I'm thinking of asking her to marry me, like Charlie did. What do you think?"

I think he'd be too young, too inexperienced with money and the workings of the ranch. Where would he plan to live? In the big house with me and both his grandparents and his brother and wife, a mere boy bringing another wife there? The place was beginning to look like an anthill. "Well, son, I haven't met her yet."

I suspect having Udell in Harland's house seemed as natural as having me, to my little brother, so it went along that with Gilbert bringing a guest to supper, we would send Aubrey an invitation, too. It went along with that, that Rachel put on a fresh dress and combed her hair for a second time that day. In the late afternoon we waited Gilbert's return in the parlor, talking of the heat and yesterday's little thunderstorm, and the plague of mosquitoes it left behind.

At the table, Blessing made a big process of showing me her mosquito bites and counting every one, except two, which, she whispered, were on her backside. Then aloud she said, "The skeeters in the outhouse are terrible fierce, Aunt Sarah."

I wanted to laugh, but Rachel frowned at her.

At six o'clock, Gilbert drove up in the buggy and helped a girl, taking her arm on his own, to lead her up the steps. I took a deep breath. After all, my oldest boy had chosen to marry Elsa Maldonado without any more thought to the whole scheme of things than a whim. Why would I be surprised that here came Gilbert leading that woman from the stage wreck, Miss Charity James?

She squeezed his arm several times, and when he introduced us as if we'd never met, she tried to smile. I don't know whether I managed to look pleasant or not. We sat down to supper with roast mutton, a plate of vegetables and another of risen rolls, and chocolate cake. Charity didn't seem as ragged as she had when I first met her, but I reckon surviving a stage wreck would be trying on a woman's features.

"Mrs. Elliot?" Charity said. "This was a fine supper."

"Well, I didn't make it," I said. "Harland has a hired cook."

"Oh. I cook some. Not as fancy as this. Plain fixings."

"Plain is all right, isn't it, Mama?" said Gilbert.

"Plain is fine," I said. "Better, mostly."

"Gil says you make the best pies in the state. I never could get a hand on pie crust except to get it all tough and it comes out like hardtack."

I said, "Well, maybe you need a little lighter touch, that's all. It's not hard."

Charity giggled. "Mine is. Maybe if I was to try to make hardtack I'd come up with something else for crust."

We all started to laugh, and then Gilbert interrupted, just sober as a judge. "Well, Miss Charity, make biscuit dough and put that on top. Cobbler's as fine as pie any day."

After supper, Charity and Rachel and I got to talking while Gilbert, Udell, and Harland went to the front room. According to her story, Miss James made her living in a ladies' boardinghouse, sewing fancies for rich women in town. I asked her which one, as there are *ladies'* houses and then there are the *other* ones.

"It's Velasquez's Rooming House," she said.

I knew the place, and too easy to check on for her to lie. She used her sewing machine in her room, creating a trousseau for one of Tucson's debutante's coming-out ball, and the girl's mother allowed no flirtatious clothing, but tasteful linens and wools with piping and no lace. She spoke slowly, as if it took more effort than it ought.

Well, then she and Rachel got to talking of dressmaking and pattern fitting, and by the time Gilbert went to carry Charity home, I didn't feel so opposed to her company. When he got back to the house, he asked me straight-out, "Mama, what do you think of this marrying a widow woman a year and a half older than me?"

"She's a widow? I thought she was *Miss* James." I tried to stay calm. Was that the reason she always seemed to be hiding something?

"No. She said 'Mrs. James' to them professors and they called it wrong, and she just never fixed it, because they were so uppity. She was afraid to tell you you'd had it wrong, too. She was scared of everything back then, heading out to start life over and all. There seemed to be so much explaining, she said she just let it go by."

"I know you too well. There's something else. What's she running from, son?"

He paused a long minute. "She told me her husband tried to break a union picket line to find work in California, and got his skull cracked and died. The old boys that did it called her husband and her scabs—isn't that the nastiest thing you ever heard?—and said they'd kill anyone crossing their line *and* their family, to boot. So she packed up her clothes, walked away from their house one day, and bought a ticket east. She never had children, as they'd only been married a couple of months and were waiting until he had steady work. Her folks are dead and she's making her own way in the world. Seemed like a strong upstanding gal to me. I guess I figured to trust her, that's all."

"Where were you planning the two of you to live?"

"Town, I reckon. I'll find a job. I got some ideas."

"Thought you gave up school to be a rancher."

"Maybe I'd start a job as a ranch hand. Work up to foreman. Know anybody hiring?" He grinned.

"I've got eleven cows and twenty-five horses. Zachary could foreman my place. I can't pay you a nickel, either."

"There's another thing I'm thinking doing. I talked to a couple of the old fellows that knowed our pa. Knew Pa. About schooling back East. Did you know I could go to the same academy he did, just like that, account of he took those medals?"

Took medals? Took? Jack paid for them in blood and scars, in time gone from home, in war and death and sickness. Lord. This boy is still a child, trying to make up his mind to be a man. I tried not to sound as irritated as I felt when I said, "Military academy? When you couldn't abide the torment of doing your lessons at a second-rated territorial college where half the pupils are less than fifteen and they can't even qualify most students for degrees?"

He bristled, but tried to keep still. "I'm older now. Got something different on my mind."

"You can't take a wife to West Point."

"I'll just write them and see. Surely not everyone there is a kid fresh from grammar school."

It took all my strength not to reach over and pet his arm like the little boy he seemed. I declare, if there was one of my boys I might have pictured in a uniform, it wasn't Gilbert but Charlie. Taller and stiffer. Rugged, harder stuff. Gilbert was the one who'd pet a newborn horse for months just to temper him for being handled later on in life. Not that the army couldn't use a few fellows with some human kindness, but I reckoned wars were not won on kindness but hard bursts of frightening power that some men seem to have inborn. Like Jack. Like Charlie.

I knew that if I asked Gil whether he was trying too hard to fill Charlie's boots, he'd take offense. Likely run off and do it to spite my words, though he's not a spiteful boy. He's just a boy trying to figure what boots to fill. There was no way for him to do that but try them on, same way Charlie had done with the Rangers. So, I said, "Gilbert, you have to make your own choice on these things. I can't see my own future nor yours. Sounds to me like you have done some growing up, thinking about all this. You just go ahead and write them. Remember, though, if they let you in and you choose to go, you have got to do your papa proud. You've got to show them the stock you come from every step of the way. You'll come out an officer, but you're going to have to shed being a country boy before you ever put on their uniform. Remember who you are. That's all. Make your papa proud."

"I aim to make *you* proud. Miss Charity? Do you like her, then?"

"Well, I reckon if a widow woman was good enough for George Washington, one's good enough for Gil Elliot," I said.

### August 30, 1907

I drove the one-horse buggy to school, to see how long it might take to get there, then I tried the trip riding Baldy, searching out a place to tie him with some shade and water. I looked in the residencies, and wondered if applying for a spot there wouldn't be better, so I could be right next to the library and classrooms. How wonderful to be so close, in case I needed to ask a teacher a question or read extra books to catch up with all the others who have gone to school their whole lives. Yet since my old house is closer to the Carnegie Free Lending Library, it may do well being halfway between so I can use both.

I got a list in the mail of all my studies to put in my scrapbook. I thought I didn't know any teachers, but the names of Professor Osterhaas and Professor Fairhaven fairly jumped off the page. Lands. Never in my days would I have imagined meeting those two haughty rascals again, both of them useless as wings on a toad when I tugged them out of the wrecked Wells Fargo stage. Well, this will be some kind of adventure.

*September 2, 1907. Monday. The University of Arizona. The first of my college days. I have opened this tablet of genuine Collegiate Blue-lined Composition Paper, to keep a record of this, as I am sure by the time I finish here, I shall think upon these—my first—days with fondest memories.*

I drove my buggy to the school just as I'd practiced, my hands trembling, my heart racing. But at the hitching rails this morning not a square inch of open space remained for me. I ended up going down the road, so I'd have to come get my horse at lunchtime and take him to some water. I kept a list printed with the times and titles: "Domestic Science, 8:00, Mathematics, 9:30, General Science, 10:45, English Composition, 1:00, and Latin and the Classics, 2:30–4:00." I had a lead pencil, an erasing rubber, a pen holder, and a little jar of ink in my draw purse, along with my kitchen pistol. Out of sheer habit, I reached under the buggy seat for my rifle, then I smiled to myself and put it back. They have a rule against rifles. I didn't figure they'd mind the pistol, though. It was still Tucson.

Going to school was almost like getting married for the first time—walking in a strange land, surrounded by strange people and smells and a flurry of schedules and names of things that everyone seemed to understand except me. I put on my best face, wore my best dress. I determined to sit at the very front of the class in each room, and copy down every word every teacher spoke.

As I strode across the grounds, some students already had their cadets' uniforms and were marching and singing in a formation. Most of the women are not in a school uniform, and the ones that do wear them have variety, depending on the college each is doing. I'm not sure where I will fall, as I have studied the list of all classes and I want every one of them. Only found a few I don't care to take up—those being Men's Gymnastics, Men's Singing Society, and the football league. There are societies for every pastime under the sun, and some are pure mystery; I cannot feature what a Junior's Glee Club could discuss. Just how much glee can a person contain, day in and day out?

My first class of the day was Domestic Science. Mrs. Everly said we should learn to make white sauce but first we had to sew ourselves the school apron and cap, a little flat getup like April's maid Lizzie wears. I got to wondering if this class taught only becoming a maid, doing someone else's cooking and scrubbing, but Mrs. Everly did not let anyone ask questions. She passed out paper patterns and a hank of white muslin to each one, said they attached the directions to each pattern and for us to get to work, but class let out.

The mathematics professor, Alice McGinty, said we might all call her Miss Alice. Seeing such a friendly and helpful teacher was pleasant. She talked about how some ancient Indians invented the zero, then we started in on sums. I put all in my tablet and looked forward to the next day's learning, added the arithmetic book to my parcel.

A little sawed-off man named Professor Fergus Brown taught General Science. No bigger than a boy, he was dressed up prim in a black suit and a bow tie. He asked twice whether I was looking for someone, and when I said I came as a student, he said, "Well, you should sit by the door," then gave a speech about how important science was, which I took down in my tablet. At the end, he asked if we had any questions about the class, and since Miss Alice was so kind, I asked how we should call him. He gave me a stare and said, "Professor Brown will do." The students around me got very quiet.

After noon, I got to Professor Osterhaas's class. He also asked why I'd come, and did I need something, but I said again, I was a bona fide student. So he showed me to a seat, then read some poetry and talked about things called narrative points of view and how we'd be expected to pay strict attention to them. I wrote that in my tablet and underlined "pay attention." Then came Professor Fairhaven's class in Latin and Classics. I took my usual front row seat, ready for any questions. He kept looking at me like he couldn't place my face. Then he called off the names of students, and when he came to mine, he paused so long that it made me feel plum foolish when he finally said it.

The first Monday came and went so fast I hardly knew what happened. At home I got out my scissors and thread, pulled a line in that hank of muslin and whipped up my apron in about half an hour. Then I studied everything I had written down, sparing a new page of paper for each class, and memorized all of it. Then I went to help fix supper.

Tuesday morning, I wore my new school apron in Domestic Science class, expecting she'd show us that sauce she wanted us to learn. Mrs. Everly asked why hadn't I brought my pattern and cloth to work on. I stood and said, "Here it is, I'm finished." Well, you'd have thought I just shot her best housecat. What I had on was not the school apron, I had not used the directions, nor was it useful that I saved the pattern for someone else, nor did she care that I've been making aprons since my mama taught me at the age of six and could do it with my eyes closed. I couldn't possibly learn sauce if I couldn't learn aprons and since there was only one hank of muslin per student, I was not allowed to try again. I had failed apron.

My first Friday of school, Miss Alice gave a test in mathematics on foundational skills, and since my skills amounted to figuring pounds of moving hoofstock and praying for rain, I failed that too, but in somewhat better form than aprons: three correct answers out of the ten. In Science, I got most of the answers and came out on top of the class. In Osterhaas's English class we read a poem and answered questions, and then in Fairhaven's Latin, I got best in the class. Soon as school was over I headed for Harland's place to pack up my duds for the trip home. Sitting on the front porch as I drove up, Gilbert and Charity James were on two separate porch swings, having lemonade and talking. Gilbert was sitting up stiff as a board, and Charity looked only a little bit less troubled. I nodded to them both. "Evening. You heading home with me, son?" I said. "For I am making tracks to get there before dark."

"No, ma'am. I was fixin' to stay in town until tomorrow. Maybe take a stroll in the morning. Isn't that a nice hat Miss Charity has on?"

"I made it myself," Charity said eagerly.

"It's real fine, hon. I'm just tired and have to hurry or I'd sit and visit with you both." I left them with just a wave a few minutes later.

The sun had gone but it was still summer so I got home by twilight, though it was nine o'clock. Well, when I got there, Chess threw a ring-tailed conniption that Gilbert had stayed in town when he should have been riding with me for safety. But I said Gil wasn't seeing quite straight as he'd had some fine handmade millinery in his line of vision, and I'd give the boy a little room to be smitten for the first time. I'd had too much on my mind to think of needing a rider along, too. Seems we were both served well by our inattention, this time, at least.

Saturday afternoon, as promised, Gil showed up just fine. Later on, Udell and I took a ride. He said he knew how to settle our troubles with Rudolfo without it coming to blows. But his plan to get Rudolfo to settle down was to give over to him and sell out. "I can't sell my mama's land," I said.

"She sold a piece of it to save your ranch. Don't you think she'd sell a piece of it to save her own life?"

"She's pretty stubborn. Still, it's *me* that doesn't want the blessed railroad coming through here."

"Help me push my cows back home. Then we'll go have a talk with Rudolfo," he said, "and see if we can't do this peaceable."

I didn't like feeling as if Rudolfo had some kind of sinister power over my family. Lands, I'd forgotten all about this during my week of school. Now it felt as if school had never happened. After we got the cows moved, I breathed up the smells of the desert. The evening air touched my face, cool and sweet, as we rode toward Rudolfo's place.

When we got over the first hill away from my place, Udell pulled reins and reached for my hand, held it for a minute, then said, "I've been missing you."

I leaned toward him and we shared a kiss. Lands, I wanted to wrap my arms around him, but our horses stepped apart. "I've missed you, too. I need to talk to you, about everything."

"And school?"

"Some of it is better than I imagined. I like my composition and Latin classes."

He smiled and clucked to his horse and moved ahead, not waiting for the rest I intended to say.

We followed an old wagon rut. New tracks cut north before we got to Rudolfo's border, in a direction I speculate could meet the end of that rail spur. I turned my horse toward the next hill so I could see. Udell followed without asking what I had in mind doing. Below that hill, a wash had cut deep and filled with sand. During rain it drained into the Cienega but now it lay dry. Lizards slithered past, changing places from bush to bush at the fringes of sand. The sky faded to green in the east; we had but a couple of hours of light left. The hill itself formed part of the ridge that went up by my place and shifted into loose scrabble where the stage had wrecked, and another half mile up caught up with the stage road. Someone had cut a wide, even place down the side of the wash. We got off our saddles and eased the horses.

"I was going to go see the other side, but I reckon there's no sense in following this," I said. A flicker of light, bright as gold, caught my eye. A coin. I turned it in my hand, passed it to Udell. "What do you expect that says? Due-etch? It's not a peso."

He studied the coin. "Looks like Dutch but spelled odd. Hear something?"

The squeak of wheels echoed up the draw we stood in. We pulled our mounts deeper into the wash and hid, waiting around a bend. Until a month ago, I'd have just continued on my way, but it felt too risky of late. It didn't take long, and I was glad we hadn't poked along slow, because here came a long train of men pushing horses strung together on a tether straight down from one side of the new-cut road, through the bottom of the wash and back up the other side. No sooner had they got clear of the top than a heavy wagon followed by three more just like it rode right through their dust. Teams of twelve mules pulled each dray, and they made good time, straining against the loads, though their passage scarred deep ruts in the dirt up the sides.

"I can tell you where they're headed," he said. "Mexico."

I said, "Those wagoners weren't Mexicans. I heard them talking." I'd heard something like that before, but couldn't place it.

Udell still had that coin in his palm. He looked at it again, saying, "Those were like the ones I saw exchanged south of here a few weeks ago. Why would a bunch of Dutchmen be taking rifles to Mexico?"

"What makes you say rifles?" I said.

"Sarah, I did for the U.S. Army exactly what they are doing, carried hundreds of crates just like those—the very same size and shape—in Cuba. If those aren't boxes of rifles, I'll eat my boot."

I'd not have been surprised to see Rudolfo gathering horses or cows for his new rancho in Cananea, nor wagons full of miners or farmhands. Yet rifles enough for an army? I shuddered with a feeling of recognition mixed with terror. "Springfields?"

He held out his hand to help me mount my horse. "I'll tell you what I do know. If there isn't already some kind of trouble in Mexico, there's going to be soon. The mine strikes and the killings last summer were only the start. And it's all coming right through our back forty. That means it could seep back up this way, too."

I climbed on and took my reins.

"You have business here, amigos?" a voice said.

A man on a bay horse, his outfit glimmering with Mexican rondelles and tassels, waited halfway down the far wall of the wash. He had a Sharps across his lap and leaned over the piece lazily, as if he didn't need to worry whether we understood the threat he made. He must have followed the wagons a mile back, staying out of the dust. We'd stepped out of our hiding place right in front of him without checking for more people coming.

Udell swung into his saddle and said, "No, sir. We were out for a pleasant evening ride and got knocked off the road by some mule teamsters. You look out for them, if you're headed that direction. They're not going to slow down for anybody. Good evening, mister." He clucked to his horse and we headed for the side of the wash.

The click of that Sharps hammer nocked back on its spring stopped us. "I think you'll wait here a while," the stranger said. "You've got no business watching here."

"Watching?" I said. "This is my land. You're the one who should be answering about business."

The Mexican laughed. "Señora, it's just a little road through a little piece of land. No fence. Do you see a fence anywhere? I think it's not your land. I think it's Maldonado land."

"Well, I think you should ask Rudolfo Maldonado about that," I said. The man's eyes widened at the sound of Rudolfo's given name, as if he didn't expect I'd know him.

Udell cleared his throat, trying to get my attention. "We're headed home, mister. We mean no harm to you or anyone else. Out for a ride. Like you said, no fence. It's just a little road across a little piece of land. We have no weapons, so you'll oblige us and put away yours. We've got no intentions other than a nice evening ride. Now, we'll be going home, and bid you farewell."

"Pinkerton?" the man said.

Udell looked from me to the man. "No," he said, "name's Hanna. Don't know a Pinkerton."

The Mexican laughed and unnotched the rifle. "Let us all pay our respects to *el don*. Perhaps Señor Maldonado will want to offer you his hospitality. Perhaps not." We rode ahead of the man to Rudolfo's front yard. Then he motioned us into the house itself, where we waited at the doorway. I kept wondering if obeying every whim Rudolfo got under his hat was something in Udell's character I had missed before. In a room full of men, our fancy-dressed escort spoke to Rudolfo in whispers while the both of them watched us.

None of the fellows in the room stood nor made any move as Udell and I stood in front of Rudolfo's big desk like scolded children. I kept picturing the time Rudolfo'd been shot, and I helped him get dressed, union suit and all, and it helped me not feel so shaky in front of him now. He stared at me a long time, without any expression, ignoring Udell's presence. After a bit he said, "I want to make this very clear to you, Sarah Elliot. From now on, anyone who sees your people on my land will shoot first and talk later."

"I was on my own land," I said. "Unless you've forged papers to steal that, too."

He didn't so much as blink. "This man found you spying on my business. Now you accuse me of theft and fraud. These are very serious charges."

Mighty fancy words he tossed out. I couldn't think of anything to say, but I knew him enough to know that a long silence would make him squirm just like he had been trying to force me to do. So I waited. Someone behind us cleared his throat.

Udell fidgeted, too, and then when he couldn't stand the silence anymore, he said, "We were out for an evening ride. Far as we knew, we were on Prine land. Don't know how you can call that spying. This man of yours pulled us in here at gunpoint. We could call that kidnapping."

Rudolfo looked at Udell with hatred. "I have in my possession signed and sealed government surveys. Documents, deeds, and records. The land is mine. The road is mine. The railroad tracks that will soon stop there are mine. Trespassers could get hurt. It will be too easy for people who aren't on their own land to . . . be hurt."

"Why, Rudolfo," I said, "what are you up to, cutting through my place, there? All those mules? You must have bought a load of brand-new furniture for your new baby. Is that baby born yet? Not much longer, eh? Did you know you are also going to be a grandpa? *Abuelo 'Dolfo.* Do you think he'll call you *tata*?"

"Go home, Sarah Elliot," Rudolfo said. His eyes glistened. Yet just as I might have felt afraid of him, I saw a wisp of sweat on his temple. I knew better than to back down from a cur's threat at that moment. So I waited. I cocked my head at him and glared straight into his eyes, listening to a clock somewhere ticking. Fourteen seconds.

He blinked.

Then I turned to go. Udell followed me, silent. A man just coming into the room blocked my way and I nearly bumped him. He stood taller than Udell or Rudolfo or any other man in there. His hair was blond as new corn silk, with fair skin and golden-green eyes. I'd never seen a person that color before, and it startled me. *"Con permiso,"* I said, and tugged at Udell's sleeve. We made a hasty retreat to the border of my property.

•

Sunday morning, Udell came to my place before we got the dishes laid out for breakfast. He just opened the door and came in, too, without a knock. He was breathing hard. Finally, he said, "The garden's salted." He pulled a handful of coarse salt from his pocket and held it so I could see.

I felt tears of panic coming, so I turned from the sight. "Have some eggs and biscuits. We'll come help you with it. It's not tilled in, is it?"

"No."

"This land is ninety percent alkali. We'll save it. After breakfast."

So on our only day of rest, the boys and Chess and I worked with Udell on our hands and knees, picking rock salt out of the topsoil, one grain at a time. Even Granny got down and helped, although Udell about had a conniption and told her to rest. By sundown, we were aching and tired, ready for a big supper and a bath, but no one had stopped to make it. We ate bread and apple butter sandwiches with canned beans and coffee before we all went our way. When the fellows went out to do the feed, Gil came back to the house looking sorry and worn.

He found the rest of my chickens dead in the pen. This time it wasn't the heat. Maybe last time it wasn't, either. Not one pullet had been left alive. My heart broke. Now we had to go out and build a bonfire to get rid of them, because we couldn't risk one of the dogs getting poisoned from them. The clock chimed ten before we got cleaned up for bed. That was the first time it crossed my mind that I should have been back in town before that hour. It was Sunday.

I had a hundred reasons not to return to town. I declared I wouldn't, but everyone put up such a fuss, giving reasons for me to go, that Monday I packed up as usual, just a day late. I felt plenty of guilt loading my books into the buggy. Nary a one had been opened. May as well have left them in town.

Since I'd miss the day of school, I decided to go to the land office first thing. I made a loop down to Udell's place to check on the garden again. He was out watering it as I drove up, and the culprits must have thought they'd done all they needed, for it had been undisturbed during the night.

The second Tuesday of my schooling, at eight in the morning—an hour at home that usually saw me having made and cleaned up a full breakfast for anywhere from five to twenty people, fed chickens, gathered eggs, watered the stock, hauled water to the garden, weeded it, and put on beans to cook for supper, Mrs. Everly scolded me like a little child for not having made a maid's cap. That woman surely needed some castor oil. There wasn't a thing I could put my hands to that she didn't have a hard word about. Alice McGinty made up for it by having some fun, and while I scratched my head and erased my third mistake on the same problem, I got to thinking how much studying mathematics resembled taking castor oil.

Wednesday I went with April to a tea, and to supper, and those were hours I should have spent with my eyes in my books. For the first time I worried whether I could get used to studying on a timetable instead of finding minutes for reading wherever they lay, weeks and days apart. I must study more and visit less, though I've already promised her I would look after the children Thursday while she and Morris go calling.

Friday, after Mrs. Everly's morning scold, I went to the president's office to request a move from Domestic Science to the science of biology or, hopefully, botany. I told him I own books on botanical studies myself, and that was a subject I was acquainted with and should not involve making a foolish headcap. The president said that if I couldn't manage to learn the simple lessons of domestics, I'd be a complete failure in botany—a man's subject.

I tried to make my stand, but he just kept saying how I, like each new student, was on a trial run. My teachers had held a meeting about me and they had discussed my future. No, he said. It was absolutely to my *educational* benefit to make a dang-blasted tussie-mussie mobcap! Then, to step back into Professor Brown's classroom when half the lesson was gone, why that man was in a dander for another entire hour.

Professor Osterhaas gave us an assignment for next week, a theme on the nature of cosmic elements such as spring, dawn, or starlight. I have read plenty of pretty words over the years, but never in my life had to "reflect" on cosmic elements. Professor Fairhaven had grown as charming and pleasing as a man could be. Most of those young people had not heard of Homer, much less owned all his works like I did. When he asked a question, I knew the answers and found myself proud that my hand went up plenty of times.

My searching at the land office was useless. I couldn't find any proof that Rudolfo had my land nor that the railroad had bought anything. Yet I'd seen those papers with my own eyes.

By the end of the second week of school, I felt glad to head home, but I needed a packmule for all the books I carried. I spent the weekend on studies.

Every Monday from now on there will be an exam in mathematics. Tuesday, in Domestic Science we had a test on white sauce, nothing but pan gravy made with butter instead of drippings and so bland a hungry dog wouldn't care for it. I put red pepper in mine. Mrs. Everly claimed I'd done a mortal sin. The students call our science teacher Brownie, behind his back. There's no call to be disrespectful, I'd say.

Professor Osterhaas handed back my cosmic essay, then spent a while explaining how I hadn't paid attention to my points of view. Lands, how many can a person own? My point of view is the one I have and no other, and I am lost like a bat in the sunlight here in this place. I found myself looking toward the little watch pinned to my blouse, and the Regulator hanging on the wall, wishing the time would evaporate so I could drive home.

### September 30, 1907

April's boy Vallary was waiting for me when I got to Harland's, saying the baby was sick and April needed me to come. Instead of heading to the ranch, I spent the weekend with April and her family. Tennyson, still not as long as her name, snuggled feverish and quiet in my arms as if she were my own. By Sunday, as I got set to return to Harland's house and set things right for school, Tenny seemed worse. April said she quit nursing, too, and so we put some hot packs on her bosom in case her milk backed up. I stayed all night, and Tennyson cried most of it. By the time we got the poor babe asleep, the children fed and dressed in the morning, I was ragged. I missed Domestics out of exhaustion.

I rode Baldy to school and dashed to Professor Brown's General Science. When I hurried in, plum tired out, a few minutes late and embarrassed to boot, Professor Brown paid so little attention to my coming through the door I expected it had not interrupted him a bit. He went on and on about chemists' compounds and what things make alloys. He always took the longest route on any short talk, saying a hundred words when five would do. When he asked the class for someone to name a chemical part of water, without thinking I blurted out, "Gas."

The only thing that had been in my mind had been getting on to the next point, but he came to my desk, which sat just beside his, and said, "Why are you still here?"

My heart pounded. "Do you want me to sit somewhere else? Professor," I added.

"Why don't you plant yourself on your rocking chair at home and make room for a real student? This is not a hobby room, Mrs. Elliot."

My face flushed with heat. The room fell silent. "I apologize, sir. Professor Brown." I watched as he walked behind me, his hands balled in fists behind his back. For the first time I turned around. The students looked away from my gaze, nervous and picking at their books.

At lunch I went to check on Tenny and see how she fared. Not much changed, still a slight fever, still fussy. I rocked her a little and thought about Professor Brown. Then I had to hurry back to the school.

At home in my bedroom, the harder I worked the further behind I seemed to fall. I just couldn't balance all the reading and papers and studying with Truth and Blessing dashing up and down the stairs being musketeers one minute, and Honor and Story staging Gettysburg under the dining table the next. "Rachel, please," I begged. "Would you let me have two hours of quiet? At least try to keep them off the stairs and out of my room." So off they went to the park, but in the silence, the very ticking of the clock confounded my mathematics and thundered in my aching head.

One Friday afternoon when Professor Osterhaas got called away during the reading of one boy's story about an Indian fighter, the class got talking. Someone said, "Well, I happen to know Geronimo killed a hundred men. And two hundred women. Some worse than killed."

"No he didn't," another boy said. "It was only a hundred of each."

"Say, Foster, that was a great story you wrote. Sure was realistic."

"No it wasn't," I said. All eyes turned to me. Someone grunted.

Foster, the boy whose story they had interrupted, said, "What about it, lady?"

I straightened my paper and laid down my pencil before I spoke. Jack had been there. Had chased the Apache chief across Mexico and through the Dragoon mountains, until he finally gave up. It had rained so much. Jack came home burning with fever. I said, "Geronimo killed four people after Army soldiers slaughtered his family and all his uncles and aunts and cousins. Reckon I hardly blame the man. I didn't want them to capture him. Ulzana was the one to be afraid of."

Someone muttered, "Ha. I'm glad they killed them all. Redskins are better dead than fed."

"That's not what I said." I felt my face grow warm.

The room got quiet and stayed that way for a very long minute. The door opened, Professor Osterhaas returned and flexed his eyebrows with a smile. "Having a good discussion?" he asked.

Foster said, "Some people in the room didn't like my story, Professor."

"Well," Professor Osterhaas said, "let's have some pro and con, then." So he lined people up to say they liked or didn't like the story.

The boy named Foster asked me, "Lady, who was that you said? That other redskin? I never heard of him."

"Ulzana. He was a Chiricahua Apache. One of—"

The Regulator on the wall chimed. People folded their books, but Professor Osterhaas held up his hand. Foster said, "And he was meaner than Geronimo?"

A scene of chaos and stumbling horses ran before my eyes like a dream visited in a breath of time, complete with the deafening war cries of Indians, shots fired, the crackle of a burning house. "He was a fierce warrior," I said.

"How do you know that?" he asked.

My rifle had gone empty. Ulzana rode toward me, spear raised, and I pulled the trigger twice, uselessly. Jack Elliot had fired the shot that crippled Ulzana's horse and saved my life. I caught a glimpse of dusty blue uniform, the glint of a saber through clouds of dust and gunpowder, heard the squeak of saddle leather and soldier's boots grinding against stirrups. Jack's hands, bandaged and bleeding, touched my cheeks, and his eyes pierced my heart. I stared into the unlined, never-shaven face before me, wide eyes as innocent of pain and experience as April's new baby. "I just do," I said.

"Aw, you're making that up," he said, and left to catch up with the other boys.

# Chapter Fourteen

*October 5, 1907*

The school term is near halfway through and I can hardly believe it. Every moment I'm in town, I worry about what is happening at home. Udell has got up a garden after all, and he is keeping watch with his small flock of chicks and cows until he is so tired he can't work on the house. I fear the work at home piles up. Granny and Chess are not able to keep up, Elsa is touchy with baby sickness, and while Charlie and Gilbert handle the rougher work, no one has made soap nor scoured the floors nor a hundred other things that need doing.

I write letters every few days to Udell, each time thanking him for his gift of schooling, although each one I close brings a heavy feeling of betrayal, for my doubt in my ability to keep on with this schooling grows daily. Along with it, strangely, grows hunger for more. I want not to return home at all. I want to stay and find more classes, let out on the ones too tormenting to abide and just take the wonderful ones. Still, I notice often how separate I am from the other students.

On my way to my horse one afternoon, three boys on bicycles nearly ran me down. For some reason I can't tell, I stopped that very day and bought some Hagan's Magnolia Balm: "Guaranteed to keep a woman from looking like a hag before her time." I planned to put it to use while I was a student. Heaven knew it wasn't my "time."

Every minute of every weekend at home, I spend thinking of school. My unfinished assignments pile up like laundry from a dozen children. Then there's the work I give to myself, such as after Professor Osterhaas told each person how to fix their essays I rewrote mine twice, determined to get a decent mark in that class. Also, I worry that Harland's children need more care than Rachel can manage alone. April needed me there in town more than I realized. Once Tennyson's fever left, April wanted my opinion about wallpaper or diaper rashes and thumb-sucking. Gilbert came to town too much to visit Charity, and makes himself at home at Harland's place. When I asked if he wasn't leaving too many chores to Charlie, well, Chess said to let the boy go to town if he wanted. Fine way to raise a spoiled fellow, if you ask me, but no one did.

Letters from Mary Pearl tell me of her successes. I see through the handwriting more than her words, for she is homesick but not lonely, challenged but not defeated, and so I write her about my professors, and tell her all sorts of things I'd never say to another soul. When I headed for the ranch, I took her letters and the drawings she sends and I put them there in my bureau drawer.

Friday I rode home in a drizzling rain. By the time I got there, my throat was sore as if I'd been swilling lye. It rained all night and all morning, Saturday. The rain finally quit and the air is prickly with cold, and when we go out to feed, damp needles of ice stab our faces. Mighty cold for this early. After lunch, Charlie left to ride to Udell's place to check on the ten head of cattle he had there and to have a look around. He said they'd come back for supper, so Granny and I put a roast of beef in the oven with some onions and carrots, and settled in for a couple of hours of sewing. It was all I could manage, feeling poorly enough I wished I was in bed.

The fellows cleaned and sharpened knives and tools, fixing boots and playing checkers. I felt raw and poorly, but tried to study, out of desperation, I suspect.

Gilbert picked halfheartedly at his guitar, staring into the fire, starting pieces of song and never settling on something we could hum to. I worked arithmetic problems until my head ached, and I had to put the books aside. I stared out the window at the gray and dismal sky. I started a pot of coffee to have something hot on my throat. Gilbert got tired of plinking his guitar and went to the book room.

Granny has been piecing another quilt, this time a redwork piece. Granny had dozed off, quilt scraps still between her fingers, needle poised for duty but quiet when a distant rattle caught my ear. "C- C- Comanches," she said.

"Chess!" I hollered. "Chess! Where are you?" The sound of running horses grew louder, and two more shots sounded near at hand. Then a whole string of shots followed like firecrackers. "You all, get away from the windows. Elsa, take Granny to the kitchen. Gilbert—" But Gilbert ran out the door with no coat and a pistol in hand, headed toward the gate. "Gilbert! Charlie!"

Before I could get a rifle in my hands, the door was flung open from the outside and in rushed Charlie. "Maldonado's boys. They killed one of Udell's cows and then chased us off his land, Mama," Charlie gasped. Then Gilbert came in, bringing the last of a hard chill clinging to him, and he closed the door, pulling the bolt in place. It moved stiffly, since we had only latched it once or twice before. Charlie went on, "He had five sorry-looking vaqueros waiting there, and when we stopped them to ask where they were going one of them pulled out a shooter. Like *we* were trespassing. I should have never gone down there without a pistol."

"Anyone following you, waiting for someone to stick their head out the door?"

"They turned tail when Gil came running out and winged one of them with his first shot."

We heard a rattling sprinkle of more gunshots, not far away. I turned to Gilbert, who looked pretty trembly. He gulped and said, "I'm going down to the old *señor*'s place and tell him a thing or two."

"No you're not!" Charlie hollered the same words just when I did.

Elsa ran to Charlie's side and the two of them whispered for a minute. Then Charlie said, "Mama, this is about him being angry with us. We're going to leave. We knew this might come. We've got to go away to keep you all safe."

Here came Granny, lugging a box that looked to weigh as much as she did. It was the shot box we used to carry, about half full of ready-loads. None of them needed packing or loose powder, thank goodness.

"Mama, what are you doing?" I asked, taking it from her.

She said, "Put this by the window. It's full of shot and lint and powder. I'll load for you. Always did it for your pa and before that, too. We'll teach them who's got the pluck *and* the lead." She shook her little bony fist toward the window. "Just show yerselves, you varmints! My Sarah can put the eye out of a tick from a hundred yards!"

"Mama," I said, "it's over, for now. Anybody seen Chess?"

Armed like bandits ourselves, we scoured the house in the next few minutes but didn't find him. Gil went to the barn with Clover; Charlie checked the smokehouse. Around the side of the house, it looked to me like prints from Chess's boots left the yard and went over the hill toward the south on foot, so I followed them.

I could hear a man's voice. The muddy ground made tracking easy enough. I looked everywhere but behind myself, and listening as I was to the voice, heading toward it, I stopped to turn around. I felt plum startled to find Elsa trailing after me. We walked on, following the sound, and came upon Chess standing with his back to us. He laid down a stream of the sorriest curses ever known, and as rangy as he can be, I never heard the like from him.

I hollered over the commotion, "What in heaven's name is wrong with you?"

"Missed every dad-blasted one of them. Damn it to blazes! Not a shot. This old rifle is bent. The sight is off and these loads are wet. Couldn't hit—and I was always a shot! Not a thing. Not a god—" He caught himself up, seeing Elsa at my side. "Son of a gol-damned—Tarnation, girls. Get back to the house. Can't you see when a man has got some cussin' to do?"

I said, "Come do it in the yard out of their line of fire," and turned Elsa around, taking her hand, and we hurried back to the house. Partway there, I chanced a peek at her face. I expected pale, well-mannered shock, but saw a smirk.

Elsa said, "Señor Chess makes me very thirsty!"

"Some men *are* saltier than others," I said. Then we just had ourselves a bitter little laugh, and got inside the house.

The night passed peacefully enough though I sank into *la grippe* and tossed the night through. In the morning I had chills that rocked me in the bed, and could not make a sound. I stayed in bed until supper, then I got up to have a cup of hot coffee. Elsa felt sick, too, but not with fever. I moved slow as cold molasses. Chess sat in his chair by the fire for a long time, watching me while I sipped the cup. I had to whisper. "Something on your mind?"

"You get that rifle sighted in yet?"

"No. Leave it in the kitchen here. I'll try it tomorrow. Maybe it got dropped."

"That Hanna's expecting you to marry soon's you get done with this dad-blasted schooling. Isn't that why you were asking me about Texas? Ready to run?"

I lifted the coffeepot using my skirt wrapped around the metal handle, poured him a cup next to mine.

"You'd be free of an old worn-out boot. Charlie and his girl will be here. Gil, too. *You* shouldn't run off to Texas. *I'll* go back to Texas. You'd be free."

"I'm not taking up living with Udell to get shed of you. It's already settled with him. He's building you a room. I'm not going without you, Chess. Mama, either."

"Fah!" he said with a wave of his hand.

"That's exactly the kind of conversation I couldn't live without," I said. "The curious vocabulary of a right ornery man."

Then he said, "I saw that house there. He said he's thought of a deal where you keep this here place and let your boys live on it. Sell it to 'em for a dollar. He asked me what I thought and I told him it was the damnedest thing."

Udell hadn't said a word of this to me. "Only he didn't mention where you fit in," I said, and went to fill our cups again. "What'd you say?"

"Nothing. I came home to pack my duds and head east."

"Not while I've got this tornado brewing with Rudolfo, you're not." I started to feel my voice coming back. "I can't go to school and have to worry about this here, if you're gone."

"Can't hit the broad side of a barn. No use staying around. You're leaving, too."

I stood and put my hands on both hips, saying, "Well, aren't you the sorry old buzzard? I haven't asked you for fancy target shooting in all these years and suddenly your aim is off one day and you're cashing in and heading out, and never mind what in thunder I'd do without you? If that isn't the lowest, cussedest thing. I knew you were a tough old bird, Chester Elliot, but I never thought you'd slip so low as to leave me when the chips were down. Just because there's change on the wind and lightning in the air, you aim to take off and desert the family that's counted on you all these years. Never mind the patches I sewed on your behind nor the biscuits I cooked nor a fireside that's been your home as much as mine all these years, you are just leaving me to the wind, just like that! Well, I swan!" Then I left the room and went to find Granny.

I woke her from a nap in the parlor, and said, "Mama? You know if I marry Udell Hanna, you're going to have to move to his new house. Are you going to come, or not?"

"Oh, one chair is as good as another," she said. "Never had no root to speak of."

"Fair enough," I said. "If I don't marry, we'll stay put."

"You sure are in a fuss. Indians again? I'd sure like some soup for dinner."

"I'll make you soup, Mama, tomorrow." Chess had followed me into the room and stood right behind me. "Chess?" I said. I took hold of the sleeve of his shirt and pulled it. "If you won't come with me, I won't marry him."

"Aw, honey," he said.

Then, for the first time in all our lives together, he put his arm around my shoulder. His hands patted my back as if he thought I'd break. I felt tears heat up behind my eyes and pushed him away. I said, "Now, get along. I'm sick and I've got to get to bed. Straightening out your rope was all I had in me."

Sunday afternoon, I couldn't go back to town. I felt so weak and ill it was hard to breathe. I'd have to quit. Well, the boys told me students were allowed to be sick and stay home, and to just lay up and get well, so I did. It was pretty near accepted that with all the new folks around everyone would be sharing their sickness, too. For near a week I got coddled on by my family and by Friday I grew plum right again. All the while in bed, I caught up on all the papers and readings, too. I felt joyful when Sunday rolled around and it got time to head back to town. Until I got to school.

*October 21, 1907*

Although Brownie was mean as a boot full of cholla, Mrs. Everly made me want to draw swords every time I laid eyes on her. The harder subjects may have been things I didn't understand, but that Everly woman just made me feel a fool over things I've been doing as natural as breathing, my whole life. I decided to let myself out of Domestic Science to preserve the common good and keep myself out of jail.

In mathematics I scored a passing mark on a paper. I felt pleased, but such a stack of work awaited and they were so far ahead, by the time I got to Brownie's class I was pure sorry I had laid off sick. His rambling lectures have nothing whatever to do with the tests he gives, and I kept remembering that when Charlie and Gilbert dropped out of school last year, three weeks before final examinations, Charlie had complained that I didn't know what they were up against, and swore the geology professor had been unfair and cantankerous. That teacher had been this Fergus Brown, a little squirt no bigger than my right arm. Brown had quailed my boy Charlie, a man who had been an Arizona Ranger and was tough and smart as anyone you'd care to know. I piled up my books and notes and lugged them to Professor Osterhaas's class feeling like the tail end of destruction.

Professor Osterhaas asked us to write a theme on "What I Want." It seemed simple enough. He would require us to read them aloud, and each person must learn to express himself well. I put that on the top of a new page in my tablet. What I Want. I thought about schooling, and my family, and my home. I thought about going on to more schooling, mostly, and the railroad should go bankrupt. Rudolfo should get friendly again. My mama to get her thinking back. I made a list and connected the things on it with dashes. I was ready. I quit carrying the pistol. The place was like home.

Days later, after two people read their essays on "What I Want," and the whole class discussed them, I decided to write mine again. Then I went to Professor Fairhaven's class early one day, and sat clear to the back to watch and see if folks filled in around me or moved away like I was a snapping turtle thrown in their fish pond, just like in Brownie's class. I took out my Latin primer and the notes I had, for I'd translated the lessons for the rest of the week.

Fairhaven closed the door, fiddled with things on his desk then walked around the room. I shifted my feet as he stopped in front of me and sat on the desk across the aisle. "Afternoon, Miss Elliot—Mrs. Elliot—so easy to forget. Doing well in this class?"

"I like your class fine, sir."

"You haven't made many friends, though."

"I 'spect not, sir."

"Well, count me as one, would you? I find you are quite the student, after all."

After all? Had I struck him as a lunatic before I took his tests? He kept talking but I quit hearing what he said. Others came in and I felt glad for the interruption, for he was just too smiley. They did sort of shift away from my seat, but eventually the seats filled because there were so many students.

After class, Professor Fairhaven asked me to ride him in my buggy downtown after school. He said, "Since you've been sick, I'd be happy to provide extra tutoring." Well, a nervous blush rose on my cheeks, the way he stared at me. After a nice talk he shook my hand when I left him at the bank.

As I drove, I made a decision. It wasn't so bad I couldn't handle this just like I'd handled every other mountain I've come across. I would write Udell and tell him to wait until I had all the school I wanted. He could wait for me and I'd find a way to keep on going to school until there were no classes I hadn't tried. I planned to stay in town this weekend to study, so he would have time to think on it before next we met.

When I got home, Harland's household exploded in sheer pandemonium. Story and Honor had Truth's picture book and dangled it out the attic vent just as Blessing fell off the back porch rail where she'd been trying to walk with her eyes shut. Rachel called the maid who broke into tears and nearly swooned at the sight of Blessing's bloody neck and pinafore. I got Blessing on Baldy and jumped on behind, and told Rachel to follow us to the doctor. Yet Rachel didn't ride, couldn't hitch a harness, couldn't leave the three little ruffians without them burning the place to the ground, so I, along with two nurses and a doctor, held Blessing down until they could give her a breath of chloroform while they put two stitches in her chin. The poor child felt in a terror when she awoke, and both of us were wringing wet with blood, but we had no choice but to ride through town looking a mess. The nurses were kind and gave us sheets, so we wrapped our bloody dresses in white sheets. I told Blessing we looked like we were wearing big tortillas, and she laughed, holding her chin. To keep her mind off anything sad, every few minutes I'd give her a squeeze and call her *burrito,* or ask her if she was a tortilla filled with beans. All the terror was over when she proudly displayed her war wounds to her brothers. The boys gaped in awe, begging permission to touch the stitches, which of course she denied.

I got Blessing to bed that afternoon by promising to do my reading in her room while she slept. I stared at the stack of books and papers I trucked into her room and spread across the dresser. I stood lost in a dust storm of schooling and family, a constant panic at being so far behind in some areas, so yearning in others.

The next day after two tests in mathematics to catch up with the class, I knew even if Professor McGinty turned my scores upside down so that 17s were 71s, I'd still not pass numbers. I felt more akin to my boys' sentiments when they let themselves out of school than I ever thought possible. When Miss Alice asked me to stay behind the other students, I sat at my desk as they tiptoed out, feeling childish and scalded. Well, we had a good long talk. By mutual agreement, I have now let out of Mathematics, too. That leaves only General Science, Composition, and Latin. I never knew you could take part of school, but Miss Alice says to go ahead and finish the rest, and try again next term, so I promised I would. Next term? Of course. I'll take it next term. By the time she and I finished, I'd missed half of Brownie's class again, so I went to the library to study.

I sat amidst row upon row of books. I ran my fingers across some leather bindings. I pulled out *The Life of Major General Andrew Jackson,* by John Henry Eaton. Why couldn't I drop Brownie, too, and take up some good history class? I sat and read and read, until I'd missed Osterhaas's class and half of Fairhaven's. I slipped in just before class let out, purely numb with indecision.

Professor Fairhaven asked me to ride him downtown again. He told me I was clever, and quite charming. Purely filled my ears with flattery. If he'd tried that when I first met him, I'd have scorned him good, but I found myself lapping it up as if I longed to hear more. I left him at the barber shop with a wave and went on home. That evening, when I carried a letter to Udell to the stand by the front door where Rachel would take it with her own letters the next day, I passed a mirror hanging by the entry and paused. The face that looked back at me appeared startled, and not for want of Magnolia Balm.

From inside looking out, I had no sensation at all that I looked or spoke differently than other students. More than that, my clothes were not stylish, Magnolia Balm did not change the fact that I had passed eighteen some years back. That boy Foster had awakened memories with a story he knew nothing about. I fought Ulzana before some of those students were born, never mind that I had been just a child then, myself. Sitting in the classroom, I had felt sure I belonged in the company of like minds. I tried to be one of them, forgetting the miles traveled, miles that must have contributed to having failed equally at aprons and mathematics.

I slipped my letter back into the pocket of my apron. I went to the kitchen, and dropped it into the stove. I should just go home, back to what I understand. From upstairs, Blessing's voice called me.

Rachel was beating eggs for a cake. Aubrey Hanna will join us for supper. He came early to visit while she and I put food on the table. He must resemble his mother, for he was very different from his father. When Harland, Aubrey, and Rachel went to the parlor to talk after supper, I asked them if they'd excuse me so I could study my lessons and write a letter for Aubrey to take to the ranch tomorrow.

I held my pen above the paper for a great while. I wanted to quit school and go home. I wanted to run to Udell and at the same time to hold him at arm's length—make sure no more cows got killed, no more old folks had shot at the clouds—I wanted to stop time so I could go to school, but only the way I wanted it, not the way they gave it. I was not a schoolgirl.

I said to the bureau, "I shall write this: 'My Dearest Udell, your gift of the one thing I've spent my life hanging all my wishes on, a University education, cannot be more appreciated by another living soul, and yet I would like to throw it away because the students shun me, and I am in sure peril of failing this semester due to having learned at my mother's knee the difference between pan drippings and churned butter. I have unnaturally enjoyed the attention of a professor on an innocent buggy ride although I appear to be somewhat over the age of all students, and I have lost my backbone. I feel as childish as Blessing Prine, who is even now pitching a fit in her bedroom, being made to go to bed at half past seven, even though the doctor told her to rest.'

"Or this. 'Dear Udell, I cannot go back, as I am unpopular as a goat in church and between General Science, Mathematics, and Domestic Science, this school has reached a level of unpopularity *with me* that is beyond measure, therefore I plan to act an ungrateful wretch and waste your gift and quit and come home and marry you if you'll still have me and forget this nonsense.' "

Blessing slipped into my room without a word, stared at me for a moment, then crawled up on my bed and wiggled herself into the covers, from which she faced me. I put down the pen, blotting the tip, and waited.

"Who were you talking to, Aunt Sarah?"

"Myself, I reckon."

"Did she answer you?"

"No, not directly."

"Story pinched my arm. N' I have stitches in my chin, n' ever'thing."

"You'll have a scar," I said, forgetting her age.

"I will?" A smile formed as she touched the threads with her fingertips.

"Your first."

"I'll get more," she said, rather than asked.

"Likely. Are you going to sleep in here with me, punkin?"

She nodded. "May I?"

"Stay there and keep it warm for me." I hurried to the parlor. "Aubrey," I said, "if you're going tomorrow, will you be back before Monday morning at nine?"

"Yes, ma'am. Is there something I can get for you?"

"Take me with you. I had been going to stay in town this weekend but I need to go home, even if it's just for a few hours."

He smiled and his eyes flickered toward Rachel. "At your service, Mrs. Elliot. Miss Rachel wanted to visit her folks, too. We can make it a fool's run and back."

I saw them chance another look at each other. I drew in a breath. Sparks flew through the air between Rachel and him! For Mary Pearl's sake, I'd better be sitting in the front seat next to Aubrey Hanna, I could see that.

*October 26, 1907*

After I said enough to be polite to Chess and Granny and the boys, I rode to Udell's place, my heart heavy and my backside sore after the ride from town.

When that stone house came into view, I threw back my shoulders and took a deep breath as if the sky opened above me. That big, lumpy gray house seemed a kind of castle. I know Jack always loved me, but we each carried our own loads. He always expected me to be strong enough for my own, and sometimes for his, too. Udell expects me to crumble, and seems surprised when I don't, and yet, I believe in many ways he may be closer to knowing my mind than Jack had been. No matter what happened around me, at that moment I looked upon that house, that hill, and that man, as a refuge. I planned going to tell him so. Tell him I'd chosen him over the university after all.

I found Udell standing on a ladder around back, putting up the double-hung windows that had come in at last. A stack of them leaned against the house below him and for a moment I had a real dread that he might slip off the ladder into that pile of glass. I dared not call out and startle him, so I waited, watching two men moving around the place. They were putting a door on, drilling bolts into the rock-and-mortar walls.

Udell saw me and his face lit up. As he came down from the ladder, he called, "Oh, Mrs. Elliot! My friend and scholar! What a fine morning *this* is," and stood in front of me. I'd have rushed to his arms, but both those workmen were in plain sight and propriety kept us from even shaking hands.

"I see you've got work going," I said. He nodded, so I went on, "How is your—*our*—garden?" One of those fellows came up and asked if Udell had any more cement, then left us. The other man, though, stayed within earshot. Heat flushed up my neck and my face burned. I said, "I've been meaning to talk to you, and I'd like to sit a spell. Would you take a walk with me?"

Udell stepped over the feet of the man mixing a can full of cement to patch some holes, and opened the front door, sweeping his arms toward the room inside. "Come on in first. I want to show you how I've got some of the furniture in. Things Frances's mother left behind. You're going to like this. It's real fine." I stepped through the opening into a fine, large room. Stuffed chairs and couches nicer than in a hotel lined two walls. Tables—with lamps on every last one—filled every corner. Beyond the front room in the parlor, a big square piano crouched like an animal waiting to jump forward on fat carved legs. He said, "You'll want to move things around, I suspect, to suit you. Just point and I'll push and carry them wherever you want. There's her square Chickering there in the parlor. Frances always wished she had that piano she'd played when she was a girl. Don't know how we'll get it tuned up. Maybe someone out of Tombstone."

"I don't play a piano. It won't matter."

He climbed halfway up the stairs, looking toward the higher landing, waving his arms. "Come on up. Of course, you have your own furniture you want to bring, but we'll have plenty of chests and all. This one here is full of linen sheets and embroider-ied pillow coverings. Some of them are the best ones Frances ever made. Lace all around."

I stood at the foot of the stairs, looking into a small room off the front parlor while he peered into the open chest of Frances's needlework. "What is this room?" I said. It was too small for a parlor or a kitchen, and a fancy mahogany bed sat against one wall with a tiny washstand near it. A mirror perched above it and across the room hung a framed picture print of cows grazing under a tree. The only rug in the house covered the brick floor in there. A delicate lace counterpane lay across the feather bed.

He fairly galloped down the stairs in his excitement. "That's for your mother. That's a good heat stove in the corner, with the damper built right into the wall. See this crank? Rock walls, small windows. Cool in the summer, and safe as she can be. See that bed? Metal-spring frame. No ropes. It'd make her real comfortable. 'Course, we'll need blankets and such, but she might want to bring along the fine quilts she's got now."

I followed Udell through the house he'd built, looked in every room and at his prodding inspected the insides of every chest of drawers. With each opened door I felt smaller and smaller until I nearly disappeared into my own shoes. On one wall by the stairs hung a framed doily with a carefully woven and knotted hair wreath all done up like flowers. Frances's hair, no doubt. From the piano she'd always wanted to the lace curtains in the bedrooms and the gilt-framed daguerreotype of her in the hallway, this wasn't a bower house for me.

He'd built himself a house . . . for Frances.

I lost all track of what I had come for. I told him I had to get home and start supper, and of course, he must come share with us. Then I headed home to think without anyone else's opinion included.

I changed to an old house dress and worked up the row of buttons on the bodice, staring into my little looking glass. I couldn't marry Udell Hanna. Not for anything. He wasn't building that house out of loving me. The man was marrying his dead wife. Building *her* a house. Filling it with her things. He'd sent me off to school as if he had been daring me to find some excuse not to come home. Now I didn't want to. I tried to remember the words I had so easily rattled off to Mary Pearl, caught in just such a fix.

But I was not Mary Pearl. I had my own land and house, my own children. I didn't need Udell Hanna's money, or his land, or his stone house. If I couldn't have a man on my own terms, just for the preference of his company, I wouldn't have him at all. It wasn't the same as a young girl thinking of her future and needing a man to provide it. I wanted the things my own hands had provided, and I didn't want to be seeing shadows in the halls nor wondering if he closed his eyes and thought of her at times.

Lord. I'd never live in that house. Yet oh, what have I done? Lain with him as if we were married, promised him, too, and spoke words as if I'd stand by them or bust for all time. Gave my word and now was weaseling out. Maybe what both of us had thought was love was just lonesomeness for the past.

When I got back to town, riding alongside Rachel in the back as Aubrey drove, I knew Aubrey had spent time at Albert's place, but I couldn't worry about whatever was brewing between those two. Hearing Aubrey's voice as he and Rachel cheerily talked, I heard Udell's voice, too. And Lord, I knew I loved him. But to spend my life there, with him, oh! My thoughts spilled on the floor like two sacks of loose buttons, never to be sorted out, and I stayed quiet the whole way.

All week that blamed piano kept popping up there on the page of my general science book betwixt the geologic structures of North America. By the end of Brownie's class Tuesday I decided it seemed only fair to Udell to break the promise between us. In town I felt too far from my home and from him, misplacing my trust and my real feelings.

Life seemed better without Mathematics. Definitely better without Domestic Science. I wrote letters to Mary Pearl, and finally in one of them pressed her for some feelings toward Aubrey. I didn't know if she were writing him, too, so I merely asked if she'd heard from him. Since I had fewer classes and more time, I went back to taking the buggy to school.

Brownie's lecturing got more addled with each day and when he sent back our papers, a note written on mine said that I hadn't any idea how to back up my thesis. That detestable little canker sore. Every time I thought of him, from then on, I remembered I had a setting hen named Brownie with a much nicer disposition and a good deal more intelligence.

Mister-Doctor Fairhaven acted kindly, even attentive. Too smiley, yet somehow his kindness was comforting, too. In Osterhaas's class two more students read their "What I Want" themes. We discussed their way of putting words on paper as if no one cared what the students had put down that they'd like to own or sought to become. I looked again at the list of stuff I wanted, put it aside and rewrote the page, prettied it up with adjectives and such. Then I went to April's house and had tea and read stories to her children while she nursed Tennyson. That little toot is tiny, but now that she is well, what a holler she's got on her! She'll be one to keep her mama busy, I reckon.

That week, Harland's children all got rashes and a cough so they were kept out of school and fretful. The doctor has been to the house and said it was the eight-day measles but they were not quarantined because it isn't the bad kind. Before I headed to Brownie's class each day, I made sure to check on the children, especially Blessing, who is doing fine and playing quietly with her toys for a change.

One morning, having to feel obliged to drive Professor Fairhaven downtown suddenly seemed real inconvenient to me. I rode Baldy instead of driving the buggy and I determined I would do so until the end.

Instead of being run over by bicyclers, I found that now students parted for me the same way they did for the teachers. I sensed it meant something. As I arrived at the classroom, the train downtown blew its whistle. It reminded me of little Blessing running away from home. I stopped with my hand on the door to Brownie's room. I detested the very knob, hated the man behind it, the stupid way he made me feel. The whistle moaned, dropping at the end with a sigh like a mourning dove. Which home was I running from?

We went over last week's test in Brownie's class. Mine had a large F on the top margin but not another mark. I'd long before swallowed any pride I'd owned about my scores. I'd gotten Cs and Ds all along, but never completely failed. I waited until after most of the students asked questions about the test answers they'd missed, then raised my hand. He called upon everyone he could find, even calling out names for their opinions, while my hand stayed up. When silence took over the room and my hand had turned to stone, I stood and said, "I'd like to know which of my answers is wrong, Professor Brown. I answered every question right. There isn't a dot on this page except the F."

"Someone in class please explain a grading curve to Mrs. Elliot. I haven't time." Brownie camped behind a battered old painted wood desk that like to swallowed him. He fiddled with some bent brads while I stood listening to a boy in the back explain that I failed because most people got a C, a percentage got a B, and one person could get an A, so someone else had to fail. I felt my breath go cold.

I walked toward the desk. "Professor Brown?" I heard my hen cackling as I spoke.

"Take your seat." His eyes widened. The brads clicked on the desk as he shrank into his chair. He watched those little metal brads and pushed them around as if they were important as bullets.

"Maybe you'll have time to write something else on my paper," I said.

"No. Class is almost over. The lecture—" He stopped, his eyes darting, his thin, unevenly shaved little mustache quivering like a cat sniffing something putrid.

I screwed up my eyes and quieted my voice, taking my sternest posture, the one I'd practiced on Rudolfo Maldonado. I felt almost as angry as then, too. "I got every answer correct and yet you tell me I've failed. I've read more books on geology and geography than anyone in this room, I'd lay a bet. Maybe even you. Professor Brown, you write on my paper that there are no incorrect answers. You don't have to change the grade, just write the truth." The little weasel squirmed in his chair. His inkwell was so dribbled on it had stuck to the desk itself. I placed my paper before him, dipped his own pen in the well, and held it toward him. "Everyone in this room is going to sit here until you write it," I said. Then I gave those students a look that could defy the Magnolia Balm right off a woman.

Brownie trembled and breathed noisily. He stared at the pen. He looked around the room, but none of the students made a move to shoulder him up. A drop of ink hit the blotter in front of him and made a spider of blue. One tiny droplet dashed onto his knuckle and spread in the wrinkles. I waited, counting seconds, like I'd done with Rudolfo, never taking my gaze from his face. He coughed after nine seconds of pure silence. The faint smell of urine rose from under his desk. A clock in the hallway chimed. No one moved. Someone dropped a pen and a handful of papers, but didn't retrieve them.

Brown's face reddened and sweat beads formed on his lip where they spread and ran. He wiped at them with the back of his hand, leaving a thin, crooked line of blue across his mouth. With a trembling hand he took the pen and with great spasms of penmanship, he wrote, "There are no incorrect answers on this paper."

"Sign it," I said.

"I wrote what you wanted."

"Sign it."

He scribbled something that might have been his signature.

Then I went to the desk where I'd been sitting, put the paper between pages of my geology book, stacked it with everything else, and walked out of the room. I heard a few of the students follow me. One or two even called out my name and someone said, "We agree it isn't fair," but I kept walking and didn't stop until I found Baldy.

I rode out of town, north to the Rillito riverbed, feeling murderous, hoping to fill my lungs with clean air before I could face any more school. A little rivulet snaked through the bottom of the sand. I stopped and let Baldy drink, and fished in his saddlebag for the book with the geology test. The big F stung me again when I saw it, but the scribble beneath salved it. I tossed the paper into the trickling stream. Two classes will be easier than three. Only Fairhaven and Osterhaas remained. I did not fail Brownie's test, no matter what grade he wrote, but I will not go back. I have no respect left for that rascal. I should have listened to Charlie!

Then I got on Baldy and clucked to him. As we moved downstream, a clattering, honking noise filled the air. I heard dogs barking, some banging like cow bells. I kneed Baldy and we went toward the noise, slowly. Around a jutting boulder and clumps of dead trees filled with flood debris, waited a herd of dirty, noisy sheep. Two Mexican boys were herding them.

All this time I never knew people raised the critters around these parts and here a huge herd of them stumbled and bellowed and drank! Well, I called hello to the boys and got off Baldy. That afternoon I shared tortillas, green peppers, and the cheese and apples I had with two half-grown boys, the Uribe brothers, and learned some about sheep and sheep dogs in a broken mix of English and Spanish and even some Latin I'd improved in Fairhaven's class. By the time the sun started to get low and Tonio Uribe said they had to get the animals home to their pens, I had plenty of knowledge to add to my time spent in town.

The air seemed cool. Baldy pranced now and then, happy to have a chance to stretch his legs and wind. Soon as I got to the house, Harland ran down the steps and said, "You're home! I've been to the university looking everywhere for you. I've hitched up my big wagon. We got word there's been shooting down at your place."

I packed to head home in two shakes. Harland could not take the children, measles and all, he said, especially into something that could be dangerous. I fussed at him, "You stay here with your children. If something happened, they'd be orphans," but he wouldn't listen.

Then he surprised me and pulled a brand-new Winchester out of a closet. "I've been meaning to ask you to show me how to use this," he said.

"This isn't the time for you to learn."

"Just load it up and you take it. I'll drive."

Blessing came running in and threw her arms around my legs. "Take me, Auntie Sarah. Make Poppy take me. You need me."

"I need you to stay here and get well," I said. "Poppy can't watch out for you and me both."

"You're watching out for him, aren't you? I'll help."

I pulled her hands loose. "Blessing, go to bed."

Rachel dragged her away, sobbing, as Harland and I exchanged sad glances. "Stay here, Harland."

"I've made up my mind."

"I'm surrounded by ornery men."

"Well, we're cut from the same cloth."

Rachel came back in a few minutes and said, "Uncle Harland, Blessing has a fever again. She says her throat hurts, just like before."

"See?" I said. "You must stay."

"You know I'd come."

"I know. Mama'll know, too."

I tied Baldy on the back of the buggy and headed south toward home.

# Chapter Fifteen

*October 27, 1907*

I swan. A bunch of men have blocked our road. Soon as I passed, they must have dragged all those beams and posted guards to keep us here. Another of Udell's cows has been shot down. I didn't think to bring extra provisions on that run home. Short of shooting our way through, there was no way to return to town. Part of me would like to run through them as if these were the old days and they were Indians, take down a few and keep on going. However, the railroad's outlaws seem more willing than Apache warriors to shoot back, and outnumber us twenty to one, and there's not a one of my family I'd be willing to sacrifice just to get back to town and fail school.

Eventually, supplies are going to run out. We can live without sugar or coffee and even salt. Still, sooner or later, saltless beans and cornbread are going to taste pretty tiresome, and then there's Elsa's expectations, and my schoolwork. This nonsense just had to stop. I managed to get to Udell by a roundabout coyote trail that went past the south windmill down and back up over some steep hills to his place. I had a desperate notion that this was a kind of siege. We just hadn't come to grips with it yet.

Charlie said they also watched the mail route to Marsh Station. We're so far out, this capture could go on until we starved to death or they forged papers to take the whole territory from us, and no one would know to come looking. Gilbert was willing to try slipping through the brush on foot to get to Marsh

Station with a letter to Sheriff Pacheco asking help not to leave us caught like this. I told him we'd all think it over.

Udell tried to talk with Rudolfo but twenty riders met him, forming a half circle between him and the hacienda. They answered his questions with stone silence, though he asked half a dozen times. He reckoned the bunch to be the ones we saw murder the two fellows they outran last fall. When he described the brands they wore, I knew it was Rudolfo's men. Everything I'd planned to say to Udell would have to wait.

### *October 29, 1907*

Between our houses, from Udell's farthest south, to mine between, and Albert's on the north across the Cienega, we pass freely. This morning Udell rode up and said he felt useless and so he went with Charlie before dawn to see how far south they could travel. When they returned, Charlie told us that they have cut a route through the farthest south section of our land, and he and Udell had watched from some hills. Before long six drays moving south from Maldonado's came to a stop at a clearing. The wagons were met by riders who switched places with the drivers, exchanged parcels from their packhorses, and then the drays continued south while their former drivers, now mounted, headed northwest. Udell and Charlie followed them as they crossed from our land to the Cujillos' place, until they cut off the Cujillos' land and onto Maldonado's, heading straight for the main house.

That afternoon, Granny sat rocking on the porch next to Elsa, knitting baby soakers. They talked softly and the sound comforted me. I put some lard in four bread pans and set the loaves in to rise. No doubt Mrs. Everly would have had something to say about the way I did that, too.

At the very second I stood straight up, three shots from something powerful and close range slammed into the front of the house. Elsa and Granny screamed. Two more shots hit the adobe bricks, then, and one of them splintered the windowsill right by where I'd been standing, sending glass and wood slivers into the bread dough sitting in the pans.

Udell rushed out, scooting Elsa through the door and lifting Granny like a baby. Cradling her in his arms, he set her on her feet in the kitchen. I barred the door. Granny stood for a moment, then fell to her knees and slumped to the floor. I cried out and knelt by her. "Mama, Mama! Have they killed you? Oh, Lord. She's shot." Red soaked her apron pocket.

Granny lay on the floor, shaking and moaning, her eyes closed and her mouth open, as if she neared death. "They shot m' finger."

The first finger of her left hand looked fine except that it abruptly ended at the first knuckle and blood flowed from it as if it were a fount. Udell took her hand and pressed on the finger. She whimpered again. "Hold this tight," he said to me. "Right on the wound." Then he took off.

I wrapped her finger with a clean towel, and Elsa and I carried her to her bedroom. Elsa set to bandaging it while I pulled curtains across the windows. Together we dragged her bed to a corner as far from the window as we could, then pulled a highboy in front of the glass. A bullet hit the window just as I did, shattering the glass and making spiderwebbed cracks on the mirror of the highboy. From the side, I could see a ball of lead sticking from the back of the mirror. I heard other shots, too, farther off, and waited by the door with my pistol in my hand.

Suddenly I realized that I didn't know where Charlie, Gil, or Chess were. They should have been no farther than the barn. Should have heard the shooting, yet no one came. Our dogs were going crazy in the yard. The thought flickered in the back of my mind that my men all lay dead in their tracks, already murdered by the person trying to kill my mother, but I put that aside; it was simply too terrible to imagine. The girl sat on the edge of the bed. "Elsa, get in this corner and keep down." I glanced from my poor mother to my pregnant daughter-in-law and pictured Elsa shielding Granny with her own body. "She's low in the bed. The bureau will make it a hard angle to hit. Pull this chair in front of the door when I leave and stay in the corner. I won't have you shot, too."

A dozen shots came from every direction outside, then. Running to the front of the house, I took my rifle and crawled under the windows, trying to see as far as I could without being right in somebody's line of fire. Shots came from the barn and the side of the house. I reckoned my boys might be in the barn with Chess, so I crept around back and slipped around the side. A man sat in shadows before me. I raised the rifle and drew on him as he hunkered low, aiming to the barn. Udell. I got to him after stumbling over the length of my skirt, nearly tripping headlong just as Chess had done. He didn't look up nor seem surprised to find me at his side.

Udell said, "Look between that saguaro and the smokehouse, just to the right there. That's where the shots came from. Someone in the barn is holding them down, but there're bullets coming in high from somewhere I can't see." Without warning, he pulled up and fired twice. A thud and a groan came from the distance, followed closely by the sound of brush being trampled. A man lay in the bushes beyond the smokehouse.

A fast volley of gunfire went off again from the barn itself, and a man rolled—dead before he landed—off the very top of the barn and into the round corral, spooking horses. Then all grew quiet. I stood. Udell held his hand up and motioned me back to my knees. He laid a finger on my arm then pointed to the smokehouse again. Then he hollered, "Charlie? You boys all right there in the barn?"

The barn door swung wide and Chess stepped in plain sight just like he was trying to draw fire. Udell fired a single time toward the smokehouse, and a man fell to the dust, his own rifle still in his hands, pointed toward the barn door. Then we heard loud hoofs, riding away, saw dust rise in the west. From the opening of the barn came Gilbert riding Baldy, barebacked, shotgun in hand, followed by another horse carrying his older brother holding a pistol. Udell and I had just risen to our feet when we heard the shotgun go off, several shouts, and then all got quiet. No birds were calling, no animals lowing.

Udell rushed to check out the three dead men. My heart grew quiet. I searched carefully for more shooters. Dead men posed no problem to me. I had to keep hold of my senses until my sons rode back to the house. Time stretched long, and I couldn't think, except to pin up the thought that someone had decided it was time to inherit Granny's land.

They'd come to kill my mother. No more meanness in the woman than a little gray dove on a nest; the vision of her bleeding finger loomed in my eyes while I watched the horizon for the return of my sons.

Behind me, I heard "Charlie!" and saw Elsa run from the house across the yard to him. Charlie and Gilbert were both on a single horse. Hatch. Chess and Udell joined Charlie and Gil. They came to me, talking, laughing nervously, talking more. Finally, I could bear no more, and I said, "Anyone else hurt?"

"No," they answered, all around. Then Gilbert said, "What do you mean 'else'? Who *is* hurt, Mama?"

"Granny. Took off her finger, but she's old and a touch of sepsis could kill her."

The whole family gathered at Granny's bed, and she seemed revived a bit. While she told her story, the boys told theirs. Gilbert had let go with both barrels from the back of my best horse. He'd served justice on the shooter, but Baldy wanted nothing to do with cannons going off over his head and he'd left Gilbert riding a clump of prickly pear.

When I heard that, I said, "All right. Gilbert, you get in yonder and drop your drawers, and your brother and your grandpa are going to take out any thorns you got left. Then you are going to draw yourself a hot bath and put some witch hazel in it and make sure *you* don't get septic, too. If you get so infected you can't sit a horse, you're going to be in a mighty fix if anything else happens. And don't make that face at me, 'cause you aren't too big to strap, the mood I'm in. Elsa? Look after Granny." And I put my hat squarely on my head. "Mama? Do exactly what Udell tells you and soak that finger. Bandage her up and I'll be back in two shakes."

"Where are you going?" Udell said.

"Get my horse," I said. I heard someone calling me but I kept walking.

I didn't have to go far. I hopped on Hatch and followed the trail west. I turned north at the only clear place between the scrub and cholla. I reined up hard and put my fingers to my lips, whistling as loud as I could. Hatch tussled around but I didn't give her any slack. I whistled twice more, and there came Baldy, looking rank and shaking his head as if his ears were still ringing. It was a miracle he'd even heard me, what with a shotgun going off over the poor animal's skull. I took his reins and he balked, bit at Hatch, made sure we all ate some dust. Then I kicked us into a run and we got home. I planned to have a long talk with Señor Maldonado. A very convincing talk.

I chopped vegetables feverishly, making minced pieces that would cook down soft for my mama to eat. The kitchen was empty and quiet except for the rhythm of the knife. Udell came in. With a glance around, he took my hand and I dropped the knife. He said, "We're going to figure this out, Sarah." He put his arms around my waist and pulled me close. "I'll keep you safe, if I have to perish doing it."

I pushed away and took up the knife again. "Don't think it," I said. "No perishing of anyone allowed from now on." Lands. I needed to have a long talk with Udell, too.

"I could just go ask them if we can pass by. Just neighborly. You need to get back to school."

"Just go ask them? They're not joshing. Think you can reason with them?" It seemed too easy to go crawling to some man and ask for passage down a free road we have traveled for twenty years. I didn't want lead flying but I'd have understood Udell more if he'd a-wanted to order the man to let us pass or taste steel. Jack would have taken the high road with them and put those men in irons by now.

"I'm going to go ask 'em to be reasonable. Usually I can talk to folks—"

"Besides. I won't go back. I've missed so much. They won't let me catch up and I wouldn't leave Granny no matter what. I reckon I'm not cut out for schooling, anyway."

"Why do you say that?"

"What on earth made you give me schooling as a present? Anyone else would have bought me a ring or even a horse or a bolt of calico." I couldn't hide the tone of my voice, yet I knew I wasn't angry at him.

"I don't know. Maybe 'cause you wanted it so. Everybody knows it. I thought at the time it was like giving a woman a bathtub. Even if she asked for it, you'd be half afraid she'd think you're telling her she needs it. Seemed like you wanted it. If you don't want it no more, well, it isn't like you needed it in the first place."

"Fiddlesticks. Carry that soup for me." The things I wanted most in the world could tear me asunder. I took Granny hot biscuits loaded with butter and swimming in sorghum, and she ate one then fell hard asleep. Udell stayed in the room with me as I watched over her. I finished then, as if nothing had interrupted, whispering, "I *do* want it. But I never in my life had to be someplace and know something by a time of day. I learned everything in smidgens between tending babies and hauling horse feed. Never set a clock by my learning and it took me away from my home and family. If I'da been here this wouldn't have happened."

"But you were here."

"I can't go back to town, now."

"I know."

"You angry with me for quitting?"

"I figure you'd know when you had enough."

It hadn't been two days since I declared to myself that I wanted to keep on at school forever. To do that it would have to come my way, not me change to its way. Still, so much was left, those papers due, the pages of Latin I'd translated, the essays and all. I was doomed to fail school. And that troubled me as much as every other trouble hereabouts, as if I gave some half-addled notion equal weight with the peril of my family. Rain and hail in Beulah land. I must have lost my senses, but I longed to go back even as I told myself I'd already failed out. I took the plate and cup from Granny's table and Udell followed me into the kitchen. I said, "Reckon I haven't quit entirely yet. Just missed some. What's that look on your face mean?"

"You are a hard woman to figure, is all."

"Well, I can't quit."

"Stubborn as the day is long. Chess is right."

"Better you know what you're getting, if you still want to marry after this is over." If it were his choice to quit on me, I wouldn't have to say the words to him.

"Harder-headed woman you'll never find," Chess tossed in.

Udell smiled. "Leave off this talking to Rudolfo, then."

I said, "Fact remains, you've all tried before. I think I'm the one Rudolfo will listen to. You fellows load up their dead in the buckboard. Haul 'em down to the big ocotillo and turn 'em out. Let them bury their own."

### October 31, 1907

While Udell and the rest of the family had prayers in Granny's bedroom, I got myself fixed up in some of Charlie's old clothes. Wearing a man's pants and shirt, I felt uncovered. I didn't need a coat, but it was cool enough to wear my Stetson instead of a bonnet. Then I put two dishtowels together with pins and mounted them to a fishing pole. It made a white flag to get me in the door to talk to Rudolfo.

Just as I got set to go out the door, Udell and I had a fuss about me going down there. He declared I was the most ornery woman full of grits and gravel he'd ever met. I hollered right back at him that I was plum fed up with folks making assumptions about my character then having no more manners than to tell them to my face, while those same people waited for hell and high water to come right to their front porch. I was in no mood to simmer down. All the ruckus brought the rest of the family out, and pretty soon they were talking battle tactics I had no intention of running.

This time I needed a horse I could trust so I saddled Baldy, put a rifle in my scabbard and a pistol in my belt. All those danged men on my place wanted to ride with me like we were a posse, and sure as I'm standing I know that will bring destruction to all of us because we'll look like an opposing army, so I allowed for them to follow but not ride beside me. If Rudolfo's men were going to let me in, it was going to be alone, under a flag of truce. Baldy wasn't appreciative about my flag, thinking less of it than he had of the basket I took the other day. I did my best to hide it as I went down the hills toward Rudolfo's place, and soon as I came to the big ocotillo, I pulled the flag and held it high, and the horse kept going. The men we'd left there yesterday were gone.

Well, three of Rudolfo's men came on foot from out of nowhere, stopping right in front of me. One of them said, *"Alto, amigo. ¿A dónde va?"* As if he thought I was a man.

I said, "To the big house."

He peered at my face and met it with a wide, evil grin. "Are you lost, *mujer*?" His eyes swept down my legs and made me shiver. "*¿Sola?* Alone?" He chuckled and brought his horse closer.

I took the rifle from the scabbard. "I come to see Rudolfo Maldonado. I've had enough of being held prisoner on my own land." Two men came from behind him and took my reins. One of them was that fellow Tick, the other was Caldo, the coach driver.

One of the men said something that included my name. The three looked at each other, and the lead man nodded toward the hacienda. He led the way while the other two followed me. I sheathed the rifle and held the flag over my head. When we got within twenty paces of the front door, the leader turned so fast I couldn't react to stop him, and he slipped my rifle from its place, saying, "I'll hold this. There is no hunting here."

I felt as certain of my own doom as any chicken that lays its head on a chopping block as I followed the man to Rudolfo's doorway. Rudolfo stepped out from a room farther back as I walked in, and the look he greeted me with could stop a rattler in its tracks.

"I've come to talk to you. Get this settled once and for all. I'm tired of being a prisoner in my own house, and I want to know why you had your men take shots at my mother," I demanded.

He waved his hand as if I were a squawking chicken and then grunted. "No one here has done this. Perhaps they were hunters." Rudolfo's white linen shirt hung open to the waist. He untied his fancy cuffs and loosened the ruffles. "Sarah, you weary me." With that, a heavy gold pin fell from his collar and he reached to retrieve it as if we were just having a merry chat.

"Your men have us trapped. They shot Granny. Udell carted all those dead fellows to the road by your place. They've disappeared so I know you know about this. What has happened to you, Rudolfo, to make you stoop to this?"

"Ah. Coyotes are bad this year. *¿Y tu madre?* She is well?" He approached me, pulling a sash from his waist and dropping it on the floor. "Why are you dressed in man's clothes?"

I backed up a step but gritted my teeth and said, "Coyotes, railroaders, what you call them makes no difference. I aim to get to town, Rudolfo. I aim to tell Nabor Pacheco that your outlaws tried to kill my mother."

"El Nabor? He's a good friend of mine. Give him my regards."

I didn't believe it. Sheriff Pacheco was our best hope. "Rudolfo? You will turn this into a feud. A range war. I don't want us taking shots at each other."

Faster than a rattlesnake, he had me by the shoulders. I shook to get him off, but his fingers dug into my skin so hard it felt he would pull the bones loose. "You should have married me, Sarah."

I jerked under his grip. "Why? So you could steal my place legally?"

"I don't like being insulted." His hands pressed harder, and he drew me toward him. Someone opened the door. "Get out!" he threw over his shoulder, then turned back to me.

I fought to free a hand and swung it toward his face. He gritted his teeth and let me slap him, then snatched my hand and twisted my arm, crushing himself against me. I gasped. "Take your hands off me."

"You are a fool."

I wanted to holler just like a child, "Am not!" but I held my peace. His breath was hot and smelled of tequila. His clothes were expensive and his chest broad and menacing, this close. I felt his hand run across my side and down one leg where he pulled the derringer from my pocket. I squirmed and said, "Let go, you."

He held the derringer to his lips, kissed the barrel, and raised one eyebrow. Pressed as I was, so close against him, when he drew a breath I had to stop breathing. I struggled for air. He leaned against my temple as if he were a lover, and whispered, "I could kill you right now."

"No you couldn't. You're not a murderer. That's why you send others."

He flung the gun at a chair. Fire smoldered in his eyes. He pressed his lips against mine, though I fought and strained. I felt no passion or desire, just repulsed and dirty. "I could do more than this, Sarah. More than you know. I have given you every chance to make the right choice, but you do not. You think you are clever and strong but you are a fool." Suddenly he loosed his hold and forced me back over a chair as he did.

I caught myself before I fell and spat on the floor. "Two-bit snake," I called him. "Vile contemptible snake."

"Oh, you have learned some new words, making a joke of yourself, sitting in school next to children."

"Don't you ridicule me, Rudolfo Maldonado. I remember I used to pay you in tortillas for cleaning stalls, *mi peón.*"

He raised his hand as if to strike me but halted before my flinched expression at the last second. "You wear clothes like a man. Maybe you think you are a man, but you are still a woman, in a man's land. Opportunity is placed before you and in reply you insult me before important men like a bad child. You can't do business like a man, you have no sense, but maybe you have been drinking, ah? *La Llorona* comes to you at night? Makes you think you have power? There is more to all of this than your pitiful scrap of desert. Those were powerful men you insulted in my house, soon to be even more so. And I will rise with them. Your land? I can have it all, any time I choose."

"This is really because you are angry about Charlie and Elsa, isn't it?"

"Charlie and who? Your son's whore doesn't interest me."

"You're never going to get my land, Maldonado."

He thrust his finger at my nose. "I already have. You will not stop me." Then he paused and laughed, adding, "A locomotive is a very hard thing to stop."

"I'll die trying."

"A fool's choice." With a sneer he added, "Your business is finished," and turned away. Sitting on a chair, he tugged off his boots.

"No it isn't." I shook with rage. He planned to take the land from us no matter who he killed. His greed spread across the desert like a plague. He was capable of destroying everything we owned or ever thought we wanted. My schooling was the one private dream I ever held and he'd torn it from me by his threats to my family and our land. He was playing some kind of terrible game, something south of the border that would ignite what—a war? He'd tried to get me into it, but I'd been too stubborn to bite. I wanted to fly at him and choke him. My voice trembled. "This is really about Mexico! You would align yourself with Don Porfirio, when for twenty years you have cursed his name? Those Mexican generals and Germans, the guns you carry, are they to crush more people under his whip? So, you are the *peón* of *el don* now? Or for the railroad? You've become what you used to hate the most. Whipping boy for the rich and powerful."

Standing suddenly before me, he whispered, "I am no one's slave, woman. Porfirio will soon be gone. I will own all the land between here and Cananea. The railroad works for me, not I for them."

"The railroad works for no one but the gold eagle. Do *you* plan to overthrow Porfirio? And to do this you would destroy my family for the sake of your wealth, then? I came here to reason with you, but instead, you'd better listen to me. You have declared war, Rudolfo. Anyone sets a toe on my land, or Hanna land, or Prine land, is going to be fixed up for slow traveling. I know where my borders are."

"Caldo!"

The three men rushed in and then escorted me to the border of my land where my men waited, under the aim of Maldonado's vaqueros. The leader handed me back the rifle. I was surprised to see it was still loaded. Then he said, "Señor Maldonado extends his best wishes for the health and long life of your mother. He hopes that she will be well enough to travel, too. Perhaps to see a doctor. *Adiós*."

### November 1, 1907

In the small hours of the morning under a moonlit sky, I watched through the windows of our dark front parlor as two figures snaked from shadow to shadow toward the house. Both wore heavy blankets and moved as if one had to wait for the other, so I figured they must be different in size. Might be those two fellows from the road. When they got to the porch steps, I tapped Charlie on the shoulder and he woke with a start. He got next to the window and I aimed at the doorway. A birdcall—a whistle I remembered from my childhood—made the skin on my neck tighten. Albert and Ernest and I used to signal each other that way when we were just spuds. I cupped my hands over my lips and fluttered a rusty trill in reply that was anything but birdlike.

A woman's voice called out softly, "Sarah?" I lifted my finger off the trigger. Charlie pulled the door open while I stood back in the darkness. Savannah stood in the doorway, holding forth a wide plate covered with a cloth. She took three more steps and then stopped, saying, "Sarah? Where are you? We heard the shots."

"Get inside, quickly," I said. Albert had a pack on his back. They slipped in and we bolted the door. The plate in Savannah's hands was wrapped in red gingham and smelled of hot bread. She placed it on the table.

Albert said, "We sent the boys to town to Harland's place. They're scared."

I said, "Granny's hurt. Just her finger but she's got a fever."

Albert said, "We were worried . . . We brought quinine and headache powders."

Charlie said, "Is there any to spare? I've got a bell-ringer."

Albert and Charlie sorted out the bag while Savannah and I looked in on Granny. "Oh, oh, my," Savannah whispered. "She's burning up." Her frightened expression cast a weary shadow on her face. Savannah seemed to have aged since I saw her last. We got the quinine and woke Granny so she could take some. Then we sat in the darkness in silence. The boys had nailed boards across the window so it kept out the moonlight. We turned a lamp low in one corner; thick shadows loomed around the bed and danced upon the walls. Men's voices came from beyond the door.

Udell put his head in and said, "I'm going to go home to feed my stock. I've got more shells, too."

I rubbed my eyes. "Be careful," I said. I heard the door close. Hairs on my neck and arms stood straight up.

"Sarah?" Savannah began. "What started this?"

"Gunrunners and railroaders. They figure to take Granny's land one way or another. Since we drove 'em away from buying it proper, they found a way to steal it. If Granny's dead, there'd be an inheritance."

"To the gunrunners?"

"To Rudolfo Maldonado. He's made a deal with Felicity. It isn't legal, but he's done it and he's got some skunk of a judge to back him up. When Granny dies he gets a fourth of her place. By the time we get it straightened out in court, the tracks and all of us will be in the ground."

"Oh." There wasn't a sound for several long minutes. During that time, I thought about how I'd said "when" instead of "if " about my own mother.

Granny moaned. Savannah turned up the light a bit. We tucked the covers again. Savannah bent over Granny and kissed her, then let out a sob. I turned to go, thinking she'd maybe want to be alone, but Savannah stood in my way. She reached for my hands and held them with hers.

"Sarah? Now, let me say my piece, or I'll never get it all said the way it ought to be. I've come to ask your forgiveness. I've been mule-headed and blind. Mad as a wet hen at myself, and blaming things on you that weren't your fault. I asked you to help school my children. We never spent money on books, having so many shoes to buy. It just seemed natural. You were right. Albert said I was trying to resurrect Esther. That I had to let her rest in peace. I fed that anger with memories of every hard thing I've suffered, though heaven knows my life has been so easy compared to yours. You—you were always so strong. Always bearing the rest of us—me, especially, I mean—on your shoulders. And then Mary Pearl going so far, and then you were going off, too! I was so lonesome. All my children went so soon. All I've ever done was mother. I just went crazy wanting another child. So I hung all the blame on you, too, for things that aren't your doing, and maybe aren't even wrong. To everything, there is a season. I just never expected the fall to come so soon." Tears painted gleaming streaks on her cheeks and left dark stains on her blouse.

"I never said I was blameless," I said.

"This wasn't your fault. I'm the one who's been fortunate, to have my husband and children this long. It was no wonder you found other things—I mean, Mr. Hanna. He is a good man. Yet he was taking you away from me. I didn't want you to leave. Not for school or for him."

"Well, I'm sorry, Savannah. If you think I shouldn't—"

"No, I'm sorry. Is there any way you can forgive me for this? I've been so unfair. I'm so very sorry." Outside, the sky was fading to pale green. We turned the lamps off and sat in shadow. "Can you forgive me?" she asked.

I crushed Savannah to me, and she threw her arms around my shoulders. We held each other for a long time, soft, hot tears running from our eyes. I said, "Let's go and let her sleep in peace." Hand in hand, we pulled up chairs around the kitchen table.

I said, "Reckon it made me pretty mad, trying to forget you were there. Should have come over and tried again. Now that I think of it, I should have never quit trying. Because, the truth is, there's nothing you could do that I couldn't forgive."

"I've been stubborn."

"It's a family trait. It's not really fall, yet, is it? For us, maybe, just summer?"

"Oh, I don't know. End of July at least. Maybe mine's August, 'cause I'm older." We both smiled. After a pat of my hand she said, "Those chickens laying?"

"Maldonado's men killed 'em. Salt mixed in their feed. Salted Udell's garden, too, but I think we saved it. Yours?"

"That heathen! No wonder they didn't make a sound as we crossed the yard. Well, that kept us safe, at least. Tomorrow I'll bring more."

"Not until we settle this feud."

Savannah fiddled with a dishrag that had been laid crosswise upon another one, atop her basket from home. She straightened and folded it then, and set it on the stack, making all the corners meet perfectly straight. Then she sighed and said, "Mary Pearl does have to go her own way. Despite all my trying to keep her in rag curlers and pinafores, she's become a woman."

"What changed your mind about her, Savannah? What Albert said?"

"No. I finally read the papers she's sent from the college. I felt cut to the bone. I'd been so wrong about Wheaton School. It is not a cesspool of bohemians. Everything they stand for is the highest virtue. It's a place my own mother would have wished for me. The sorry thing is, I went harsh on you for giving her the head it takes to grow up."

"Well, I did tell them to go to school. Your children are the ones who listened. My own don't care a hoot."

She smiled. Fresh tears squeezed from her eyes. She pulled that dishrag from the basket and refolded it, in thirds this time. "It's all gone so fast. There are only the two boys left at home. Know what Zachary told me? He's determined to become an aviator. He said that a real flying machine was going to stop in Tucson someday and he's going to get on it and sail up into the sky and look out on top of the clouds. Lands, I hope I'm in my grave first. I couldn't bear knowing he was up there."

I waited a few minutes, then I said, "Well, I am sorry I didn't tell you about her writing to that Wheaton place, after all."

"No, no. You were sick. You forgot. I just didn't want to hear it. It had seemed just like Esther, writing secret letters to that man."

Savannah and Albert's girl Esther had fallen in love over some letters and poems from a boy who delivered them every night by way of a ladder and a rosebush. When I look back on it now, it was not much different than my April running away with Morris. But Esther and Polinar ran into trouble, not into town. Morris had done fine by my April, and she by him. There was no reasoning out why one had gone so well and one so bad. I said, "Polinar was only twenty years old, honey, and he got murdered, too. It wasn't *his* fault, either. They fell into a terrible fix."

Savannah nodded. "I'm hungry," she said. "Are you hungry?"

"Well, coffee's made. We could cut some bread. It'll be daylight soon."

"I brought pie, too. We could eat that." She fished into that basket and pretty soon we cut up the pecan pie that had been packed under the loaf of bread. I poured coffee and milk into cups. "This is no temperance pie. It's got two drams of vanilla in it."

"Why, Savannah!" I sniffed at the pie. "It'll be intoxicating!"

"I do love the taste."

I laughed. So did she. Then she burst into tears and flung herself on my neck, and we both had a good, long, crying hug. Afterward, we went back to eating our pie, all crunchy and runny at the same time. Savannah said, "Sarah, I've missed you so. Then when we heard the shooting I got so terribly afraid! Afraid I'd lose you without ever telling you how sorry I was. Granny was right about that other, too. Last year when I thought I was going to have a baby, it wasn't anything but the change. Comes on you slow like that. Now things are back to normal, and then sometimes not."

"But you're not crazy."

"I hope not. Touchy some. I was always afraid I'd end up like—"

"My mama? I am, too. I don't blame her a bit, but I don't want to be that way."

"No. Neither of us."

"We won't, will we?" I said.

"No. We won't. It's only our summer."

# Chapter Sixteen

*November 2, 1907*

Savannah and I were sisters again—deeper than blood-born—though I remained puzzled by her actions, her love lost and now found as if it'd been mislaid like a glove. Although I understood her fears, a little corner of my heart bears a scar, as if she had hurt me in a place no one else on earth could touch. I told myself what came between us boiled down to that she had her upbringing and I had mine. Chess and I exchange cross words five times a day and never question our ties. My bunch can make a noise like a shivaree any time of the day or night, but it never included the shunning of the others. Until this year, it always seemed like she and I were two parts of a set. While the set is whole and the pieces still work together, it's been broken and glued. Still, I can bear anything if Savannah is there.

Udell loaded up his old Springfield and brought a couple of bands of ready-loads to my house. He looks like a man set for war, as if he has put off being a farmer, and with a change of his hat and a sad but cold look in his eye, become a soldier. He stayed, bunked in the front room, on guard.

In the morning, when he got ready to return to his place to take care of the feeding, I followed Udell to the yard where he saddled his horse. He was tied near the ocotillo fence and cropping at tufts of grass. I lifted a hoe leaning next to the fence and fiddled at some weeds with it. He spoke without turning toward me. "Sarah, marry me now. Let's don't wait. I won't mind if you take off and spend a while in town finishing your school term. We could ride down to Benson this afternoon yet."

"Why, Mr. Hanna," I said, mocking him. No cheery teasing rested in his face.

"I can't watch out for you here. Take a look at the pommel on my saddle."

A deep U-shaped cut ran through the leather clear down to the wood.

He went on, "I shot back and hit one of them, but he just kept on going."

"How will marrying change that?"

"I'm thinking about your old people. Your mama and your father-in-law. Your boys ought to come here, too. This thing is about to blow up in our faces like dynamite. We can only hope to hold out until some wandering soul sees the fix we're in and brings help."

For the first time, I let myself think beyond my own nose and saw how everything I did, whether I married Udell or not, went to school or not, fussed with Rudolfo or kept my peace, all of it concerned my children and my old folks, none of it was about my happiness. I'd been giddy, mooning over Udell like a schoolgirl, all right. Going to school instead of tending to my business. Thinking young girl things and feeling young girl shivers every time I saw him. Now this put a new wrinkle on everything. Would I marry him for the sake of the others? Yet the only certainty in my life was that nothing stood forever. I had to put off denying him.

"You know," I said, "we've been letting this all turn around on Rudolfo's say, but why don't you and I ride down to the Cujillos' place and see where they stand?"

"His daughter is Maldonado's wife. No matter what, Cujillo stands with her."

"And Charlie's wife is Maldonado's daughter. If Rudolfo felt that way about his own daughter Elsa, we wouldn't be having this talk."

"You've changed your mind, haven't you?"

"About riding to Cujillos'?"

"About marrying me. Something's different. I don't know what. You don't look at me the same. The house isn't finished, you know. It'll be better when I'm done."

"It's not the house, Udell. And I look at you the way I always did." Even as I said it, I couldn't face him.

"But you won't marry me now, just to be safe? Or if you aren't pleased to marry yet, would you . . . live there . . . to be safe, I mean? You'll have your own rooms anyway. No one . . . well, no one needs to know. I'd respect your privacy."

I put down the hoe and studied the ocotillo limbs that made up my fence. Green openings formed on some of them, hints of the leaves to come on a plant that refused to die even when made into an ordinary old fence. I took a hard breath. "I don't know if I can marry you, Udell."

He rested his gloved hand against the thorny fence and looked to the distance. "How'm I going to watch over you and your folks with you living in another house?" Udell took my hands in his. My garden gloves in his leather work gloves seemed a portrait, there in the sun, the hands of two people who worked hard but counted on each other. I wanted to count on him, down to the marrow of my bones. But I felt all loose ends. He said, "But you said you'd marry me. You mean later?"

"Come on to the house. Let's talk this over with the family. I—I can't think straight."

He stopped. "Because you don't want to come? Is it because I took advantage—"

"No! I can't think straight because I want to run to your arms, and stay there the rest of my days. But it's got to be for the right reason. There's more to think about. That house isn't mine. Besides. Besides. You said yourself anything I do affects a passel of folks, and they've got a right to a say."

"So you haven't lost affection for me?"

"Udell, I feel so weighed down, so haunted by this mess with Rudolfo. I won't stand up and promise to love and keep you and then turn away. I've got to be sure before I give you my word and oath."

A warmth flooded up from his collar, turning his face dark under the tanned skin, and his lips tightened. He said, "I never had any faith in life being easy or simple. I knew trouble was coming and I built us a house I could defend. The door is on. Top floor almost finished. The shutters have gun slots. I'll fix screening in the holes to keep out flies. Plenty of furniture in the two sheds, too."

"I can't because there is the thought of us spreading out too thin. That would leave only Charlie and Elsa and Gilbert at this house. They are so young."

We stood talking by the door so long, Savannah and Albert, my sons, and Elsa all came to the front porch. I knew I had to draw up some gumption and tell Udell I was not going to marry him. I tried words out in my imagination this way and that, pretending to see his reaction. I said, "Udell? You have been nothing but good to us all, from the day we first met."

Udell's expression looked hopeful and then somber. " 'Twas always my intention, Sarah."

"I've been thinking, honestly. Sincerely, I must tell you something. With all you've done with the house and all—maybe it is better for us not to come there." I wanted to rush and hug him. To protect him from the hurt I planned to deal him.

"Oh. No, I'm sure Maldonado intends to run me out, too. He needs your land. Me, he wants gone on principle."

"I am talking about marriage. Reckon the formal way is to release us from our, our promise of betrothal." I could as much as feel every soul gathered there hold their breaths. My head spun. Sweat broke on my forehead. "There is no simple way to say it. I can't marry you. I can see it now. I was rushing headlong."

"Sarah, if I led you to this, if it's too fast—is it because of Aubrey and Miss Rachel?"

"Rachel?" I looked quickly to Savannah. A handkerchief to her eyes, she shook her head.

Udell said, "Well, I told the boy he was casting Miss Mary Pearl aside too soon, not giving her a chance to come home and see her again and all. I've done all I can with the boy—man. Well, you know he's grown. They've got a will of their own. He's said he's wanted to marry Miss Rachel since he got to know her better. Says they're more suited, more equally yoked. Closer, you know, agewise and education and—"

"Udell, we can't move Granny and everyone to your place because I can't marry you because I think we're going about this all wrong. I think I was just wishing you were Jack, and that you were thinking I'd turn into Frances."

"Into Frances?"

That parlor on the hill was full of Frances, her mother's tables and lamps, under every lamp antimacassars that Frances had embroidered with flowers and frippery. "It's that piano, Udell. That house full of lace doilies."

He shook his head and pulled a hand through his hair. Then he reset his hat, picked up his ammunition and rifle.

"I'm sorry," I said.

Udell peered at me, glanced around at my family, turned back to face me. "Were you just toying with me, Sarah?"

"No. I was just caught up. I'm sorry."

He put his hat on and left without another word. I went inside, sat and stared into the fireplace all day, while around me, people talked and ate and slept. I told myself telling him straight-out was more honest. Oh, Lord, my heart was as black as the firebox, cold as iron, too. Now I'd have to face all this without him. The loss felt worse than losing Savannah. All the dark, hard places of my heart shook with angry tears that refused to fall. I cursed myself for hurting a truly kind man. A decent man. A man who deserved better than to be too easily, too comfortably had. I shivered and missed him, ached for the easy, simple way of him. Still, it was better this way. It must be! Had to be, because there was no future here with him, there was only that bleak house on that hill, that bower of the dead wife's, in a future with him. I wanted the man but not what he'd created, wanted the friend but not the husband. In the midst of my agony, passion for him swept over me in currents so strongly I wanted to seize the nearest horse and gallop to him.

After that night, we didn't see Udell again for three days. Every other minute of each long day, I told myself I was glad to be shed of him. The minutes in between, I longed for him, pined for him the way I've pined for Jack. I wasted half my day looking over my shoulder to the horizon, hoping to catch sight of him coming on one of his big workhorses.

Finally, I packed up a basket lunch and changed into a clean dress and took myself a walk in his direction. I held a conversation with my shadow, tromping over rocky ground, thinking aloud about that man living on that hill in that stony castle. "Do I love him," I said to the quail trying to beat my path clear before me, "or do I just want to love someone—anyone—so much I can't see straight? How in the name of heaven can anyone know if it's love until you've climbed a few hills together? And isn't Charlie right? Marriage is the hardest, cussedest thing a person can do."

When the house came into view, I slowed down and took a good, long look. Nothing much seemed to have changed except the dark boulders now seemed less menacing. I climbed up the steeper steps right on the front, straight up to the door, and banged on it with my knuckles. There was no answer. I hollered, "Mr. Hanna!"

I rapped on the wooden door with a stone he kept on the porch as a doorstop. "Udell?" He might have been out in the barn. It was down the hill in the back, every bit as huge and ominous as the house. I rounded the curved path to it. Then stopped in my tracks. No sound came from the barn. No cows. No bleating of the four calves. I hurried to the door and found it standing open, swinging on a breeze.

"Udell?" I ran from stall to stall. No animals. None of the cow mess was fresh, either. "Udell!"

A cactus wren squawked at me from a beam overhead. I left the basket outside the door and went around the hill, going in the top level of the barn. Eight cows and five horses stood there, eating. But no Udell. The pepper plants in the garden drooped like willows from want of water.

I hurried to the house, flinging wide the back door. I couldn't remember where anything was. I rushed into storage rooms and the privy, calling up the stairs, and at last found him prone at an angle on a bed on the top floor. He lay fully dressed across the counterpane, drenched in sweat. The room felt still and stifling, the smell of sickness came from his breath.

His lips moved but no sound came out. Fever made him start at the touch of my hand, which must have felt like a cold rag on his burning brow. "Udell," I said, "let me get you into this bed."

"I got the stock fed," he said.

"I know. Stretch your arm out." I pulled his shirt and pants off him, tossing them into a corner. There wasn't a bureau or chair. "When did this come over you? I should have checked sooner. I thought you'd had enough of my company for a while."

"Malaria. Since . . . Cuba."

"Malaria?"

He nodded. "Thirsty."

I searched the top floor. No canteens or water pitchers, not a thing to bring a drink in. Down in the kitchen, I found dirty pans and a couple of spoons, slimy with old water. In a chest, then, I discovered several cups that matched, and though there wasn't a pitcher, there was a flower vase, so I ran the pump in the washroom and filled it. Then I hunted through the chests he'd pointed out before for some kind of flannel I could use. I took the big pillow off the bed in the room he'd set aside for Granny under one arm, a china cup and the vase in both hands, and went back up the stairs.

By the time I got done fixing him up and wrapping his forehead in cool, wet flannel, he fell fast asleep.

I fetched my lunch basket from the yard. I watered the animals and the garden. I checked on Udell every half hour and damped the flannel to cool it again. I washed the pans and straightened the kitchen up, setting the cups in rows instead of all piled together waiting to fall over. I swept the kitchen, then the whole downstairs. Then I hefted a chair over my head and got it up the stairs. I set it beside his bed, and stayed in it a while, thinking. It was high time

I headed home, but I couldn't move him. I reckon if someone at home starts to wonder where I am, they'll come a-looking.

Late in the afternoon, I wandered through that house. The room where he lay must be the one he meant for himself. I remember that old bed from the shack he'd built after his old house burnt down last fall in the range fire. I had sat on it once to put on some boots. The other rooms stood wide and roomy. The windows needed opening, though, so I pulled up the sashes and a good breeze came in. In the center of the house, next to the chimney that branched off to each room, a second flue was built, and it had a double damper that moved from a box in the kitchen on the bottom floor.

Opening that flue drew fresh air in every window at once and out the top as if it were smoke, so the place went from stuffy to pleasant in no time. I thought of my brother Harland, figuring to put that air vent in a house, and figured just like my old place in town that he had designed, this one must have a dumbwaiter somewhere. I found it in another room off the kitchen pantry. There, a genuine washing machine had been set up, looking like a churn turned sideways, with a big dasher by which you could sweep the clothes back and forth.

It wasn't until suppertime Charlie came riding toward Udell's house. I met him outside and told him how I'd found Udell sick with malaria. I don't know if Charlie wanted to be sure of my words or Udell's fever, but once he saw the man, he said he reckoned if he was that sick, someone ought to stay with him.

"The only other bed in the place is downstairs right off the front parlor. It's for your granny," I said.

"I'll come check on you in the morning. Elsa will bring food."

"Ask her to fetch me some clean clothes, too. I didn't expect to work so hard in this dress and have to sleep in it, too."

When I went to Udell's room again, he had curled up on his side, shaking and moaning. "Cold," he managed to get out. I covered him with the lone blanket on the bed, closed his window, and went to hunt more coverings. I found three beaten-up quilts and a light feather counterpane in a chest. I carried them all up the stairs and tucked him in. Then I went down to the room reserved for my mama and sat myself on the bed, hoping to fall asleep. I lay in the darkness, listening to the night sounds. Gnat-catchers trilled in the sky overhead. A bat squealed. From the barn, the contented murmur of horses sounded like friends talking low. A thump overhead jarred me wide awake.

I had to find a lamp. Find a match. Then find the stairs and get back to

Udell's room. "I'm coming," I called out. "Don't walk around in the dark, you'll trip down the stairs!"

"Sarah?" Udell's hoarse voice cried. "I can't find you."

I held the lamp high as I came through the room. The room was large and the flame seemed swallowed up in darkness. I almost tripped over him. Udell sat on the floor, holding the back of one hand to his face. He pulled it away and blood trickled from his lip.

"Did you fall out of bed?" I said.

"Dreamed I couldn't reach you and you needed me."

"Looks like you hit your face on the chair I left here. I've been sitting with you."

"I'm all right. I'm all right. I'll just go put my cows in the barn."

"They're in for the night. Fed, watered, and tucked in like babes in a bunting. Let me help you back into bed."

He leaned on me and I grunted under his weight. Udell was heavier than he looked. He must have carried the weight of a taller man, compacted in a shorter frame, for I'd swear he'd outweigh either of my sons. "Thank you, thank you," he said. He smiled at me as I arranged the cold flannel on his head again. But no sooner had I settled it and dried my hands, than he fell to sleeping hard, his body laboring, drawing in deep, bottomless breaths.

I looked at the doorway, imagining the long stairway and the trip across the four rooms to Granny's bedroom. Now that my eyes had grown used to the dark, here in his room, the stars flung across the inky heavens seemed almost light, coming in the window. In squares at the sides leaded cut glass made prisms, but the center glass was large and no curtains spoiled the view.

I moved the chair away from the bedside and set the lamp on it so there'd be light if he woke again. Then I sat on the bed beside him, and moving so as not to wake him, I slid my feet down and stretched out. I leaned my arm against the wall and my head upon my arm, then put the other hand on Udell's arm where his fever gave me a feeling of heat so strong I would not have needed a blanket. I still had my dress on. I'd left my shoes downstairs. The man was nearly unconscious. And where I couldn't close my eyes downstairs, the next breath I took, I drifted away, lost in slumber.

"Mrs. Elliot?" a voice said.

I opened my eyes.

"I've been a nuisance," Udell said. He scratched his head and turned away as if he were embarrassed.

"It was too far away, that other bedroom. I needed to be nearer to you. Is your fever gone?"

"When it comes that way, usually it's one day on, one day off, for about a week. This will be a good day, then tomorrow I'll be sick again."

I felt so drawn to him. I tore myself loose from the feeling and got off the bed, straightening my clothes. I said, "Hungry?"

"No."

"You should eat. Maybe just a little soup or some porridge." I pulled at my hairpins and the whole thing tumbled to my shoulders.

"I'm surprised you're here."

"You didn't come when I called. I found you sick in bed. I fed your critters for you."

"I need a shave."

"No you don't. Just wait it out. Don't go to that trouble on my account."

"Naw, if I skip a day it's just harder to do the next time. If . . . if you'll excuse me. Seems I've got undressed somehow. I'll wait until you leave to get up. I'll get dressed if you're determined to fix breakfast."

I made him a bowl of oat porridge, and Udell came downstairs to eat it, though I sent him right back to bed when he was done. Charlie and Elsa came with quinine, clothes, and a plucked chicken so I could make soup. They had to walk past the parlor where an open door showed the bed downstairs sufficiently rumpled to pass inspection.

I stayed with Udell two more days, and the next morning he awoke and seemed quite a bit revived. That afternoon he sat in the front parlor and watched while I pulled some weeds in his garden.

The fever did not return that evening and it seemed far outside the corral of proper behavior I've set for myself to stay in the same room with him then. I lay on the bed he'd saved for Granny, reckoning that my idea of "proper" had fallen into some disrepair. Over the years my propriety has been battered by hail and death and fears, so a few boards are missing in that corral fence. Still, there was a difference in what happened between us before as an accident of time and place, and what might happen by forethought and opportunity. Especially since now I was determined not to marry him. So the next morning after I fed Udell and then the animals and watered the garden, I got myself home.

All the way there I remembered every moment I'd spent with him, as if I were living it all again. When Udell was awake he had been polite and I was courteous. We hadn't talked about anything except weather. His house was clean, his animals fed. That was all I concentrated on. While Udell had slept, sometimes fitfully, I worked. Swept. Climbed the outer walls and spied on Rudolfo's house. We'd passed those days avoiding each other's eyes, merely a patient and a nurse. He wore the hurt on his face as clearly as the sickness, and I carried that rock of guilt and sorrow in my chest every step of the way home. It weighed even more by the time I got to my own porch.

### November 10, 1907

Savannah and I sat up all night. Granny still lay in her bed, moaning, crying out, for something or someone we could not understand. We couldn't comfort her in any way we tried. Savannah and I talked about all the things that have come to us since the railroad turned Rudolfo Maldonado evil with greed. When morning dawned, the sun brought a kind of special healing to my mama, and she woke me up with a pat, saying, "Did you girls make any coffee yet?"

Well, Savannah ran to start it and Granny said she was fed up with being made to stay in bed. She'd survived on our doctoring her finger with Epsom salts and Coca-Cola and wanted some by-gum steak and scrambled eggs. When I told her all the chickens were dead, she had some words for Rudolfo I was glad Savannah couldn't hear.

First light, this morning, the boys and I spread out on horseback and scouted. When we got to the north quarter, off in the distance as far as we could see, a fresh scar of railroad tracks led from the regular SPRR set heading west. On Granny's land there had been a heap of digging done. Trash left all around the place, too. Greasy papers blew in the wind, mismatched old boots lay here and there, a canteen with a bullet hole in it hung from a tree, and dozens of cigarette papers fluttered around like butterflies.

At the new track, I got off Hatch and kicked a broken whiskey bottle just as Gilbert got to me. "Where do you reckon it heads?" I said. We started walking.

Charlie went ahead, and after a quarter mile, pulled a scope from his pocket and drew a bead to the west, standing in line with the track. "It's going to take off the corner there, beyond what Granny sold. Farther is Rudolfo's. You reckon that's all this fuss is over?"

Gil said, "Lordy. They'd shoot Granny for a half acre of land?" His face reddened; he turned away.

I stared down the shallow trench to where stakes marked the meeting of

Rudolfo's spread. This was the flattest corner any of us owned. Just flat enough that a little scraping had made it perfect for the tracks. Had Rudolfo ordered someone to steal that phony inheritance claim from Granny's land, or had he just blindly told some two-legged rattlesnake to earn his keep, and the man figured that was the way of it? A half acre of land. I swore under my breath. Then I said, "Let's ask Granny to sell it to him. A gentleman's agreement for a dollar or some such. This isn't worth anyone dying."

"Well, what is it they think they got the right to? More'n this?" Charlie asked.

"A fourth of all of it," I said. "So, yes, more than this."

Gilbert said, "Let's get Sheriff Pacheco. We'll go out with a posse and clean 'em up. I'll get to town, Mama. I can make it."

Charlie set his elbow on his brother's shoulder as if he were thinking hard and needed a place to rest while he did. Gil didn't move. Then Charlie said, "Bud, you and me will go get mail and take a letter to Sheriff Pacheco. Maybe one to Rye Miles." I knew that old Texan. Tougher than rawhide. No bigger than Brownie, but a sight more useful. Miles would be a big help to us, if he would come.

I started, "Maybe Chess—"

My sons looked hard at each other, then Charlie said, "Ma, it's not that Grandpa Chess, well, not like he's gone mushhead on us, but you shouldn't—"

Gilbert interrupted, "That'll leave no one watching Granny and Miss Elsa."

I searched my boys' faces, then said, "We can't leave the place unprotected. One person should go to Marsh Station. I'm thinking it should be Gilbert." I turned away so he wouldn't see my face after saying it. If he wasn't home in a few hours, we'd send someone else after him.

We wrote our letters quickly, as clouds gathered outside and rain fell, with everyone putting in their two bits' worth. Then we ate a cold lunch in Granny's room so we could keep her company. The rain quit. Clouds hung low and the air was as damp as wash day.

When Gil left, I watched him ride away and a terrible, hollow feeling followed him out of the yard and over the hill, as if a shadow remained of his passing.

Then I got Hatch and went up into the hills where I could see the hills running east toward Benson. A light rain made fluttering noises on the brim of my hat and stained Hatch's neck from bay to brown. By the time we reached the top of a hill, the rain had turned to mist, so thick in the air it seemed as if the very clouds had come to the ground to rest from their efforts. Eastward, a band of white cloud draped over a familiar sawtooth ridge of rock in folds, straight on top just like a blanket laid on a fence rail, making the jagged mountains into an even line where they touched the heavens. I pushed toward it, amazed at the air that moved about as if it were smoke.

So many things, just now, were sitting on a fence rail, I thought. Asking my mother to sell her land, our first homestead here, went against my grain down to the core. And there was that schooling lost. Gil wanting to run off and be a soldier. And I'd wasted my tuition same as my boys had theirs. Wasn't I supposed to be older and wiser, as their mama? And there was Rudolfo to keep fighting; my kinfolk to protect. The railroad. I was still broke, too. And there was Udell. I'd chased after him like a spring filly, but wanted to keep him at the end of a tether, like a good dog. Just wait, Udell. Go home. Stay. Shoot, maybe that was why Aubrey was making eyes at Mary Pearl's sister Rachel, because Mary Pearl had said wait, Aubrey. Go home. Stay. So let Udell find some other woman to wear his wife's clothes.

I was a hard woman, Chess said. Well, what else could I be? I'd had to hurt Udell. It was more than a woman's embroidery and a hair wreath on the wall. It was the way he'd laid them out as if he were expecting I'd take up where she left off. Wasn't at least half of loving someone knowing they loved you in return? The real you, though. Not the one they made believe you were.

I slid off Hatch and sat on my haunches, breathing deep of the creosote and clay perfume. Right at the toe of my boot, hoping to keep so still I wouldn't see him, a silver-dollar-sized horny toad froze in his tracks. Those critters are the only animal I ever knew that could hold its breath like a person. I picked him up very tenderly, mindful of my leather gloves so I wouldn't hurt him. I rolled him over and admired his soft belly. He was so white and silken underneath, so crusty on his back he looked like he was coated with gravel. He hissed and squirmed, trying to bite me with his toothless gums. Then I put him down and he darted away, kicking up little pebbles in his hurry. I went to get back on Hatch, but as I reached for the pommel, reins in my left hand, I just laid my head against the skirt leather and sighed. Hatch turned her head and bucked me with her nose, hard. I fished for the stirrup and got on, and said to her, "Danged cayuse. Mind your own business. He just doesn't love me, that's all. That's one problem solved, anyway. Let's go home, lunkhead."

I gritted my teeth and the rain began to fall again. This time I tipped my face toward the sky and let the rain soothe the burning in my eyes.

Gilbert was home in three hours with no word other than he'd delivered our messages, and he'd picked up the mail. He'd got word from West Point that they accepted him, but that all cadets had to be unmarried men. He was torn. That's sure. He didn't think to write his girl a letter, too, we'd been so worried, and there was no way for him to talk to Miss Charity for a few days, at least. The town paper, the *Weekly Star,* said there had been more killings in Cananea. Rudolfo Maldonado owned ten thousand acres between Cananea and Naco. My old friend seemed to be growing horns and a tail, getting meaner every minute. I didn't know how much Elsa knew about her father's dealings, but after we read that paper, I left the room and went to my rocker in the parlor. My head ached and the soreness went down my back like I'd been pinned with two iron rods.

That evening, Albert and Savannah, Ezra, Zack, Clover, and Rebeccah joined us. They carried everything they owned that'd put a hole in a man, but I couldn't help thinking if it came down to pitchforks we were lost before we started. We ate biscuits and gravy for supper and washed it down with coffee and peach pie. No one talked much that supper.

I made the gravy with milk that Albert brought, and told Elsa to have plenty, as a woman expecting a baby ought to have milk. She is starting to look plump and real pretty, getting that ripe, risen-dough look of being great with child. Rebeccah was staying real close to Savannah, I noticed, and kept brushing against her mother, petting her, as if something had gone between them before they arrived. Well, time enough for family gossip later, I reckon.

We had just reached the groaning stage, pouring more coffee, when Udell drove up with a wagon, offering to get us to town. When I asked him why, he said he'd seen two dozen riders at Rudolfo's place, armed up like *juarístas.* Elsa gripped my arm. The men all looked at each other, but Udell wouldn't look me in the eye.

Charlie said, "Coming here?"

"Don't know. Just came to help out if they do."

Chess came to the parlor carrying Gilbert's guitar. "Here, boy," he said. "Pick us some tunes. I'm tired of this war already." He squinted at me.

Gilbert did as he was told, sitting at his grandpa's feet, and Chess closed his eyes, tapping his fingers on one knee to the music, lost in some thoughts far away. Well, the whole family drifted in then. I went to see if Granny had cobbled up some of her old spunk and wanted to get out of bed. Everyone cheered when she walked in and then my mama took her nightgown and made a curtsy. She came and sat on a stuffed chair, listened for a bit, and took the bowl of soup Elsa brought her. Other than the guitar's strings, no one spoke. Reckon we were all contemplating our vision of war.

As the sun went down, Charlie spread all the weapons in the house in a circle on the floor in front of him and commenced checking and cleaning each one. He had the trigger out of his own pistol and went over the works with a rag dipped in alcohol. As I watched him, a cold, shadowy hardness took over my insides, and I didn't lift a finger to help or speak a word, as if I'd been strapped to the chair.

Elsa, Rebeccah, and Granny went to bed down. Ezra and Zack nodded in their chairs but were not sent away. They were to sit up like men. The soft music of the guitar seemed to make the light in the room yellower, and the flames in the lamps danced. A sharp pain in my head beat to some awful rhythm Gilbert could not hear.

At midnight, the dogs set up a racket just as three slugs of lead hit the side of the house. We flew into readiness, all of us with guns drawn. The men and I held pistols and rifles. Charlie and Elsa took Granny to the pantry where many layers of wooden and adobe walls would protect her. We made Zack and Ezra sit in there with her.

All was quiet for a long time. A night owl trebled off in the distance. The wind blew a shutter against the window frame. Then I heard Charlie say in a strained whisper, "God in heaven, no. Come back, Elsa!"

We craned our necks from the edges of windows to see the front porch. Elsa had donned her novice's white robes and stepped out into the wan moonlight. Under the pale light her milky gown looked as if light came from it. Her hair was long and black, flowing down her back. A thin blue shawl wrapped her head and slid to her shoulders. She held her hands forward, palms together and fingers pointed to the stars, as if she were in prayer, then spread her hands as her voice rang out, "*Virgencita de Guadalupe, quiero ser tu ferviente devota . . . In nombre de tu hijo.* Where are my friends? You men there, do not lay this sin to your count. *¿Cuanto? ¿Uribe? ¿Caldo? ¿A dónde mi amigos?*"

She kept on talking, to the wind and the stars, to the shadows in the barn, sometimes in Spanish, sometimes in English. Horses roused and whinnied, stamping. Somewhere, a bucket overturned. A cow lowed as if the animal mourned from some dark pain of the soul. Charlie crawled beneath the window to the door, lay on his stomach, then pulled it wider ajar.

"Call yer wife in, boy," Chess hissed.

"Too late. They ain't shot at her; maybe they'll listen. She ain't one to argue with, 'specially not now." He aimed his rifle through the slot made by the door and its jamb, waiting for any movement toward Elsa. I nudged the window up and pushed the block of wood we kept there into the sash to keep it up and trained my Winchester to Elsa's right, trying to wish a form out of the darkness upon which to level an aim.

Well, our crippled and scarred old dog Nip, poor beat-up fellow nearly trampled to death in the stampede last fall, wandered up from the corral to see what Elsa was doing. He came within ten feet of her, so that he faced her straight-on. Elsa didn't move. Her arms were still outstretched. When he satisfied himself who it was, the old boy laid down, his nose in her direction, too sore and weary to move on without a reason. When Nip goes down, because of all his broken legs and ribs, it always looks as if he were making a gentlemanly bow, lowering the front first, then his back end with perfect dignity.

Maybe those outlaws saw the dog bow before Elsa as if a supernatural being were kissing the ground before a saint. No one could say, but Nip had done just the right thing at that moment. A burst of hooves clattered on gravel, and in the shadows before the barn, five horsemen bolted for the hills toward Rudolfo's land.

Charlie flung that door wide and followed them with three shots. Then he turned on Elsa and hollered at her to get in the house, and said, "Don't you care about me at all? How can you risk yourself? Don't you love our baby?" until she was crying so hard I feared for her health. I wanted to calm him and comfort her, too, and lands, caught between them I couldn't speak a word. Thankfully, Savannah put her arms around Elsa and told everyone it was time for bed; all the women would be staying together. The men would have to decide who kept watch.

Charlie grunted and pounded his fists on the kitchen table as we left the room. I was caught up in the flutter of dovelike sounds from the women's room—Granny's old bedroom—as we made up beds for the night. I left them to return to the kitchen and bank up the fire and found Charlie alone in the parlor.

"Others sleeping?" I asked.

"Gone south. Spying on Maldonado. Watching Udell's place."

"Chess, too?"

"What could have possessed her, Mama? How could she think they wouldn't shoot her?"

"I don't know."

"This having a wife is the damnedest thing. Half the time I'm crazy in love and half the time she just keeps me crazy mad. Why I'd have torn a man apart with my bare hands if anyone had . . . I could eat nails."

"Reckon women don't think like men."

"Why on earth don't they learn how?"

I rubbed my face. "Ain't meant to, honey." I smiled and kissed his brow. "It occurs to us to ask the same thing. Keeps the world turning, I suspect."

# Chapter Seventeen

*November 12, 1907*

As the sun rose I put the morning's leftover pancakes out for our penitent dog hero, Nip, and his cohort, Shiner. They were busy eating when I saw a rider coming up from the west. He circled up on the sandy ridge, disappeared for a bit, then returned. After a long, slow ride in, a stranger got off his horse.

We had a new hand on our side! Rye Miles was good to his word. He bunked in the book room where the dandy professors had slept, and all of us felt better with him there, too. Mr. Miles went with Gilbert and Charlie down to Udell's place. They were gone about three hours and I was starting to worry when they finally came home. I went out to talk to them as they unsaddled their horses by the trough. They said they had helped Udell finish a wooden platform he has built up from the second floor with stairs and a short ladder. It's high enough that it makes a third-floor watchtower. From there, with a long glass, they watched Rudolfo's ranch compound. Gilbert said half of Rudolfo's men had deserted him after the "vision" of Nip bowing before Elsa got told around.

Miles told me, in language as colorful as any I have heard and some I wouldn't repeat, that they had a buzzard down there dressed up like a priest who took a shotgun to two of the deserters. "That's one damned evil son of a gun," he said.

"I know him," I replied. "Odd scar on his face."

Rye Miles shot a look at Charlie, who glanced at me and turned his eyes away. Both of them had the same dry expression. Charlie said, "Don't mention him to the other ladies, Mama."

"Well, come on in and have some beans and bacon," I said. "Savannah's made cornbread for an army."

Over dinner, Savannah confessed what Udell had already hinted at. Rachel and Aubrey Hanna were to marry before Thanksgiving. Mary Pearl had been sent for and someone needed to wire a ticket to her. After two hours of the family putting in each one's two bits of thoughts on it, our plan became simple. All the women would take the stagecoach to town. The men would stay to guard and keep up chores. Gilbert made each of us promise to call on Miss Charity.

The one person I most feared for, however, was Granny. Bandits who'd shoot through windows would have no qualms about stopping a stage and finishing the job. We had until the Butterfield came through again, to get everything ready.

### November 16, 1907

Heavy clouds greeted our start to the day. We waited at Marsh Station for four hours before Pancho Dailey showed up driving an eight-hitch of mules. It was a good thing he had to trade one out, for if we'd had to board in the usual way, jumping onto a slowly moving coach, Granny would have been in danger. Five other people were on the stage, and with Rebeccah, Elsa, Savannah, Granny, and myself, it seemed right packed. I was glad it was crowded, though. Granny all but disappeared in the petticoats and wrappers, and I doubted Rudolfo or his men would guess we'd take her to town, much less on a stage when we'd always driven ourselves.

Under the dark softness of the cloudy sky, with the rocking of the coach and the constant rumble of the wheels, I felt stupefied into calm and peace that I hadn't known in ages. I slept the entire trip away. When we stopped in Tucson, I let everyone else get off before me. As I alighted, the rain which had threatened all day finally began. I stood in the door of the stage and grasped the handles. As I did, raindrops speckled my fingertips, and I raised my face to let the fresh water touch my cheek.

We exchanged a wave with Mr. Dailey, and watched while he pulled in at the corral. Savannah hired a buggy to get to the house.

We arrived at Harland's front door with no warning to him that we were coming. The quiet when Rachel opened the door was alarming. She welcomed us in with a finger to her lips. The children were all in bed again, this time with mumps and dysentery. It had gone through town without mercy, the dark finger of disease marking several doors of folks we knew.

We were shown to the parlor, and in a few minutes, a nurse in a uniform came to report something to Rachel. The woman's eyes opened wide when she saw us. Elsa was obviously round, now. Elsa could not stay there, not in her condition, she said. Though the rest of us had had mumps and every other childhood ailment, the nurse feared the unborn child might take the disease somehow. It was late, and it would be another imposition, but Elsa must be sent to April's house. I said I would take her.

Rachel said, "I think you all should go. I've been ill, too, along with Uncle Harland. I think this is more common than mumps, and more catching. We are worn to exhaustion nursing children. Our first round of grippe seemed to take two weeks to come and go, then Story came home with mumps. Now, this bowel complaint is dreadful. The Taylor boy, two blocks over, died last week, and one of Morris's cousins lost a baby. April's house has been spared. Our Blessing just began to get well when she got it again." The end of her words brought the echo of some child upstairs, crying. "I'd better go see who that is," she said.

Rain drummed upon the walls and the window glass, shushing the world outside. Savannah finally spoke. "You all go to April's. I'll stay here and help Rachel." After a little discussion, it was agreed. I wanted to see Harland and his children, but it would be better not to take any chance of illness to April's home with a new baby.

We got to April's house just as they finished their supper. We were drenched. April and Morris were surprised. At least, though, it was dry indoors, and warm, and plenty spacious for Elsa, Granny, Rebeccah, and me.

The next day was Sunday. I helped my mama get dressed and she went to the parlor. While the rest of us listened, she told old stories, just like she used to do when I was a girl. She always called it "Sunday School," though none of us knew if the stories were from the Bible or not. They always were told with fervor, though, and the plots were lessons about good and evil. While their mother left to tend baby Tennyson, April's children, Vallary, Patricia, and Lorelei, gathered around and listened as if they'd never heard the like.

I slipped out of the room when everyone seemed intent on the story, and went to the front to peer out the viewing glass at the wet, gray world. The wind blew drops clinging to the wooden overhang and flung them against the bulbous front of the glass, further distorting what was already an odd reflection of the world on the other side. Every few seconds, a drop illuminated a distant picture right before my eyes. It was the last half of a billboard sign painted on the brick wall of a livery, just the word "Fargo" in bright green.

Singing coming from the parlor interrupted my concentration. I opened the front door and stepped outward, shielding my eyes with one hand. The sign was gone. There were no colors at all, just a dingy, smoke-colored wall of rain. Closing the door once again, the rain on the viewing glass lit up again. I smiled. This would have been one for Professor Osterhaas's essay on cosmic elements: raindrops that can clarify a dreary world. I turned toward the parlor and halted as if my feet suddenly took root in the rug. Fargo.

I knew a way to fight Rudolfo.

Maybe there was no power bigger than the railroad. No evil greater than greed. But there was another power I could enlist. The stage company had been here since before we came. All these years I'd given Wells Fargo a sort of squatter's right to cross below that sandy cliff. All these years I'd watered their mules and fed their drivers when they asked it. Maybe the Eastern money that fueled the coal-smoke-belching railroad was in a bigger bank, but the Wells Fargo had roots here. If the land didn't belong to Granny or to me, but to the Wells Fargo company, then let the giants storm heaven, and I will be like Artemis and Wells Fargo will be my Apollo. I'll never quit fighting for my land.

I thought about it all through the morning and by noon I knew just what I would do. The hardest part would be waiting until tomorrow when the bank opened up.

Well, that afternoon we were all surprised to find Savannah and Rachel at the door. Savannah explained, "I just wanted to let you all know and ease your worries. Their sickness is no different than trail fever. Bad water, if you ask me. I boiled up a dozen kettles of water and started dosing everyone with plain, clean-boiled water. Within two hours, all the stomach complaints began to calm. Tomorrow I'm going to boil the linens and all their clothes, too. April, you must boil all the water your children touch."

April said, "Well, that probably isn't necessary, Aunt Savannah."

"Why not?" I asked.

"Because, Mother. Because, really, I hate to say it, but, well, this is a better part of town. Our water is always cool. Sometimes theirs is hot. All the best people build on this end of town."

"But that was my house. It's a good house. There's nothing wrong with living there."

"No, of course not," April said. "It's just that this is healthier."

"If you asked me, I'd say the problem wasn't the class of people living in a place but the class of plumbing fixtures they had." I said, "Ladies? Will you join us in rescuing Rachel and her charges?"

Savannah ducked her head. "It is the Sabbath, Sarah. I didn't mean to create work for you all."

I patted her arm. "And if thy neighbor's ox fall in a ditch on the Sabbath? I can be ready in two shakes. We've got sheets to boil."

Elsa and Granny remained with April. The rest of us took to Harland's house in a way that would have made prim and starched Mrs. Everly seem to be a sloven harridan. All the bedding was laid out on the back porch, rain and all. Sheets dried in rows in the kitchen, and one by one, warm and pristine makeshift pallets held the sick of the household. That evening, we sent both Rachel and Rebeccah to April's, and Savannah and I stayed. We bathed the children and rubbed them with alcohol spirits and water, and threatened Harland with the same if he refused to have an hour's soak in a tub of the same mixture. Of course, his children thought that was riotously funny, though I wonder if they doubted my ability to make good on the threat.

Blessing's drawn and sad appearance was hardest to take lightly. The girl had grown thin and narrow, and her large eyes were seared with heat, staring from a fevered brow. Still, she grinned when she saw me, and after her bath, climbed into my lap and soon was fast asleep. All day as I tended my family, I thought on my plan. Calculated my acreage. Did sums in my head that would have made Miss Alice proud.

### November 18, 1907

Monday morning, early, after finding Harland dressed and sipping tea, I proposed my idea to him.

"There are two parts of this, Harland. First, you know I own a few thousand acres, and leases on more. Some of it runs east of the line they have drawn across Mama's land, although they've cut a swath on my property too, near where the stage line runs. But some of the best flatland is far south, beyond

Rudolfo's place and due north of the Mexican border. I figure once they get tracks laid on Mama's land he'll run me off the rest, too. So why not sell it? To the stage line. If Rudolfo wants it that much, someone else will, too."

"But Sis, you have spent your life building that ranch. It's your legacy. You've said as much yourself."

"I don't mean all of it. Just the south lease and a couple of sections north of the border. Some people keep money in a bank. I have kept mine in the ground. We can't eat dirt and I can't buy stock. I need to draw out some cash to keep going. That's all. Good times, bad, they will both come again. Also, I can't pass down a legacy to ghosts. I think Rudolfo will gladly see us all in the ground before he'll quit. The only way I see to come out on top is to find a buyer.

"Second thing is Mama's homestead. She doesn't live on it nor work it, and I think she'd as soon sell it as let the railroad take it for nothing. Since we—you, Albert, and I—are the beneficiaries of it, if we agreed to ask her to sell it now—"

"But it's the principle of the thing."

I got my back up. Did he think principles could stop bullets? "That only holds up if both sides have the same principles, Harland."

He took a sip from his cup of tea. "What does Albert say?"

"I hadn't thought of this when I left home. Savannah's here. She'd know how he would decide. She can speak for him."

"We can't take Mama's place from her."

"I'm not saying take it. She lives with me and likely always will. She's not crazy, you know. I have seen how she aches for every one of us that has died. Each one in the ground pushes her farther into the shadows of her mind. That land is not so important and her reason isn't so gone she can't figure it will save us a bloody range war."

"I don't want any of the money from it, then."

"No. I don't either. It's hers. I'll keep strict accounts and show them to you whenever you please."

"All right, then. It has to go to making her life as sweet as it can be for the rest of her days."

"Anything she wants. If you're agreed, then I'll go ask Savannah."

"We can ride to the bank in my new horseless carriage. I will go put the top on in case it rains again."

I stopped at the door and turned.

"The thing is, Harland," I said, "that I want everyone to hear us ask her and

I don't want anyone to put words in her head or push the idea. It's got to be her free and clear choice or we've railroaded her, same as Rudolfo."

"Agreed," he said. Are you sure we're healthy and it's all right to go to a house with a baby?"

"Look how you all have changed with twelve hours of absolute cleanliness."

"But April won't know about that. It's possible she'd blame us for bringing it."

"I think it will be all right," I said. "It has likely run its course by now."

We drove to April's and laid our plan before our mother. Addled as she could be, yesterday with the Sunday School and singing, why Mama seemed to have lost fifteen years and was bright and sassy. She listened closely, then shut her eyes for a whole minute, nodding. Then with a pound from her tiny fist, she hollered, "Sell it all, then. Sell whatever it needs. You put yours in, and we'll show those blackhearted thieves who's boss."

"Agreed?" I said.

"I'm coming, too. Fetch my shawl," Granny said.

"But Grandma," April said quickly, "won't you stay and tell the children more stories?"

"Fiddlesticks. You tell 'em. You're their ma. Get me to the bank, girl."

Harland, Granny, Savannah, and I rode in his horseless carriage. We stopped at the telegraph office to send a wire to Mary Pearl, along with purchasing a round-trip ticket home and back with a week's stay in between. From there to the bank, Harland and I argued every foot of the way about what my land was worth. He said prices had gone up. That I could get six or seven thousand for what I wanted to sell. I told him I'd take a thousand dollars just to have this settled and know the railroad wouldn't cross my place, and though the tracks were on Granny's land, no engine would ever roll on them. Then we pulled deeds on Mama's land and every parcel I owned. Finally, we came to a halt in front of the Wells Fargo office, and walked right upstairs to the manager's office, barging in on Mr. Thompkins.

The other three sat quietly while I laid forth my plan. We would sell the stage coach company the western half of Granny's claim, and incorporate the eastern parcel into Albert's land. I told Thompkins there were rail tracks already laid there, although the rail company had no valid deed to it. "This here is the original deed to the land. Free and clear, homesteaded and patent filed. So there'd be some kind of tussle with Santa Fe. But no matter how it came out," I said, "the stage company would own the land the rails went through." We offered Granny's parcel for two thousand dollars. That man's eyes lit up like firecrackers on a dark night though he said nothing. "Then," I added, "I've got another parcel for sale here, due south in a direct line that stops just north of Benson and runs eleven hundred acres, see along this line here?" I pointed on my deed map. "It's cattle land, and there's a windmill already there. Plus a four-thousand-acre lease east-southeast of that. You'd have a straight shot to Fort Huachuca."

A cocky look spread across his face as if the man were sure we'd come to boondoggle him. "And what, pray tell, do you want for that? A million dollars? Five million?"

I glanced at Harland. Then I said, "I figure with what I put into it, and what I paid for it, and that there's nothing much on it, I'd take two thousand for that one, too."

"And what?"

"I said two thousand. For the eleven hundred clear and the four-thousand lease. Long-term."

"What's the matter with it? Indians? Squatters?"

"Let's just say I'm running fewer head of cattle. I'll still have sixteen hundred acres and two other leases. That's enough for me."

The fellow looked Harland up and down. He said, "I saw what you came here in. Somebody here's got money. What's the real truth, Mr. Prine? What's on that land?"

I could see he was intent on doing business with Harland over my very land, just because Harland had on the only pair of pants in the room besides his own. I leaned forward, resting my arms on the desk. Harland followed suit. Savannah sat up straight, and our mother just grinned, watching it all. Harland said, "Railroad."

"Yes," I followed. "Nothing's cut yet but the first road across a half-acre section. There's a cattle track used by some smugglers a while back. But the Santa Fe men are eyeing the whole way. The Wells Fargo could buy it from me outright and then sell them the right of way to use it."

He stared at each of us in turn. Studied the deeds before him. "Why aren't you selling it to them? You make them that offer, they'd take it, I can almost promise you." Then he made a tent with his fingertips and leaned back into his spring-loaded chair. Waiting.

I straightened. "It's my land. I'll sell it or not to whomever I please."

Thompkins touched his chin with the tips of his finger tent. "Truth is, folks, we're not really interested in this right now. It's a nice offer, but no thanks."

My foot clunked against the chair, betraying my surprise and dismay. I held my chin firm and started to say he *had* to reconsider, or offer to lower the price, but I felt something jerking at my skirt. I looked down at my side to see Harland's hand motioning me to leave the room. My brother stood and tipped his hat, escorting us to the door, thanking Mr. Thompkins for his time, and hurriedly shooed us to the horseless carriage.

"Harland, where are we going? What are you doing?"

"Taking us on a ride. That was a tactic, sister. He's seeing if you're really desperate, if you'd come back again. Didn't you see his hands touch his chin? So we're going to go for a little ride. A nice run up and down Speedway Road. I'll show you where they've actually put a limit on how fast you can drive, while Thompkins sends some red-hot wires back East. You saw his face. We'll hear from him later."

We pulled onto Speedway Road. Savannah said, "Brother Harland, you aren't really going to go seven miles an hour, are you?"

He laughed and said, "I'll behave, for your sake, dear sister." Harland drove us up and down the length of it, and then we motored home. Now all we had to do was wait.

### November 19, 1907

Blessing was at last sitting up and playing quietly with some paper dolls. Now we'd spend time putting some meat on the poor child's bones, and then let her return to school. In my room in Harland's house, my stack of schoolbooks called out to me. I didn't own them. I needed to return them, at least, so I hitched up the buggy and drove to the college in the early afternoon. A cold wind whipped the ties of my hat around. It was a sad but good feeling, a finalness, to go one by one past the mathematics room and the science room and leave off the books. Classes were in session, so I just stood them against the doorjamb. Someone would take them inside. Then I stopped at Professor Fairhaven's room. The door was closed, but the early class wouldn't start for half an hour, and my session wasn't for two hours. I didn't plan to wait that long, so I pushed it open. Professor Fairhaven turned sharply at the sound. A young woman I didn't recognize stepped backward from him, blushing, shielding her face with a hand.

"I won't be needing this," I said. "Can't finish the classwork."

"Oh, Mrs. Elliot! The faculty has been so worried. We were quite distressed when you failed to return."

"Thanks, I'm sure."

"Have you been ill?"

"I was detained out of town. Personal matter."

Professor Fairhaven asked me to stay and said he'd help me catch up on my grades. While the girl cleaned the slate boards, I told him that there had been bandits down our way and I couldn't leave my family. He listened very sympathetically but couldn't believe I didn't want to continue his class even with his special help.

By the time I got clear of that long-toothed rascal, Professor Osterhaas's class had actually begun. I intended to leave the book by the door but that boy Foster came late and opened it up, holding it for me to enter. Well, the professor's eyes seemed so kind, so like I remembered my papa's when he'd ask me what I'd done wrong, I felt like telling him some of what had really happened. The whole class listened.

Finally, Osterhaas said, "All of us know, or will someday, that education is a precious privilege, and not to be taken for granted. Events of late have conspired against you, Mrs. Elliot, through no fault of your own."

"That's true enough," I said.

"Have you brought your essay? If you could only read your essay for us. You are the last one yet. That would be nice."

"My essay?"

"The 'What I Want' essay?"

"Oh, that. Yes, well." I leafed through the pages of the book. My essay had grown from one page to eight, and then over the last days I'd been in class it had shrunk until it was hardly a paragraph. I looked at it more closely. The sentences around were all crossed out, too, and I'd never repenned it. The paper was ragged and hashed this way and that. "Oh, it's nothing much, anymore. I haven't had a chance to work on it."

"But you have it? Read it. Read it aloud so I can give you a grade. There are only three more weeks of this school term. I can pass you on this class if you'll read it."

I eyed the other students. Then I turned to the professor. "You'll give me a grade, when I haven't been here?"

He shrugged. "You did a great deal of work. If you have your essay, then? The floor is yours."

"But it's just a sentence. Nothing much."

"Please."

The paper shook in my hand. My throat turned parched. I read my silly excuse of an essay very slowly, for my eyes had to chase the trembling page for every syllable. "What I want. I dream of land, cut only where streams glistened with birdsong wander through quiet hills burnt hard by the scrape of wind, and of a porch from which a single road leads only homeward." Then I looked up. "That's all there is."

Professor Osterhaas had tears in his eyes. He raised both his hands and gave a faint clap, which the other students joined with soft applause. He said, "Will you stay so we may discuss the writing of it?"

"I think, sir, there isn't much to discuss. It started with a whole list of things. Then pretty soon it was about folks, health, and money, and good marriages and friendship, and all, and then it changed. The harder things got at home, the shorter the list went. Reckon you can take anything away, even happiness. In the end, this is all I want from the world. The rest, a person's got to make for themselves."

"I'll give you your class, Mrs. Elliot. I think a B minus is in order. Your grades will be posted at the end of the term with the others. You have passed this class."

I simply nodded and slipped out. I was so overcome, I rushed to the library and dashed down the stairs, looking for an empty corner in which to hide. I slipped into a dark little storeroom that smelled of must and mice, and propped myself on a chair. I'd passed a class. I'd gone to college and done it. Not everything, not like a girl might do with the world at her feet, but I'd done one. I held my shoulders and squeezed. A powerful joy filled me. A single class was something. A little piece of a dream was still a dream. No one could ever say I hadn't learned a trainload of things, most of it not from the books. I'd gone to school at last. And I'd made it.

"Ma'am?" said a boy. "We usually practice in this room about now. It's nice and quiet down here, you know. And the echo is good. May we ask—"

I smiled. "I was just leaving," I said.

But I didn't leave. I lingered outside the door to the little room. Five boys went in, one carrying a ukulele. He plucked a string and they began to sing. They did a ragtime and "Sweet Caroline," and then while the others hummed, one young fellow alone sang "Rose of Tralee" in a way that like to melted me from the inside out. His voice was like the sound of pouring water. I hurried to the steps, wanting to leave that place while I could still hear the music, ever so faintly.

After supper, I stretched my legs downtown, taking a peaceful stroll along the boardwalk, pausing to eye the goods in Corbet's store. I was still out of cash, so I kept myself from going inside. As I headed home, I passed a little restaurant. There in the corner, I saw the back of a head I recognized. Professor Osterhaas sat at dinner with his back to the window.

I hadn't thanked him for what he'd done, so I stepped inside. As I went toward him, I stopped short. Across the table from him, facing me, sat a man I knew from Rudolfo's parlor last Christmas, Herr Von Wangenheim. He glanced up but then returned to his conversation. He hadn't recognized me. The two were in hushed conversation, speaking German. A chill understanding seeped through me. Von Wangenheim had sat with the men scheming to overthrow the Mexican government. It didn't matter what I thought of don Porfirio; they were dangerous men. Now he sat with my favorite professor. The two of them spoke the language of the men running guns through my land. No matter what else might bind them, in this country a man is known by the men he rides with. I turned away. Trusting I hadn't been seen by Professor Osterhaas, I rushed from the building and didn't slow until I reached Harland's house.

# Chapter Eighteen

*November 20, 1907*

Granny and I stayed at Harland's place, Savannah, Rebeccah, and Elsa at April's house. To fill the waiting, I bought some saucy blue calico with little white kittens chasing balls of black yarn and I'm sewing Blessing a new frock. Mary Pearl will arrive Friday at noon, and I promised Blessing she could probably have it by then. It hasn't mattered much that she has missed school. The whole place had closed down for a week and a day, due to mumps. Even a few of the teachers were out with it. Sad to say, April was right about the water, too. They have notified half the town to drink boiled water until further work is done on the fresh-water system. Meanwhile, I try not to worry or even think about my sons and their uncle and grandpa, and of course, Udell, down there holding off Rudolfo's raiders. Sheriff Pacheco was not around his office, and the deputy, Oscar Carillo, wouldn't tell me where he had gone, but I reckon it is a big county.

*November 21, 1907*

Thursday afternoon we gathered in the parlor. Rachel was running Story, Honor, and Truth through their spelling lessons; I had Blessing standing on a chair in her dress so I could pin the hem. A sudden sharp rapping at the door startled me so that I dropped the scissors and the button bag at the same time, making a terrible racket, too. "Blessing," I said, "will you help me and collect these again while I get the door?"

There stood Mr. Thompkins and two other men. One was a stranger. The other was Mr. Richards from the railroad. Thompkins held his hat and said, "Mrs. Elliot? I trust you are well? May we speak with you and your brother and sister?"

"Come in, gentlemen," I said. "I will have to send for them. Harland is at his office and Mrs. Prine is up the road at my daughter's home."

Before I knew it, Rachel had sent for tea and told Truth to ride his bicycle to his papa's office, and to ask him to rush to April's house and have Aunt Savannah come. She really did manage everything well, and I could see how she might be a good wife for a prominent young lawyer. Mary Pearl would have some stretching to do to reach her sister. They were different as could be. "Have him fetch Aubrey Hanna, too," I said. The men smiled as if they knew the name.

It took half an hour to get us collected. Thompkins introduced his engineer, a man named Travis Bondurant, and Mr. Richards, who doffed his hat and nearly dropped it in his haste.

I said, "But Mr. Richards, I thought you worked for the railroad?"

Richards said, "Not exactly, ma'am. The firm I'm employed by will of course negotiate rights of way on this land and the sections that separate them. That initial survey and staking that was done was because of the flatness of that parcel. If we have access to the larger parcel, well, it changes everything."

Mr. Thompkins said, "Well, now, we've got experts working on the changes right this minute."

"Angles and trajectories," the third man said. "Travis Bondurant, engineer, ma'am. With this wider upper acreage, we can drop the angle of the tracks crossing the Cienega Creek and head west another mile then south-southeast to connect right down to your parcel. It will bypass that silty loam deposit and the—"

Thompkins interrupted. "What Mr. Bondurant means, Mrs. Elliot, is that is a problem our men will work out to everyone's satisfaction. Just do not worry yourself about it. Our men have everything under control. We are so pleased you came to us, and we could do business with you on this. Our colleagues at the home office already knew of your good character, the way you saved the travelers, the coach, even returned the mules from last year, so when a chance came to assist you, they would not in good conscience have passed it up."

With Aubrey watching, Granny made an *X*, and the three of us signed our names to a document that turned over half my mama's original homestead to the company. Instead of the two thousand we asked for it, they paid two thousand dollars each, six thousand total. "Now, in lieu of negotiations my secretary has drawn up a check for you, payable immediately," Thompkins said. For the eleven hundred acres of my own, and rights to the land lease, instead of two thousand dollars, Mr. Thompkins opened a leather secretary and took out a bank check made out to me in the amount of fifteen thousand dollars. Wells Fargo and Company was taking up my offer and then some.

"But why?" I asked. "If you could have had it for a song, why pay this kind of money?"

Aubrey spoke up. "Of course, Wells Fargo and Company would wish to avoid the appearance of any conflict of interest. It is a fair market price for the property."

Richards, who always did strike me as slicker than a pan full of cold bacon, said, "I would never rest peacefully again if we were to give any less to you, a soldier's widow, dear Mrs. Elliot."

I took the check in my hands, reading the sum again as if the ink might evaporate right off it before my eyes.

Richards said, "They will use the spur already laid, of course."

"Will they cross the land between?" Savannah asked.

I looked from her to my brother, and back to the check. We all knew Rudolfo owned the land in between. If they were in league with him anyway, they would have free rein of it. I sure hoped Udell wouldn't be able to hear trains crossing from his house.

We bid those men good afternoon, and then Aubrey and Harland took Savannah and me to the bank to put the checks in our accounts. Seventeen thousand dollars would keep my ranch solvent for six years or more. I could restock my fields and Udell's, too. I took five hundred back in cash for some operating money.

By the time supper was done, we all felt as if we'd had a party. As he was fixing to leave, I asked Aubrey if he thought me getting those folks out of the wrecked stage was really enough reason for them to pay ten times my price on the land.

He just grinned and said, "A stage wreck is no small matter, especially when someone dies. Mrs. Elliot, the things you did that day saved them several potential lawsuits. That wasn't about a conflicting interest or any scruples because you are widowed. The company figured they owed you plenty. Why, they could easily have paid out a hundred thousand or more in damages by the time it was all settled. You just trussed up those birds and served them supper and no one thought to make a fuss. This is peanuts compared to what you could have had if you'd wanted to hold your foot on their necks for a while."

"I'd never do that."

"I know, ma'am. Thing is, they don't know it."

"Good night, Aubrey."

"Evening, Mrs. Elliot."

I liked that young man. I just wished he wasn't playing so lightly with my girl's feelings.

### November 22, 1907

The whole herd of us showed up on the train platform at a quarter to noon. When that engine steamed in and those brakes squealed, we all held our breaths as one, searching the passengers. Finally, there she was. No longer slender as a flower stem, Mary Pearl's figure had blossomed into womanhood. She wore a new dress, or one that had been made over. Her face seemed different, too, her smile more fetching and her hair perfectly tucked under a lovely, flowered wide hat. She kissed and was kissed until all were satisfied she was still our girl.

Saturday, we persuaded Deputy Carillo to ride along with our family back to the ranch, to see if any trouble had come up. Just because there was no longer a need for anyone to falsely inherit my mother's land, that didn't mean some long-necked renegade mightn't keep on trying. It would be just what I would expect of Rudolfo not to call off his dogs even when the fight was over. Feeling as if I were back on top of at least half my trials, we had a fine ride home, and heard wonderful things about Mary Pearl's time in Wheaton. She pressed me for my own stories, and I told her how I'd kept the one class, and that it was enough for me. She smiled, but I don't think she understood me.

April and Morris drove behind us in their own coach with all their children. Every little while, I thought I heard Tennyson make a racket. Rachel came along, too, of course, only she rode in a separate carriage with Aubrey. He would spend the night at Udell's, and then they would declare the wedding Sunday. The only one missing was Harland. He'd said that without Rachel there, he was caught short, because he didn't want to risk taking the children all that way and back in two days so he could return to work Monday. They'd been too sick too long, he said, and so would have to miss the wedding. Then he promised he'd come down for Thanksgiving next week. It would have to do.

Chess and the boys whooped and hollered when they saw us coming. We brought food and supplies, too, so it was a fine evening and we stayed up late, telling all that had passed in town. If only Harland and his brood had come, everything would be perfect. Deputy Carillo kept on going, said he'd take a ride down to Naco and Nogales before coming back this way.

Then I looked through the faces. Udell was not among them. Tomorrow, he would come for his son's wedding day. That night as I lay in bed, trying to see stars out my window, I hoped Udell was safely home. Not shot, or sick. I wished he had come tonight. He could sleep somewhere, though there was a crowd. Having him here with us was only normal and right. First thing, I would tell him about selling part of my land. I'm sure he will think I've done the right thing.

### November 24, 1907

It was cold as December as we crowded into Albert and Savannah's parlor. Aubrey and Rachel held hands. Both of them nearly glowed with happiness and the sweetness of their age. I watched Mary Pearl for an hour, as she smiled and teased and hugged everyone she got nearby. Then she disappeared and I figured she must have been tired. I worked my way through the long legs and talking voices toward the kitchen, where Rebeccah and April stood cake duty. April said Mary Pearl had gone to catch her breath outside.

I slipped out the door, heading first for the outhouse. Finding it empty, I went to the barn and then the pecan house. I thought I heard a kitten, and went in the door, leaving it ajar. Mary Pearl sat on a stave barrel, weeping in broken-hearted sobs. "Oh, honey," I said, and threw my arms around her. "Oh, honey," was all I could get out.

Mary Pearl fell onto my shoulder, crying, "He's married her, Aunt Sarah. He's gone and married. Why couldn't he wait for me?"

"I don't know, Mary Pearl."

"He was *my* beau. Not hers. Rachel took him from me. Stole him. I hate her."

"She's your sister. Do you really think she meant to fall in love with him?"

After several more sobs, she said, "No. I don't hate her. This is his fault. He said he loved me. He *kissed* me. And I kissed him—back!"

"I know, I know. Still, if you loved him, honey, did you ever tell him? That letter sounded like he didn't mean a thing to you."

"Of course he did. He knew that. I kissed him! I'll love him for the rest of my life, Aunt Sarah. I know he loves me, too."

"No, now don't go saying that. You just quit loving him! He doesn't love you any more and you get that through your head. You released him from his promise, just like you wanted. Sometimes for men, it's different. They can kiss you just because they like kissing. Then sometimes it isn't the girl they're after, they're just in the mood to get married. Remember. Now Rachel's going to live her life in town, not out here. You go through your life telling yourself he carries a torch for you, and you'll know nothing but bitterness and hurt the rest of your days."

She wept again, while I held her and patted her back. "Now, then," I said. "We'd better be getting back before someone else comes out to hunt you. I've got to say, the way you stood up in there and smiled and petted everyone, no one would have known you cared a hoot. Were you just pretending to be happy?"

"I—I couldn't hurt Rachel. It is her beautiful day. I couldn't spoil it by being a fool in front of her. I tried to be happy for them, but I just couldn't."

"Don't, then. No one requires you to feel happy about someone else's life. Just brave about your own."

She snuffled into her handkerchief and smoothed her hair. Mary Pearl said, "You know what he did? Remember when he promised me he'd buy the Wainbridge ranch for us to live on, and then wanted to go live in town anyway? Well, he gave me the ranch as a token, he said. I own a stupid ranch, all to myself. It was in my name anyway and he said he wanted there to be no bad blood between us. Ha."

"You mean there still is bad blood, far as you're concerned?"

"I was worth a few hundred acres of tumbleweed, at least."

I shook her by the shoulders, gently. "Listen to me. I never told you this, but my first husband married me when he loved another girl. She wasn't handy, and I was. I told myself he loved me but he never cared for me. Never lost one second of thought over anything I wanted or needed. I was nothing but a brood mare to him, a thing to use. No more count than a hired hand he didn't have to pay. If Aubrey had wanted to wait for you he would have and no one could have stopped him. Your sister Rachel, look at me, now, Rachel is more like him in every way. He is not the man for you, and you as good as said it yourself before you left."

"Why can't a man have any sense?"

"Ask your cousin Charlie."

"I don't want anyone to think I've been crying. Do I look like I've been crying?"

Her eyes were awfully red. "I'll tell you what I did on my last day in Brownie's class, and then you can tell them all you've been laughing until you cried. Let's go back to the house."

## November 25, 1907

"Sarah?" Granny's voice was a whisper, but I had just gone to sleep and I awoke startled and filled with dread at the tone of it. "Sarah, get up. Somebody's pot-shot at the house again. We got to move from this wild town, get out to where it's peaceful. Too many strangers hereabouts and them cowboys drinking and carousing is going to kill someone."

The moment my feet touched the floor I heard a loud gunshot and then Chess let out a roar. "Gotcha! You sons a guns! Eat that for yer supper, snake in the grass!"

We spent a wakeful night. In the morning, we found that whoever Chess had shot at had been hit. Sign was there, as if he'd been deer hunting and not gotten a clean kill. We examined the slugs left in the adobe wall, and Granny told us repeatedly where she'd been standing when they found their mark. Luck was all that kept her alive. One bullet had been too far right and the other only missed because she'd turned to see what was the noise on the wall. Had she been daydreaming and not concerned, the second bullet would have hit her square in the chest.

"Ain't it been about half a week since we signed them papers?" Granny asked. Before I could answer, she said, "Well, likely Maldonado's found out now. Three, four days. Don't take long to get a letter from Tucson to here. He's mad as a hornet. That's all. Pure-D mad."

"I was thinking the same thing," I said. "We out-foxed him and he's boiling over. Given some time, he'd simmer down."

Chess said, "Well, not if he's coming to gun us all down first."

"Starting with Granny," I said.

Charlie was the first one to say aloud what I was thinking. "What do you suppose is going on at Hanna's place?"

"We'll need to ride down there. But I think we'd better get Granny and Elsa to town until things settle."

I wanted Granny with me, but the only way for her to be safe was someplace else. Moving Granny up the road less than a mile to Albert and Savannah's place only brought the danger to their doorstep. I didn't want to leave Chess and the boys here with Elsa. Didn't want to leave Udell without checking on him regularly. The only thing I knew to do that didn't involve running to marry in too much hurry, was to take Granny to town.

Everyone but my mama favored it. Granny got plum tired, she said, of all this wrangling over her like she was some old stray cat. She knew what she wanted, she said. She wanted to go live with Udell Hanna.

"Oh, now this puts a new wrinkle in everything," Charlie said. "Granny, I believe you're sweet on the old boy."

"Come over here so's I can paddle you, boy," she said.

Charlie'd make two of his granny. He laughed, looking down at her, and swelled his shoulders out so he looked even bigger. Then he obliged her, crossing his arms over his chest, which was higher than her head, and turning his back pockets toward her, to which she gave a good slap.

She pursed her lips at him, a move made all the more silly by her lack of teeth. Then she said, "That young feller needs tending if he catches another fever. You said yourself, Sarah, he's gone 'n builded me a room. What's wrong with it?"

"Well, Mama," I said, "you'd have to go cooking and cleaning for a man, instead of taking your leisure like you do here. You'd be plum worn out from work."

"Hard work never kil't anybody," she said.

I smiled and said, "I just don't believe it's a good idea to move in on his hospitality until we get some things ironed out. I don't want anyone taking shots at Udell's place, either, and here, we've got more folks around to keep watch."

"Who's to say," said Chess, "that Maldonado won't send his men to murder the lot of us? That'd make it easier for him to take the whole place, wouldn't it? Just 'cause he's sore. I say we stick. Dig in. Not retreat."

Charlie shot a look toward Elsa. "I think we could make use of that watchtower that Udell's built. Ask him to keep watch from there and signal if there's trouble."

"Easier to fight from here than on the road again," Chess said. "These walls'll stop a shell. Nothing you can hide behind out there."

That man has always had a knack of laying bare a thing I couldn't see.

### November 26, 1907

We got a wonderful surprise this morning. Sheriff Pacheco rode up with two deputies and told us he'd just been down to Rudolfo's and that everyone was "straightened out." They stayed with us long enough for some biscuits and beans and coffee. When I asked what he meant by that, Nabor Pacheco just said we'd have no more problems with our neighbors. As they got ready to leave, though, the sheriff turned to Chess, I reckon because he figured him to be *el patrón,* and said, "If there are any more troubles, Mr. Elliot, you do what you have to do." So then, after figuring that everything would be all right, Rye Miles decided he'd mosey on down the road toward Naco, though we told him he was surely welcome to return for Thanksgiving supper if he was of a mind to.

All is peaceful and silent, save for the noises of cooking and cleaning. Rudolfo's men have drawn back and we think we are free to come and go at last. Gilbert went to town to bring his girl here for Thanksgiving. I told him to buy sugar, too, as we have pies to bake. He was there and back in a single day. Miss James—Charity—acts nice and friendly but he came home nervous and touchy. Chess tells me to leave the boy alone, that he's got his grandmother's eyes, whatever that means.

Granny seems healed up, and is back to her regular sewing and snoozing habits as if little has changed except the bandage on her finger now and then getting in her way. She tried for two days to sit in the center plaza and enjoy the geraniums and purple wandering Jew plant I've got potted there, but says she just can't abide not having a horizon and a road to watch. So, against my stern warnings she has resumed her perch on the rocking chair out front. Though all has remained quiet, I worry for her safety after that fool plot of Rudolfo's. If we get through the next couple of days without any lead flying, a genuine Thanksgiving will surely be in order this year.

I've been missing Udell something awful. With Rachel and Aubrey gone on a honeymoon trip, he's down there in that house alone. I wanted him to come for supper Thursday so I took Hatch and went for a ride to his place. I got off the horse by the garden fence, where I found him hard at work.

He waved and pulled off his hat. "Mrs. Elliot?" he called. "Morning. Just stringing some vine stakes. How goes *your* garden?"

"Pretty well, thank you. Are you putting in peas already?"

"Going to be cold next week. I feel it in my bones. Time to get them in is now, I believe."

I agreed. "If you have troubles with black worms, mix some snuff tobacco and cayenne in water, shake that on the leaves. Not too heavy though, the plants don't care for it, either. What is this, here?"

"Believe it's called chard. Greens of some sort. I ordered some things in a catalog. Just liked the looks of it. Might give it a try."

"Would you have Thanksgiving supper with us, then?"

"I'd be obliged."

I waited. He looked down at his gloves and worked some mud off one of the fingers. Hatch leaned her head in and tried to get a sniff of a cucumber vine. "Get out of there, Hatch," I said. "Well. Reckon I'll be going, then."

"Thanks for the invitation. I'll be along, Thursday. Good day, Mrs. Elliot."

"Good day, Mr. Hanna."

I gave Hatch too hard a nudge and she bolted a few steps before I settled her. What had I expected? I had freed him from his promise, just like Mary Pearl had done with Aubrey. A man had to have some pride, after all. One of us was a danged fool, and I didn't believe it was the fellow in the garden.

I tried to stay too busy to think about Udell coming for supper. Or Thanksgiving, or anything. Harland and the children would come, and Gilbert could sit with Miss Charity alongside his brother and Elsa. Everyone would be there but Rachel and Aubrey.

### November 27, 1907

Thanksgiving Day. This house has never seen so much flurry. Ezra and Zack have forgotten that they were ever banned from this place, and Ezra is lying under the kitchen table with a twig of broom, tickling anyone that catches his fancy. Zachary made himself a slingshot and was in the yard trying to aim rocks at the chopping stump, so I asked Savannah to tell him to shoot at something else. He could get bits of rock buried in my stump so the axe might go dull or split off a piece of steel. Savannah has brought me another start of chickens. Five hens and a rooster. Clover was out raking and cleaning the old coop for us, so that none of the salt might accidentally get into new chicken feed. Finally, after Ezra wouldn't leave Rebeccah's ankles alone, I sent him to help Clove. Last thing we needed, I told him, was someone to get tickled and drop a pie.

*November 28, 1907*

The day of our great thankfulness has come and gone. We had a fine time. Savannah gave me a gift of a cloth for the table cover, all fancy embroidered, heavy linen, two layers thick, with roses on every corner. I told everyone the first galoot to spill something on my fine new tablecloth was going to rue the day. Everyone laughed, but everyone was careful, too. The only cloud on our horizon was that empty seats called out amongst us. We waited dinner until nearly two, and then ate it, hoping Harland and his children would arrive before we got to the coffee and pie. Udell came, brought a bowl of that chard he'd cooked up with some dried bacon and it was real tasty. He smiled and was polite, and then left for home. Watching him ride slowly toward the horizon, I felt a huge emptiness fill the air around me. By suppertime when everyone else went back to the table for more, we all kept looking out, hoping to see Harland drive up in his fine buggy.

Friday came and went and still he didn't appear. I spent the day at Savannah's place, helping to get Mary Pearl's things washed and ironed for her ride back to Illinois until Christmas. She'll bring her horse with her, then, but for now, we had plenty to do. We'd leave at dawn the next day to get her to town to catch the six-thirty north.

*November 29, 1907*

Albert drove Savannah and Mary Pearl in their surrey. I drove behind, fighting a brisk side wind. After we saw her off and the train puffed and rumbled away, Gil and I carried Miss Charity to her little boardinghouse. Albert and Savannah drove on to April's place. In a devilishly cold wind that stung my face with rain and ice, Gil and I finally pulled our buggy in at Harland's yard. It was nigh on eight in the evening. The house was dark, except for a dim light coming from an upstairs window.

Gil said, "Something looks wrong," as if he could hear my own thoughts. We went about unhitching the team together, making quick work of it, though my sense of worry grew with each little chore. Harland's horses were out of food and water both, and so we tended them, too. I'd have a word about these poor horses with my brother, grown or not. No woman who'd been raised on a ranch, lived on one still, and intended to be put to rest on that same land would make a move to her own comfort until the creatures entrusted to her care were tended. Those poor animals drank as if they would gladly drown themselves, as if they had been thirsting for days. The smell of them wasn't clean, either. The floor was rancid and terrible. I grabbed a handful of the oats in their mangers and smelled rust and mold on it. That meant cleaning it all out for them, too. It was a good half hour before we could even get to the house. By then, I was near panicked with worry over what could have possessed Harland to let this happen.

As we finally left the barn, the night's full blackness eked into every crevice around the house. The light from that single window on the third floor now glowed brighter against the pitch of shadows.

Gil got to the back door a step ahead of me and held it ajar. The two of us fumbled in the kitchen, looking for lamps and sulfur matches. The stove was hot, so we put more kindling and a good log in it, to bring some flame back up. The first two lamps we found were dry, but the third was full and we lit it with a sprig from the fire in the stove. Gil held the lamp high. Dirty dishes were piled about. Rags lay in heaps in the corners, as if a quick escape had happened, some days before we arrived. We made our way toward the broad staircase and went up it, fear prodding our steps to a lively pace. "Harland?" I called out.

A door crept open as if pushed by someone very timid, or old, or—sick. My brother stood before me, his hair dampened, his skin glowing and wet, his clothes a matted wreck. "Is it night already?" he asked. "Sarah, see if you can do something. Please? See."

I took him by the arm and shook him. His clothes were so damp I wondered if he had gone plum insane, had the windows open and was standing in front of them, catching the rain. He was beside himself, quivering, worse than I'd found him when his wife was dying of cancer. "Harland, get hold of yourself. Do something about what?"

"I need more steam kettles. The stove may have gone out. Some of them aren't hot enough anymore."

I gave him a shake and shifted my shoulders down, bracing for some kind of nightmare in the room beyond him—beyond the door to Blessing's room. I flung it open and entered a damp, clammy world. The very air hung with cloying mist, the curtains sagged, the counterpane was stained with brown, and the place smelled of kerosene and dank old woolen clothes. First thing I wanted to do was throw open a window and let in the fresh air. A young woman in a nurse's uniform, equally exhausted and shriveled with steam as Harland had been, stood by the bed, and she whispered, "Now, take this. Open your mouth. Your daddy wants you to take this. Don't be naughty. Be a good girl."

"Blessing!" The word flung itself from my lips. In one step, I was at her bedside. "What is the matter with her?" I demanded.

The nurse said, "Influenza again. And pneumonia. Came right on top of the mumps. The child has been so ill. Her defenses were down. Would you please see if you can make Mr. Prine fetch some more steam kettles?" The thickened air felt as if it crawled into my lungs carrying pestilence along with it. How could anyone believe this vile air could save a child? Yet the only alternative was the bitter winter storm outside.

"What medicine are you giving her?"

"Right now, just water. Doctor ordered a teaspoon of water every fifteen minutes. We are quite stubborn, and what little we get in her, we spit up. Our congestion of the lungs and bowels is severe."

"Gilbert, take that lamp and this teakettle here, fill it up and set it to boil. Fetch everything else you can boil water in, and then come get these others and start them, too."

"Ma'am," said the young woman, "you shouldn't expose yourself to this. This house is quarantined. The other children were sent to some relative's."

"April's house? With only the maid there? Where in blazes is the doctor?"

"He's been with her day and night, ma'am. There is little else he could do. He's left me in charge, to keep trying, at least, until the end."

"The end? There isn't going to be an end!"

The girl cowered, drawing back. "I'm sorry, ma'am. Of course not. We're going to have our little cherub right again in no time. Doctor said we must have some water every fifteen minutes to keep our kidneys from drying up."

I could hear the falseness in her voice, though I could barely see her face. I hated the way "we" were sick and "we" were congested in "our" kidneys. The cow couldn't possibly feel the dragging effects of Blessing's illness.

I said, "Why don't you go and fetch more water, too? I'll stir up the stove and put on more wood."

"It's coal, ma'am."

"Coal, then! Go ahead. I'll tend her for a spell."

When she left, I made that fire roar. Then I sat in the nurse's chair at Blessing's side and laid my hand across her brow. She was ablaze with fever. No wonder that she had dry kidneys, for any water in the girl was leaving her in sweat. "Blessing?" I called, trying to sound cheerful. "Blessing? Won't you wake up? Aunt Sarah is here."

Her eyelids flickered. "Mommy?" she croaked.

"Aunt Sarah."

"Oh."

"Have some water, precious." I held the teaspoon to her lips and drizzled it in. She swallowed, choked, then coughed with a racking rattle that vibrated my own ribs. Stubborn? The child wasn't being stubborn. I knew my little Blessing. This was not contrariness here. She was horribly sick. Her chest heaved up and down, gasping for air. Every hair on my arms stood upright. I placed her tiny hand in mine and held it. She didn't respond. I patted and stroked her hand and arm.

I sat there the night through, while Harland and Gilbert and the nurse shuffled in and out with coal and kettles of water. The storm outside broke down into a tumultuous rain, and close to four, it tapered off and stopped. Trying to force water down Blessing's throat always ended with the gasping and coughing, and finally, I asked the nurse if we had to continue it. Yes, she said. Doctor's order.

Dawn broke through a clouded sky, looking again like one of those paintings I used to love. Blessing rattled and struggled for air. And then she drew in one shallow breath and let out a very long one. Her tiny, wracked body sunk ever deeper into the coverlets. She grew very still. I watched that little body. The struggle for breath was finished. Our Blessing was no more. I stepped away, holding my head in my hands.

Harland knew what had happened, the moment I did it. He dropped to his knees at her bed, sobbing. Gilbert stood at the door, crying in strangling sounds, half-man, half-boy sounds. The nurse left the room. Her shoes echoed on the stairs. I went to the window and rubbed a circle into the steamed glass with my sleeve. A set of double, shimmering rainbows circled the damp town outside.

I opened the window just an inch, and the cold air sent a chill to my damp skin and clothes. The practical things, now, would fill my day, and the grief would shatter all the practical things, minute by minute. There would be the funeral to arrange, quietly, because of the quarantine. There would be the coffin to order. The dress to choose. April's family must be kept away for the sake of Tennyson and her big sisters and brother, Harland's three sons staying there. All this swirled in my thoughts, until I sank to the floor by the window, peering out through the inch of fresh, cold air, to those vivid rainbows. They grew brighter the way a flame will, with new fuel added, more air pushed at them. I held to the window skirt and leaned against the wall. Then I gave over to the tears I could hold off no longer. Blessing had finally caught the long, black train home to her mother.

### November 30, 1907

We dressed Blessing in the blue calico. I curled her hair. Harland had a photographer take a picture of her, lying there as if dressed for a play party and suddenly taken with sleep. The icy rain returned with vengeance and stayed the day through, forcing the service miserably short.

It would still be a fortnight before we could allow Harland's sons to return to the house. It had to be aired and cleaned, top to bottom. I got Harland to agree to letting me take the boys home with us, and coming along, too, to stay until after Christmas. If they wanted for clothes, they could wear castoffs from Savannah's boys. My dear April promised to bring her children for Christmas, though she didn't dare even hug me until the two weeks' spell was past.

### December 1, 1907

Sunday, the rain quit, so after we gathered for prayers, somber and silent, I drove my buggy filled with quiet little boys behind Albert and Savannah's and we made our way home. The arroyo was not running but puddled, and we decided to cross it, letting everyone out on foot while Albert drove first the surrey then my buggy up the side. Harland didn't seem to be good for much of anything, and no one would fault him for it, so he watched from the side next to me. Right before us, Story punched Honor a hard clip on the back, and the two fell upon each other like wildcats. Harland grabbed Honor and I wrangled Story, and we made sure to keep them apart the rest of the trip.

Though the sky cleared and the birds sang, dark clouds loomed over my heart, long after we got to the house and settled everyone in.

The sheriff and Mr. Miles had departed, so it was just our family at home. Chess said all had been quiet. When he found out Blessing had left us for heaven's arms, he retreated to his hole in the barn and would hardly answer when I spoke to him, except to say he had to hurry and get this new saddle finished. It was truly as fine as ever I have seen him make. I told him so, standing at his elbow, and like to got my head knocked off for the trouble. Chess was busy hammering cut designs into a piece of wet leather.

I waited a while and asked, "Are you planning to sell it? It ought to bring three hundred dollars, a nice work like that."

"This one's for my boy. Gilbert. 'N' don't you go telling him, neither."

"When are you going to give it to him?"

Chess pounded that hammer three more times before he said, "When I'm done. Before he goes off to the Point."

"Ah. You don't think he'd marry that girl instead?"

"Either way, he could use a good saddle." The thing was more than a good saddle. It was going to be too nice to use. He whacked into that leather with a punch, his shaky old fingers making a true and straight line with the tool.

"Think we're finally safe from Maldonado?" I asked.

"You're asking me?"

"I am."

"First time for ever'thing. No. I don't." Chess rubbed a wet rag across the leather. "If Gil goes to the Point he'll need this. It's a gentleman's saddle. Not cuttin' and workin'." His mallet rattled the bench again and again, as if he'd lost track of me. Then he hammered and banged and swore and threw the broken mallet so it bounded off the wall and was lost in the hay rake. "Why in tarnation would anyone think we needed a little old flower around this house?"

I didn't ask what he meant. It was clear enough. We did need our flowers. Our Blessings. How tender are the girls in this family. So treasured and fragile as glass. "The sickness was just more than she could fight."

I went to Baldy's place, got him a blanket on, and threw my old work saddle over him. He puffed out his belly and I blew on his nose until he exhaled to cinch up. Then I pulled him from the stall toward the door.

Chess looked up, tools in his hands, one metal poker behind an ear, and he said, "Railroad man came around again. Said they were changing the route again, wanted us to know. I told him he already had what he wanted and offered to nail his tail to a six-foot board. He skedaddled quick enough. You can't fight the damned railroad. It's trying to argue with the air. Them gunrunners to

Mexico ain't about to listen to no one, neither. Then you got Maldonado who thinks your boy stole his girl from the convent where he had her stashed. Now you've went and sold out and our Blessing's—well, I'd say it's time to go to Texas."

"Wish you'd a heard him out. Where they're aiming it now, and all."

"Well, there 'as nothing I wanted to hear from him but his feet making tracks."

"We're staying, Chess. That means you, too. It's settled," I said. "Rudolfo's backed off because I sold to the Wells Fargo Company to get the railroad off our front porch. Mama was in agreement. You don't have to worry about it, Chess. We'll let the giants either fight it out or work hand in glove. It isn't going to touch us anymore."

Then I got on Baldy, pulled my hat low, and rode to the gate. I left it open for my return, and headed south, toward the far windmill I'd had so much trouble with last year. Now it was someone else's problem. To Chess, Texas still seemed a long way from all of it. But there was really no escape. There'd only be a different kind of trouble. There'd always be a railroad, always the rattle of a saber someplace not far enough away, and always be a neighbor I couldn't predict. You couldn't have children and not lose some of them. The air was cold but the sun beat on my shoulders. I rode, just ambling, thinking about the pains of the last year.

I passed reminders of last year's fire that cleaned out the brush left from three years of drought. Here and there a down and rotting saguaro, charred stumps of mesquites, and among the newly grown but dry grasses, bones. Cattle, lean and starved, dying of thirst, had been overcome by the rampage of fire and dropped where they stood. Their bones lay, picked clean before winter was through, bleached white under the suns of summer, and stark against the dark, sodden ground.

I wished for a heavier coat. Thought about Udell's lambskin overcoat, how toasty it had been. The calico on the back of my shirt was faded near to white, but it was still blue on the front. Even under my cloth coat, the frost in the air felt as if it burned the flowers into my skin in little tattoos. A little old flower. Oh, Blessing. Little rosebud. I rode on across lowlands and then into some hills that marked the newly sawed-off end of my property and the beginning of my lease land. From there, a rider could make Mexico in two hours in the winter, being careful with a horse. Summertime, it would take only four hours to the border. Farther down, beyond my vision, was the old windmill and the place I'd sold to Wells Fargo.

It was good to be alone, and to feel safe being alone. After an hour I rode back up and before long I found myself in the shadow of Udell's stone house, now finished, the second-story walls painted and trimmed, smoke curling deliciously from two chimneys. I rapped on the door. Buttons came barking from the side of the house, and I petted his back and rubbed his tummy. In just a few minutes, Udell opened the door, and the scowl he'd worn for a half second vanished. "Mrs. Elliot? I, I mean, come on in and warm up."

"Just passing by and thought—"

"I've got coffee made. Have a seat there by the fire."

I followed his orders. Something about the place had changed. The lamps in the big room were lit, for one thing, but the lace trifles, doilies, and chair covers had disappeared. Could he have only set them about thinking to charm me with pretties? Were they not something he wanted to see around himself to remind him of her? Udell placed a large cup of coffee wrapped in a thick cloth in my hands. He didn't let his fingers touch mine for an instant.

I told him about selling the land, first. It was a good choice, he said. He'd been watching after we left for town, and the hacienda had grown still and quiet. For now, at least, the wagon caravans of rifles had ceased. Then I told him about Blessing.

Udell put his cup down and came to my side, sitting at my knee. "I'm so sorry."

I nodded.

"Sarah?" he whispered as he took my hand. "Are you sorely grieved?"

"Yes, reckon so." Tears rushed forth I hadn't even expected.

"Sweet, precious little Sunbonnet."

"Yes."

"I wish I could have been there for you."

"I do, too."

"You aren't plum mad at me, then?"

"No, Udell. I just didn't think it was right for us to marry."

"Ah."

"I was thinking, riding here, of something to even up the debt between us."

"What debt?"

"To pay you back for the school, you know. I want to give you a gift, but it's not the kind to give if the person isn't inclined toward it. Like a bathtub, the way you said it. I'm back in the black, now, good for a few years even if I don't sell so much as a single egg. I found some boys herding sheep, Udell, and they told me the sheep do right well hereabouts. I would buy you a herd of sheep; lock, stock, and dogs. A hundred head. If you built a higher corral, with the boards closer, you could keep 'em."

"You don't have to do that."

"Would you take them? It'd make me real happy to give them to you."

He thought a minute. "Suppose so. I'd like that. If you wanted to, I'd like it."

"The place is looking good."

"Finished, I suppose. Mostly. Could paint upstairs, maybe."

"Nice and warm."

"M-m, yes."

A chasm spread between us, wide as the great arroyo. I wanted to sit on the floor beside him, before the imposing rock fireplace, to regain what had slipped away. "Suppose I should go on, then," I said.

"I'm really sorry for your little girl. Your loss, I mean."

"Obliged. I'll head home, I reckon." I stood.

Udell rose to his feet, too. Though he didn't really move, I imagined his arms reaching for me, recollected the feel of resting against his shoulder, the shaving cream smell of him and the stubble on the tiny place he always managed to miss. "I'll start building a pen, then. And I'll have to clear a place and plant some good pasturage for spring."

"Come to supper?"

"All right."

I smiled. He did, too. The expanse between us closed by half. So I let my smile widen, and then I had to go.

In a few minutes I crossed the corner where Rudolfo's land met my place and Udell's, next to the spreading ocotillo.

"Wah . . ." a soft voice whispered.

I couldn't see anyone. "Who is that?" I shouted.

A soft, breathy voice said, *"Agua . . . por favor . . ."*

I got down and took the rifle from my saddle rig. Slowly, I walked around the big ocotillo. On the shady side, a man lay curled in the dirt. He appeared to be dead, but when my shadow crossed him, he moved. I stepped back, quickly scanning the brush and trees around the place and keeping myself more than an arm's length from him. This could be a trap.

*"Agua . . ."* he said again. He raised a scratched and torn hand; up to the elbow covered in brown stain and caked with sand. He had crusted, dusty hair

and wore battered sandals. They were the work clothes of a ranch hand, coarse cloth, sewn nothing fancy and often patched. He tried to straighten himself, and when he did I saw the brown from his hands was on his shirt, too. In the center of a large brown ring was a darker, brownish-red one. *"Muerte. Agua . . . poquito,"* he said with eyes closed.

Still watching the brush around me, I fetched the canteen from where I'd left Baldy, then scrunched down closer to his level. He revived just seeing me take the cork from it, and reached, throwing water into his mouth clumsily with both hands. I said, "Do I know you? Caldo? Isn't that it? You drove Maldonado's coach."

"Aye. *Sí.*"

"You've been shot? Who did this? Bandits?"

He gasped out, *"El señor."*

"Rudolfo shot you?"

*"Sí."*

"Why would he do that? Let me help you onto my horse." I reached for him, but he hollered.

"Maybe he say I tell you. Maybe he think I say."

"Say what, Caldo?"

"The train she is coming."

"Where?"

"To the door of the big house. *Un año. El jefe* is angry. In a year these train she is going through his *cocina.* He is wanting all you *familia* to be dead. And he is coming for . . . *la niña . . . religiosa. Mas agua . . .*" He drank again, gasped, and for a moment, I thought he had died.

"Why did he shoot you, Caldo?"

"I witness. I see *la Virgencita* is guards you *casa.* She call my name. *Mi nombre* come from the lips of the Blessed Mother. I not kill any more peoples. I tell him, let train come, I will not kill. Let *la Doña* Elliot in peace. He no listen to poor old Caldo. *Agua.*"

His head slumped against the rocks.

"Caldo, here's more water. Won't you let me help you?"

Only silence and the buzzing of a wandering bee answered me. I touched his shoulder and Caldo slid, lifeless, to the ground. I looked for track, then, and saw he'd clawed his way from a place beyond the brush, dragging his legs. He had been there a while. If I'd come the usual route, I'd have passed him long ago. I was halfway between Udell's place and mine. Could Rudolfo have passed me by on a more direct path, as I wasted the day riding around? I listened to the sounds of the brush. There was no rumble of hooves. Finches chirped and fussed with each other. A thrasher annoyed a woodpecker who'd been hard at work. If something were going to happen soon, it hadn't come about yet. From Udell's upper room, I would be able to see down to Rudolfo's house, and from another, clear to the graveyard at my place. I could only hope the ground was dry enough to give up dust between the two, if someone were headed that way.

In one movement, I poured the last of the water on the ground and corked the canteen, shucking the rifle into the scabbard as I mounted the horse. Then I held my heels to Baldy's sides and my face to his neck and headed back toward Udell's place. Baldy got in a frenzy and started pulling the reins himself as if he were outrunning the Devil. The horse would run himself to death for me, and I had to pull him in to save him from himself.

Baldy started to foam. I hauled back on the reins and it took all my strength to turn him enough to get his attention. I jumped to the ground and took off running, tugging his reins. The horse balked and stamped his hooves. "Come on, you loco cayuse. You're not running yourself to death but you are not stopping here, either. Come on. I'm saving your life." I sort of half ran, half walked as fast as I could go. Halfway up a hill I slipped in the gravel paving the ground, and missed catching myself, too, landing hard with my left shoulder and cheek into the rough. That made Baldy more frantic and he jerked away from me, running off to one side. I let him go a minute and then whistled for him. Ornery as he was feeling, he came at his whistle, and I said, "You're going to get a bushel of apples for yourself, for doing that, boy."

My skirt had ripped at the left knee, too, and there was a hole in my long winter drawers underneath. I found a splinter in my knee, and pulled it but it wouldn't budge; cholla thorns don't let go nice. My knee felt fiery as I ran. Finally, from the top of that rise, I saw Udell's place clearly. There, I got back on the horse and gave him his head, leaning into his neck again, and we made for the stone house. Stopping in a spray of dirt, I whipped the reins at the first post I came to, snapping a ring that would hold Baldy, who now was rank as I'd ever seen him.

"Udell!" I hollered. I hurried to the house and flung open the door. I called at the top of my lungs, but he was not in the house. "Udell Hanna!" I pushed aside the thought that Rudolfo's men had already dragged Udell away and shot him the way they had killed Caldo. I looked in Udell's bedroom and the storage room that was next to it where he kept his Springfield. It was gone. So were the bandoliers he often carried. I spun around to leave and saw the hat peg on the wall. It stopped me in my tracks. His army hat was gone.

I rushed through the top of the barn, making a ruckus I knew would draw him out if he were in the bottom, too.

"Sarah!" came a shout. "Soon as you left, I was in the attic looking for something and looked out the window. There are twenty men gathered at Maldonado's place looking for blood. I wish you'd have gone on home. What are you doing back here?"

"I need you," I gasped. "They're going to my place. I found Caldo, near dead. He told me Rudolfo's going to . . . I'll carry one of those." I took a bandolier from him and slung it across my shoulder.

"Let's go. Sarah, I'm not going to wait for you, and you don't wait for me. Both of us ride, but if my horse falls behind, you keep on. If yours falls back, you just hide in the brush and wait until he can go again. One of us has got to get there."

I dashed for the house, caught up the reins, and threw myself up onto Baldy's back. He reared and danced a minute, then we headed for home. A noise came from my throat, like a groan, a cry of pain held down, panic moving my spirit beyond what I could see, and I rode for home. I cut off the corner by the big ocotillo, taking Baldy wide away from the dead body of Caldo and off the road and toward a stand of mesquite and palo verde. We slowed. I had to let him catch his breath, or the poor animal would die under me before I got there. I heard hooves, saddle rigs, and jingles. Likely they moved up on the road, abreast of where I was flanking them. Rudolfo's army. My chest hurt, but panic forced me to go toward home even if I had to walk. Clouds gathered. What had been a blue sky scattered with a few puffs of white became gray.

I took the rifle from the scabbard again and made sure there was a round ready to fire. I walked Baldy over raw desert, curling around cholla and barrel cactus. We came to a rift in the soil and he strode down in as if it were nothing at all. Moving up toward the back of my house, I heard closer hooves, a single rider. I got off and wedged Baldy into a copse and waited, rifle ready. The bandoliers across Udell's chest and the Montana hat gave him a look of being not natural, out of place.

I was a hundred and fifty yards away. I waved a hand, carefully and low. At last, he recognized me in the brush. He kept moving, said nothing, only waved a finger the way you'd throw a rope, toward the house. I climbed on and followed him. We reached the barn at nearly the same time. I was breathing so hard, I didn't know who'd succumb first, me or the horse. Poor Baldy needed brushing, but all we could do was put the animals in the barn, collect Chess, and head for the house.

"Charlie! Elsa!" I hollered. "Gilbert? Everybody, come on in here."

Udell said, "I saw them mustering in the field there. Watched for a while, then Rudolfo himself came out, wearing pistols, and took a horse, leading the way. I grabbed my kit and came ahead."

I added, "Caldo, that fellow that drove his coach, got himself shot coming to warn us. Wells Fargo got in cahoots with the train and changed the route. According to him it's going to run straight through Rudolfo's front parlor. Caldo wouldn't fight us because of what Elsa did the other night. He said Rudolfo's going to kill us all and take Elsa back. He won't rest until this entire family is dust."

Granny came in, moving slowly, hauling a twelve-gauge shotgun. "I'll load," she said. The light in the house lowered, as if the clouds themselves felt the coming of this storm.

Charlie moved quickly around the room. "There's nothing over these windows," he said. "Gil, pull that table over here and stand it up. Elsa, you get in the pantry and stay there. Grampa," but Chess had already left the room.

"They've got a small army with them," I said.

Udell said, "Nineteen, counting Maldonado. They're bringing an empty horse, too. I don't think they aim to leave with 'im empty."

"They'll stop at nothing, then," I said. "Harland, get your boys hidden. Take them to the pantry, too."

"Give me a gun. I'll fight," Harland said.

I wanted to send him to a bedroom like a child but I said, "In the kitchen, there, top shelf behind the can of soda and the medicinals."

As he left to get it, the front door opened. Savannah, all a-smile, stepped in. "Hello, everyone. Sarah, I got a new pattern for . . . what's happened?"

Charlie spoke first. "Aunt Savannah! Take Elsa home with you. And tell Uncle Albert we need him. Maldonado is on his way to take Elsa by force. Udell saw nineteen mounted riders carrying guns. Elsa! Come here, quick!"

At that moment a low thud hit the wall of the house, then a dozen more shots. Some of them found windows. One went clear through from the parlor and into a bedroom, where it hit the wash pitcher and caused it to explode as if it were a charge of dynamite. We rushed to find cover, keeping low to the ground. There was a spell of silence, then a volley of gunfire, I'd reckon two or three shots from each man, hit the front of the house. I heard a housecat screech.

Rudolfo's voice boomed loud in the silence that followed. "I want my daughter. Elsa Maria Ramirez-Valdon Maldonado, come out here, before I kill the rest of them. Carlos, Charlie Elliot, you bring out my daughter! I will have you dead."

Charlie was by a broken window. He hollered, "She's married, Señor Maldonado. Go home."

I crawled on hands and knees to where my son stood. I called out, too, "Rudolfo? Go on home for now. You hear me? This doesn't have to be this way. Why don't you just come over for supper? Come visit her. She's married. She chose it. You can see her as much as you want and we don't have to be enemies. Go on now, and come back later."

"Yes, Papa!" came Elsa's voice. She stood at a window, her form in full view. "Come to me, and let us talk!" she said.

Our answer was a roar from a Sharps, like the boom of a cannon, and something huge crashed through the window showering Elsa with glass, immediately speckling her face with blood. I watched then as Rudolfo swore and pulled his pistol, shot the man through the head who'd fired haphazardly at his daughter. As he fell, the man's horse went wild with fear. Inside, Charlie surrounded Elsa with his arms and tugged her to the floor in a far corner. Gilbert called then, "Someone's around the back. I saw two men." Chess went to Gilbert's side. Harland's boys peered from around the pantry door, one above the other like three heads without bodies.

"Rudolfo!" I hollered. "Let's talk this over. You've got the land. You got what you wanted, passage for your . . . goods to Mexico."

"My Elsa did not come freely to your house. You have stolen her. A hostage . . . *tu rehén* . . . I will take her back. No one leaves here alive. That is my final word."

Granny hefted the big shotgun to her lap. "Let 'em in. I'll let a vent in the skunk before he gets in the door."

Savannah went to her. I thought she'd drop to her knees and pray, or tell my mama to put away the shotgun, since firing it would likely kill her from the recoil. Instead, Savannah herself took it from Granny's hands and pointed it toward the door. She said, "Albert will hear this ruckus and come running, and right into their sights. I'm not letting them harm a hair on his head. Tell them, Mr. Hanna, that no one leaves here at gunpoint. That this family stands for its own. Tell them they'll answer to me or to the devil, but they'd better leave."

I wanted to laugh. To cheer. To cry. Udell did as she asked, and hollered those things at Rudolfo. In reply, they opened up shooting at us as if we were squirrels caught in a trap. Gilbert and Chess fought from one wall, Charlie and me from another, while Udell fired from his wall and Elsa and Savannah reloaded everyone's weapons. This new house of mine, this house Rudolfo himself had helped build, was getting beaten to dust. We stopped to reload again. The smell of sulfur and black powder filled the rooms. A loud explosion shook the house, raining dust from the ceiling, and something burst into flames out in the center plaza.

"Bombs," Udell said. "They're throwing bombs on us. Charlie, come help me put out the fire."

Chess turned as they hurried to the center of the house, and said, "No! It's a diversion . . ." but his words were cut off as the front door fell from its hinges, rammed from outside by men with a log. Rudolfo and two other men got into the parlor, and seemed to be everywhere. Shots ricocheted off the stove.

Elsa ran forward, saying, "Papa! I'll come with you. Stop the shooting. Don't kill anyone. I'll come. Only stop. Please stop!" She ran toward him, and Rudolfo caught her arm, pulling her toward the doorway. The two men stood in our way.

Savannah let go with both barrels. Udell and I took down another man as Savannah sank to the floor and moaned. The two men who'd come in with Rudolfo lay dead in their tracks, but somehow he had gotten in and out without being hit. Another bang came from back of the house and we heard all the children scream. Charlie dashed toward the noise and returned to the room to see Elsa being dragged toward the group of men by her father. He charged out the door, pistols in both hands, firing, and four men fell from horses. A quarter of our attackers lay dead. More than half Rudolfo's men had already gotten to the gate, and the rest were moving away from the house toward it.

Rudolfo dropped Elsa's arm and aimed his pistol at Charlie. In that second, Elsa saw what unfolded before her, and ran like a deer, arms outstretched, toward Charlie. We held our breaths. The pistol in Rudolfo's hand was a Colt .44. It went off like a cannon. Charlie sidestepped as if it were instinct, and the bullet hit Elsa square in the back with a dull thump as loud as a bat hitting a baseball. She stumbled and fell into Charlie's arms. In the span of half a second, my first thought was oddly separated from what was happening, and that it looked like the same wound I'd seen on Caldo. No doubt, the same gun had done him in, too. My second thought was horror at seeing her fall. Thirdly, I pictured the bullet had pierced Charlie, too. They would both lay dead. His mouth open in shock, Charlie stood in his tracks, dropped his guns. Picked her up from the ground. She was as limp as a rag. Dead before she hit the ground.

Charlie screamed in concert with Rudolfo, their voices fierce as mountain lions'.

My son's anger tore through me like a Bowie knife. There was no time to cry. Rudolfo charged at him, firing, but as Charlie moved toward Rudolfo with Elsa in his arms, bullets seemed to bounce off him. He was covered with blood, but walked on and on, toward the man who'd murdered his wife. Rudolfo's gun clicked, loud and empty. Charlie laid Elsa on the ground and ran to pick up his pistols. Rudolfo's men closed in, and then I moved out on the porch with Udell at my side and we rained lead on them. Hand over hand, Charlie shot. I fired my rifle and took down three of them. In a shower of bullets, Harland took one and Udell hit another four. Bullets peppered the metal trough and water gushed into the yard, swirling around a dead man, forming a red pool. Between us, all of Rudolfo's men except two standing by him had either fled or died, and those two stood amidst frightened stomping horses, petrified, watching. Two of the animals fell and groaned.

Then the noise stopped. Silence blanketed the yard. Charlie, tears streaming from his eyes, again laid his pistols in the dirt and groaned with a sound that seemed to rend the very air, leaning over Elsa. Rudolfo thrust his men aside and raced toward him.

Gilbert ran straight into the reddened mud between horses and men and all, and grabbed Rudolfo by the throat. Rudolfo reached for his guns, and that hesitation kept his hands busy long enough for Gilbert to knock him to the ground. They rolled and rolled. Both of them soaked in mud, they grappled for their lives. Rudolfo outweighed him by fifty pounds of pure meanness. I couldn't get a clear shot without hurting Gil. Then I saw a flash of metal. My heart stopped beating. Between the two of them, twisting like snakes trying to kill each other, a long Mexican dagger went from one hand to another. Red began to flow between them. Mud made them slip and slide together, made the blade handle slick as glass. A sound punch flew from one man to the other, and one mud-coated form rose above the other, knife in hand.

A bang and a loud "Hah!" from beside the house made my knees shake. The upper man jerked back, mouth opening in shock, knife upraised. His form slumped forward onto his enemy, and the knife fell. Chess's voice hollered, "I got him!" followed by a string of curses.

The lower man shoved the dead one over. Looking straight at me, venom in his eyes, Rudolfo stood.

He ran to his horse and mounted it. Udell rushed forward and shot at his back once, then fired again but the gun was empty. He pulled the trigger again, then lowered his rifle as horse and man galloped away.

Chess yelled, "I got him," again, and came toward the mud where the final fray had taken place.

I outran him.

I lifted Gilbert's head and shoulders into my lap and screamed and screamed until my voice gave out. Chess's face was a knot of horror.

Gilbert opened his eyes. "I'm shot through the chest, Mama," he said.

I hugged his head to my face, groaning like a wild animal. "No," I said, repeatedly. Udell crouched at my side.

Chess made a fierce moan, dropped his rifle and stumbled away.

Gilbert winced. "Am I going to die?"

"No," I said.

"I can't breathe much, Mama. Damn, it hurts." After a bit, he said, "Is everyone all right? Granny's not killed, is she?"

"Granny's fine."

"Mama, can you give me anything for the hurt? I'm on fire inside."

I crushed my face with my hands and let go a sob. Then I shrieked at Udell, "Get him a blanket! Get him inside!"

Udell bent and lifted Gilbert as if he'd been a child, as if he were strong as a bull, the same way he had carried my mama, he carried my son into the house. Past Charlie crying in the yard, cradling Elsa to his shoulder, past Savannah, horror-stricken, trying to console Charlie. Udell laid Gilbert on the kitchen table. Gilbert coughed and blood dribbled from his lip. All that was left now was his dying.

# Chapter Nineteen

*December 3, 1907*

Gilbert moaned, half crying like a child, half stifled—the way I remember soldiers at the fort doing—as if he were scared like a little boy but still knew he was grown and was trying to brave up to the pain. I got my shears and cut through his Christmas shirt, opening the seams to release his arms without him having to move. Granny, Savannah, and I rinsed the mud away and wrapped him in clean linen with a folded soaker under his back. The bullet had not pierced his heart or he'd never have spoken a word, but it could do terror to the lights or other things. It had surely gone clean through, but too low to think there was a chance he'd live over this.

Cold wind assailed us through the broken-out windows and somehow I was aware that Granny was busy stuffing rags and old clothes into the holes. She stoked up the fires, too, moving around, hovering, spiritlike, more than I'd seen her move in years.

Harland and Albert, Zack and Ezra have ridden to the four corners of the earth to find a doctor who'll come out here. Albert's gone to Tucson, the boys to Benson. We told them to promise any amount of money to a real doctor willing to come, as I'm sure Gilbert would not live through the wagon trip to one of them.

Savannah said she knew of something, and she ran on foot all the way to her house. She brought back a jug of apple cider that had turned. She was keeping it to dose her chickens if they got the sheds, so Udell is helping me dose Gilbert with quinine and hard cider. I put my two best feather pillows under my boy's head. Then I kissed his face and sat by him. From where I sat, I could see light from the window kissing his face, too. The makings of a beard formed a gold line raised just above his skin.

Charlie and Chess have buried Elsa in our graveyard. I stepped away from Gilbert's side for a while, to attend her. Later, they hauled the Maldonado men in a wagon to the edge of Rudolfo's land and there they threw them out like dead animals, to rot in the desert sun. I told them that was uncommon poor to do, but Charlie's anger is bigger than he can abide. He said he went all the way to the hacienda to kill Rudolfo, but the place was empty. It is as if Charlie could easily mow down every living thing around him, and if he's got no Christian spirit to dig graves for them, I can hardly blame him. Yet, I am sitting at his brother's deathbed and I won't have him bringing anger into this kitchen. It can't be any help to his brother.

I sent Charlie to Marsh Station to send word to Miss Charity about Gilbert. It's something for him to do, and I reckon we'll see if she cares.

### December 4, 1907

A day and a night passed. By morning, Gil had fever rages, hotter by far than Udell's had been with the malaria. He tossed and thrashed sometimes. I held him with my whole strength, then sometimes Savannah did, too, keeping him from falling off the table, mopping his brow and holding him still until he lost consciousness.

Charlie should have come back by now. Don't know where Chess is, either. He must be tormented beyond all reason, thinking he's killed Gilbert. I wakened, my arms numb and spidery-feeling from sleeping with my head upon them, stretched out onto the kitchen table, holding my boy.

Oh, God, my spirit ached. My heart was rent in two, my mind stilled and black. As the sun rose, my son trembled and his breath rattled with his death fever. His face had grown yellow and thin.

"Sarah?" a man's voice said. "Sarah, wake up, please. The doctor is here. It's a Dr. Pardee from Benson." A young, gentle-eyed man, with a tidy swatch of beard and mustache that made a triangle around his mouth was bent over Gilbert and didn't acknowledge me. Udell took my arms and lifted me from the wooden chair that felt as if it had grown into my bones. Then it seemed as if the room spun as he pulled me up, lifting me toward him. I reached for Udell and held his shoulders, and slid down a black, deep well, a tomb I had only thought I knew; this grief had become a newer, blacker, more menacing place than any grief I'd yet encountered. I sobbed into Udell's shirt and he held me on his lap in a chair, like a child.

Then I straightened my shoulders and rose from his grasp. "I'll go back to him, now," I said. We stood by Gilbert while the doctor unwrapped the bandages I'd made. He prodded the bulletholes, front and back, and Gilbert cried out. Udell and I held him down while the doctor pulled a splinter of bone from his back. I retched, dry, for I hadn't eaten in days, and turned my face. Then the doctor patched his wound again with cotton lint, bales of it, it seemed, and we laid the boy on his back again.

Pardee propped his leather bag on the sideboard and searched through it. Chess came into the room, then, standing shriveled and meek by the door. Dr. Pardee said, "Give him these every three hours. Crush one for him if he can't swallow."

"Will it cure his fever?" I said.

Ezra stood by the stove. He had ridden to Benson. He was proud of himself for getting the doctor, just he and his brother, and now he took responsibility for his cousin. Pardee shook his head, saying, "It'll ease the pain." Ezra's shoulders slumped and his face twisted and grew red. He left the room, stumbling over Zachary, who just stared, wide-eyed, at the doctor.

Udell said, "Doctor?"

The doctor faced each of us and simply said, "No. There's infection. I swabbed it with sulfur and Mercurochrome. We can't do anything else. Eventually the infection will take his brain, and the pain will get bad. No sense in letting him go that way. I know you're decent people, but have you got any hard spirits? That'd be good for him. Anything? Even some vanilla. There's nothing else I can do. I am truly sorry."

"There's a little of that cider left, that went hard. We gave him some before you got here." I turned to Zack. "Boy? Go run to your mama's pantry and bring the vanilla bottle. Don't you drop it." I drew a shattered breath. "Will you stay, Dr. Pardee? Will you stay with him? I'll pay you to stay, anything you ask. Please?"

"I have patients in town." He looked from Gilbert, sweating, shivering, groaning, to me. Then he said, "Yes, ma'am. I'll stay with you until it's over."

"Can we move him to a bed?"

"No. That'll cause more bleeding."

We dosed Gilbert with vanilla, and then the house smelled like sulfur and cake.

I went to make the doctor some coffee. I heard him ask Udell how Gilbert got shot. Udell told him we'd tangled with some Mexican bandidos, nothing more. While the coffee heated, I went to change my dress; I still wore the same dirty one I'd had on all these days. I heard a muffled bump of wood against wood. In Charlie's room, I found him roughly stuffing things into two small wooden crates. I went to him and laid my hand on his shoulder. He froze stiff for a moment. Then he gasped two short breaths, hard sobs he choked down into his boots. He wiped at his eyes.

"It ain't fair, Mama. Should be me dead there. I as much as dared him to kill me. Walked right through every bullet. I want to be dead with my Elsa. I want to be with her." He set one hand on mine and squeezed.

I could only bite my lips from the inside. We stood like statues for five minutes, just aching. I glanced into a box he was loading. It was full of the baby soakers and wrappers Elsa had been knitting. I wept, too, and sat beside him on his bed.

Finally, Charlie said, "Mama, I ain't staying here. I can't."

"Where you going to go?"

"I'm going to go kill Rudolfo Maldonado and then run. Disappear to somewhere there's lots of space. Montana, maybe. Argentina."

"Listen to me," I said, shaking his shoulder. "Don't you go thinking that way. That isn't going to bring her back."

"It'll put him where he belongs."

I held Charlie's arm. "You've got to stay with me awhile. Watch over Gilbert."

"I'll see Maldonado in hell. I swear it."

"But not today."

Charlie bent and tugged at his hair. Then he straightened himself. He put an arm around my middle. "Mama, you are nothing but skin and bones. Go get some dinner. I'll sit with him awhile."

Granny came into his room. She said, "Boy? You listen to your old grandmother. There was a time when all this was going on, when I was a girl, and the neighbors killed each other, too. Can't even recollect who was on whose side, now. But this here, we got the law on our side and the right, you being a Ranger and all. Don't you go off to the Argen-tine. You catch that varmint and bring 'im here to hang."

Charlie scratched his head. "I can't stay here."

"You think on it, though, Charlie," I said.

"He's probably gone to Mexico. I'll go find him."

Granny said, "With all his army and guns? Ain't ye' got no sense left? You gotta get some men to go with you. Take that Hanna feller. And that Miles."

I said, "Take some time, son. Catching Rudolfo isn't our biggest worry. You'll make the right choice. I know it."

I tried to rock a spell on the porch. The flies annoyed me too much. I went back to sit by Gilbert where the doctor kept watch. Now and then my eyes would flood with tears that did not flow. Heat sweats and cold shivers swept over me. Shocks like splashed cold water rolled over me every time Gil made a noise.

Rebeccah and Savannah moved in and out of the room lighting candles. The doctor snored in the chair, his head against the wall. Harland left to fetch April.

*December 5, 1907*

In a while, Rebeccah put the candles out, and another night had passed. Gilbert still breathed, rattling and liquid. In Gil's room Charlie leaned, staring out through the piece of broken window that was now stuffed with rags to keep out flies.

I went to him but didn't touch him. "You still planning to kill Rudolfo?" I said.

"Won't right nothing."

"No, it won't."

"Mama?" he said. But it seemed as if he knew I could see the trembling in his lip, and that was enough talk for him. He just shook his head and bit the inside of his jaw.

"I know," I said. "I know."

From somewhere in the house I smelled coffee. Rebeccah brought me a cup and I tried to sip at it. She fetched more wood for the stove, and I let her fill it without lending a hand, just watching and drinking coffee, lost in a twelve-foot-square room. I'd lost track of everything and everyone. As she finished, Dr. Pardee leaned over Gilbert, rubbing his chin. "That right lung is gone, I think. But he's still holding on. I've got an idea. I can't tell you whether it'll help. It's just an idea."

"What?" I said. "I know some doctoring. Whatever it is, we'll do it."

He said, "I was watching a hot air balloon one time at a fair. The thing accidentally landed in a duck pond. The picture of it made me wonder. Your boy here is strong, and hanging on, but he's drowning. I'm guessing pooling blood is crushing the lung like that balloon, so he can't breathe. I am wondering if a simple surgery might drain that out."

"We'll do whatever you say, Dr. Pardee."

He rushed to the water pump and washed his hands, using nearly half a cake of lye soap. "Wash your hands, too, Mrs. Elliot. I shall need a nurse."

I scrubbed my hands, shaking hard, weak in the knees, trying to hold my stomach still. My heart pounded in my ears so loud the room seemed filled with drumming. Dr. Pardee rummaged through his leather bag. He pulled out metal instruments and gruesome things I never laid eyes on before that looked like the inventions of a tormentor. He started fixing some things together, making a metal cylinder and fixing a large needle to it. He stropped that needle several times and then rinsed the whole thing in grain alcohol. The smell of it filled the room and made the floor lift and turn. "I had morphine in here," he said. "Have you seen anybody get into my bag?"

"No, sir," I said. "No one would take it."

He scrambled through the satchel again, impatient as a schoolboy going through a lunch. He said, "We haven't got time to mess with that. Hold him over, then. I'm going to try from the back."

We rolled Gilbert on his side and Udell and I held him down. He moaned when Pardee stuck him. I turned my head away. The sounds of liquid dripping were all I could take; I could not look at what Dr. Pardee was doing. After a bit, Pardee said, "All right. Lay him back."

When we laid him down to rest, Gilbert drew a deep breath. A flush of red came back to his face for a few seconds, then left. Pardee said, "I will do that every hour or so. It does look as if it helped."

With that, though, I nodded and stepped away from Gilbert's side. Then my eyes caught on the blood-filled bowl.

I awoke in my bed with Savannah seated at my side, slowly and gently brushing my hair. I tried to get up and she pushed my shoulders back to the bed.

Savannah said, "Albert has gone with Charlie to look for Chess."

"Where is he?" Chess? Gone to murder Rudolfo?

As if she heard me thinking, Savannah said, "Well, to tell you the truth if he's gone to kill Rudolfo I would gladly load the pistol for him. Your hair needs tending, honey. Just lie back. Rebeccah is here and she's drawing you a bath. You need to eat, too."

"Gilbert?"

"Gilbert's still with us. He's improving. Dr. Pardee is a good doctor. Becca is helping, good as any nurse."

"My boy," I said, and closed my eyes. I could feel her cooling hands through my hair. I could feel every thread on the bedclothes through my skirts and camisole. I could feel the grain of the wooden floor coming through the ropes that held me above it. "Not like this. Not like this."

Dr. Pardee tapped on the door as he entered the room. "Mrs. Elliot? Mrs. Prine? You should call your family. I believe Gilbert's turned a corner."

I nearly sprang up from the bed.

"Go," said Savannah. "I'll fetch the rest."

Dr. Pardee held up one hand, a motion of gentle pause. "I didn't want you to think . . . falsely. He seems a bit more lively, ma'am, but there is a revived state that often comes just before the end." I glared at him.

I rushed to Gilbert. Albert, Clover, and Rebeccah were there. Harland, too. Even Zack and Ezra and all the littler fellows. Zachary and Ezra looked as if they had aged ten years, both boys gone old before being grown. I heard Savannah's voice calling from outside, and pretty soon Charlie came in.

"Where are Chess and Udell?" I asked him.

"Working."

"Working? At what, in heaven's name?"

Zachary came and took hold of my hand. He tugged me down and when I leaned forward he whispered in my ear, "Aunt Sarah, they are digging a grave."

I bit into my finger so hard it left a mark. I couldn't feel it. Watching Gilbert sleeping there, looking gently at rest instead of fevered and tormented with pain, he seemed so regular, so natural, except that he was still stretched out on the kitchen table.

Like a spark lighting dry brush, the thought came to me that I had to find Chess before Gilbert was gone. That quiet but rumbling desperation that I'd lived in for so many months suddenly drummed in my head. The air swirled with banging louder than cannonfire. My eyes saw everything at once and all around me creation flowed like a river of sights and sounds.

From the front porch, I heard water being poured. I stumbled off the last step and hurried toward the splashing at the outdoor pump. Udell was there with his shirt off, soaking wet, just wiping the last of the soap off his arms. "Udell," I called, "where's Chess?"

His somber face instantly changed, mirrored the panic I felt. "I don't know, Sarah. We finished a while ago; he said he had something to do."

I put my hands on my hips. "Did he go to the barn? Something with the saddle? I've got to find him."

We both started walking when he said, "I thought he went down by the crick. Reckon he *might* have gone to the barn."

"You go. Hurry," I said. He went to the barn. I took off toward the stream. Breaking through shady brush where I usually hunted quail and dove, the shade and sound of water were wasted on me. My heart shouted, *Gilbert, stay alive until I get back, Wait for me, boy. Wait.* "Chess? Chess!" I yelled.

A cardinal startled me with his curlicue chirp. Coming as if he'd answered my call, the bright red bird swooped toward me, cut a couple of looping strides in the air and flew on, chirruping loudly. "Chess!" I waded across the flowing stream at a shallow spot to a mossy bank where I used to send the boys to fish to keep them out of my way, when they were smaller.

I saw a pair of old boots. "Chess, I've looked everywhere," I said breathlessly, gasping. "Get on home. Gilbert needs you. The doctor says he's turned a corner. Chess? Wake up, Chess."

Chess was stretched out full, his head on Gilbert's new saddle, his feet a few inches apart. His eyes were closed. A fly poked along on his lower lip. "Chess?" I knelt by him. I gritted my teeth together and touched his arm. It slid from his chest. His right hand had gripped something that let go. A brown vial with a cork in it rolled toward my feet. Dr. Pardee's morphine. I took it up and squeezed it and beat on his chest, crying out, "Don't you do this to me, old man! You rotten old cuss. Get up from there. Don't you leave me like this. Chess! Don't die, Chess. Oh, God, don't let this be happening. I need you, Chess. Get up."

"Sarah!" Udell's voice called.

"Here," I hollered back. "I've found him." I put my head on Chess's still warm body and listened until Udell came. "Why would he do this, Udell? Why? He knows I'd never blame him. Make him stop, Udell."

Tears slid from his eyes, too, making a wet film on his face. "I didn't know what he meant. One last thing to do. He didn't say much while . . . while we dug. I thought he had a sick stomach."

"Help me carry him to the house. I've got to see Gilbert one last time."

"It's a long piece, Sarah, I'll get one of the boys . . ."

"Help me!" I ordered. Then I picked up Chess's legs and waited. Udell nodded. He put the brown vial of pills in his pants pocket and took Chess under the arms, moving his head to where it rested easy, not hanging down. Charlie and Clover saw us and ran to help. We got him laid on the floor in the parlor. Dr. Pardee hurried in and bent over Chess's still body.

"How's Gilbert?" I said.

"Still here, Mama. He's good," Charlie said. "Did Grandpa Chess fall again?"

I told how we'd found him. Shocked looks painted every face. Charlie bent over his grandfather, patting him, and hearing a crinkling sound, he pulled a note from Chess's breast pocket. "It says," he said, " 'I never was so sorry. I can bear it no more. You will all be a sight better off, shed of a nuisance that's outlived any good use or sense. I never loved any boys more than Charlie and Gilbert, so I'm gone to clear a path for my fellow. Lord love you, Sarah. You're better than a daughter. Forgive this damned old fool.' "

Dr. Pardee looked into Chess's eyes, opening the lids carefully. He shook his head. "Strange," he said.

Udell held out the vial, saying, "How many did he take?"

Pardee took it from him, shook the pills into his hand and slowly worked them back into the bottle, counting. "I had twenty-two pills in there. They're all here. He didn't take any." Pardee put the vial down and studied this new patient again, as if he still could use healing; he lifted Chess's arms, inspected the fingernails, and put his hand against Chess's still face, as if feeling for a temperature. "Whatever's killed him, folks, looks to be nature. It wasn't morphine. I'd attest to it in a courtroom."

"But his letter—" Charlie said.

Pardee nodded. "I'm telling you this man did most certainly *not* die of morphine. All the pills are here. People think it's a wives' tale, but sounds to me like the man died of a broken heart. No one quite understands it—one of the mysteries of nature."

The family got quiet. Dr. Pardee stared straight into my eyes. I remembered that he didn't know the source of our problems. If he was the talkative kind, a family caught up in a feud could be branded as trash forever. I was not going to have Chess's name in the territorial newspaper, in case I couldn't trust this stranger. At last I said, "Chess was an old soldier, and the boy's grandpa.

Their papa was killed when they were shavers. His whole life was spent trying to protect us. We had that fracas with Mexican outlaws . . ."

I saw Savannah watching me. I know she would rather I told every bit of the truth, as unvarnished as peeled wood, no matter what it showed. Then, too, if I told everything, maybe Rudolfo would hang—I'd pay money to watch—but he could have bought and paid with railroad money for some judge to hold up anything he wants to do. I weighed the words and then chose among them as if I were picking a bouquet and only wanted particular flowers when I said, "He thought he let us down. Charlie and Gilbert, he'd helped raise, and then when he—when he couldn't shoot straight—"

Pardee shook his head as if he knew exactly what I meant, and then sighed with a reassuring air. "Old soldiers just can hardly bear it when they outlast their stripes. You folks have had a tough go of it."

"Mama?" a soft voice said.

I looked to Charlie, but he'd turned toward the kitchen. I raced through the door to Gilbert, thinking I'd heard the voice of a ghost. I called, "Son?"

Gilbert's very much alive eyes fluttered, and he said, "Mama. I'm awfully thirsty."

### *December 7, 1907*

Well, this afternoon a rattling Mexican carreta, pulled by a donkey so small it looked to be a toy, stopped at our gate. A woman got out. The carreta driver pulled away, flicking at the animal with a string tied in a knot on the end hanging from a bent pole. It wasn't long before I heard a knock on the door and footsteps coming to Gilbert's room. I wasn't all that surprised to see the flushed and dusty face of Charity James.

She tipped into the room. "I came soon as I could. I had to hire a man with a donkey. I'm sorry I smell awful. Mrs. Elliot? May I see him?"

I nodded.

She knelt by the bed and took Gilbert's hand, brought it to her face and kissed his fingers. Then she spoke to the fingers as if they had ears. "I got here as fast as I could. I've been two days on the road to see you, my Sweet Boy, and I'm so glad you've stayed for me. Oh, Gilbert, I do care for you. I love you." Tears rushed from her eyes as if she'd been holding them back during the long trip here. "I'm so very fond of you but it don't do for me to tell you right out. I been praying for you and sending you my heart ever' since I heard. Please keep on living, Gilbert, my dear, my sweet. Try hard." Then she laid his hand carefully on his bed. "Mrs. Elliot? Mind if I stay in your barn or some other? I wouldn't be a bother to you." She stood. "I brought some dried apples and hardtack, so you don't have to worry about me at all."

"Well, honey, I won't hear of it," I said. "You'll have a bed in the house. We'll fix it up nice for you. You can take my bed. I'll sleep somewhere else. Are you tired? You look plum ragged."

She hadn't taken her eyes off Gilbert. "No, ma'am. Not much. That is, now that I see he's alive."

I went to her and patted her arm and said, "You're worn out. If you want to pull a bath, there's a little room there with a pump and a tub and all. We'll set you a place at supper. You wash up."

The sun was setting when there came a racket that scared every horse on the place and jarred me plum out of my thoughts. My first thought was that the train was here already, had leapt its tracks and was heading straight for my parlor, just as I'd feared. In the yard, here came Harland in his horseless machine, with April sitting beside him, holding baby Tennyson. She held me tight for a second, the only greeting we needed then. Harland just stood there, looking haunted. I pointed April toward his room where Gilbert was in bed; she handed Tennyson to me, then ran to Gilbert's side and nodded a quick hello to Charity. I followed just one step behind her. "Morris," April whispered, "will be down tomorrow with the other children. I just couldn't wait."

At the doorway stood my little brother; the four of us made a strange mirroring of my daughter and her own little brother. He was gaunt and thin, and his clothes unpressed and shabby. I pressed Charity's shoulder and she smiled admiringly at little Tennyson.

"Harland?" I asked. "Where are your boys?"

"With Morris. They'll be along tomorrow."

Tennyson fussed and squirmed in my arms as I went to April's side. "Honey, you'd better feed her," I said. "Just go sit in that chair."

Her eyes darted back and forth. "Well, not in here. Anybody might come in."

"It's all right. It won't bother Gilbert or the doctor, I'm sure."

"Mama, she has to have perfect peace while she eats or she gets colicky. I'll have to go to the book room. You tell everyone to stay out until I say so."

"Sure," I said. Heavens, as if a mother couldn't nurse a baby in a house full of family.

"And Mama," April said, "he's going to be well. I know it. Little brothers like him are too special to . . . to go away." Her face reddened. "We'll talk later. Now, I have to compose myself. I have to be calm. We'll only think of daisies and butterflies and perfect spring mornings while Tenny has her nummy."

Charity and I exchanged glances as April left with the baby. But I saw my brother had gone, too, so I went after him.

"Harland?" I called. A few minutes went by before I found him on the front porch by Granny's rocker. She was sleeping soundly. I whispered, "Want some coffee?"

"Sure."

"It's cold, though. You all right?"

"I should never have taken the children to town. This would never have happened if I'd listened to you. I'd have been here to help. Blessing wouldn't have been exposed to every disease that came down the pike."

I couldn't feel his pain anymore, I was too numbed with my own. I looked back toward the door where Gilbert lay dying. My voice came out dry as the desert on a June afternoon, with not a lick of feeling for him remaining. "Hush, now. You didn't do anything wrong. A man has got to make a living to have some self-respect. I believe you did the best."

"But . . ."

I brought the cold coffee and handed him a cup. I suddenly felt angry at him. "No one blamed you for Gilbert's being shot. Stop leaning so blasted hard on me and stand on your own two feet."

Harland looked shocked, then mad. Granny stirred between us. Then abruptly his face changed. "It's getting late. You got any chores that need doing?"

"Feeding and watering, just like always." I pictured his poor horses in town.

"Best somebody do 'em," he said, and he put the cup on the rail and went to my barn.

*December 8, 1907*

I had hung Gilbert's new saddle in the barn hoping he would see it someday. We buried Chess at sunrise in the grave he had dug for Gilbert.

December 9, 1907

Gilbert's fever broke last night and his breathing was good and sound. Dr. Pardee can barely quit smiling. Gil was still weak and had lost a washtub full of blood, most of it into a pan held by Rebeccah, and some on the kitchen floor, but he was sound enough to be moved into his own bed where he could sleep much more safely, not being so far from the floor and all. Pardee had performed a near miracle.

I went to Gilbert's room and pulled up a chair next to Charity who sat watching over him. Rebeccah moved soundlessly around, tending things as if she had been a nurse her entire life. Gil's cheeks were drawn but pink. Udell slipped quietly in and sat by me. He patted my knee. I turned to look down at him, and he reached for my face. I touched his arm, and then he took my hand and held on tight. I leaned into his shoulder and rested there. I didn't shed a tear, though. My face was hard and unmoving, and my heart had turned to stone. I'll cry no more in this lifetime, I expect.

December 12, 1907

Dr. Pardee left, saying Gilbert was mending and was in good hands. I tried to give him fifty dollars, but he said no, his fee would have been twenty-seven, after all the days he stayed with us, and since he didn't have any change for the bills I gave him, he was obliged to take thirty, but if we needed him again, he'd come for free. I told him he was a fine man and a good doctor. He just smiled and left, tipping his hat as he climbed into his buggy. But I watched from the kitchen window as the buggy stopped in the yard. Pardee removed his tall hat and stepped out again, to say farewell to Rebeccah, who'd just come to the yard with a basketful of washed and folded linen bandages. They shared some words, nods, and lastly, timid smiles. As he drove away, he turned and waved discreetly to her, and she lifted a hand in response.

December 13, 1907

For days I have wandered through a dark world of shadows and voices, hearing Chess calling for me in the middle of the day, and wide awake, barely sleeping, unsure of leaving Gilbert alone for more than a couple hours at a time. If that old man walked into this kitchen this very minute, I'd give him the sharp side of a scolding, I swear it.

Now that her brother has recovered somewhat, April and Morris and their children are headed home. Harland and his boys have decided to stay awhile, but they are bunked at Albert and Savannah's place. I don't know exactly why, but we have houseful enough, and so I don't mind at all.

Udell has stayed with us, afraid of Rudolfo returning to finish the job. He only goes home to tend his animals. I don't think Rudolfo will return. He killed what he had come to take. Finally, Udell and I decided to have a closer look, a sneak-peak, at the hacienda. On foot, we edged closer and closer to Rudolfo's house. When at last we came to the yard, an old man and a very fat young woman came out toward us. Using a few words of my broken-up Spanish, I found out Rudolfo had moved his family overnight down to his rancho in Cananea. They left many nice things behind, the woman said twice. She and her father were watching over the place until the train came through. She said she was going to have a cantina in Rudolfo's front room. They must have been *peóns* for Rudolfo. No more love for the man than any *hacendado,* they were proud now, elevated to running a cantina in his parlor and sleeping in his bed.

Udell gave me the merest wink of one eye.

As we turned our horses toward home, the plump woman called out, "*¡Vaya con Dios, amigos!*" I turned to see her and she wore an open smile, nothing but neighborly cheer on her face.

## *December 20, 1907*

Mary Pearl has made a safe trip home and she'll be here a month. Gilbert has gotten up and wanted some clothes on. Dr. Pardee called again and he said it was a true miracle that he has pulled through. He told me it must be from healthful food and clean living. I told that Dr. Pardee he was the genuine article, a caring and curious man with the grit to try to help and the knowledge to make a clever experiment. Heaven knows, we've lost plenty of family due to doctors who had neither. Rebeccah stays by his side. I do like the man.

Miss Charity—reckon I can't get used to calling her "Mrs. James"—is sleeping, what little she sleeps, in my room, at my insistence, while I've taken a pallet behind a sheet in the parlor. But she works as if she'd come to be a housekeeper for us, so we have to tell her to quit and rest. Charity made a fine roast beef supper last evening. While the others were cooking, I went through my chests where we'd raided every scrap of cloth to make bandages for Gilbert.

This afternoon, Udell came to the house and asked me to walk a spell with him. Buttons tagged along at his side. "I got word the herd of sheep will be coming down by wagonloads, starting next week," he said. "They're bringing dogs, too. Don't know if we could get Buttons to come back here again after all this time. He'll have to learn about sheep if he stays with me. I kind of like the little feller. If you don't mind me trying him out."

The sound of hammering floated through the air. Charlie and Albert, along with Ezra and Zack, were fixing the door and taking out broken windows. Harland's boys played in the yard. I said, "It's all right. They're due for some new puppies up at Savannah's place."

Quiet surrounded us for a moment. A quail, sitting perched on the edge of the roof where a chunk was missing, gouged out by a bullet, let out a soft call.

I said, "Still quiet from Rudolfo's?"

"As a church. You doing all right?"

"I'm all right."

"Really?"

"I miss Chess."

"I do, too. Aubrey and Rachel are coming down today, but they'll be staying with her folks for Christmas."

"Mary Pearl told me that yesterday. She's at my place. Helping Rebeccah and Miss Charity nurse after Gilbert."

Then we said each other's names at the same moment. We laughed and began again, and the same thing happened.

Finally, smiling, he nodded for me to speak.

I said, "I have something for you. I bought you this as a Christmas gift last year. Then you were gone, and I was in town so much." I reached into my pocket and took hold of the spirit level. "I had it under some things in a chest, and I haven't looked in there all this time. I'd never have found it if I hadn't had to make so many bandages for Gilbert." I pulled it forth, and shrugged, feeling silly. "I plum forgot I'd bought it to help you build your house. It's to check levels of things. See? It's held with a string so you can balance the bubble between the lines and make sure the walls are straight and the floor is flat."

He took it and admired the little box. "Don't know if anything is straight there, but nothing's fallen down. Maybe we could have used this. Sure is a fine-looking instrument. Maybe they used the old-fashioned way. Just sightin' it in."

"Reckon it doesn't matter so much if it's not so level. Reckon a thing doesn't have to be perfectly straight to do the job."

"Maybe a man doesn't have to be perfectly right, either." He cradled the little thing in his hands, watching the liquid spirit slop back and forth in its tube.

"For what?" I said.

"Oh, I was just thinking."

"Well, I was thinking I don't like being so far away from you all the time, Udell."

He stopped walking and turned to face me. "I'd be always good to you, Sarah."

I knew he would, too. That was the thing. I knew him now. Knew just what he was made of. I swallowed, hard. "I'd be always good to you, too. If you'd let me. I'm not soft and womanly."

"You are, more than you want to admit."

"You're a fine man, Udell Hanna."

"I've got a lot to live up to. You set the marker high. I'd be pleased ever to have the pleasure again of calling on you."

"I'd be pleased ever to have a chance again to be your wife."

He moved his head, slowly, back and forth, while his eyes watered up and his lips, though they smiled, turned inward against his teeth. When at last he spoke, his voice was but a whisper. "There's nothing in the world I'd like better. We could do a Quaker wedding, like Aubrey and Rachel. Just invite the folks out to the place and raise a cheer."

"Even after I turned you away, you'd still do that?"

"I knew you had your reasons."

"And now?"

"I haven't changed my mind. Just quit asking you."

I reached for his hand. We held tightly to each other and went to tell the family.

# Chapter Twenty

*December 26, 1907*

This Christmas Day was a quiet one. We had no gifts to exchange. We had decorated no cholla skeleton. Nevertheless, plans had to be made and so this morning, right after breakfast, wagon after wagon took beds and blankets, crates and chests of drawers from my old house to Udell's stony fortress. The place wasn't homely, it was a monument. And it was ours.

Soon as her quilt and dresser arrived, Granny got up a fire in her little room and took a snooze, just happy as a cat. We made Gilbert sit and rest while the others scurried like ants, making the place up. Charity called out with delight, "A piano!" and sat before it, coaxing some little song from its soured old keys before she left to unload another box.

Udell took the box from her and placed the crate on the piano. It held my brush and comb, my carved box full of years of diaries, the picture of Jack and me from long ago, even April's old doll, the one she called "Mrs. Lady." He placed Jack's daguerreotype on the mantel, next to a similar one of Frances, then set the diary box beside the two, next to a lamp. He fished in his pocket and took out the spirit level. When he placed it on the mantel, the liquid settled and the bubble came near to one line and crossed the other one just a tiny bit. It wasn't truly perfect. We smiled at each other. Then I took the box upstairs to set out the last few things.

Albert had set up my bedstead against the outside wall, but I dragged it over in under the window. I pulled the mattress on, and went to tighten the ropes. Though we each had our rooms, I set it a little loose. A bit of sagging meant two would slide together.

April helped me fix my hair into a nice, stylish roll in the front. Mary Pearl had gotten a photographing box with a hood and a whole crate of silverplates, and she set them up and took a picture of me sitting in front of Udell. Then Udell said he had found the perfect spot for the wedding, and the weather was just fine for it, so he led the way and off we walked down the hill from the house. He must have worked many long days and nights to make this special place, for we were all amazed and said so, with each step we took.

Udell had cut a pathway and carefully placed stone steps, all lined and mortared in, right down the slope to where we'd sat and admired his house long ago. Each step was chiseled square and flat, laid in level as if he'd had the use of the spirit level all along. At the bottom next to the gurgling Cienega, where in another month the bank would overflow with wild purple irises that looked so like stars in the grass, he'd set bricks and wide beams to make permanent benches in a circle under a tall cottonwood tree. Stones had been set into the creek bed enough to build up a little pool and cause a waterfall that sounded like a music box to me. A nice ramada was set to one side, and streamers of red and white papers were nailed to its posts, while hanging from the inside beams of it were dozens of white-painted wooden stars. To save the grass and the flowers, the only places where the ground had been cleared were under the benches themselves, likely so a snake wouldn't be waiting there under a person's feet.

I could see betwixt the dry clumps of grass the shoots of irises already wakening. A fringe of green surrounded the dry grasses, promising to replenish the beauty of the spot.

Savannah came to me and hugged me then took my hand, saying, "This is sure a pretty place he's made. A sweet little garden for picnicking or reading a book or sewing. I don't doubt you'll have plenty of fine times here."

I felt the heat of a deep blush on my face. No one here except Udell and me could know what this spot meant to the two of us. I smiled then said, "It's mighty pretty when the flowers bloom between the grasses. A regular star garden."

"Sarah, you look as fresh as a daisy," she whispered. "Why you're blushing no end!"

I lowered my face. "I'm just happy, I suppose."

"When Udell told me he was building this place, I planted some daffodil bulbs here, too, for you. And look, nothing has dug them up at all. Maybe they'll bloom alongside the iris under the shade here. It'll be so beautiful."

Arm in arm, she and I sat upon the large stone where I'd once gotten a good look at the house. I said, "Reckon that house isn't too ugly anymore. From that watchtower, we can see your place along with my old house and the graveyard. All the way down to the new railroad tracks, too." After a bit, I said, "Never thought I'd marry again, after Jack."

"Well, I think Udell will take good care of you. Much as you'll let him, of course."

"I'm sure sorry about Aubrey and the way he broke Mary Pearl's heart. Udell tried to have a talk with him, too, but it did no good. Look at her there. Isn't she a vision?"

Savannah nodded. "Oh, me. She's made photographs of the whole family with that thing. Just look at her. She's taken on a whole new life. I wanted to keep her by my side, make sure she did things my way. Now I can see she'd never have been happily married to him the way Rachel is. Maybe it was meant to be."

"Our children are all fine folks, Savannah, every one of them."

She shook my arm and looked deep into my eyes for a moment, as her own filled with tears. "I'll tell Albert it's time to get this wedding going," she said. "Promise me you won't stay too many days away from my kitchen table, though."

"I promise, honey."

When we got everyone sat down for the wedding, Savannah and Albert sat by Dr. Pardee who sat next to Rebeccah. Granny and Savannah kissed my cheek and Albert gave my hand to Udell. Gilbert held hands with Charity. Harland's boys and April's children rolled about the place like tumbleweeds. Then, back at the house, while Zack and Ezra discovered the dumbwaiter was big enough to ride in, we dished up pies and roast goose and potatoes to serve an army. Then everyone sang and we had a fine time until late in the evening.

When all our guests had gone and Granny was tucked in bed, I went up and combed out my hair. I tiptoed to his room and found Udell on his knees before his bed. His voice said softly, "Thank you, sir. Amen."

"Udell?"

"Yes, Mrs. Hanna?"

"It's chill up here, Mr. Hanna. I was wondering if you'd mind to keep me warm?"

"Why, no, Mrs. Hanna. I—I don't mind."

"I'll just change, then. Won't take a minute."

He nodded again with a look as if he were about to weep with joy.

## January 10, 1908

Gilbert told me this morning that he and Charity will wed next week, just before Mary Pearl returns to Wheaton. Gil and Charity plan to live at the adobe house and work on patching the rest of the holes and the glass. Rebeccah has asked her parents to invite Dr. Pardee, too, though it will hardly be a change for him since he has come to the house twice a week and not charged for the visit. Whether he's calling on his patient or Rebeccah Prine, it would be hard to say.

Charlie goes to the station to look for mail every day. He has written a dozen letters, and heard back from all, even got a letter from the territorial governor. After him explaining to colonels and commanders, politicians and lawmen alike that his brother is no longer able to take the commission, and him sending his own recommendations from Burt Mossman and even John Slaughter himself, the Army has settled that Charlie will take his brother's place at the West Point Military Academy. All his experience and knowing all those fellows stood him in good stead, I reckon. It's hard for me to look in his face and see the boy I raised replaced with an iron-boned man. There's a deep crease, just like his father's, between his eyebrows that wasn't there when he came home with his bride last year.

Charlie will leave tomorrow for his new life. He put on his cadet's uniform for me, and though another mother might have fought back tears, all I felt was pride in him. He promised me he will stop in town and have a daguerreotype done and sent home to me. A person could ride the length and breadth of this country and not find a better man than Charlie Elliot.

We read in the *Daily Star* and *Citizen* papers that Mexico is headed for all-out war. It will be no small wonder to me if the resistance will be long and bloody, for old Don Porfirio has more enemies than friends, Rudolfo Maldonado among them, and surely the blood spilled will reach from Mexico City to Cananea.

For us, many miles north of the fracas, here in Arizona Territory, we have fought and won a hard battle. Peace reigns through our days now. Someday, softer women like my April will be more common than my kind. One day, too, the far-off sound of a locomotive will remind us of what it took to own this peace, the lives lost, the dreams spent and gained. No one made a life here without backbone and perseverence. It's a place with no forgiveness, this Territory, this land that I love.

Though tonight I lie here alone, I hear my husband breathing hard from the other room after a long day spent penning his sheep. The critters mumble and nag each other constantly, but we are secure in the two good dogs that guard them. As I lie here in bed, I am alone but not lonely. When I pressed Udell to tell me why he created my own room, he told me it was simply because I was a lady, and ladies just needed such things. If that doesn't beat all. A lady at last.

I see from this high window, Udell Hanna has given me a sky full of glittering diamonds. Walls tall and secure as only a castle may be. I can hear the nighthawks trill a lullaby. A little bat is bouncing through the air, taking bugs for his supper. Downstairs, Buttons lies curled at the front door, king of his domain. From the front porch, a single road leads straight to the people I love, and brings them straight to me.

# Appendix

## Arizona Pecan Pie (one 9-inch pie)

Begin by putting 3 ice cubes in a measuring cup and add water to at least ½ full. Melt 2 tablespoons of real butter in a small bowl or pan; set aside for filling. Assemble ingredients and have at hand: flour, salt, shortening, sugar, syrups, eggs, vanilla, pecans, measuring utensils, and rolling pin. Heat oven to 350 degrees.

One-crust Pie Shell
*1 cup (rounded, unsifted) unbleached white flour*
*½ teaspoon salt*
*¼ cup Crisco shortening (Granny used 3 tablespoons lard)*
*½ cup (+/-) iced water*

Mix flour with salt, cut in shortening until it looks like heavy meal. Drizzle in ice water a little at a time, about ½ cup, mixing lightly just until it sets up in one piece. Pop it out onto a floured counter. Roll about ¼ inch thick, about 2 inches bigger than pan all around (9-inch pie plate), lay it in, trim to make an even rim, pinch up the edge, and poke the middle with a fork in 6 or 8 places. Let it sit in the refrigerator for 15 minutes or so while assembling the filling.

Pecan Pie Filling
*4 large eggs*
*1 cup sugar*
*1 big pinch salt (about 1/8 teaspoon)*
*2 tablespoons butter, melted, cooled slightly*
*2 teaspoons vanilla*
*1/2 cup Light Karo Syrup*
*1/2 cup Dark Karo Syrup*
*1/4 cup clear maple syrup*
*2 1/2 cups shelled pecan halves, do not chop*

Beat eggs lightly in a big bowl. Stir in sugar and salt, butter and vanilla. Blend well. Then add all three syrups and mix well. Put pecans in and stir. Pour into crust and bake for about an hour at 350 degrees.

After 55 minutes, start checking for doneness. Slide a table knife into the syrup mixture an inch from the edge. When it pulls out clean, pie is finished. Let cool slowly; the center will finish cooking on the table. Good served warm with vanilla ice cream.

This makes as good a pecan pie as you can get if made with real sugar, butter, and maple syrup, even better if you have a tree out front to shake, and kids to pick and shell a bowl of fresh pecans, like my grandmother had. Don't substitute artificial sweetener, vanilla, margarine, or anything else that's not the real thing.

1. Why does Sarah feel so responsible for all the people in her life, even Rudolfo Maldonado? What changes with each one?

2. How does finally achieving her dream of a formal education change who Sarah is?

3. Why did Savannah plant the flower bulbs?

4. What did Sarah really learn from her classes?

5. Why did Sarah feel as if she "disappeared into her own shoes" when going through Udell's house?

6. Discuss the evolution and meaning of Sarah's freshman English essay "What I Want."

7. In what ways does the symbolism of gift giving run through the novel?

8. How do Sarah's struggles relate to modern life?

9. Throughout the novel, illness sweeps through the town of Tucson in waves. Children died of dysentery, and Gilbert's gunshot wound was treated with sulfur and vanilla. Can you picture a world without modern medicine, vaccines, and antibiotics?

10. What role does Blessing play in the novel?

11. What do you sense when Sarah, grieving over Blessing, wishes for Udell's coat?

12. Within a year of the end of the story, the men around Rudolfo's Christmas dinner table will put in motion a plot to overthrow the hold of Porfirio Diáz on the Mexican government. How does the looming danger that Sarah knows but can't define affect the tension of the idyllic last scene?

*A Reading Group Guide*

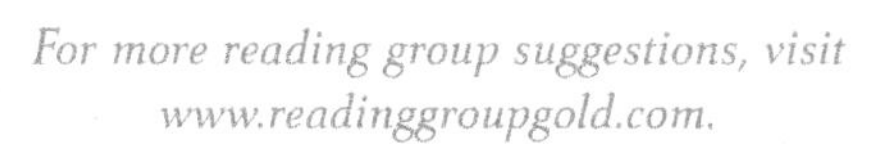

# "Authentic . . . reminiscent of Larry McMurtry's *Lonesome Dove*."

—*THE DENVER POST*

Our indomitable heroine Sarah Agnes Prine shares her homespun wisdom and her heartache as she contends with life-threatening drought and the great San Francisco earthquake.

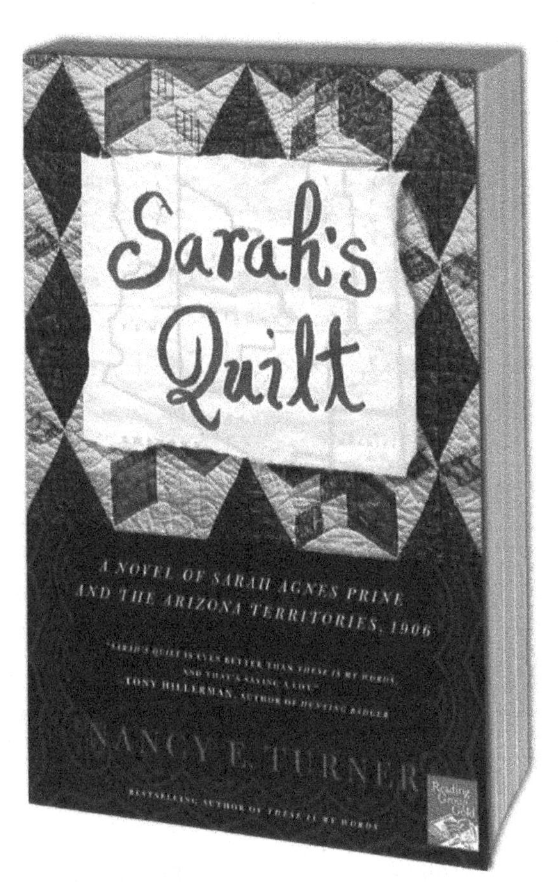


*"Older, tougher, wiser, Sarah enchants . . . as straightforward, gritty, and persistent as the woman who inspires it."*

—PUBLISHERS WEEKLY

*Available wherever books are sold*

Reading Group Guide available at www.readinggroupgold.com

www.stmartins.com
www.thomasdunnebooks.com

St. Martin's Griffin